PENGUIN CLASSICS

THE GILDED AGE

SAMUEL LANGHORNE CLEMENS was born on November 30, 1835, in Florida, Missouri, about forty miles southwest of Hannibal, the Mississippi River town Clemens was to celebrate as Mark Twain. In 1853 he left home, earning a living as an itinerant typesetter, and four years later became an apprentice pilot on the Mississippi, a career cut short by the outbreak of the Civil War. For five years, Clemens lived in Nevada and California as a prospector and a journalist. In February 1863 he first used the pseudonym "Mark Twain," as the signature to a humorous travel letter. A trip to Europe and the Holy Land in 1867 became the basis of his first major book, *The Innocents Abroad* (1869), *Roughing It* (1872), his account of experiences in the West, was followed by a satirical novel, *The Gilded Age* (1873), *Sketches: New and Old* (1875), *Tom Sawyer* (1876), *A Tramp Abroad* (1880), *The Prince and the Pauper* (1882), *Life on the Mississippi* (1883), and his masterpiece, *Huckleberry Finn* (1885). Following the publication of *A Connecticut Yankee* (1889) and *Pudd'nhead Wilson* (1894), Twain was compelled by debts to move his family abroad. By 1900 he had completed a round-the-world lecture tour, and, his fortunes mended, he returned to America. He was as famous for his white suit and his mane of white hair as he was for his uncompromising stands against injustice and imperialism and for his invariably quoted comments on any subject under the sun. Samuel Clemens died on April 21, 1910.

CHARLES DUDLEY WARNER (1829–1900) is remembered chiefly for his collaboration with Mark Twain on the novel *The Gilded Age* (1873).

LOUIS J. BUDD, James B. Duke Professor of English (Emeritus) at Duke University, is the author of *Mark Twain: Social Philosopher* (1962) and *Our Mark Twain: The Making of His Public Personality* (1983). Among other Twain-related collections, he has edited *Mark Twain: The Contemporary Reviews* (1999). He is the founding president of the Mark Twain Circle of America.

MARK TWAIN
AND
CHARLES DUDLEY WARNER

The Gilded Age

A TALE OF TO-DAY

*Edited with an Introduction
and Notes by* LOUIS J. BUDD

PENGUIN BOOKS

PENGUIN BOOKS
Published by the Penguin Group
Penguin Group (USA) Inc., 375 Hudson Street, New York, New York 10014, U.S.A.
Penguin Group (Canada), 90 Eglinton Avenue East, Suite 700, Toronto,
Ontario, Canada M4P 2Y3 (a division of Pearson Penguin Canada Inc.)
Penguin Books Ltd, 80 Strand, London WC2R 0RL, England
Penguin Ireland, 25 St Stephen's Green, Dublin 2, Ireland (a division of Penguin Books Ltd)
Penguin Group (Australia), 250 Camberwell Road, Camberwell,
Victoria 3124, Australia (a division of Pearson Australia Group Pty Ltd)
Penguin Books India Pvt Ltd, 11 Community Centre, Panchsheel Park, New Delhi – 110 017, India
Penguin Group (NZ), cnr Airborne and Rosedale Roads,
Albany, Auckland 1310, New Zealand (a division of Pearson New Zealand Ltd)
Penguin Books (South Africa) (Pty) Ltd, 24 Sturdee Avenue,
Rosebank, Johannesburg 2196, South Africa

Penguin Books Ltd, Registered Offices: 80 Strand, London WC2R 0RL, England

First published in the United States of America by American Publishing Co. 1873
This edition with an introduction and notes by Louis J. Budd published in
Penguin Books 2001

12

LIBRARY OF CONGRESS CATALOGING-IN-PUBLICATION DATA

Twain, Mark, 1835–1910.
The Gilded Age : a tale of to-day / Mark Twain and Charles Dudley Warner ;
edited with an introduction by Louis J. Budd.
p.   cm.
Includes bibliographical references.
ISBN 0-14-043920-X (pbk. : alk. paper)
1. City and town life—Fiction.   2. Washington (D.C.)—Fiction.
3. Legislators—Fiction.   I. Warner, Charles Dudley, 1829–1900.
II. Budd, Louis J.   III. Title.

PS1311 .B84 2001
813'.4—dc21   2001021514

Printed in the United States of America
Set in Stempel Garamond

CONTENTS

THE GILDED AGE

CHAPTER XLVI

CHAPTER XLVII

CHAPTER XLVIII

CHAPTER XLIX

CHAPTER L

CHAPTER LI

CHAPTER LII

CHAPTER LIII

CHAPTER LIV

CHAPTER LV

CHAPTER LVI

CHAPTER LVII

INTRODUCTION

OUT OF THE FLOOD of books that mostly rolls on toward oblivion, *The Gilded Age* will last for at least three reasons.

First of all, it's associated with Mark Twain, whose fame is refreshed continually through TV documentaries, multipurpose use of his sayings, impersonators now aching for the title of "impressionists," cameo stints in sitcoms, and other stagings of pop culture. Of course, *Adventures of Huckleberry Finn* keeps his fame alive at all English-speaking levels of U.S. and even world society.

But fairness demands emphasizing that *The Gilded Age* had a co-author, Charles Dudley Warner. In a sociocultural calendar, *The New York Public Library American History Desk Reference* (1997) lists for 1873: "Author Mark Twain names an era when he writes a novel called *The Gilded Age*, which describes the extravagance and corruption of post–Civil War life." This entry might have suited Professor Thomas R. Lounsbury of Yale, who ignored *The Gilded Age* when supervising the fifteen volumes of Warner's *Complete Writings* (1904). Perhaps Lounsbury, an old friend, knew about Warner's apology to an earlier literary oracle just as *The Gilded Age* was ready to issue: "I have already found out that it is not much of a novel. It is rather of a raw satire on recent disagreeable things. You would only waste time on it." Warner could have spoken out of postpartal fatigue. But Charles Neider agreed with him about his share in the recombinant. So with the air of performing an aesthetic service, Neider spliced out *The Adventures of Colonel Sellers* (1965), which reduces the (supposedly) separate chapters by Warner to bridging passages. Since then, Warner's presence has kept dwindling toward the footnotes.

Though Twain's name came first on the title page, some reviewers in 1873 and 1874 put Warner ahead of him in literary height and weight. But by the 1880s, such a ranking had already become shaky. After World War II, as Twain rose toward canonical status academically, Warner grew as inconspicuous as ethical congressmen in their novel. This process fed on contempt for the genteel tradition, and the consensus now holds that the satire in *The Gilded Age* would have cut far deeper and more vitally without his timid hand. At times, Twain encouraged that judgment even if he eventually, to his brother Orion, rated the joint product as the "best-written and best-abused book of the age." Two months after publication, sensing that a cultural tutor didn't "like" it, he listed for her the chapters that he considered far livelier and wanted to claim. He made much the same listing for a Scottish friend and soon marked up a copy that way. Though Warner never staked out his own property, the lines looked fixed.

Nobody has discredited Twain's claim on chapters 1–11, 24–25, 27–28, 30, 32–34, 36–37, 42–43, 45, 51–53, 57, and 59–62, along with parts of 35 and 56 and the opening pages of 49. While less than a scattered half of the handwritten manuscript has yet turned up, it supports Twain's bookkeeping. In humanized terms, his devotees like to claim for him the doings of Beriah Sellers and the Hawkins family and the maneuverings in the Capital, while happy to lose territorial rights to the Boltons, the Montagues, Philip Sterling, and Harry Brierly. Twain also encouraged a simpler and catchy, if false, division: Warner "has worked up the fiction & I have hurled in the facts." Anybody beguiled by it ignores that Warner, six years older than Twain, had functioned since 1860 as an editor of leading newspapers in the capital of Connecticut. Before that, he had worked in Missouri as a surveyor for a projected railroad and, still earlier, had clerked in a bookstore. A college graduate who had practiced law in Chicago for two years, he handled the details for Laura Hawkins's trial.

The Gilded Age comes across best when readers take it as a joint, sometimes well-joined, text. More discreet than Twain, Warner never depreciated his co-author; instead, late in the process, he confided to a friend that "Mark and I are writing a novel. . . . We have hatched the plot day by day, drawn out the characters, and written it so that we cannot exactly say which belongs to who; though the styles will show in the chapters." That more complicated accounting is demonstrably closer to the emotional and practical truth. Warner carries on with Sellers convincingly after Twain's first block of chapters. An impartial reader might even enjoy the humor in Warner's first block (chapters 12–23) as more effective satire.

As close neighbors, Twain and Warner could easily confer "day by day." At night, each read his fresh batch of manuscript to a joint family circle. Their intelligent and literary-minded wives, who had supposedly goaded the husbands into the project, commented freely—and firmly. Specifically, private letters prove that they saved Ruth Bolton's life rather than having a bereaved Philip eventually reward Alice Montague for loyalty and that they argued for having Laura die rather than escape into obscurity after her lurid acquittal. Through their very presence, their approving nods, and even their silences, they shaped many touches. Most basically, they thickened the underlying consensus of middle-class certainties about how society and its morals should work—the consensus of superiority that Twain embraced when he agreed to locate in Hartford, where his wife and he were currently planning a lavish home. Both wives probably appreciated the vignette of the Montague household as a temple of self-confidently refined culture, and they surely seconded their husbands' advice about uplifting public behavior, ranging from the parlor to the sidewalks, from politics to Sunday schools, from Manhattan to piney-woods villages.

One scholar-critic who has minutely dissected *The Gilded Age* decided that it "gained in conviction more than it lost in artistry" from its communal matrix. Actually, the rushed course of the writing caused major flaws of shape and polish. When finishing up in April 1873, Warner admitted that "we conceived the design early in winter, but were not able to get seriously at work on it till some time in January." In 1877, Twain reminisced that he "once wrote 55 pages at a sitting—that was on the opening pages of the Gilded Age novel" (with a flowing script on small sheets, of course). His letters to friends give a sense of rush verging on improvisation to finish a text that printed out to 575 pages—helped by wide margins and 212 illustrations. Working with, even for him, hyperenthusiasm "6 days a week—good full days," he overextended scenes that Warner had to cut back. Their collaboration fits the exchange between Thomas Wolfe and F. Scott Fitzgerald about "putter-inners" and "taker-outers."

Characteristically, by mid-May 1873, Twain was intent on another project—getting a family group off for a tour of the United Kingdom—so he let Warner do the final tidying up. On the other hand, he tweaked the British edition alone. Some reviews would decide, even complain, that the co-authors had smoothed out each other's distinctiveness. Very few contemporary reviews would perceive it to be a well-made novel. Today, a critic could argue that the gallop from casual idea to group-think to revising proofs resulted not so much in greater conviction as in a baggy freshness. Ultimately, *The Gilded Age* carried enough of Twain's instinctive qualities—here, his air of overflowing energy, pivots of mood, and audacities of phrasing—that collected editions of his work will always include it.

A second source of longevity for *The Gilded Age* rises out of its title, now the favored name for a dubious period of the American past. A search of "The Gilded Age" as "Subject" in the database of the WorldCat Web site produces over seven hundred items. Twainians have always liked to puff the "book that named an era"; they now have support from the Society for Historians of the Gilded Age and the Progressive Era, formed in the late 1980s. Meanwhile, the name has worked its way down to middle-school textbooks for social studies. Still, Twainians, like their human subject, can get too emphatic. The period between 1865 and 1890 (or 1900 or 1914) has also figured as the Age of Confidence, or else of Cynicism, Energy, Enterprise, Excess, Gentility, Innocence, Negation, the Politicos, Pragmatic Acquiescence, Reform, or the Robber Barons; or as the Brown Decades or Era of Good Stealings or the Tragic Era. But Twain and Warner's name is building its lead. In 1990, G. B. Trudeau gathered some of his contemporary satire as *Recycled Doonesbury: Second Thoughts on a Gilded Age.* Current newspapers and magazines—the *Wall Street Journal* or *New Republic*—have started to recognize a "new Gilded Age." Less abstract than its competitors, the name implies amused tolerance more than revulsion, and visual-tactile experience more than preachiness.

Twain's admirers have assumed that he came up with the title and, increasingly, so do historians, but nobody has proved it. A search of e-texts shows that he was quick to use "gilded" elsewhere, while Warner's book of European travel, *Saunterings* (1872), had passed up obvious chances. Curiously, neither author worked the title into their text. When the Mark Twain Forum (a scholarly e-mail list) raised the question of credit for it, surprise dominated, counterpointed by the argument that if Twain had thought it up, he would have loudly claimed so later.

Support for Twain as brilliant namer of the age overlooks the dull fact that the phrase had broad currency only after Twain's death. When Charles and Mary Beard used it to head a chapter in *The Rise of American Civilization* (1930), they implied a priority of reissue while thanking Twain and Warner's "coinage." However, V. L. Parrington (who featured the "Great Barbecue") and his students had already been using the label to cover its times. In fact, Van Wyck Brooks's *The Ordeal of Mark Twain* (1920), without fanfare, used it to denominate his thesis that "business enterprise was virtually the only recognized sphere of action" during Twain's career. In our day, it prospers because of its figurative looseness. A recent critic discovered that the title of *The Gilded Age* underlines its prescient emphasis on "the gap between appearance and reality." Parapolitical discourse holds if not millions then dozens of possibilities for reinvesting it.

The third source of longevity for *The Gilded Age* feeds on the ongoing debate over one of the most interesting periods in electoral politics and federal policy. After the Civil War, wrenching tensions rose out of many conditions: social mobility, urbanism and secularism, headlong entrepreneurship, a boom in railroads, and large-scale manufacture and marketing. Though change in western societies had grown always more constant, it accelerated after the peace brought the tangle of "reconstructing" the South through the insecure dominance of the Republican Party. Above or beneath all else throbbed the intensified priority of getting rich and its obverse, a fading moral standard when doing so. The new problems and the new ways to rob the public overwhelmed the antebellum patterns for governing. Historians would begin to discuss *The Gilded Age* as the sharpest mirror of the 1870s because, with thin disguise, it refracted the scandals about the biggest hustles and hustlers.

The novel now gets mentioned in reference guides, which define the Gilded Age through get-rich-quick raids on a stock, "corners" in gold or commodities, milking the federal treasury either directly or through a front, and systematic bribery—all of this tolerated by the stupid, venal, or apathetic voters. Twainians have run down its major allusions: to the Tweed (here Weed) "ring," the Crédit Mobilier payoffs (here through Congressman Fairoaks for Oakes Ames), the buying of senatorships (egregiously by Samuel Pomeroy of Kansas, here Dilworthy, though earlier Bumeroy in the manuscript), the partisan harvests led the most boldly by Ben Butler (here Sutler), the web of petty swindles such as the abuse of the franking privilege by Senator James Nye (here Balloon, though first Bly in the manuscript). The name of Congressman Trollop is generic.

Most readers today need only to know that the topical jabs kept coming, usually heavy-handedly; that, for instance, historians have pointed out two close models for Sellers's "Salt Lick Pacific Extension." Any regular consumer of the news not only recognized the strutting original of Laura's defense attorney, but also caught the casual pun on "simony" aimed at Simon Cameron. Curiously, the closest sleuth of real-life targets found no source for the scheme to set up a Knobs Industrial University, that is, to make educating the four million freed slaves just another front for boodle. While the few congressmen honestly trying to help needed support, *The Gilded Age* sacrificed them to indignation over naked, take-home graft.

Though *The Gilded Age* has emerged as the most insightful novel about the public life of the 1870s, it had several competitors—such as Henry Adams's *Democracy* (1880), now practically forgotten. Overall, in accumulated touches of dialogue, complexity of character, and plotting, it comes much closer than the rest to a convincing realism. While common sense may discount some of its broadax satire, the worst swindles during President Grant's first term made exaggeration both hard and unnecessary. Incredibly to the Liberal Republicans, the voters gave Grant a second term in

1872. Postbellum democracy disillusioned even Walt Whitman. Likewise, some of the first court verdicts accepting a plea of insanity did look dangerous to and for the law-abiding citizen; Twain raged about "lionizing murderers" on up through *The Adventures of Tom Sawyer* (1876). Overall, the tone and pace of *The Gilded Age* matched the frenetic quality of the decade's political-legal-economic issues.

Obviously, this novel doesn't fit into William Dean Howells's budding school of commonplace realism. Its romping burlesque of manners in the Capital's "high" society merely stated that a middle group, later exemplified too briefly by Representative Schoonmaker and his wife, functioned sensibly and routinely. Other touches implied that the mass of citizens trudged on loyal to the work ethic and some code of religion. Nevertheless, *The Gilded Age* achieved the key purpose of literary realism—to challenge whether day-to-day behavior and results measure up to conventional ideals.

As for the sterner criterion of historical realism, or accuracy, humility must admit to the advantages of hindsight, which the authors themselves envied: "The eight years in America from 1860 to 1868 uprooted institutions that were centuries old, changed the politics of a people, transformed the social life of half the country, and wrought so profoundly upon the entire national character that the influence cannot be measured short of two or three generations" (chapter 18).

Still, it's fair to charge that *The Gilded Age* blurred the important differences between the Republican and Democratic parties. That binary drove policy toward the South, where the emancipated slaves were trying to narrow their huge deficit in education, income, and civil rights; the difference between the parties about paperback money, merely mentioned in chapters 40 and 44, affected the price of credit, increasingly burdensome on farmers.

The Gilded Age ignored the bottom-scale workers, swelling into millions, for whom—a historian decides—it was an "Age of Iron" of "crushing weight"; their resentments were mounting toward the Great Strike of 1877. However, any charges of oversight should concede that literary critics already deplore the novel as overcrowded. It packed in more matters of the day (Grant's ambitions about Santo Domingo, the "salary grab," or the Steamship Subsidy Bill) than a modern reader can follow. Combining old Missouri Know-Nothingism and current New England anxiety, it also packed in anti-Irish caricatures whenever it could.

Twain as well as Warner accepted the Victorian principle that literature, whatever its pleasures, should benefit its community, should enlighten it or, at the very least, do no harm. They would have disliked to think that the topical criticisms in their novel, when extrapolated into precepts, exacerbated an ahistorical myopia that saw a sudden flabbiness of moral fiber—reversible by a willing conscience—rather than a massive, qualitative shift in economic patterns and power. More narrowly, by focusing on corruption, it encouraged a cynicism about office-holding that would abandon power to those "who, in the slang of the day, understood the virtues of 'addition, division and silence.'" Though corruption did flourish during Grant's terms, Twain and Warner, both trained in journalism, headlined it beyond its importance and yet implied that civic zeal could root it out now and forever. Their righteousness undermined respect for universal suffrage, respect that needed support—sometimes still for white males, much more for blacks and women; and their ideal of a politics cleansed of self-interest helped to make disillusion bloom perennially in the reformers' garden.

From our perspective deepened by more than a century, *The Gilded Age* deflected attention from long-range policy, from national strategies for an increasingly complex society, from the need, for instance, to follow through on the emancipated slaves' progress in a cash-nexus culture. In effect, it argued for protection against supposedly spendthrift government, that is, against the operators who made it a machine for sucking up the taxpayers' money, rather than against the privileges that big money was legitimizing for the increases in its dividends. Read simply, it posed the central issue as clearing away the parasites in the "National Asylum for the Helpless" rather than controlling the ravenousness of free enterprise. Just as reverently as the clergy disguised as "political economists," it assumed that laissez-faire capitalism ranks as a "natural law."

But whatever a reader's criteria for socioeconomic justice, he or she should agree that *The Gilded Age* agitates still-important issues. At the least, it constitutes a memorable warning to analyze the protean energies of social power and to calculate in whose interest it operates, to follow the money—whether hard cash or tax break—and not the parade of bombast. Historians of the later nineteenth century will keep *The Gilded Age* alive for anybody trying to learn from the past.

The Gilded Age will also pay readers who prefer to engage its intrinsic qualities. Maybe above all, they can enjoy it as a roller-coaster of humor that zooms into vaudeville farce or subsides into quiet irony (as when Trollop pontificates that "time is money" and Laura agrees sweetly, "Yes . . . especially in Congress"). Twain's chief intention was forthright: he hoped to hire Thomas Nast as the illustrator because his "one *first-class* talent" was "caricature." Yet the authors' touch with Dilworthy improves on cartoonish obviousness, leaving us as much impressed as amused by the senator's self-disciplined hypocrisy and by their self-restraint. While satire does dominate, its tone ranges through the frivolous and tolerant (Washington Hawkins as a lion of D.C. society) to the savage (the senators' pseudo-trial of Dilworthy for bribery). Its pace varies from sideswipes to elaborated scenes of the raw ignorance in Obedstown or Stone's Landing, the gaffes of the newly rich, the Meredithian duel between Laura and Buckstone (chapter 37), or the stacking of a jury. It touches almost everybody—relentlessly with Harry Brierly (first, Golightly in the manuscript) and cautiously with a determined yet frail feminist.

Paradoxically, pointing up the workings of humor soon grows dull or else stirs resistance. Most readers will break up here and there; Twain himself laughed hard when revisiting the Micawberish feast of turnips and water years later. The style itself constantly amuses, with more credit belonging to Twain than Warner, whose review of *Roughing It* had appreciated that "there is a use of vigorous English and often a quaint use of it that gives the effect of humor in the soberest narration." To subverted sobriety, Twain added irreverence, blunt sarcasm, brashness, loud understatement, and a fundamental, instinctual élan. Bernard DeVoto, the supreme connoisseur of Twain, acclaimed his "gusto"—that "inexhaustible delight in its subjects" without which "great art seldom exists." Robert Hughes could have included him in this tribute to Thomas Jefferson: "Reading him, you feel his enthusiasm and curiosity on your face like sunburn."

Of course, Warner knew that he was teaming up with—according to his review—"our most mirth-provoking storyteller" or, more precisely, the top graduate of the school of "literary comedians." But Twain considered Warner capable of a duet, as did their contemporaries. A review of Warner's *Being a Boy* (1878) asserted that "the more evident quality of his style is humor." He would get well above the average number of items into *Mark Twain's Library of Humor* (1888). So neither author felt like a contortionist when they tried to blend their tones. Warner cavorts with Sellers more broadly than in his own previous or later writings, while Twain never again held so long to the self-restraint that keeps Dilworthy almost enigmatic. Anybody who forgets to allot each chapter will admire many a passage by Warner as good-enough Twain. Still, again, spot comparisons disrupt what they both called a "partnership" novel.

Some reminiscences state that *The Gilded Age* intended to burlesque either the sentimental domestic or else the "sensation" novel of shocking action, whether physical or emotional. Nevertheless, its burlesque dwindles to comments about the disconnect between fiction and actual experience, about the flawed practices and values in vaguely current novels. In its own practice, *The Gilded Age* exploits such favorite scenes for sentimental melodrama as the death of Silas Hawkins or Laura and the sickbed recovery of Ruth from the brink. Anybody who senses "camp" in those scenes is applying much later sensibilities. Rather than burlesquing current fiction, Twain and Warner aimed to outclass it through superiority of purpose. The fake judgment of Laura as criminally insane makes not a literary but a sociolegal point. Likewise, a reformist purpose shapes the foolhardy race between the steamboats. Failure to find Laura's father resulted from inept plotting or just hurry, rather than deliberate anticlimax. Though parading an arcane motto for each chapter did aim for burlesque, that comes across, boringly, as the real thing.

The Gilded Age also can engross readers who favor convincing, significant, and intriguing characters, humor aside. Dressed in leaner prose, Senator Dilworthy could fit into Dos Passos's *U.S.A.* His mind trained to cover his portly back, he stays calm when Laura catches him with his Bible upside down. The closest the authors come to outing him is to wonder about the "cant terms which the Senator employed, perhaps unconsciously, and mistook, maybe, for religion" (chapter 52). As for his dishonesty—besides, of course, his buying votes for reelection—the closest actionable evidence is that "perhaps" Laura "had some hold on him." He operates as a perfected spoilsman while insisting privately as much as publicly on his purity of motive. Certainly, Laura has no sexual "hold" on him, yet after she murders Selby, he does not denounce her—for reasons left to interesting conjecture because they exclude loyalty or altruism. Crafty, unflappable, patient, and tireless, Dilworthy ends up as far from a literary cartoon as from a sincere public servant.

Likewise, recourse to stereotype will miss the subtleties enhancing Ruth Bolton. Though the heroine, she sings with a "slightly metallic" timbre and has "common-place and unformed hand-writing." While Philip "never exactly understood" her smile, she "thoroughly scared" a "young gentleman" with "the little laugh that accompanied a puzzling reply to one of his conversational nothings." Ruth's character has a respectworthy, self-respecting rationale. Determined not to swoon into marriage and give up studying medicine, she puts off Philip until she can achieve a "certain equality of power." Always somewhat frail, she does succumb to a melodramatically dangerous illness, aggravated by working hard to help out her parents ("Ruth's course was vindicated now"). Finally booked for marriage, she will nevertheless practice as a physician. If somewhat subdued at the end, she has established not only a far more likable but also a more effective personality than Henry James's feminists in *The Bostonians*. Memorably, Philip declares her "the most gay serious person he ever saw."

The Gilded Age paired Harry Brierly too obviously with Philip Sterling (and his too obvious name). Harry is best enjoyed as a more polished but less excusable Beriah Sellers, who—in a running joke—discounts him as "a little too sanguine, may be, and given to speculation." The authors avoid melodrama with him, however; "madly in love" with Laura, he behaves passively, feck-lessly, after the murder. She issues a belittling verdict: "He is a moth singed, that is all—the trifler with women thought he was a wasp." For Philip, the authors claim at least a phase of youthful misbehavior and warn—disingenuously—that readers "looking for a real hero would have to go elsewhere." They do make him more puzzled than perceptive with women. But, inevitably, his mettle pans out genuine. Van Wyck Brooks especially responded to Philip's tunneling to a bonanza in coal, and in his autobiogra-phy would imagine that his father had "felt like Mark Twain's young man . . . to whom the paths to fortune seemed innumer-able and open." Though for Brooks the bitch goddess Success would distort Twain's genius, the paradigm of making good through imaginative grit held its communal, quasi-religious cachet for generations.

For the later nineteenth century, Colonel Beriah Sellers over-shadowed all the other characters. Our mind-set may see a windbag, a know-it-all who never catches on, a cadger of drinks and cigars, or just a cheerful psychopath. Yet, sanguine, shabby poseurs once had transnational appeal: Oliver Goldsmith's Beau Tibbs and Charles Dickens's Micawber, along with many of Twain's charac-ters, were Sellers's first cousins. Several times—with varying atti-tudes as well as facts—Twain identified a favorite relation of his mother as the living model. But besides Warner's share, Sellers had richer sources that included Twain's own personality. So thought Howells, and when Twain sent home hopeful bulletins about the mechanical typesetter that he was backing, she admitted to her sister: "They make me laugh, for they are so like my beloved 'Colonel.'"

Beneath the diapason of Sellers's oratory, his character shifts spasmodically. Warner's private summary featured his "kindly na-ture" and an "untruthfulness" born "of the imagination and not of the heart." Several times over the years, Twain insisted that Sellers evoked "pathos"—on his own account, not that of his often hun-gry family. Twain also insisted on rating him a "gentleman," an honor he never awarded casually. But Sellers wavers in dignity, principles, and intelligence. When explaining how politicians do business (chapter 51), he sounds almost sensible yet also naive.

And thickly naive or just clueless when, constructing his awe-somely unique map and fantasizing about the itinerary for his railroad, he praises the village of Corruptionville: "And patriotic?—why they named it after Congress itself." In his domi-nant effect, he now comes across as the most laughable of Twain's rationalizers, but he then embodied the get-rich-quick-and-big schemes that meshed with corruption to debase the nation's ethi-cal currency. "Speculators" carried a baggage of antisocial meaning opposed to "producers," who turned raw materials into crops and usable goods.

His final flourish about becoming a lawyer is personal, treated amiably. Enough of his likability carried over for Howells—who had refused to puff the novel despite his warm friendship with both authors—so that he would talk up the play that Twain soon hacked out. Boomed as *Colonel Sellers*, it paid fat real-life profits for twelve years. The drama critics who proclaimed that Sellers acted out the spirit and behavior of a major American type were evidently right; C. Vann Woodward decides that "Sellerses thrived" in the Southwest "by the thousands in the seventies." Though at his funniest during his speech to the jury, the ebullient stage Sellers—now first-named Mulberry—made "There's millions in it!" a catchphrase for the rest of the century. Unfortunately, Howells encouraged Twain to keep him alive. After a second, aborted play, an old, far more eccentric Sellers wandered through *The American Claimant* (1892), which didn't deserve to earn even hundreds of readers. Still, however dim Sellers has grown, he ra-diated a cultural self-identity for his times, so "Attention, atten-tion must finally be paid to such a person," a happier and more expansive Willy Loman.

Modern readers will probably wonder most about Laura Hawkins. So late as chapter 60, the authors kept trying, without any demeaning satire, to give her complexity of emotion and mo-tive. First cast as an ingenue, sweet-willed during her "romantic age," she nurtures a "devil in her heart" after Colonel Selby mis-uses her. Shrewd enough to understand that an effective social presence will require a base of general knowledge, she puts herself through a "tireless and elaborate course of reading," which coun-teracts the fanciful novels that had misled her virginal judgment.

However, does she grow too knowing, too aggressive, too determined to control outcomes, too successful at handling men (except for her old seducer), perhaps even too cynical?

Critics, currently more interested in Laura than any other
character, puzzle over whether ineptitude, design, hurried car-
pentry, or male chauvinism blocked empathy with her. Her death
focuses the issue. Suicide or heart failure? In either case, an eva-
sive, plausible, realistic, or punitive move by the authors? While
their wives favored her dying, some readers surely hoped for better from or for her. Though she just may have palmed some graft
from lobbying (chapters 34 and 47), she had too much self-respect
to become a bird in a gilded cage by marrying for money. Though
she played hardball with the wiliest pitchmen on Capitol Hill, she
never used altruism as a mask. One critic argues convincingly that
the authors, instinctively reluctant to let her win against males on
the field of public affairs, make her regress into the reminiscences
of a fallen angel before getting rid of her. Nevertheless, while the
eventual standard is low, Laura ends up (*pace* Warner) the most
maturely perplexing of Twain's female characters.

Anybody who goes to fiction for vicarious morality likes to
see the good win out—in believable ways, to a believable extent.
Anybody who accepts matrimony as an option with integrity can
feel happy for Ruth, sorry for Alice. Though Philip finds a bonanza, he did earn it by digging long and hard. Is Washington
Hawkins punished or rewarded by his awakening to the reality
principle? The "Moral" of *Roughing It*—depend on "faithful dili-
gence"—applies still better to Harry. However, only the sternest
moralist could wish much worse for Dilworthy: at least, unlike
Dreiser's Charlie Drouet, this prairie vulture won't be as light on
the wing as before. As for Sellers, ironists can settle for assuming
he will go on talking multimillions and running any success into
the ground. Cynics can assume gratefully that the tide of boodle
will roll on as unstoppably as Melville's "great white shroud of
the sea."

Committed readers want to know about a novel's share in the
author's career. *The Gilded Age* was Twain's first long work of
fiction—his only novel, proclaimed Brooks provocatively. It's

unarguably now an anomaly. Twain's many books seldom engaged a contemporary United States. Much more characteristically, *The Gilded Age* grounded itself in his personal history. His father did build the family's prospects on seventy-five thousand (or more) acres of Tennessee hills; the early years of the Hawkins family parallel those of the Clemenses in Missouri. Whatever the broad similarities between Si Hawkins and John Marshall Clemens, Twain explicitly identified dreamy Washington with his own older brother, Orion. Starting with the family-run newspaper in Hannibal, Twain had learned about legislative politics in the Nevada Territory and then in the Capital as a reporter before a stint as associate editor of the *Buffalo Express*. Only *Personal Recollections of Joan of Arc* (1896) would (almost) suppress the injecting of his own experiences.

Less directly, *The Gilded Age* incorporated the latest phase of his sociocultural values and intertwined style of living. Having felt vaguely superior to the upper crust of Buffalo, his wife and he wanted to blend into the crypto-highbrow ambience of the Nook Farm community in oak-solid Hartford. Having gypsied for almost twenty years, he himself wanted to settle down into a more stable pattern—like that of the Montagues in Fallkill—a pattern supported by and supporting the values of Victorian domesticity and rooted enterprise. Encouraged by the Nook Farm attitude of earned superiority (deferring only to the Boston-Cambridge elite), *The Gilded Age* elevated the standards that Twain applied to American society. These standards now acquired a hauteur toward the nouveau riche, ironically, and even still more toward the lowest classes, toward their politics, manners, and tastes. Especially condescending are the squalid, torpid-motion sequences in rural Tennessee, Missouri, and Pennsylvania. Crucially different, *A Connecticut Yankee in King Arthur's Court* (1889) would recruit a spokesman from a working-class neighborhood of Hartford who attacked all levels of snobbery.

An in-depth census of Nook Farm will explain away surprise over Twain's proposing or else agreeing (the alleged facts differ) to collaborate with Warner. Hoping, more than he would admit, to impress his neighbors by developing into a "man of letters" (as the phrase went), he valued the confirmed respectability that

Warner carried over not only from the *Hartford Courant* but also from the genteel magazines. He surely expected Warner to tone down both his humor and his vehemence. Reasonably, he assumed that the well-educated Warner knew more about the "rules," about how to shape properly the plot and characters of a novel. Better at analyzing his own appeal than most writers, Twain recognized that his success so far depended on sketches cantilevered beyond the laws of literary physics and connected shakily by his persona.

That Warner decided to collaborate is genuinely surprising. He was already an eminent journalist and had published through the most prestigious firm in Boston. By the time that sales agents delivered *The Gilded Age* door-to-door, he felt regrets, perhaps because respect for his previous work was accumulating. In 1874, solemn essays about him ran in *Scribner's Monthly* and *Appleton's Journal*. But he was wanting more income, and Twain was bragging about his profits by the subscription route. Nook Farmers built houses and took trips abroad that bookstore sales to the discriminating minority could not pay for. To a friend who was weighing mission against moola, Warner apologized in 1874: "I think if you were to see your dainty literature in such ill conditioned volumes, you would just die. There is no doubt, however, that 'by subscription' is the only way for the author to make any money." He had guiltily compromised for a marketing rationale that, as intensified by Thorstein Veblen's time, promised as much and delivered as little as it dared. And he would do so again; conspicuous consumption was getting virulent just as its physical counterpart, the "white death" (tuberculosis), started to recede.

Except for the royalties (potentially large for a best-seller, of course), why did Warner, successful with three books of travels and informal essays, sign on for his own first novel? With belles-lettres challenging theology for sanctity in Nook Farm, the Victorian novelists had risen almost as high in prestige as the poets. Since 1868, furthermore, appeals for the Great American Novel had started ringing through the newspapers and magazines. Warner, at least a captain in the home guard for refinement, may have aimed to raise the ambitions of native fiction, seemingly relapsed after Irving, Cooper, and Hawthorne. Of course, he also felt obligated to improve the quality of social results, as his later activity for several philanthropic causes would demonstrate. (That record deepens the puzzle of why *The Gilded Age* impugned the motives behind helping the freed slaves; perhaps he opposed applying federal legislation and money.) When Warner came back to writing novels in the late 1880s, they solemnly were intended to correct basic ethical values.

Though only Twain would grouse for the record, Warner got the lesser benefit from their collaboration. Most reviewers assumed that Twain deserved all the credit for the fresh, knowledgeable episodes in Missouri and for any daring passages elsewhere. But while expecting him to mix soaring with belly-landings, they knew Warner's previous work as balanced and controlled. The *Literary World* of Boston huffed: "We have read enough of the book . . . to fill us with wonder as to how a man of Mr. Warner's literary reputation could lend his name to such cheap and feeble stuff." *The Gilded Age* came to be remembered as a mistake for Warner, who, during the next ten years, would still rank higher than Twain, especially in the East. Probably Warner felt relieved letting him take over the dramatic rights for the book (and not just the Missouri characters). In 1887, the *New York Critic* explained that "through badinage and for a joke," Warner had "collaborated with Mark Twain on that monstrosity, *The Gilded Age*. The shrewd Mark made his private arrangements with Warner, whereby Mark possessed the sole right to dramatize. The book was a dreadful failure." Critically, that is, not financially, and debatably so, moreover.

The Gilded Age also engages the reader who likes to judge how well a topical novel moved with the sweep of history. Twain and Warner were helping the push for reforming the Civil Service (or ending the "spoils system") that would benefit Hayes in 1876, Garfield in 1880, and—the first Democrat elected president since Buchanan—Cleveland in 1884. But *The Gilded Age* also contributed to the eventual nadir for American blacks. Except for the cadaver that upsets Ruth briefly, African Americans get no active sympathy. Irony destabilizes the exchange about the "niggro" (chapter 20) between the volubly racist Sellers and supple Dilworthy (whose real-life model was a Radical Republican). In sober effect, the novel joined the rising shift of priorities that would let so-called Redemption negate the progress of Reconstruction and lay the track for the New South of the 1890s.

Surprisingly early, ahead of the country's mood, *The Gilded Age* reconciled Yankees and Confederates. Colonel Selby, whom the book never forces to apologize for bad faith toward the Union, gets a cotton claim approved—honestly, the reader can assume. Fully aware of past animosity, Sellers and Dilworthy collaborate amicably (just like Warner and the ex–Confederate "ranger" Sam Clemens). Sellers "was one of the Southerners who were constantly quoted as heartily 'accepting the situation.'" While both the characters and their authors engage again in unstable irony, practicality overrides the past, as when the estimable Mrs. Schoonmaker corrects Laura: "You know we don't say 'rebel' anymore. . . . I find we are very much alike, and that kindness and good nature wear away prejudice. And then you know there are all sorts of common interests. My husband sometimes says that he doesn't see but confederates are just as eager to get at the treasury as Unionists" (chapter 38).

In literary politics, Twain and Warner moved away from regionalism and the gathering school of "local color." Their Washington doesn't display the Southern atmosphere that visitors would sense until the 1950s or later. When Sellers introduces himself to Harry and Philip, he proclaims: "Eastern born myself— Virginia." *The Gilded Age* vigorously unrolls the first panorama of the United States in fiction, with its geographical spread and its range of locales from a surveyors' camp in the boondocks to a Quaker household in Philadelphia to P. Dusenheimer's "hotel" to a courtroom in Manhattan. By showing a variegated, raw, and turbulent country, it invited a dilemma, however, keener for Twain because of what his crony Howells would deplore as his "Anglomania." From 1872 to 1879, England impressed him as far better governed, groomed, and mannered, far more appreciative of authentic talent than his United States. (He was already selling briskly there.) Yet he had kept enough national pride to worry about giving proof for exulting about the failures and vulgarities of New World democracy. He tried to blunt the dilemma with his "Author's Preface to the London Edition," which acknowledged "the shameful corruption which lately has crept into our politics" but professed "a great strong faith in a noble future for my country." Nevertheless, most British reviewers chortled over the crude misrule endemic in a democracy while those American reviewers Anglophobic since the Civil War scolded *The Gilded Age* for confirming English aristocratic smugness.

Twain and Warner stumbled into a comparable dilemma when they decided to commit to the subscription trade. Books sold that way typically settled for a plebeian level of content—"patently subliterary," decides Hamlin Hill. Visually, they aimed for cut-rate showiness with, conceded Twain, such "wretched paper & vile engravings" that *The Gilded Age* was "rather a rubbishy looking book." The *Literary World* declared that the author who "resorts to the subscription plan . . . descends to a constituency of a lower grade and inevitably loses caste." Yet, surely puzzling some of its subscribers, *The Gilded Age* pulses with elitism ranging from the harshly expressed to the clearly implicit. It mocks the "great public" for its gullible head, sometimes misled further by a kind heart. That public reveres the windbags who make the perceptive few nostalgic for the founding heroes of America's Golden Age of civic leadership. The name of Cattleville fits its human stock, and *The Gilded Age* sneers long and loud when impaneling a jury. In between the set outbursts, the narrative persona looks down on most persons and their behavior. Thomas Hobbes would have found continual support for "sudden glory" as the trigger of humor.

The hauteur includes a superiority of taste that carries over into the social niceties. Resenting both a lack of deference from the poorly paid and "a certain vulgar swagger and insolence of money," it comes close to the Bostonian snootiness that Howells had just deplored in *A Chance Acquaintance* (1873). While the idealized Montague household keeps a margin of cheerfulness, it cohabits with a sedate New England seminary. Hypocritically for a subscription book, *The Gilded Age* derided mass-cult splendor, commenting irrelevantly, for example, that the main salon of a steamboat "was more beautiful than a barber's shop." Chapter 24 flaunts a standard offended by every physical side of Washington—its hotels, the arts decorating the interior of the

Capitol, and both the outside and the inside ("bad taste reduced
to mathematical completeness") of the White House. Just as hypocritically, *The Gilded Age* warns against eager-to-sell novels
("Are all books lies?" mutters Laura) and derides their clichés obvious to a truly educated and discriminating mind. Still, *The
Gilded Age* sold well enough to prove that many readers found its
main effect respectful toward them; and some were eager for
pointers in refinement, anyway.

The word "gilded" invites if not another dilemma, then a dis-
sonance. Who should laugh at people too poor to buy solid gold
for enjoying a thin layer of it? But most readers of the novel to-
day judge gilding simply as a practice of the decorative arts. (The
cover of *New York* magazine announced a makeover as "The
New Gilded Age at the Russian Tea Room.") Gilding can add el-
egance; a high-priced binding of the novel offered gilded edges.
Yet gilding loses luster when deceptive or overdone. In the 1920s,
a consensus developed that the decorative arts of the later nineteenth century had overused gilding among too many faux effects;
a historian quips that the only thing its showy plutocrats could
not afford was good taste.

Twain and Warner now appear prescient—in the title of their
novel, not in the decor of their homes. But Warner, consistently,
and Twain, sporadically, could have agreed with the elitist E. L.
Godkin, editor of the *Nation*, that "Chromo-Civilization" described their times best. They did not flaunt their own choice. Of
the uses of "gild" or its cognates in the text, the most dismissive
goes into the "great gilt sign" that "betokened the presence of the
'Columbus River Slack-water Navigation Company.'" Throughout Twain's writings, natural gildings from sunrises or sunsets delight the eye while applied ones reflect his sense of humor, most
strikingly with the gilded pate of the schoolmaster in *The Adventures of Tom Sawyer*. He made the charge of pretense strongest
with *A Connecticut Yankee*, which berates the aristocracy as a
"gilded minority."

By 1880, *The Gilded Age* had sold sixty-five thousand copies
(twice as many as for *Tom Sawyer*). Regularly, despite the short
run for topical novels, the plates were hauled out of storage until
the "uniform" editions of Twain's works started coming. Various

runs of those editions, along with solo reprints, have kept *The Gilded Age* buyable and presumably read. Still, at some point it stopped sounding contemporary. Most historians decide that shifts during the 1890s brought a society that felt meaningfully different about itself.

Literary shifts also outmoded *The Gilded Age*. Programmatic realism and then self-conscious naturalism made it seem disjointed, garish, and sentimental. Especially after World War II, formalist critics dismissed the political novel as second-rate because journalistic. So, in a 1976 essay in the *New York Times Book Review*, Garry Wills startled them by assuming the value of the genre and then proclaiming *The Gilded Age* "our best political novel," which makes "the tie between politics and private life vivid in a way no other fiction has." He perhaps helped set off a burst of foreign editions (China, 1979; Japan, 1980; Soviet Union, 1985; Russia, 1993), though *The Gilded Age* had already migrated into eleven other languages, starting with Russian in 1874 and German in 1876. Doubtless, the translations have increasingly aimed to trade on Twain's name. But other-language readers should also approach *The Gilded Age* as a work of joint authorship, should also ponder the promise in its preface that "there is scarcely a chapter that does not bear the marks of the two writers of the book."

SUGGESTIONS FOR FURTHER READING

Andrews, Kenneth R. *Nook Farm, Mark Twain's Hartford Circle*. Cambridge: Harvard University Press, 1950.

Budd, Louis J. *Mark Twain: Social Philosopher*. Bloomington: Indiana University Press, 1962.

Camfield, Gregg. "Afterword." In *The Gilded Age*. Vol. 4 of *Oxford Mark Twain*, edited by Shelley Fisher Fishkin. New York: Oxford University Press, 1996.

Emerson, Everett. *Mark Twain: A Literary Life*. Philadelphia: University of Pennsylvania Press, 2000.

French, Bryant Morey. *Mark Twain and "The Gilded Age": The Book That Named an Era*. Dallas: Southern Methodist University Press, 1965.

Gale, Robert L. "Charles Dudley Warner." In *American National Biography*, vol. 22. New York: Oxford University Press, 1999.

Harris, Susan K. "Four Ways to Inscribe a Mackerel: Mark Twain and Laura Hawkins." *Studies in the Novel* 21 (1989): 138–53.

Hill, Hamlin. "Toward a Critical Text of *The Gilded Age*." *Papers of the Biographical Society of America* 59 (1965): 142–49.

Hoffman, Andrew J. *Inventing Mark Twain: The Lives of Samuel Langhorne Clemens*. New York: Morrow, 1997.

Kaplan, Justin. *Mr. Clemens and Mark Twain*. New York: Simon and Schuster, 1966.

Kruse, Horst. "A Matter of Style: How Olivia Langdon Clemens and Charles Dudley Warner Tried to Team and to Tame the Genius of Mark Twain." *New England Quarterly* 72 (1999): 232–50.

Lampton, Lucius M. "Hero in a Fool's Paradise: Twain's Cousin James J. Lampton and Colonel Sellers." *Mark Twain Journal* 27 (Fall 1989).

Salamo, Lin, and Harriet Elinor Smith, eds. *Mark Twain's Letters: Volume 5, 1872–1873.* Berkeley: University of California Press, 1997.

Sloane, David E. E. *Mark Twain as a Literary Comedian.* Baton Rouge: Louisiana State University Press, 1979.

Summers, Mark Wahlgren. *The Gilded Age, or The Hazard of New Functions.* Upper Saddle River, NJ: Prentice-Hall, 1997.

NOTE ON THE TEXT

The setting text here is the first edition in its second printing. However, the authors, very soon afterward and for all further printings, changed the first name of Colonel Sellers from Eschol to Beriah in order to mollify a real-life Escol Sellers. That change is followed here.

Guided by the work of Hamlin Hill and Robert H. Hirst, by my own reading, and by a painstakingly alert copyeditor, I have corrected a few errors, but I have made no speculative changes. The original text used both short and long dashes (and, rarely, a length in-between); this text reproduces that practice because Twain, who had earlier worked as a typesetter, marked up his manuscripts carefully; Warner was also closer to the printing process than most authors. The long dash usually showed a pause in conversation or inner musings. However, I do not mean to imply that I approach establishing a definitive text.

This edition omits all of the illustrations from the first edition save one—the map on pages 192–93. Reluctantly so, because the subscription trade used them lavishly, and Twain always took close interest in them for his own books—on account of sales much more than aesthetics. For purists, the facsimile edition in the *Oxford Mark Twain* (1996) is now available; even better, original-plate copies are findable, often accessibly priced. But the illustrations, done by three (actually four) artists of varying talent, present nondescript and stiff figures. As printed by the still-crude technology of the early 1870s, their effect is now antiquated and even countereffective for a novel with the subtitle of *A Tale of To-Day*.

Nobody has established Twain's or Warner's authority for the running heads of the first edition. Likewise, judging from how their publisher handled other books, he probably reshaped the chapter summaries.

It was tempting to omit the mottoes at the head of each chapter. Suggested by a set of synopses that Twain made for their erudite supplier, they fit the content only loosely. But since the reader at the time assumed that Twain and Warner had picked them, they belong to the original effect of the novel.

My thanks to Kevin Bochynski for searching out the uses of "gilded" in Twain's other works and for commenting analytically on them.

THE
GILDED AGE,
A Tale of To-Day.

By

MARK TWAIN,
(SAMUEL L. CLEMENS.)
Author of "Innocents Abroad," "Roughing It," &c.

AND

CHARLES DUDLEY WARNER,
Author of "My Summer in a Garden," "Back Log Studies," &c.

FULLY ILLUSTRATED FROM NEW DESIGNS:
BY HOPPIN, STEPHENS, WILLIAMS, ETC., ETC.

SOLD BY SUBSCRIPTION ONLY.

HARTFORD:
AMERICAN PUBLISHING COMPANY,
1873.

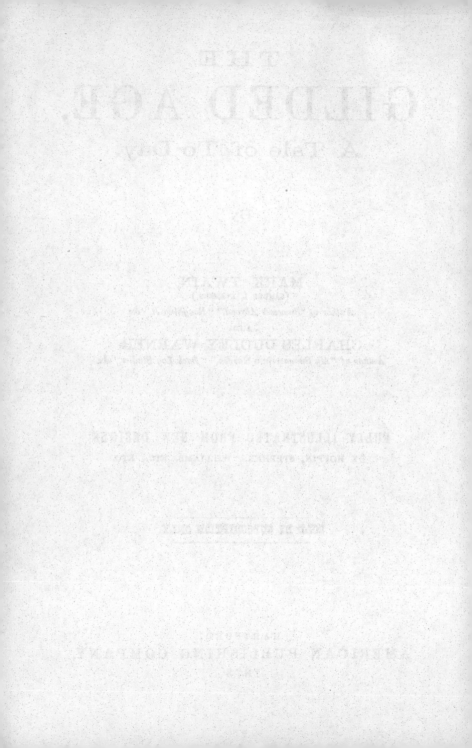

協力山成玉
同心坭變金

PREFACE

THIS BOOK WAS NOT WRITTEN for private circulation among friends; it was not written to cheer and instruct a diseased relative of the authors'; it was not thrown off during intervals of wearing labor to amuse an idle hour. It was not written for any of these reasons, and therefore it is submitted without the usual apologies.

It will be seen that it deals with an entirely ideal state of society; and the chief embarrassment of the writers in this realm of the imagination has been the want of illustrative examples. In a State where there is no fever of speculation, no inflamed desire for sudden wealth, where the poor are all simple-minded and contented, and the rich are all honest and generous, where society is in a condition of primitive purity and politics is the occupation of only the capable and the patriotic, there are necessarily no materials for such a history as we have constructed out of an ideal commonwealth.

No apology is needed for following the learned custom of placing attractive scraps of literature at the heads of our chapters. It has been truly observed by Wagner that such headings, with their vague suggestions of the matter which is to follow them, pleasantly inflame the reader's interest without wholly satisfying his curiosity, and we will hope that it may be found to be so in the present case.

Our quotations are set in a vast number of tongues; this is done for the reason that very few foreign nations among whom the book will circulate can read in any language but their own; whereas we do not write for a particular class or sect or nation, but to take in the whole world.

We do not object to criticism; and we do not expect that the critic will read the book before writing a notice of it. We do not even expect the reviewer of the book will say that he has not read it. No, we have no anticipations of anything unusual in this age of

5

criticism. But if the Jupiter, who passes his opinion on the novel, ever happens to peruse it in some weary moment of his subsequent life, we hope that he will not be the victim of a remorse bitter but too late.

One word more. This is—what it pretends to be—a joint production, in the conception of the story, the exposition of the characters, and in its literal composition. There is scarcely a chapter that does not bear the marks of the two writers of the book.

S. L. C.
C. D. W.

CHAPTER I

Nibiwa win o-dibendan aki.

> *Eng.* A gallant tract
> Of land it is!
> *Meercraft.* 'Twill yield a pound an acre:
> We must let cheap ever at first. But, sir,
> This looks too large for you, I see.

JUNE, 18—. Squire Hawkins sat upon the pyramid of large blocks, called the "stile," in front of his house, contemplating the morning.

The locality was Obedstown, East Tennessee. You would not know that Obedstown stood on the top of a mountain, for there was nothing about the landscape to indicate it—but it did: a mountain that stretched abroad over whole counties, and rose very gradually. The district was called the "Knobs of East Tennessee," and had a reputation like Nazareth, as far as turning out any good thing was concerned.[1]

The Squire's house was a double log cabin, in a state of decay; two or three gaunt hounds lay asleep about the threshold, and lifted their heads sadly whenever Mrs. Hawkins or the children stepped in and out over their bodies. Rubbish was scattered about the grassless yard; a bench stood near the door with a tin wash basin on it and a pail of water and a gourd; a cat had begun to drink from the pail, but the exertion was overtaxing her energies, and she had stopped to rest. There was an ash-hopper by the fence, and an iron pot, for soft-soap-boiling, near it.

This dwelling constituted one-fifteenth of Obedstown; the other fourteen houses were scattered about among the tall pine trees and among the corn-fields in such a way that a man might stand in the midst of the city and not know but that he was in the country if he only depended on his eyes for information.

"Squire" Hawkins got his title from being postmaster of Obedstown—not that the title properly belonged to the office, but because in those regions the chief citizens always must have titles of some sort, and so the usual courtesy had been extended to Hawkins. The mail was monthly, and sometimes amounted to as much as three or four letters at a single delivery. Even a rush like this did not fill up the postmaster's whole month, though, and therefore he "kept store" in the intervals.

The Squire was contemplating the morning. It was balmy and tranquil, the vagrant breezes were laden with the odor of flowers, the murmur of bees was in the air, there was everywhere that suggestion of repose that summer woodlands bring to the senses, and the vague, pleasurable melancholy that such a time and such surroundings inspire.

Presently the United States mail arrived, on horseback. There was but one letter, and it was for the postmaster. The long-legged youth who carried the mail tarried an hour to talk, for there was no hurry; and in a little while the male population of the village had assembled to help. As a general thing, they were dressed in homespun "jeans," blue or yellow—there were no other varieties of it; all wore one suspender and sometimes two—yarn ones knitted at home,—some wore vests, but few wore coats. Such coats and vests as did appear, however, were rather picturesque than otherwise, for they were made of tolerably fanciful patterns of *calico*—a fashion which prevails there to this day among those of the community who have tastes above the common level and are able to afford style. Every individual arrived with his hands in his pockets; a hand came out occasionally for a purpose, but it always went back again after service; and if it was the head that was served, just the cant that the dilapidated straw hat got by being uplifted and rooted under, was retained until the next call altered the inclination; many hats were present, but none were erect and no two were canted just alike. We are speaking impartially of men, youths and boys. And we are also speaking of these three estates when we say that every individual was either chewing natural leaf tobacco prepared on his own premises, or smoking the same in a corn-cob pipe. Few of the men wore whiskers; none wore moustaches; some had a thick jungle of hair under the chin and hiding the throat—the only pattern recognized there as being the correct thing in whiskers; but no part of any individual's face had seen a razor for a week.

These neighbors stood a few moments looking at the mail carrier reflectively while he talked; but fatigue soon began to show itself, and one after another they climbed up and occupied the top rail of the fence, hump-shouldered and grave, like a company of buzzards assembled for supper and listening for the death-rattle. Old Damrell said:

"Tha hain't no news 'bout the jedge, hit ain't likely?"

"Cain't tell for sartin; some thinks he's gwyne to be 'long toreckly, and some thinks 'e hain't. Russ Mosely he tole ole Hanks he mought git to Obeds tomorrer or nex' day he reckoned."

"Well, I wisht I knowed. I got a prime sow and pigs in the cote-house, and I hain't got no place for to put 'em. If the jedge is a gwyne to hold cote, I got to roust 'em out, I reckon. But tomorrer'll do, I 'spect."

The speaker bunched his thick lips together like the stem-end of a tomato and shot a bumble-bee dead that had lit on a weed seven feet away. One after another the several chewers expressed a charge of tobacco juice and delivered it at the deceased with steady aim and faultless accuracy.

"What's a stirrin', down 'bout the Forks?" continued Old Damrell.

"Well, I dunno, skasely. Ole Drake Higgins he's ben down to Shelby las' week. Tuck his crap down; couldn't git shet o' the most uv it; hit warn't no time for to sell, he say, so he fotch it back agin, 'lowin' to wait tell fall. Talks 'bout goin' to Mozouri—lots uv 'ems talkin' that-away down thar, Ole Higgins say. Cain't make a livin' here no mo', sich times as these. Si Higgins he's ben over to Kaintuck n' married a high-toned gal thar, outen the fust families, an' he's come back to the Forks with jist a hell's-mint o' whoop-jamboree notions, folks says. He's tuck an' fixed up the ole house like they does in Kaintuck, he say, an' tha's ben folks come cler from Turpentine for to see it. He's tuck an' gawmed it all over on the inside with plarsterin'."

"What's plarsterin'?"

"*I* dono. Hit's what *he* calls it. Ole Mam Higgins, she tole me. She say she warn't gwyne to hang out in no sich a dern hole like a hog. Says it's mud, or some sich kind o' nastness that sticks on n' kivers up everything. Plarsterin', Si calls it."

This marvel was discussed at considerable length; and almost with animation. But presently there was a dog-fight over in the neighborhood of the blacksmith shop, and the visitors slid off their perch like so many turtles and strode to the battle-field with an interest bordering on eagerness. The Squire remained, and read his letter. Then he sighed, and sat long in meditation. At intervals he said:

"Missouri. Missouri. Well, well, well, everything is so uncertain."

At last he said:

"I believe I'll do it.—A man will just rot, here. My house, my yard, everything around me, in fact, shows that I am becoming one of these cattle—and I used to be thrifty in other times."

He was not more than thirty-five, but he had a worn look that made him seem older. He left the stile, entered that part of his house which was the store, traded a quart of thick molasses for a coonskin and a cake of beeswax to an old dame in linsey-woolsey,[2] put his letter away, and went into the kitchen. His wife was there, constructing some dried apple pies; a slovenly urchin of ten was dreaming over a rude weather-vane of his own contriving; his small sister, close upon four years of age, was sopping corn-bread in some gravy left in the bottom of a frying-pan and trying hard not to sop over a finger-mark that divided the pan through the middle—for the other side belonged to the brother, whose musings made him forget his stomach for the moment; a negro woman was busy cooking, at a vast fire-place. Shiftlessness and poverty reigned in the place.

"Nancy, I've made up my mind. The world is done with me, and perhaps I ought to be done with it. But no matter—I can wait. I am going to Missouri. I won't stay in this dead country and decay with it. I've had it on my mind some time. I'm going to sell out here for whatever I can get, and buy a wagon and team and put you and the children in it and start."

"Anywhere that suits you, suits me, Si. And the children can't be any worse off in Missouri than they are here, I reckon."

Motioning his wife to a private conference in their own room, Hawkins said: "No, they'll be better off. I've looked out for *them*, Nancy," and his face lighted. "Do you see these papers? Well, they are evidence that I have taken up Seventy-five Thousand Acres of Land in this county—think what an enormous fortune it will be some day! Why, Nancy, enormous don't express it—the word's too tame! I tell you, Nancy———"

"For goodness sake, Si———"

"Wait, Nancy, wait—let me finish—I've been secretly boiling and fuming with this grand inspiration for weeks, and I *must* talk or I'll burst! I haven't whispered to a soul—not a word—have had my *countenance* under lock and key, for fear it might drop something that would tell even these animals here how to discern the gold mine that's glaring under their noses. Now all that is necessary to hold this land and keep it in the family is to pay the trifling taxes on it yearly—five or ten dollars—the whole tract would not sell for over a third of a cent an acre now, but some day people will be glad to get it for twenty dollars, fifty dollars, a hundred dollars an acre! What should you say to" [here he dropped his voice to a whisper and looked anxiously around to see that there were no eavesdroppers,] *"a thousand dollars an acre!*

"Well you may open your eyes and stare! But it's so. You and I may not see the day, but *they'll* see it. Mind I tell you, they'll see it. Nancy, you've heard of steamboats, and maybe you believed in them—of course you did. You've heard these cattle here scoff at them and call them lies and humbugs,—but they're not lies and humbugs, they're a reality and they're going to be a more wonderful thing some day than they are now. They're going to make a revolution in this world's affairs that will make men dizzy to contemplate. I've been watching—I've been watching while some people slept, and I know what's coming.

"Even you and I will see the day that steamboats will come up that little Turkey river to within twenty miles of this land of ours—and in high water they'll come right *to* it! And this is not all, Nancy—it isn't even half! There's a bigger wonder—the railroad! These worms here have never even heard of it—and when they do they'll not believe in it. But it's another fact. Coaches that fly over the ground twenty miles an hour—heavens and earth, think of that, Nancy! Twenty miles an hour. It makes a man's brain whirl. Some day, when you and I are in our graves, there'll be a railroad stretching hundreds of miles—all the way down from the cities of the Northern States to New Orleans—and it's got to run within thirty miles of this land—may be even touch a corner of it. Well, do you know, they've quit burning wood in some places in the Eastern States? And what do you suppose they burn? Coal!" [He bent over and whispered again:] "*There's whole worlds of it on this land!* You know that black stuff that crops out of the bank of the branch?—well, that's it. You've taken it for rocks; so has every body here; and they've built little dams and such things with it. One man was going to build a chimney out of it. Nancy I expect I turned as white as a sheet! Why, it might have caught fire and told everything. I showed him it was too crumbly. Then he was going to build it of copper ore—splendid yellow forty-per-cent. ore! There's fortunes upon fortunes of copper ore on our land! It scared me to death, the idea of this fool starting a smelting furnace in his house without knowing it, and getting his dull eyes opened. And then he was going to build it of *iron* ore! There's mountains of iron ore here, Nancy—whole mountains of it. I wouldn't take any chances. I just stuck by him—I haunted him—I never let him alone till he built it of mud and sticks like all the rest of the chimneys in this dismal country. Pine forests, wheat land, corn land, iron, copper, coal—wait till the railroads come, and the steamboats! *We'll* never see the day, Nancy—never in the world—never, never, never, child. We've got to drag along, drag along, and eat crusts in toil and poverty, all hopeless and forlorn—but *they'll* ride in coaches, Nancy! They'll live like the princes of the earth; they'll be courted and worshiped; their names will be known from ocean to ocean! Ah, well-a-day! Will they ever come back here, on the railroad and the steamboat, and say 'This one little spot shall not be touched—this hovel shall be sacred—for here our father and our mother suffered for us, thought for us, laid the foundations of our future as solid as the hills!' "

"You are a great, good, noble soul, Si Hawkins, and I am an honored woman to be the wife of such a man"—and the tears stood in her eyes when she said it. "We *will* go to Missouri. You are out of your place, here, among these groping dumb creatures. We will find a higher place, where you can walk with your own kind, and be understood when you speak—not stared at as if you were talking some foreign tongue. I would go anywhere, anywhere in the wide world with you. I would rather my body should starve and die than your mind should hunger and wither away in this lonely land."

"Spoken like yourself, my child! But we'll not starve, Nancy. Far from it. I have a letter from Beriah Sellers—just came this day. A letter that—I'll read you a line from it!"

He flew out of the room. A shadow blurred the sunlight in Nancy's face—there was uneasiness in it, and disappointment. A procession of disturbing thoughts began to troop through her mind. Saying nothing aloud, she sat with her hands in her lap; now and then she clasped them, then unclasped them, then tapped the ends of the fingers together; sighed, nodded, smiled— occasionally paused, shook her head. This pantomime was the elocutionary expression of an unspoken soliloquy which had something of this shape:

"I was afraid of it—was afraid of it. Trying to make our fortune in Virginia, Beriah Sellers nearly ruined us—and we had to settle in Kentucky and start over again. Trying to make our fortune in Kentucky he crippled us again and we had to move here. Trying to make our fortune here, he brought us clear down to the ground, nearly. He's an honest soul, and means the very best in the world, but I'm afraid, I'm afraid he's too flighty. He has splendid ideas, and he'll divide his chances with his friends with a free hand, the good generous soul, but something does seem to always interfere and spoil everything. I never did think he was right well balanced. But I don't blame my husband, for I do think that when that man gets his head full of a new notion, he can out-talk a machine. He'll make anybody believe in that notion that'll listen to him ten minutes—why I do believe he would make a deaf and dumb man believe in it and get beside himself, if you only set him where he could see his eyes talk and watch his hands explain.

What a head he has got! When he got up that idea there in Virginia of buying up whole loads of negroes in Delaware and Virginia and Tennessee, very quiet, having papers drawn to have them delivered at a place in Alabama and take them and pay for them, away yonder at a certain time, and then in the meantime get a law made stopping everybody from selling negroes to the south after a certain day—it was somehow that way—mercy how the man would have made money! Negroes would have gone up to four prices. But after he'd spent money and worked hard, and traveled hard, and had heaps of negroes all contracted for, and everything going along just right, he couldn't get the laws passed and down the whole thing tumbled. And there in Kentucky, when he raked up that old numskull that had been inventing away at a perpetual motion machine for twenty-two years, and Beriah Sellers saw at a glance where just one more little cog-wheel would settle the business, why I could see it as plain as day when he came in wild at midnight and hammered us out of bed and told the whole thing in a whisper with the doors bolted and the candle in an empty barrel. Oceans of money in it—anybody could see that. But it did cost a deal to buy the old numskull out—and then when they put the new cog-wheel in they'd overlooked something somewhere and it wasn't any use—the troublesome thing wouldn't go. That notion he got up here did look as handy as anything in the world; and how him and Si did sit up nights working at it with the curtains down and me watching to see if any neighbors were about. The man did honestly believe there was a fortune in that black gummy oil that stews out of the bank Si says is coal; and he refined it himself till it was like water, nearly, and it *did* burn, there's no two ways about that; and I reckon he'd have been all right in Cincinnati with his lamp that he got made, that time he got a house full of rich speculators to see him exhibit only in the middle of his speech it let go and almost blew the heads off the whole crowd. I haven't got over grieving for the money that cost, yet. I am sorry enough Beriah Sellers is in Missouri, now, but I was glad when he went. I wonder what his letter says. But of course it's cheerful; *he's* never down-hearted—never had any trouble in his life—didn't know it if he had. It's always sunrise with that man, and fine and blazing, at that—never gets noon, though—leaves off and rises again. Nobody can help liking the creature, he means so well—but I do dread to come across him again; he's bound to set us all crazy, of course. Well, there goes old widow Hopkins—it always takes her a week to buy a spool of thread and trade a hank of yarn. Maybe Si can come with the letter, now."

And he did:

"Widow Hopkins kept me—I haven't any patience with such tedious people. Now listen, Nancy—just listen at this:

"'Come right along to Missouri! Don't wait and worry about a good price but sell out for whatever you can get, and come along, or you might be too late. Throw away your traps, if necessary, and come empty-handed. You'll never regret it. It's the grandest country—the loveliest land—the purest atmosphere—I can't describe it; no pen can do it justice. And it's filling up, every day—people coming from everywhere. I've got the biggest scheme on earth—and I'll take you in; I'll take in every friend I've got that's ever stood by me, for there's enough for all, and to spare. Mum's the word—don't whisper—keep yourself to yourself. You'll see! Come!—rush!—hurry!—don't wait for anything!'

"It's the same old boy, Nancy, just the same old boy—ain't he?"

"Yes, I think there's a little of the old sound about his voice yet. I suppose you—you'll still go, Si?"

"Go! Well, I should think so, Nancy. It's all a chance, of course, and chances haven't been kind to us, I'll admit—but whatever comes, old wife, they're provided for. Thank God for that!"

"Amen," came low and earnestly.

And with an activity and a suddenness that bewildered Obedstown and almost took its breath away, the Hawkinses hurried through with their arrangements in four short months and flitted out into the great mysterious blank that lay beyond the Knobs of Tennessee.

CHAPTER II

መፍትው፡ሐዝበ፡ክርስቲያን፡እላ፡አልሮሙ፡ውሉደ፡
ይሕፀንዎሙ፡ለእጎ፡ለ፡ማውታ፡ወራዙት፡ወደናግል፡
ወይረስደይዋሙ፡ከመ፡ውሉደሙ፡ወፈድፈደ፡፡

TOWARD THE CLOSE of the third day's journey the wayfarers
were just beginning to think of camping, when they came upon a
log cabin in the woods. Hawkins drew rein and entered the yard.
A boy about ten years old was sitting in the cabin door with his
face bowed in his hands. Hawkins approached, expecting his
footfall to attract attention, but it did not. He halted a moment,
and then said:

"Come, come, little chap, you mustn't be going to sleep before
sundown."

With a tired expression the small face came up out of the
hands,—a face down which tears were flowing.

"Ah, I'm sorry I spoke so, my boy. Tell me—is anything the
matter?"

The boy signified with a scarcely perceptible gesture that the
trouble was in the house, and made room for Hawkins to pass.
Then he put his face in his hands again and rocked himself about
as one suffering a grief that is too deep to find help in moan or
groan or outcry. Hawkins stepped within. It was a poverty
stricken place. Six or eight middle-aged country people of both
sexes were grouped about an object in the middle of the room;
they were noiselessly busy and they talked in whispers when they
spoke. Hawkins uncovered and approached. A coffin stood upon
two backless chairs. These neighbors had just finished disposing
the body of a woman in it—a women with a careworn, gentle face
that had more the look of sleep about it than of death. An old lady
motioned toward the door and said to Hawkins in a whisper:

"His mother, po' thing. Died of the fever, last night. Tha warn't
no sich thing as saving of her. But it's better for her—better for
her. Husband and the other two children died in the spring, and

she hain't ever hilt up her head sence. She jest went around broken-hearted like, and never took no intrust in anything but Clay—that's the boy thar. She jest worshiped Clay—and Clay he worshiped her. They didn't 'pear to live at all, only when they was together, looking at each other, loving one another. She's ben sick three weeks; and if you believe me that child has worked, and kep' the run of the med'cin, and the times of giving it, and sot up nights and nussed her, and tried to keep up her sperits, the same as a grown-up person. And last night when she kep' a sinking and sinking, and turned away her head and didn't know him no mo', it was fitten to make a body's heart break to see him climb onto the bed and lay his cheek agin hern and call her so pitiful and she not answer. But bymeby she roused up, like, and looked around wild, and then she see him, and she made a great cry and snatched him to her breast and hilt him close and kissed him over and over agin; but it took the last po' strength she had, and so her eyelids begin to close down, and her arms sort o' drooped away and then we see she was gone, po' creetur. And Clay, he—Oh, the po' motherless thing—I cain't talk about it—I cain't bear to talk about it."

Clay had disappeared from the door; but he came in, now, and the neighbors reverently fell apart and made way for him. He leaned upon the open coffin and let his tears course silently. Then he put out his small hand and smoothed the hair and stroked the dead face lovingly. After a bit he brought his other hand up from behind him and laid three or four fresh wild flowers upon the breast, bent over and kissed the unresponsive lips time and time again, and then turned away and went out of the house without looking at any of the company. The old lady said to Hawkins:

"She always loved that kind o' flowers. He fetched 'em for her every morning, and she always kissed him. They was from away north somers—she kep' school when she fust come. Goodness knows what's to become o' that po' boy. No father, no mother, no kin folks of no kind. Nobody to go to, nobody that k'yers for him—and all of us is so put to it for to get along and families so large."

Hawkins understood. All eyes were turned inquiringly upon him. He said:

"Friends, I am not very well provided for, myself, but still I would not turn my back on a homeless orphan. If he will go with me I will give him a home, and loving regard—I will do for him as I would have another do for a child of my own in misfortune."

One after another the people stepped forward and wrung the stranger's hand with cordial good will, and their eyes looked all that their hands could not express or their lips speak.

"Said like a true man," said one.

"You was a stranger to me a minute ago, but you ain't now," said another.

"It's bread cast upon the waters—it'll return after many days," said the old lady whom we have heard speak before.

"You got to camp in my house as long as you hang out here," said one. "If tha hain't room for you and yourn my tribe'll turn out and camp in the hay loft."

A few minutes afterward, while the preparations for the funeral were being concluded, Mr. Hawkins arrived at his wagon leading his little waif by the hand, and told his wife all that had happened, and asked her if he had done right in giving to her and to himself this new care? She said:

"If you've done wrong, Si Hawkins, it's a wrong that will shine brighter at the judgment day than the rights that many a man has done before you. And there isn't any compliment you can pay me equal to doing a thing like this and finishing it up, just taking it for granted that I'll be willing to it. Willing? Come to me, you poor motherless boy, and let me take your grief and help you carry it."

When the child awoke in the morning, it was as if from a troubled dream. But slowly the confusion in his mind took form, and he remembered his great loss; the beloved form in the coffin; his talk with a generous stranger who offered him a home; the funeral, where the stranger's wife held him by the hand at the grave, and cried with him and comforted him; and he remembered how this new mother tucked him in his bed in the neighboring farm house, and coaxed him to talk about his troubles, and then heard him say his prayers and kissed him good night, and left him with the soreness in his heart almost healed and his bruised spirit at rest.

And now the new mother came again, and helped him to dress,

and combed his hair, and drew his mind away by degrees from the dismal yesterday, by telling him about the wonderful journey he was going to take and the strange things he was going to see. And after breakfast they two went alone to the grave, and his heart went out to his new friend and his untaught eloquence poured the praises of his buried idol into her ears without let or hindrance. Together they planted roses by the headboard and strewed wild flowers upon the grave; and then together they went away, hand in hand, and left the dead to the long sleep that heals all heartaches and ends all sorrows.

CHAPTER III

—Babillebalou! (disoit-il) voici pis qu'antan. Fuyons! C'est, par la mort boeuf! Leviathan, descript par le noble prophete Mosis en la vie du sainct home Job. Il nous avallera tous, comme pilules. . . . Voy le cy. O que tu es horrible et abhominable! . . . Ho ho! Diable, Satanas, Leviathan! Je ne te peux veoir, tant tu es ideux et detestable.

WHATEVER THE LAGGING dragging journey may have been to the rest of the emigrants, it was a wonder and delight to the children, a world of enchantment; and they believed it to be peopled with the mysterious dwarfs and giants and goblins that figured in the tales the negro slaves were in the habit of telling them nightly by the shuddering light of the kitchen fire.

At the end of nearly a week of travel, the party went into camp near a shabby village which was caving, house by house, into the hungry Mississippi. The river astonished the children beyond measure. Its mile-breadth of water seemed an ocean to them, in the shadowy twilight, and the vague riband of trees on the further shore, the verge of a continent which surely none but they had ever seen before.

"Uncle Dan'l" (colored,) aged 40; his wife, "aunt Jinny," aged 30, "Young Miss" Emily Hawkins, "Young Mars" Washington Hawkins and "Young Mars" Clay, the new member of the family, ranged themselves on a log, after supper, and contemplated the marvelous river and discussed it. The moon rose and sailed aloft through a maze of shredded cloud-wreaths; the somber river just perceptibly brightened under the veiled light; a deep silence pervaded the air and was emphasized, at intervals, rather than broken, by the hooting of an owl, the baying of a dog, or the muffled crash of a caving bank in the distance.

The little company assembled on the log were all children, (at least in simplicity and broad and comprehensive ignorance), and the remarks they made about the river were in keeping with the character; and so awed were they by the grandeur and the solemnity of the scene before them, and by their belief that the air was filled with invisible spirits and that the faint zephyrs were caused by their passing wings, that all their talk took to itself a tinge of the supernatural, and their voices were subdued to a low and reverent tone. Suddenly Uncle Dan'l exclaimed:

"Chil'en, dah's sumfin a comin!"

All crowded close together and every heart beat faster. Uncle Dan'l pointed down the river with his bony finger.

A deep coughing sound troubled the stillness, way toward a wooded cape that jutted into the stream a mile distant. All in an instant a fierce eye of fire shot out from behind the cape and sent a long brilliant pathway quivering athwart the dusky water. The coughing grew louder and louder, the glaring eye grew larger and still larger, glared wilder and still wilder. A huge shape developed itself out of the gloom, and from its tall duplicate horns dense volumes of smoke, starred and spangled with sparks, poured out and went tumbling away into the farther darkness. Nearer and nearer the thing came, till its long sides began to glow with spots of light which mirrored themselves in the river and attended the monster like a torchlight procession.

"What is it? Oh, what *is* it, Uncle Dan'l?"

With deep solemnity the answer came:

"It's de Almighty! Git down on yo' knees!"

It was not necessary to say it twice. They were all kneeling, in a moment. And then while the mysterious coughing rose stronger and stronger and the threatening glare reached farther and wider, the negro's voice lifted up its supplications:

"O Lord, we's ben mighty wicked, an' we knows dat we 'zerve to go to de bad place, but good Lord, deah Lord, we ain't ready yit, we ain't ready—let dese po' chil'en hab one mo' chance, jes' one mo' chance. Take de ole niggah if you's got to hab somebody.—Good Lord, good deah Lord, we don't know whah you's a gwyne to, we don't know who you's got yo' eye on, but we knows by de way you's a comin', we knows by de way you's a tiltin' along in yo' charyot o' fiah dat some po' sinner's a gwyne to ketch it. But good Lord, dese chil'en don't b'long heah, dey's f'm Obedstown whah dey don't know nuffin, an' you knows, yo' own sef, dat dey ain't 'sponsible. An' deah Lord, good Lord, it ain't like yo' mercy, it ain't like yo' pity, it ain't like yo' long-sufferin' lovin'-kindness for to take dis kind o' 'vantage o' sich little chil'en as dese is when dey's so many ornery grown folks chuck full o' cussedness dat wants roastin' down dah. Oh, Lord, spah de little chil'en, don't tar de little chil'en away f'm dey frens, jes' let 'em off jes' dis once, and take it out'n de ole niggah. HEAH I IS, LORD, HEAH I IS! De ole niggah's ready, Lord, de ole———"

The flaming and churning steamer was right abreast the party, and not twenty steps away. The awful thunder of a mud-valve suddenly burst forth, drowning the prayer, and as suddenly Uncle Dan'l snatched a child under each arm and scoured into the woods with the rest of the pack at his heels. And then, ashamed of himself, he halted in the deep darkness and shouted, (but rather feebly:)

"Heah I is, Lord, heah I is!"

There was a moment of throbbing suspense, and then, to the surprise and the comfort of the party, it was plain that the august presence had gone by, for its dreadful noises were receding. Uncle Dan'l headed a cautious reconnoissance in the direction of the log. Sure enough "the Lord" was just turning a point a short distance up the river, and while they looked the lights winked out and the couching diminished by degrees and presently ceased altogether.

"H'wsh! Well now dey's some folks says dey ain't no 'ficiency in prah. Dis chile would like to know whah we'd a ben *now* if it warn't fo' dat prah? Dat's it. Dat's it!"

"Uncle Dan'l, do you reckon it was the prayer that saved us?" said Clay.

"Does I *reckon*? Don't I *know* it! Whah was yo' eyes? Warn't de Lord jes' a comin' *chow! chow!* CHOW! an' a goin' on turrible—an' do de Lord carry on dat way 'dout dey's sumfin don't suit him? An' warn't he a lookin' right at dis gang heah, an' warn't he jes' a reachin' for 'em? An' d'you spec' he gwyne to let 'em off 'dout somebody ast him to do it? No indeedy!"

"Do you reckon he saw us, Uncle Dan'l?"

"De law sakes, chile, didn't I see him a lookin' at us?"

"Did you feel scared, Uncle Dan'l?"

"*No* sah! When a man is 'gaged in prah, he ain't fraid o' nuffin—dey can't nuffin tetch him."

"Well, what did you run for?"

"Well, I—I—mars Clay, when a man is under de influence ob de sperit, he do-no what he's 'bout—no sah; dat man do-no what he's 'bout. You mout take an' tah de head off'n dat man an' he wouldn't scasely fine it out. Dah's de Hebrew chil'en dat went frough de fiah; dey was burnt considerable—ob *coase* dey was; but *dey* didn't know nuffin 'bout it—heal right up agin; if dey'd ben gals dey'd missed dey long haah, (hair,) maybe, but dey wouldn't felt de burn."

"*I* don't know but what they *were* girls. I think they were."

"Now mars Clay, you knows bettern dat. Sometimes a body can't tell whedder you's a sayin' what you means or whedder you's a sayin' what you don't mean, 'case you says 'em bofe de same way."

"But how should *I* know whether they were boys or girls?"

"Goodness sakes, mars Clay, don't de Good Book say? 'Sides, don't it call 'em de *he*-brew chil'en? If dey was gals wouldn't dey be de she-brew chil'en? Some people dat kin read don't 'pear to take no notice when dey *do* read."

"Well, Uncle Dan'l, I think that——— My! here comes another one up the river! There can't be *two!*"

"We gone dis time—we done gone dis time, sho'! Dey ain't two, mars Clay—dat's de same one. De Lord kin 'pear eberywhah in a second. Goodness, how de fiah and de smoke do belch up! Dat mean business, honey. He comin' now like he fo'got sumfin. Come 'long, chil'en, time you's gwyne to roos'. Go 'long wid you—ole Uncle Daniel gwyne out in de woods to rastle in prah—de ole nigger gwyne to do what he kin to sabe you agin."

He did go to the woods and pray; but he went so far that he doubted, himself, if the Lord heard him when He went by.

CHAPTER IV

—Seventhly, Before his Voyage, He should make his peace with God, satisfie his Creditors if he be in debt; Pray earnestly to God to prosper him in his Voyage, and to keep him from danger, and, if he be *sui juris,* he should make his last will, and wisely order all his affairs, since many that go far abroad, return not home. (This good and Christian Counsel is given by *Martinus Zeilerus* in his Apodemical Canons before his Itinerary of Spain and Portugal.)

EARLY IN THE MORNING Squire Hawkins took passage in a small steamboat, with his family and his two slaves, and presently the bell rang, the stage-plank³ was hauled in, and the vessel proceeded up the river. The children and the slaves were not much more at ease after finding out that this monster was a creature of human contrivance than they were the night before when they thought it the Lord of heaven and earth. They started, in fright, every time the gauge-cocks sent out an angry hiss, and they quaked from head to foot when the mud-valves⁴ thundered. The shivering of the boat under the beating of the wheels was sheer misery to them.

But of course familiarity with these things soon took away their terrors, and then the voyage at once became a glorious adventure, a royal progress through the very heart and home of romance, a realization of their rosiest wonder-dreams. They sat by the hour in the shade of the pilot house on the hurricane deck and looked out over the curving expanses of the river sparkling in the sunlight. Sometimes the boat fought the mid-stream current, with a verdant world on either hand, and remote from both; sometimes she closed in under a point, where the dead water and the helping eddies were, and shaved the bank so closely that the decks were swept by the jungle of over-hanging willows and littered with a spoil of leaves; departing from these "points" she regularly crossed the river every five miles, avoiding the "bight"⁵ of the great bends and thus escaping the strong current; sometimes she went

out and skirted a high "bluff" sandbar in the middle of the stream,
and occasionally followed it up a little too far and touched upon
the shoal water at its head—and then the intelligent craft refused
to run herself aground, but "smelt" the bar, and straightway the
foamy streak that streamed away from her bows vanished, a great
foamless wave rolled forward and passed her under way, and in
this instant she leaned far over on her side, shied from the bar and
fled square away from the danger like a frightened thing—and the
pilot was lucky if he managed to "straighten her up" before she
drove her nose into the opposite bank; sometimes she approached
a solid wall of tall trees as if she meant to break through it, but all
of a sudden a little crack would open just enough to admit her,
and away she would go plowing through the "chute" with just
barely room enough between the island on one side and the main
land on the other; in this sluggish water she seemed to go like a
race-horse; now and then small log cabins appeared in little clear-
ings, with the never-failing frowsy women and girls in soiled and
faded linsey-woolsey leaning in the doors or against wood-piles
and rail fences, gazing sleepily at the passing show; sometimes she
found shoal water, going out at the head of those "chutes" or
crossing the river, and then a deck-hand stood on the bow and
hove the lead, while the boat slowed down and moved cautiously;
sometimes she stopped a moment at a landing and took on some
freight or a passenger while a crowd of slouchy white men and
negroes stood on the bank and looked sleepily on with their
hands in their pantaloons pockets,—of course—for they never
took them out except to stretch, and when they did this they
squirmed about and reached their fists up into the air and lifted
themselves on tip-toe in an ecstasy of enjoyment.

When the sun went down it turned all the broad river to a national banner laid in gleaming bars of gold and purple and crimson; and in time these glories faded out in the twilight and left the
fairy archipelagoes reflecting their fringing foliage in the steely
mirror of the stream.

At night the boat forged on through the deep solitudes of
the river, hardly ever discovering a light to testify to a human
presence—mile after mile and league after league the vast bends

were guarded by unbroken walls of forest that had never been disturbed by the voice or the footfall of a man or felt the edge of his sacrilegious axe.

An hour after supper the moon came up, and Clay and Washington ascended to the hurricane deck to revel again in their new realm of enchantment. They ran races up and down the deck; climbed about the bell; made friends with the passenger-dogs chained under the life-boat; tried to make friends with a passenger-bear fastened to the verge-staff[6] but were not encouraged; "skinned the cat"[7] on the hog-chains;[8] in a word, exhausted the amusement-possibilities of the deck. Then they looked wistfully up at the pilot house, and finally, little by little, Clay ventured up there, followed diffidently by Washington. The pilot turned presently to "get his stern-marks," saw the lads and invited them in. Now their happiness was complete. This cosy little house, built entirely of glass and commanding a marvelous prospect in every direction was a magician's throne to them and their enjoyment of the place was simply boundless.

They sat down on a high bench and looked miles ahead and saw the wooded capes fold back and reveal the bends beyond; and they looked miles to the rear and saw the silvery highway diminish its breadth by degrees and close itself together in the distance. Presently the pilot said:

"By George, yonder comes the Amaranth!"

A spark appeared, close to the water, several miles down the river. The pilot took his glass and looked at it steadily for a moment, and said, chiefly to himself:

"It can't be the Blue Wing. She couldn't pick us up this way. It's the Amaranth, sure."

He bent over a speaking-tube and said:

"Who's on watch down there?"

A hollow, unhuman voice rumbled up through the tube in answer:

"*I* am. Second engineer."

"Good! You want to stir your stumps, now, Harry—the Amaranth's just turned the point—and she's just a-humping herself, too!"

The pilot took hold of a rope that stretched out forward,

jerked it twice, and two mellow strokes of the big bell responded. A voice out on the deck shouted:

"Stand by, down there, with that labboard lead!"

"No, I don't want the lead," said the pilot, "I want *you*. Roust out the old man—tell him the Amaranth's coming. And go and call Jim—tell *him*."

"Aye-aye, sir!"

The "old man" was the captain—he is always called so, on steamboats and ships; "Jim" was the other pilot. Within two minutes both of these men were flying up the pilot-house stairway, three steps at a jump. Jim was in his shirt-sleeves, with his coat and vest on his arm. He said:

"I was just turning in. Where's the glass?"

He took it and looked:

"Don't appear to be any night-hawk[9] on the jack-staff[10]—it's the Amaranth, dead sure!"

The captain took a good long look, and only said:

"Damnation!"

George Davis, the pilot on watch, shouted to the night-watchman on deck:

"How's she loaded?"

"Two inches by the head, sir."

"'Tain't enough!"

The captain shouted, now:

"Call the mate. Tell him to call all hands and get a lot of that sugar forrard—put her ten inches by the head. Lively, now!"

"Aye-aye, sir!"

A riot of shouting and trampling floated up from below, presently, and the uneasy steering of the boat soon showed that she was getting "down by the head."

The three men in the pilot house began to talk in short, sharp sentences, low and earnestly. As their excitement rose, their voices went down. As fast as one of them put down the spy-glass another took it up—but always with a studied air of calmness. Each time the verdict was:

"She's a gaining!"

The captain spoke through the tube:

"What steam are you carrying?"

"A hundred and forty-two, sir! But she's getting hotter and hotter all the time."

The boat was straining and groaning and quivering like a monster in pain. Both pilots were at work now, one on each side of the wheel, with their coats and vests off, their bosoms and collars wide open and the perspiration flowing down their faces. They were holding the boat so close to the shore that the willows swept the guards[11] almost from stem to stern.

"Stand by!" whispered George.

"All ready!" said Jim, under his breath.

"Let her come!"

The boat sprang away from the bank like a deer, and darted in a long diagonal toward the other shore. She closed in again and thrashed her fierce way along the willows as before. The captain put down the glass.

"Lord how she walks up on us! I do hate to be beat!"

"Jim," said George, looking straight ahead, watching the slightest yawing of the boat and promptly meeting it with the wheel, "how'll it do to try Murderer's Chute?"

"Well, it's—it's taking chances. How was the cotton-wood stump on the false point below Boardman's Island this morning?"

"Water just touching the roots."

"Well it's pretty close work. That gives six feet scant in the head of Murderer's Chute. We can just barely rub through if we hit it exactly right. But it's worth trying. *She* don't dare tackle it!"—meaning the Amaranth.

In another instant the Boreas plunged into what seemed a crooked creek, and the Amaranth's approaching lights were shut out in a moment. Not a whisper was uttered, now, but the three men stared ahead into the shadows and two of them spun the wheel back and forth with anxious watchfulness while the steamer tore along. The chute seemed to come to an end every fifty yards, but always opened out in time. Now the head of it was at hand. George tapped the big bell three times, two leadsmen sprang to their posts, and in a moment their weird cries rose on the night air and were caught up and repeated by two men on the upper deck:

"No-o bottom!"

"De-e-p four!"

"Half three!"

"Quarter three!"

"Mark under wa-a-ter three!"

"Half twain!"

"Quarter twain!————"

Davis pulled a couple of ropes—there was a jingling of small bells far below, the boat's speed slackened, and the pent steam began to whistle and the gauge-cocks to scream:

"By the mark twain!"[12]

"Quar-ter-*her*-er-*less* twain!"

"Eight *and* a half!"

"Eight feet!"

"Seven-ana-half!————"

Another jingling of little bells and the wheels ceased turning altogether. The whistling of the steam was something frightful, now—it almost drowned all other noises.

"Stand by to meet her!"

George had the wheel hard down and was standing on a spoke.

"All ready!"

The boat hesitated—seemed to hold her breath, as did the captain and pilots—and then she began to fall away to starboard and every eye lighted:

"*Now* then!—meet her! meet her! Snatch her!"

The wheel flew to port so fast that the spokes blended into a spider-web—the swing of the boat subsided—she steadied herself————

"Seven feet!"

"Sev— six and a *half!*"

"*Six* feet! Six f————"

Bang! She hit the bottom! George shouted through the tube: "Spread her wide open! *Whale it at her!*"

Pow—wow—chow! The escape-pipes belched snowy pillars of steam aloft, the boat ground and surged and trembled—and slid over into————

"M-a-r-k twain!"

"Quarter-*her*————"

"Tap! tap! tap!" (to signify "Lay in the leads.")

And away she went, flying up the willow shore, with the

whole silver sea of the Mississippi stretching abroad on every hand.

No Amaranth in sight!

"Ha-ha, boys, we took a couple of tricks that time!" said the captain.

And just at that moment a red glare appeared in the head of the chute and the Amaranth came springing after them!

"Well, I swear!"

"Jim, what *is* the meaning of that?"

"I'll tell you what's the meaning of it. That hail we had at Napoleon[13] was Wash Hastings, wanting to come to Cairo—and we didn't stop. He's in that pilot house, now, showing those mud turtles how to hunt for easy water."

"That's it! I thought it wasn't any slouch that was running that middle bar in Hog-eye Bend. If it's Wash Hastings—well, what he don't know about the river ain't worth knowing—a regular gold-leaf, kid-glove, diamond-breastpin pilot Wash Hastings is. We won't take any tricks off of *him*, old man!"

"I wish I'd a stopped for him, that's all."

The Amaranth was within three hundred yards of the Boreas, and still gaining. The "old man" spoke through the tube:

"What is she carrying now?"

"A hundred and sixty-five, sir!"

"How's your wood?"

"Pine all out—cypress half gone—eating up cotton-wood like pie!"

"Break into that rosin on the main deck—pile it in, the boat can pay for it!"

Soon the boat was plunging and quivering and screaming more madly than ever. But the Amaranth's head was almost abreast the Boreas's stern:

"How's your steam, now, Harry?"

"Hundred and eighty-two, sir!"

"Break up the casks of bacon in the forrard hold! Pile it in! Levy on that turpentine in the fantail[14]—drench every stick of wood with it!"

The boat was a moving earthquake by this time:

"How is she now?"

"A hundred and ninety-six and still a-swelling!—water below the middle gauge-cocks!—carrying every pound she can stand!—nigger roosting on the safety-valve!"

"Good! How's your draft?"

"Bully! Every time a nigger heaves a stick of wood into the furnace he goes out the chimney with it!"

The Amaranth drew steadily up till her jack-staff breasted the Boreas's wheel-house—climbed along inch by inch till her chimneys breasted it—crept along, further and further till the boats were wheel to wheel—and then they closed up with a heavy jolt and locked together tight and fast in the middle of the big river under the flooding moonlight! A roar and a hurrah went up from the crowded decks of both steamers—all hands rushed to the guards to look and shout and gesticulate—the weight careened the vessels over toward each other—officers flew hither and thither cursing and storming, trying to drive the people amidships—both captains were leaning over their railings shaking their fists, swearing and threatening—black volumes of smoke rolled up and canopied the scene, delivering a rain of sparks upon the vessels—two pistol shots rang out, and both captains dodged unhurt and the packed masses of passengers surged back and fell apart while the shrieks of women and children soared above the intolerable din——

And then there was a booming roar, a thundering crash, and the riddled Amaranth dropped loose from her hold and drifted helplessly away!

Instantly the fire-doors of the Boreas were thrown open and the men began dashing buckets of water into the furnaces—for it would have been death and destruction to stop the engines with such a head of steam on.

As soon as possible the Boreas dropped down to the floating wreck and took off the dead, the wounded and the unhurt—at least all that could be got at, for the whole forward half of the boat was a shapeless ruin, with the great chimneys lying crossed on top of it, and underneath were a dozen victims imprisoned alive and wailing for help. While men with axes worked with might and main to free these poor fellows, the Boreas's boats went about, picking up stragglers from the river.

And now a new horror presented itself. The wreck took fire from the dismantled furnaces! Never did men work with a heartier will than did those stalwart braves with the axes. But it was of no use. The fire ate its way steadily, despising the bucket brigade that fought it. It scorched the clothes, it singed the hair of the axemen—it drove them back, foot by foot—inch by inch—they wavered, struck a final blow in the teeth of the enemy, and surrendered. And as they fell back they heard prisoned voices saying:

"Don't leave us! Don't desert us! Don't, don't do it!"

And one poor fellow said:

"I am Henry Worley, striker of the Amaranth! My mother lives in St. Louis. Tell her a lie for a poor devil's sake, please. Say I was killed in an instant and never knew what hurt me—though God knows I've neither scratch nor bruise this moment! It's hard to burn up in a coop like this with the whole wide world so near. Good-bye boys—we've all got to come to it at last, anyway!"

The Boreas stood away out of danger, and the ruined steamer went drifting down the stream an island of wreathing and climbing flame that vomited clouds of smoke from time to time, and glared more fiercely and sent its luminous tongues higher and higher after each emission. A shriek at intervals told of a captive that had met his doom. The wreck lodged upon a sandbar, and when the Boreas turned the next point on her upward journey it was still burning with scarcely abated fury.

When the boys came down into the main saloon of the Boreas, they saw a pitiful sight and heard a world of pitiful sounds. Eleven poor creatures lay dead and forty more lay moaning, or pleading or screaming, while a score of Good Samaritans moved among them doing what they could to relieve their sufferings; bathing their skinless faces and bodies with linseed oil and lime water and covering the places with bulging masses of raw cotton that gave to every face and form a dreadful and unhuman aspect.

A little wee French midshipman of fourteen lay fearfully injured, but never uttered a sound till a physician of Memphis was about to dress his hurts. Then he said:

"Can I get well? You need not be afraid to tell me."

"No—I—I am afraid you can not."

"Then do not waste your time with me—help those that can get well."

"But———"

"Help those that can get well! It is not for me to be a girl. I carry the blood of eleven generations of soldiers in my veins!"

The physician—himself a man who had seen service in the navy in his time—touched his hat to this little hero, and passed on.

The head engineer of the Amaranth, a grand specimen of physical manhood, struggled to his feet a ghastly spectacle and strode toward his brother, the second engineer, who was unhurt. He said:

"You were on watch. You were boss. You would not listen to me when I begged you to reduce your steam. Take that!—take it to my wife and tell her it comes from me by the hand of my murderer! Take it—and take my curse with it to blister your heart a hundred years—and may you live so long!"

And he tore a ring from his finger, stripping flesh and skin with it, threw it down and fell dead!

But these things must not be dwelt upon. The Boreas landed her dreadful cargo at the next large town and delivered it over to a multitude of eager hands and warm southern hearts—a cargo amounting by this time to 39 wounded persons and 22 dead bodies. And with these she delivered a list of 96 missing persons that had drowned or otherwise perished at the scene of the disaster.

A jury of inquest was impaneled, and after due deliberation and inquiry they returned the inevitable American verdict which has been so familiar to our ears all the days of our lives— "NOBODY TO BLAME."*

*The incidents of the explosion are not invented. They happened just as they are told.—THE AUTHORS

CHAPTER V

دِيـِمـْتُرَيَ كـهِي أُتـهَارِي پَـنْهَن جِي كـهَـرِ رِهَارِي پَارِّمِيـنْدَا فـَسِّـي

Il veut faire sécher de la neige au four et la vendre pour du sel blanc.

WHEN THE BOREAS backed away from the land to continue her voyage up the river, the Hawkinses were richer by twenty-four hours of experience in the contemplation of human suffering and in learning through honest hard work how to relieve it. And they were richer in another way also. In the early turmoil an hour after the explosion, a little black-eyed girl of five years, frightened and crying bitterly, was struggling through the throng in the Boreas' saloon calling her mother and father, but no one answered.— Something in the face of Mr. Hawkins attracted her and she came and looked up at him; was satisfied, and took refuge with him. He petted her, listened to her troubles, and said he would find her friends for her. Then he put her in a state-room with his children and told them to be kind to her (the adults of his party were all busy with the wounded) and straightway began his search.

It was fruitless. But all day he and his wife made inquiries, and hoped against hope. All that they could learn was that the child and her parents came on board at New Orleans, where they had just arrived in a vessel from Cuba; that they looked like people from the Atlantic States; that the family name was Van Brunt and the child's name was Laura. This was all. The parents had not been seen since the explosion. The child's manners were those of a little lady, and her clothes were daintier and finer than any Mrs. Hawkins had ever seen before.

As the hours dragged on the child lost heart, and cried so piteously for her mother that it seemed to the Hawkinses that the moanings and the wailings of the mutilated men and women in the saloon did not so strain at their heart-strings as the sufferings of this little desolate creature. They tried hard to comfort her; and in trying, learned to love her; they could not help it, seeing how she clung to them and put her arms about their necks and found no solace but in their kind eyes and comforting words. There was a question in both their hearts—a question that rose up and asserted itself with more and more pertinacity as the hours wore on—but both hesitated to give it voice—both kept silence and waited. But a time came at last when the matter would bear delay no longer. The boat had landed, and the dead and the wounded were being conveyed to the shore. The tired child was asleep in the arms of Mrs. Hawkins. Mr. Hawkins came into their presence and stood without speaking. His eyes met his wife's; then both looked at the child—and as they looked it stirred in its sleep and nestled closer; an expression of contentment and peace settled upon its face that touched the mother-heart; and when the eyes of husband and wife met again, the question was asked and answered.

When the Boreas had journeyed some four hundred miles from the time the Hawkinses joined her, a long rank of steamboats was sighted, packed side by side at a wharf like sardines in a box, and above and beyond them rose the domes and steeples and general architectural confusion of a city—a city with an imposing umbrella of black smoke spread over it. This was St. Louis. The children of the Hawkins family were playing about the hurricane deck, and the father and mother were sitting in the lee of the pilot house essaying to keep order and not greatly grieved that they were not succeeding.

"They're worth all the trouble they are, Nancy."

"Yes, and more, Si."

"I believe you! You wouldn't sell one of them at a good round figure?"

"Not for all the money in the bank, Si."

"My own sentiments every time. It is true we are not rich—but still you are not sorry—you haven't any misgivings about the additions?"

"No. God will provide."

"Amen. And so you wouldn't even part with Clay? Or Laura?"

"Not for anything in the world. I love them just the same as I love my own. They pet me and spoil me even more than the others do, I think. I reckon we'll get along, Si."

"Oh yes, it will all come out right, old mother. I wouldn't be afraid to adopt a thousand children if I wanted to, for there's that Tennessee Land, you know—enough to make an army of them rich. A whole army, Nancy! You and I will never see the day, but these little chaps will. Indeed they will. One of these days it will be 'the rich Miss Emily Hawkins—and the wealthy Miss Laura Van Brunt Hawkins—and the Hon. George Washington Hawkins, millionaire—and Gov. Henry Clay Hawkins, millionaire!' That is the way the world will word it! Don't let's ever fret about the children, Nancy—never in the world. They're all right. Nancy, there's oceans and oceans of money in that land—mark my words!"

The children had stopped playing, for the moment, and drawn near to listen. Hawkins said:

"Washington, my boy, what will you do when you get to be one of the richest men in the world?"

"I don't know, father. Sometimes I think I'll have a balloon and go up in the air; and sometimes I think I'll have ever so many books; and sometimes I think I'll have ever so many weathercocks and water-wheels; or have a machine like that one you and Colonel Sellers[15] bought; and sometimes I think I'll have—well, somehow I don't know—somehow I ain't certain; maybe I'll get a steamboat first."

"The same old chap!—always just a little bit divided about things.—And what will *you* do when you get to be one of the richest men in the world, Clay?"

"I don't know, sir. My mother—my other mother that's gone away—she always told me to work along and not be much expecting to get rich, and then I wouldn't be disappointed if I didn't get rich. And so I reckon it's better for me to wait till I get rich, and then by that time maybe I'll know what I'll want—but I don't now, sir."

"Careful old head!—Governor Henry Clay Hawkins!—that's what you'll be, Clay, one of these days. Wise old head! weighty old head! Go on, now, and play—all of you. It's a prime lot, Nancy, as the Obedstown folk say about their hogs."

A smaller steamboat received the Hawkinses and their fortunes, and bore them a hundred and thirty miles[16] still higher up
the Mississippi, and landed them at a little tumble-down village
on the Missouri shore in the twilight of a mellow October day.

The next morning they harnessed up their team and for two
days they wended slowly into the interior through almost road-
less and uninhabited forest solitudes. And when for the last time
they pitched their tents, metaphorically speaking, it was at the
goal of their hopes, their new home.

By the muddy roadside stood a new log cabin, one story
high—the store; clustered in the neighborhood were ten or twelve
more cabins, some new, some old.

In the sad light of the departing day the place looked homeless
enough. Two or three coatless young men sat in front of the store
on a dry-goods box, and whittled it with their knives, kicked it
with their vast boots, and shot tobacco-juice at various marks.
Several ragged negroes leaned comfortably against the posts of
the awning and contemplated the arrival of the wayfarers with
lazy curiosity. All these people presently managed to drag themselves to the vicinity of the Hawkins's wagon, and there they took
up permanent positions, hands in pockets and resting on one leg;
and thus anchored they proceeded to look and enjoy. Vagrant
dogs came wagging around and making inquiries of Hawkins's
dog, which were not satisfactory and they made war on him in
concert. This would have interested the citizens but it was too
many on one to amount to anything as a fight, and so they commanded the peace and the foreign dog furled his tail and took
sanctuary under the wagon. Slatternly negro girls and women
slouched along with pails deftly balanced on their heads, and
joined the group and stared. Little half dressed white boys, and
little negro boys with nothing whatever on but tow-linen shirts
with a fine southern exposure, came from various directions and
stood with their hands locked together behind them and aided in
the inspection. The rest of the population were laying down their
employments and getting ready to come, when a man burst
through the assemblage and seized the new-comers by the hands
in a frenzy of welcome, and exclaimed—indeed almost shouted:

"Well, who *could* have believed it! Now is it you sure

enough—turn around! hold up your heads! I want to look at you good! Well, well, well, it does seem most too good to be true, I declare! Lord, I'm so glad to see you! Does a body's whole soul good to look at you! Shake hands again! Keep *on* shaking hands! Goodness gracious alive. What *will* my wife say?—Oh yes indeed, it's so!—married only last week—lovely, perfectly lovely creature, the noblest woman that ever—you'll like her, Nancy! Like her? Lord bless me you'll love her—you'll dote on her— you'll be twins! Well, well, well, let me look at you again! Same old—why bless my life it was only just this very morning that my wife says, 'Colonel'—she will call me Colonel spite of everything I can do—she says 'Colonel, something tells me somebody's coming!' and sure enough here you are, the last people on earth a body could have expected. Why she'll think she's a prophetess— and hanged if I don't think so too—and you know there ain't any country but what a prophet's an honor to, as the proverb says. Lord bless me—and here's the children, too! Washington, Emily, don't you know me? Come, give us a kiss. Won't I fix *you*, though!—ponies, cows, dogs, everything you can think of that'll delight a child's heart—and————. Why how's this? Little strangers? Well you won't be any strangers here, I can tell you. Bless your souls we'll make you think you never was at home before—'deed and 'deed we will, *I* can tell you! Come, now, bundle right along with me. You can't glorify any hearth stone but mine in *this* camp, you know—can't eat anybody's bread but mine— can't do *any*thing but just make yourselves perfectly at home and comfortable, and spread yourselves out and *rest!* You hear *me!* Here—Jim, Tom, Pete, Jake, fly around! Take that team to my place—put the wagon in my lot—put the horses under the shed, and get out hay and oats and fill them up! Ain't any hay and oats? Well *get* some—have it charged to me—come, spin around, now! Now, Hawkins, the procession's ready; mark time, by the left flank, *forward*—march!"

And the Colonel took the lead, with Laura astride his neck, and the newly-inspired and very grateful immigrants picked up their tired limbs with quite a spring in them and dropped into his wake.

Presently they were ranged about an old-time fire-place whose blazing logs sent out rather an unnecessary amount of heat, but that was no matter—supper was needed, and to have it, it had to be cooked. This apartment was the family bed-room, parlor, library and kitchen, all in one. The matronly little wife of the Colonel moved hither and thither and in and out with her pots and pans in her hands, happiness in her heart and a world of admiration of her husband in her eyes. And when at last she had spread the cloth and loaded it with hot corn bread, fried chickens, bacon, buttermilk, coffee, and all manner of country luxuries, Col. Sellers modified his harangue and for a moment throttled it down to the orthodox pitch for a blessing, and then instantly burst forth again as from a parenthesis and clattered on with might and main till every stomach in the party was laden with all it could carry. And when the new-comers ascended the ladder to their comfortable feather beds on the second floor—to wit, the garret—Mrs. Hawkins was obliged to say:

"Hang the fellow, I do believe he has gone wilder than ever, but still a body can't help liking him if they would—and what is more, they don't ever want to try when they see his eyes and hear him talk."

Within a week or two the Hawkinses were comfortably domiciled in a new log house, and were beginning to feel at home. The children were put to school; at least it was what passed for a school in those days: a place where tender young humanity devoted itself for eight or ten hours a day to learning incomprehensible rubbish by heart out of books and reciting it by rote, like parrots; so that a finished education consisted simply of a permanent headache and the ability to read without stopping to spell the words or take breath. Hawkins bought out the village store for a song and proceeded to reap the profits, which amounted to but little more than another song.

The wonderful speculation hinted at by Col. Sellers in his letter turned out to be the raising of mules for the Southern market; and really it promised very well. The young stock cost but a trifle, the rearing but another trifle, and so Hawkins was easily persuaded to embark his slender means in the enterprise and turn over the keep and care of the animals to Sellers and Uncle Dan'l.

All went well. Business prospered little by little. Hawkins even built a new house, made it two full stories high and put a lightning rod on it. People came two or three miles to look at it. But they knew that the rod attracted the lightning, and so they gave the place a wide berth in a storm, for they were familiar with marksmanship and doubted if the lightning could hit that small stick at a distance of a mile and a half oftener than once in a hundred and fifty times. Hawkins fitted out his house with "store" furniture from St. Louis, and the fame of its magnificence went abroad in the land. Even the parlor carpet was from St. Louis—though the other rooms were clothed in the "rag" carpeting of the country. Hawkins put up the first "paling" fence that had ever adorned the village; and he did not stop there, but whitewashed it. His oilcloth window-curtains had noble pictures on them of castles such as had never been seen anywhere in the world but on windowcurtains. Hawkins enjoyed the admiration these prodigies compelled, but he always smiled to think how poor and cheap they were, compared to what the Hawkins mansion would display in a future day after the Tennessee Land should have borne its minted fruit. Even Washington observed, once, that when the Tennessee Land was sold he would have a "store" carpet in his and Clay's room like the one in the parlor. This pleased Hawkins, but it troubled his wife. It did not seem wise, to her, to put one's entire earthly trust in the Tennessee Land and never think of doing any work.

Hawkins took a weekly Philadelphia newspaper and a semiweekly St. Louis journal—almost the only papers that came to the village, though Godey's Lady's Book[17] found a good market there and was regarded as the perfection of polite literature by some of the ablest critics in the place. Perhaps it is only fair to explain that we are writing of a by gone age—some twenty or thirty years ago. In the two newspapers referred to lay the secret of Hawkins's growing prosperity. They kept him informed of the condition of the crops south and east, and thus he knew which articles were likely to be in demand and which articles were likely to be unsalable, weeks and even months in advance of the simple folk around him. As the months went by he came to be regarded as a wonderfully lucky man. It did not occur to the citizens that brains were at the bottom of his luck.

His title of "Squire" came into vogue again, but only for a season; for, as his wealth and popularity augmented, that title, by imperceptible stages, grew up into "Judge"; indeed it bade fair to swell into "General" by and by. All strangers of consequence who visited the village gravitated to the Hawkins Mansion and became guests of the "Judge."

Hawkins had learned to like the people of his section very much. They were uncouth and not cultivated, and not particularly industrious; but they were honest and straightforward, and their virtuous ways commanded respect. Their patriotism was strong, their pride in the flag was of the old-fashioned pattern, their love of country amounted to idolatry. Whoever dragged the national honor in the dirt won their deathless hatred. They still cursed Benedict Arnold as if he were a personal friend who had broken faith but a week gone by.

CHAPTER VI

十 年 前 事 幾 翻 新

Mesu eu azheīâshet
Washkebemâtizitaking,
Nâwuj beshegandâguzé
Manwâbegonig edush wen.

WE SKIP TEN YEARS and this history finds certain changes to
record.

Judge Hawkins and Col. Sellers have made and lost two or
three moderate fortunes in the meantime and are now pinched
by poverty. Sellers has two pairs of twins and four extras. In
Hawkins's family are six children of his own and two adopted
ones. From time to time, as fortune smiled, the elder children got
the benefit of it, spending the lucky seasons at excellent schools in
St. Louis and the unlucky ones at home in the chafing discomfort
of straitened circumstances.

Neither the Hawkins children nor the world that knew them
ever supposed that one of the girls was of alien blood and parentage. Such difference as existed between Laura and Emily is not
uncommon in a family. The girls had grown up as sisters, and they
were both too young at the time of the fearful accident on the
Mississippi to know that it was that which had thrown their lives
together.

And yet any one who had known the secret of Laura's birth
and had seen her during these passing years, say at the happy age
of twelve or thirteen, would have fancied that he knew the reason
why she was more winsome than her school companion.

Philosophers dispute whether it is the promise of what she will
be in the careless school-girl, that makes her attractive, the unde-
veloped maidenhood, or the mere natural, careless sweetness of
childhood. If Laura at twelve was beginning to be a beauty, the
thought of it had never entered her head. No, indeed. Her mind

was filled with more important thoughts. To her simple school-girl dress she was beginning to add those mysterious little adornments of ribbon-knots and ear-rings, which were the subject of earnest consultations with her sworn friends.

When she tripped down the street on a summer's day with her dainty hands propped into the ribbons-broidered pockets of her apron, and elbows consequently more or less akimbo with her wide Leghorn hat[18] flapping down and hiding her face one moment and blowing straight up against her forehead the next and making its revealment of fresh young beauty; with all her pretty girlish airs and graces in full play, and that sweet ignorance of care and that atmosphere of innocence and purity all about her that belong to her gracious time of life, indeed she was a vision to warm the coldest heart and bless and cheer the saddest.

Willful, generous, forgiving, imperious, affectionate, improvident, bewitching, in short—was Laura at this period. Could she have remained there, this history would not need to be written. But Laura had grown to be almost a woman in these few years, to the end of which we have now come—years which had seen Judge Hawkins pass through so many trials.

When the judge's first bankruptcy came upon him, a homely human angel intruded upon him with an offer of $1,500 for the Tennessee Land. Mrs. Hawkins said take it. It was a grievous temptation, but the judge withstood it. He said the land was for the children—he could not rob them of their future millions for so paltry a sum. When the second blight fell upon him, another angel appeared and offered $3,000 for the land. He was in such deep distress that he allowed his wife to persuade him to let the papers be drawn; but when his children came into his presence in their poor apparel, he felt like a traitor and refused to sign.

But now he was down again, and deeper in the mire than ever. He paced the floor all day, he scarcely slept at night. He blushed even to acknowledge it to himself, but treason was in his mind—he was meditating, at last, the sale of the land. Mrs. Hawkins stepped into the room. He had not spoken a word, but he felt as guilty as if she had caught him in some shameful act. She said:

"Si, I do not know what we are going to do. The children are not fit to be seen, their clothes are in such a state. But there's something more serious still.—There is scarcely a bite in the house to eat."

"Why, Nancy, go to Johnson ———"

"Johnson indeed! You took that man's part when he hadn't a friend in the world, and you built him up and made him rich. And here's the result of it: He lives in our fine house, and we live in his miserable log cabin. He has hinted to our children that he would rather they wouldn't come about his yard to play with his children,—which I can bear, and bear easy enough, for they're not a sort we want to associate with much—but what I *can't* bear with any quietness at all, is his telling Franky our bill was running pretty high this morning when I sent him for some meal—and that was all he said, too—didn't give him the meal—turned off and went to talking with the Hargrave girls about some stuff they wanted to cheapen."[19]

"Nancy, this is astounding!"

"And so it is, I warrant you. I've kept still, Si, as long as ever I could. Things have been getting worse and worse, and worse and worse, every single day; I don't go out of the house, I feel so down; but you had trouble enough, and I wouldn't say a word— and I wouldn't say a word now, only things have got so bad that I don't know what to do, nor where to turn." And she gave way and put her face in her hands and cried.

"Poor child, don't grieve so. I never thought that of Johnson. I am clear at my wit's end. I don't know what in the world to do. *Now* if somebody would come along and offer $3,000—Oh, if somebody only *would* come along and offer $3,000 for that Tennessee Land ———"

"You'd sell it, Si?" said Mrs. Hawkins excitedly.

"Try me!"

Mrs. Hawkins was out of the room in a moment. Within a minute she was back again and with a business-looking stranger, whom she seated, and then she took her leave again. Hawkins said to himself, "How can a man ever lose faith? When the blackest hour comes, Providence always comes with it—ah, this is the very timeliest help that ever poor harried devil had; if this blessed man offers but a thousand I'll embrace him like a brother!"

The stranger said:

"I am aware that you own 75,000 acres of land in East Tennessee, and without sacrificing your time, I will come to the point at once. I am agent of an iron manufacturing company, and they empower me to offer you ten thousand dollars for that land."

Hawkins's heart bounded within him. His whole frame was racked and wrenched with fettered hurrahs. His first impulse was to shout—"Done! and God bless the iron company, too!"

But a something flitted through his mind, and his opened lips uttered nothing. The enthusiasm faded away from his eyes, and the look of a man who is thinking took its place. Presently, in a hesitating, undecided way, he said:

"Well, I—it don't seem quite enough. That—that is a very valuable property—very valuable. It's brim full of iron ore, sir—brim full of it! And copper, coal,—everything—everything you can think of! Now, I'll tell you what I'll do. I'll reserve everything except the iron, and I'll sell them the iron property for $15,000 cash, I to go in with them and own an undivided interest of one-half the concern,—or the stock, as you may say. I'm out of business, and I'd just as soon help run the thing as not. Now how does that strike you?"

"Well, I am only an agent of these people, who are friends of mine, and I am not even paid for my services. To tell you the truth, I have tried to persuade them not to go into the thing; and I have come square out with their offer, without throwing out any feelers—and I did it in the hope that you would refuse. A man pretty much always refuses another man's first offer, no matter what it is. But I have performed my duty, and will take pleasure in telling them what you say."

He was about to rise. Hawkins said,

"Wait a bit."

Hawkins thought again. And the substance of his thought was: "This is a deep man; this is a very deep man; I don't like his candor; your ostentatiously candid business man's a deep fox—always a deep fox; this man's that iron company himself—that's what *he* is; he wants that property, too; I am not so blind but I can see that; *he* don't want the company to go into this thing—O, that's very good; yes, that's very good indeed—stuff! he'll be back here to-morrow, sure, and take my offer; take it? I'll risk anything he is suffering to take it now; here—I must mind what I'm about. What has started this sudden excitement about iron? I wonder what *is* in the wind? just as sure as I'm alive this moment, there's something tremendous stirring in iron speculation" [here Hawkins got up and began to pace the floor with excited eyes and with gesturing hands]—"something enormous going on in iron, without the shadow of a doubt, and here I sit mousing in the dark and never knowing anything about it; great heaven, what an escape I've made! this underhanded mercenary creature might have taken me up—and ruined me! but I *have* escaped, and I warrant me I'll not put my foot into—"

He stopped and turned toward the stranger, saying:

"I have made you a proposition,—you have not accepted it, and I desire that you will consider that I have made none. At the same time my conscience will not allow me to—. Please alter the figures I named to thirty thousand dollars, if you will, and let the proposition go to the company—I will stick to it if it breaks my heart!"

The stranger looked amused, and there was a pretty well defined touch of surprise in his expression, too, but Hawkins never noticed it. Indeed he scarcely noticed anything or knew what he was about. The man left; Hawkins flung himself into a chair; thought a few moments, then glanced around, looked frightened, sprang to the door———

"Too late—too late! He's gone! Fool that I am!—always a fool! Thirty thousand—ass that I am! Oh, *why* didn't I say fifty thousand!"

He plunged his hands into his hair and leaned his elbows on his knees, and fell to rocking himself back and forth in anguish. Mrs. Hawkins sprang in, beaming:

"Well, Si?"

"Oh, con-found the con-founded—con-*found* it, Nancy. I've gone and done it, now!"

"Done what, Si, for mercy's sake!"

"Done everything! *Ruined* everything!"

"Tell me, tell me, *tell* me! Don't keep a body in such suspense. Didn't he buy, after all? Didn't he make an offer?"

"Offer? He offered $10,000 for our land, and————"

"Thank the good providence from the very bottom of my heart of hearts! What sort of ruin do you call that, Si!"

"Nancy, do you suppose I listened to such a preposterous proposition? No! Thank fortune I'm not a simpleton! I saw through the pretty scheme in a second. It's a vast iron speculation!—millions upon millions in it! But fool as I am I told him he could have half the iron property for thirty thousand—and if I only had him back here he couldn't touch it for a cent less than a quarter of a million!"

Mrs. Hawkins looked up white and despairing:

"You threw away this chance, you let this man go, and we in this awful trouble? You don't mean it, you *can't* mean it!"

"Throw it away? Catch me at it! Why woman, do you suppose that man don't know what he is about? Bless you, he'll be back fast enough to-morrow."

"Never, never, never. He never will come back. I don't know what is to become of us. I don't know what in the world is to become of us."

A shade of uneasiness came into Hawkins's face. He said:

"Why, Nancy, you—you can't believe what you are saying."

"Believe it, indeed? I *know* it, Si. And I know that we haven't a cent in the world, and we've sent ten thousand dollars a-begging."

"Nancy, you frighten me. Now could that man—is it possible that I—hanged if I don't believe I *have* missed a chance! Don't grieve, Nancy, don't grieve. I'll go right after him. I'll take—I'll take—what a fool I am!—I'll take anything he'll give!"

The next instant he left the house on a run. But the man was no longer in the town. Nobody knew where he belonged or whither he had gone. Hawkins came slowly back, watching wistfully but hopelessly for the stranger, and lowering his price steadily with his sinking heart. And when his foot finally pressed his own threshold, the value he held the entire Tennessee property at was five hundred dollars—two hundred down and the rest in three equal annual payments, without interest.

There was a sad gathering at the Hawkins fireside the next night. All the children were present but Clay. Mr. Hawkins said:

"Washington, we seem to be hopelessly fallen, hopelessly involved. I am ready to give up. I do not know where to turn—I never have been down so low before, I never have seen things so dismal. There are many mouths to feed; Clay is at work; we must lose you, also, for a little while, my boy. But it will not be long—the Tennessee land————"

He stopped, and was conscious of a blush. There was silence for a moment, and then Washington—now a lank, dreamy-eyed stripling between twenty-two and twenty-three years of age—said:

"If Col. Sellers would come for me, I would go and stay with him a while, till the Tennessee land is sold. He has often wanted me to come, ever since he moved to Hawkeye."

"I'm afraid he can't well come for you, Washington. From what I can hear—not from *him* of course, but from others—he is not far from as bad off as we are—and his family is as large, too. He might find something for you to do, maybe, but you'd better try to get to him yourself, Washington—it's only thirty miles."

"But how can I, father? There's no stage or anything."

"And if there were, stages require money. A stage goes from Swansea, five miles from here. But it would be cheaper to walk."

"Father, they must know you there, and no doubt they would credit you in a moment, for a little stage ride like that. Couldn't you write and ask them?"

"Couldn't *you*, Washington—seeing it's you that wants the ride? And what do you think you'll do, Washington, when you get to Hawkeye? Finish your invention for making window-glass opaque?"

"No, sir, I have given that up. I almost knew I could do it, but it was so tedious and troublesome I quit it."

"I was afraid of it, my boy. Then I suppose you'll finish your plan of coloring hen's eggs by feeding a peculiar diet to the hen?"

"No, sir. I believe I have found out the stuff that will do it, but it kills the hen; so I have dropped that for the present, though I can take it up again some day when I learn how to manage the mixture better."

"Well, what you have got on hand—anything?"

"Yes, sir, three or four things. I think they are all good and can all be done, but they are tiresome, and besides they require money. But as soon as the land is sold————"

"Emily, were you about to say something?" said Hawkins.

"Yes, sir. If you are willing, I will go to St. Louis. That will make another mouth less to feed. Mrs. Buckner has always wanted me to come."

"But the money, child?"

"Why I think she would send it, if you would write her—and I know she would wait for her pay till————"

"Come, Laura, let's hear from you, my girl."

Emily and Laura were about the same age—between seventeen and eighteen. Emily was fair and pretty, girlish and diffident—blue eyes and light hair. Laura had a proud bearing and a somewhat mature look; she had fine, clean-cut features, her complexion was pure white and contrasted vividly with her black hair and eyes; she was not what one calls pretty—she was beautiful. She said:

"I will go to St. Louis, too, sir. I will find a way to get there. I will *make* a way. And I will find a way to help myself along, and do what I can to help the rest, too."

She spoke it like a princess. Mrs. Hawkins smiled proudly and kissed her, saying in a tone of fond reproof:

"So one of my girls is going to turn out and work for her living! It's like your pluck and spirit, child, but we will hope that we haven't got quite down to that, yet."

The girl's eyes beamed affection under her mother's caress. Then she straightened up, folded her white hands in her lap and became a splendid iceberg. Clay's dog put up his brown nose for a little attention, and got it. He retired under the table with an apologetic yelp, which did not affect the iceberg.

Judge Hawkins had written and asked Clay to return home and consult with him upon family affairs. He arrived the evening after this conversation, and the whole household gave him a rapturous welcome. He brought sadly needed help with him, consisting of the savings of a year and a half of work—nearly two hundred dollars in money.

It was a ray of sunshine which (to this easy household) was the earnest of a clearing sky.

Bright and early in the morning the family were astir, and all were busy preparing Washington for his journey—at least all but

shington himself, who sat apart, steeped in a reverie. When the
ne for his departure came, it was easy to see how fondly all
oved him and how hard it was to let him go, notwithstanding
they had often seen him go before, in his St. Louis schooling days.
In the most matter-of-course way they had borne the burden of
getting him ready for his trip, never seeming to think of *his* helping in the matter; in the same matter-of-course way Clay had
hired a horse and cart; and now that the good-byes were ended he
bundled Washington's baggage in and drove away with the exile.

At Swansea Clay paid his stage fare, stowed him away in the
vehicle, and saw him off. Then he returned home and reported
progress, like a committee of the whole.

Clay remained at home several days. He held many consultations with his mother upon the financial condition of the family,
and talked once with his father upon the same subject, but only
once. He found a change in that quarter which was distressing;
years of fluctuating fortune had done their work; each reverse had
weakened the father's spirit and impaired his energies; his last
misfortune seemed to have left hope and ambition dead within
him; he had no projects, formed no plans—evidently he was a
vanquished man. He looked worn and tired. He inquired into
Clay's affairs and prospects, and when he found that Clay was doing pretty well and was likely to do still better, it was plain that he
resigned himself with easy facility to look to the son for a support; and he said, "Keep yourself informed of poor Washington's
condition and movements, and help him along all you can, Clay."

The younger children, also, seemed relieved of all fears and dis-
tresses, and very ready and willing to look to Clay for a livelihood. Within three days a general tranquility and satisfaction
reigned in the household. Clay's hundred and eighty or ninety
dollars had worked a wonder. The family were as contented, now,
and as free from care as they could have been with a fortune. It
was well that Mrs. Hawkins held the purse—otherwise the treasure would have lasted but a very little while.

It took but a trifle to pay Hawkins's outstanding obligations,
for he had always had a horror of debt.

When Clay bade his home good-bye and set out to return to
the field of his labors, he was conscious that henceforth he was to

have his father's family on his hands as pensioners; but he did not allow himself to chafe at the thought, for he reasoned that his father had dealt by him with a free hand and a loving one all his life, and now that hard fortune had broken his spirit it ought to be a pleasure, not a pain, to work for him. The younger children were born and educated dependents. They had never been taught to do anything for themselves, and it did not seem to occur to them to make an attempt now.

The girls would not have been permitted to work for a living under any circumstances whatever. It was a southern family, and of good blood; and for any person except Laura, either within or without the household to have suggested such an idea would have brought upon the suggester the suspicion of being a lunatic.

CHAPTER VII

Via, Pecunia! when she's run and gone
And fled, and dead, then will I fetch her again
With aqua vitae, out of an old hogshead!
While there are lees of wine, or dregs of beer,
I'll never want her! Coin her out of cobwebs,
Dust, but I'll have her! raise wool upon egg-shells,
Sir, and make grass grow out of marrow-bones,
To make her come!

B. Jonson.

BEARING WASHINGTON HAWKINS and his fortunes, the stage-coach tore out of Swansea at a fearful gait, with horn tooting gaily and half the town admiring from doors and windows. But it did not tear any more after it got to the outskirts; it dragged along stupidly enough, then—till it came in sight of the next hamlet; and then the bugle tooted gaily again and again the vehicle went tearing by the houses. This sort of conduct marked every entry to a station and every exit from it; and so in those days children grew up with the idea that stage-coaches always tore and always tooted; but they also grew up with the idea that pirates went into action in their Sunday clothes, carrying the black flag in one hand and pistolling people with the other; merely because they were so represented in the pictures—but these illusions vanished when later years brought their disenchanting wisdom. They learned then that the stage-coach is but a poor, plodding, vulgar thing, in the solitudes of the highway; and that the pirate is only a seedy, unfantastic "rough," when he is out of the pictures.

Toward evening, the stage-coach came thundering into Hawkeye with a perfectly triumphant ostentation—which was natural and proper, for Hawkeye was a pretty large town for interior Missouri. Washington, very stiff and tired and hungry, climbed out, and wondered how he was to proceed now. But his difficulty was quickly solved. Col. Sellers came down the street on a run and arrived panting for breath. He said:

"Lord bless you—I'm glad to see you, Washington—perfectly

delighted to see you, my boy! I got your message. Been on the look-out for you. Heard the stage horn, but had a party I couldn't shake off—man that's got an enormous thing on hand—wants me to put some capital into it—and I tell you, my boy, I could do worse, I could do a deal worse. No, now, let that luggage alone; I'll fix that. Here, Jerry, got anything to do? All right—shoulder this plunder and follow me. Come along, Washington. Lord I'm glad to see you! Wife and the children are just perishing to look at you. Bless you, they won't know you, you've grown so. Folks all well, I suppose? That's good—glad to hear that. We're always going to run down and see them, but I'm into so many operations, and they're not things a man feels like trusting to other people, and so somehow we keep putting it off. Fortunes in them! Good gracious, it's the country to pile up wealth in! Here we are—here's where the Sellers dynasty hangs out. Dump it on the door-step, Jerry—the blackest niggro in the State, Washington, but got a good heart—mighty likely boy, is Jerry. And now I suppose you've got to have ten cents, Jerry. That's all right—when a man works for me—when a man—in the other pocket, I reckon—when a man—why, where the mischief *is* that portmonnaie![20]—when a—well now that's odd—Oh, now I remember, must have left it at the bank; and b'George I've left my check-book, too—Polly says I ought to have a nurse—well, no matter. Let me have a dime, Washington, if you've got—ah, thanks. Now clear out, Jerry, your complexion has brought on the twilight half an hour ahead of time. Pretty fair joke—pretty fair. Here he is, Polly! Washington's come, children!—come now, don't eat him up—finish him in the house. Welcome, my boy, to a mansion that is proud to shelter the son of the best man that walks on the ground. Si Hawkins has been a good friend to me, and I believe I can say that whenever I've had a chance to put him into a good thing I've done it, and done it pretty cheerfully, too. I put him into that sugar speculation—what a grand thing that was, if we hadn't held on too long!"

True enough; but holding on too long had utterly ruined both of them; and the saddest part of it was, that they never had had so much money to lose before, for Sellers's sale of their mule crop that year in New Orleans had been a great financial success. If he had kept out of sugar and gone back home content to stick to mules it would have been a happy wisdom. As it was, he managed to kill two birds with one stone—that is to say, he killed the sugar speculation by holding for high rates till he had to sell at the bottom figure, and that calamity killed the mule that laid the golden egg—which is but a figurative expression and will be so understood. Sellers had returned home cheerful but empty-handed, and the mule business lapsed into other hands. The sale of the Hawkins property by the Sheriff had followed, and the Hawkins hearts been torn to see Uncle Dan'l and his wife pass from the auction-block into the hands of a negro trader and depart for the remote South to be seen no more by the family. It had seemed like seeing their own flesh and blood sold into banishment.

Washington was greatly pleased with the Sellers mansion. It was a two-story-and-a-half brick, and much more stylish than any of its neighbors. He was borne to the family sitting room in triumph by the swarm of little Sellerses, the parents following with their arms about each other's waists.

The whole family were poorly and cheaply dressed; and the clothing, although neat and clean, showed many evidences of having seen long service. The Colonel's "stovepipe" hat was napless and shiny with much polishing, but nevertheless it had an almost convincing expression about it of having been just purchased new. The rest of his clothing was napless and shiny, too, but it had the air of being entirely satisfied with itself and blandly sorry for other people's clothes. It was growing rather dark in the house, and the evening air was chilly, too. Sellers said:

"Lay off your overcoat, Washington, and draw up to the stove and make yourself at home—just consider yourself under your own shingles my boy—I'll have a fire going, in a jiffy. Light the lamp, Polly, dear, and let's have things cheerful—just as glad to see you, Washington, as if you'd been lost a century and we'd found you again!"

By this time the Colonel was conveying a lighted match into a poor little stove. Then he propped the stove door to its place by leaning the poker against it, for the hinges had retired from business. This door framed a small square of isinglass, which now warmed up with a faint glow. Mrs. Sellers lit a cheap, showy lamp, which dissipated a good deal of the gloom, and then everybody gathered into the light and took the stove into close companionship.

The children climbed all over Sellers, fondled him, petted him, and were lavishly petted in return. Out from this tugging, laughing, chattering disguise of legs and arms and little faces, the Colonel's voice worked its way and his tireless tongue ran blithely on without interruption; and the purring little wife, diligent with her knitting, sat near at hand and looked happy and proud and grateful; and she listened as one who listens to oracles and gospels and whose grateful soul is being refreshed with the bread of life. By and by the children quieted down to listen; clustered about their father, and resting their elbows on his legs, they hung upon his words as if he were uttering the music of the spheres.

A dreary old hair-cloth sofa against the wall; a few damaged chairs; the small table the lamp stood on; the crippled stove—these things constituted the furniture of the room. There was no carpet on the floor; on the wall were occasional square-shaped interruptions of the general tint of the plaster which betrayed that there used to be pictures in the house—but there were none now. There were no mantel ornaments, unless one might bring himself to regard as an ornament a clock which never came within fifteen strokes of striking the right time, and whose hands always hitched together at twenty-two minutes past anything and traveled in company the rest of the way home.

"Remarkable clock!" said Sellers, and got up and wound it. "I've been offered—well, I wouldn't expect you to believe what I've been offered for that clock. Old Gov. Hager never sees me but he says, 'Come, now, Colonel, name your price—I *must* have that clock!' But my goodness I'd as soon think of selling my wife. As I was saying to————silence in the court, now, she's begun to strike! You can't talk against her—you have to just be patient and hold up till she's said her say. Ah—well, as I was saying, when—she's beginning again! Nineteen, twenty, twenty-one, twenty-two, twen———ah, that's all.—Yes, as I was saying to old Judge———go it, old girl, don't mind me.—Now how is that?—isn't that a good, spirited tone? She can wake the dead! Sleep? Why you might as well try to sleep in a thunder-factory. Now just listen at that. She'll strike a hundred and fifty, now, without stopping,—you'll see. There ain't another clock like that in Christendom."

Washington hoped that this might be true, for the din was distracting—though the family, one and all, seemed filled with joy; and the more the clock "buckled down to her work" as the Colonel expressed it, and the more insupportable the clatter became, the more enchanted they all appeared to be. When there was silence, Mrs. Sellers lifted upon Washington a face that beamed with a childlike pride, and said:

"It belonged to his grandmother."

The look and the tone were a plain call for admiring surprise, and therefore Washington said—(it was the only thing that offered itself at the moment:)

"Indeed!"

"Yes, it did, didn't it father!" exclaimed one of the twins. "She was my great-grandmother—and George's too; wasn't she, father! *You* never saw her, but Sis has seen her, when Sis was a baby—didn't you, Sis! Sis has seen her most a hundred times. She was awful deaf—she's dead, now. Ain't she, father!"

All the children chimed in, now, with one general Babel of information about deceased—nobody offering to read the riot act or seeming to discountenance the insurrection or disapprove of it in any way—but the head twin drowned all the turmoil and held his own against the field:

"It's our clock, now—and it's got wheels inside of it, and a thing that flutters every time she strikes—don't it, father! Great-grandmother died before hardly any of us was born—she was an Old-School Baptist and had warts all over her—you ask father if she didn't. She had an uncle that was bald-headed and used to have fits; he wasn't *our* uncle, I don't know what he was to us— some kin or another I reckon—father's seen him a thousand times—hain't you, father! We used to have a calf that et apples and just chawed up dishrags like nothing, and if you stay here you'll see lots of funerals—won't he, Sis! Did you ever see a house afire? *I* have! Once me and Jim Terry———"

But Sellers began to speak now, and the storm ceased. He began to tell about an enormous speculation he was thinking of embarking some capital in—a speculation which some London bankers had been over to consult with him about—and soon he was building glittering pyramids of coin, and Washington was presently growing opulent under the magic of his eloquence. But at the same time Washington was not able to ignore the cold entirely. He was nearly as close to the stove as he could get, and yet he could not persuade himself that he felt the slightest heat, notwithstanding the isinglass door was still gently and serenely glowing. He tried to get a trifle closer to the stove, and the consequence was, he tripped the supporting poker and the stove-door tumbled to the floor. And then there was a revelation—there was nothing in the stove but a lighted tallow-candle!

The poor youth blushed and felt as if he must die with shame. But the Colonel was only disconcerted for a moment—he straightaway found his voice again:

"A little idea of my own, Washington—one of the greatest things in the world! You must write and tell your father about it—don't forget that, now. I have been reading up some European Scientific reports—friend of mine, Count Fugier, sent them to me—sends me all sorts of things from Paris—he thinks the world of me, Fugier does. Well, I saw that the Academy of France had been testing the properties of heat, and they came to the conclusion that it was a non-conductor or something like that, and of course its influence must necessarily be deadly in nervous organizations with excitable temperaments, especially where there is any tendency toward rheumatic affections. Bless you I saw in a moment what was the matter with us, and says I, out goes your fires!—no more slow torture and certain death for me, sir. What you want is the *appearance* of heat, not the heat itself—that's the idea. Well how to do it was the next thing. I just put my head to work, pegged away a couple of days, and here you are! Rheumatism? Why a man can't any more start a case of rheumatism in this house than he can shake an opinion out of a mummy! Stove with a candle in it and a transparent door—that's it—it has been the salvation of this family. Don't you fail to write your father about it, Washington. And tell him the idea is mine—I'm no more conceited than most people, I reckon, but you know it is human nature for a man to want credit for a thing like that."

Washington said with his blue lips that he would, but he said in his secret heart that he would promote no such iniquity. He tried to believe in the healthfulness of the invention, and succeeded tolerably well; but after all he could not feel that good health in a frozen body was any real improvement on the rheumatism.

CHAPTER VIII

—When pe borde is thynne, as of seruyse,
  Nougth replenesshed with grete diuersite
Of mete & drinke, good chere may then suffise
  With honest talkyng—
                              The Book of Curtesye.

Mammon. Come on, sir. Now, you set your foot on shore
In *Novo Orbe;* here's the rich Peru:
And there within, sir, are the golden mines,
Great Solomon's Ophir!——
                              B. Jonson.

THE SUPPER AT COL. SELLERS'S was not sumptuous, in the beginning, but it improved on acquaintance. That is to say, that what
Washington regarded at first sight as mere lowly potatoes,
presently became awe-inspiring agricultural productions that had
been reared in some ducal garden beyond the sea, under the sacred eye of the duke himself, who had sent them to Sellers; the
bread was from corn which could be grown in only one favored
locality in the earth and only a favored few could get it; the Rio
coffee, which at first seemed execrable to the taste, took to itself
an improved flavor when Washington was told to drink it slowly
and not hurry what should be a lingering luxury in order to be
fully appreciated—it was from the private stores of a Brazilian
nobleman with an unrememberable name. The Colonel's tongue
was a magician's wand that turned dried apples into figs and water into wine as easily as it could change a hovel into a palace and
present poverty into imminent future riches.

Washington slept in a cold bed in a carpetless room and woke
up in a palace in the morning; at least the palace lingered during the
moment that he was rubbing his eyes and getting his bearings—
and then it disappeared and he recognized that the Colonel's inspiring talk had been influencing his dreams. Fatigue had made
him sleep late; when he entered the sitting room he noticed that
the old hair-cloth sofa was absent; when he sat down to breakfast

the Colonel tossed six or seven dollars in bills on the table, counted them over, said he was a little short and must call upon his banker; then returned the bills to his wallet with the indifferent air of a man who is used to money. The breakfast was not an improvement upon the supper, but the Colonel talked it up and transformed it into an oriental feast. By and by, he said:

"I intend to look out for you, Washington, my boy. I hunted up a place for you yesterday, but I am not referring to that, now—that is a mere livelihood—mere bread and butter; but when I say I mean to look out for you I mean something very different. I mean to put things in your way that will make a mere livelihood a trifling thing. I'll put you in a way to make more money than you'll ever know what to do with. You'll be right here where I can put my hand on you when anything turns up. I've got some prodigious operations on foot; but I'm keeping quiet; mum's the word; your old hand don't go around pow-wowing and letting everybody see his k'yards and find out his little game. But all in good time, Washington, all in good time. You'll see. Now there's an operation in corn that looks well. Some New York men are trying to get me to go into it—buy up all the growing crops and just boss the market when they mature—ah I tell you it's a great thing. And it only costs a trifle; two millions or two and a half will do it. I haven't exactly promised yet—there's no hurry—the more indifferent I seem, you know, the more anxious those fellows will get. And then there is the hog speculation—that's bigger still. We've got quiet men at work," [he was very impressive here,] "mousing around, to get propositions out of all the farmers in the whole west and northwest for the hog crop, and other agents quietly getting propositions and terms out of all the manufactories—and don't you see, if we can get all the hogs and all the slaughter houses into our hands on the dead quiet—whew! it would take three ships to carry the money.—I've looked into the thing—calculated all the chances for and all the chances against, and though I shake my head and hesitate and keep on thinking, apparently, I've got my mind made up that if the thing can be done on a capital of six millions, that's the horse to put up money on! Why Washington—but what's the use talking about it—any man can see that there's whole Atlantic oceans of cash in it, gulfs and bays thrown in. But there's a bigger thing than that, yet—a bigger————"

"Why Colonel, you can't want anything bigger!" said Washington, his eyes blazing. "Oh, I wish I could go into either of those speculations—I only wish I had money—I wish I wasn't cramped and kept down and fettered with poverty, and such prodigious chances lying right here in sight! Oh, it is a fearful thing to be poor. But don't throw away those things—they are so splendid and I can see how sure they are. Don't throw them away for something still better and maybe fail in it! I wouldn't, Colonel. I would stick to these. I wish father were here and were his old self again—Oh, he never in his life had such chances as these are. Colonel, you *can't* improve on these—no man can improve on them!"

A sweet, compassionate smile played about the Colonel's features, and he leaned over the table with the air of a man who is "going to show you" and do it without the least trouble:

"Why Washington, my boy, these things are nothing. They *look* large—of course they look large to a novice, but to a man who has been all his life accustomed to large operations—shaw! They're well enough to while away an idle hour with, or furnish a bit of employment that will give a trifle of idle capital a chance to earn its bread while it is waiting for something to *do*, but—now just listen a moment—just let me give you an idea of what we old veterans of commerce call 'business.' Here's the Rothschilds' proposition—this is between you and me, you understand————"

Washington nodded three or four times impatiently, and his glowing eyes said, "Yes, yes—hurry—I understand————"

————"for I wouldn't have it get out for a fortune. They want me to go in with them on the sly—agent was here two weeks ago about it—go in on the sly" [voice down to an impressive whisper, now,] "and buy up a hundred and thirteen wild cat banks in Ohio, Indiana, Kentucky, Illinois and Missouri—notes of these banks are at all sorts of discount now—average discount of the hundred and thirteen is forty-four per cent.—buy them all up, you see, and then all of a sudden let the cat out of the bag! Whiz! the stock of every one of those wild cats would spin up to a tremendous premium before you could turn a handspring—profit on the speculation not a dollar less than forty millions!" [An eloquent pause, while the marvelous vision settled into W.'s focus.] "Where's your hogs now! Why my dear innocent boy, we would just sit down on the front door-steps and peddle banks like lucifer matches!"

Washington finally got his breath and said:

"Oh, it is perfectly wonderful! Why couldn't these things have happened in father's day? And I—it's of no use—they simply lie before my face and mock me. There is nothing for me but to stand helpless and see other people reap the astonishing harvest."

"Never mind, Washington, don't you worry. I'll fix you. There's plenty of chances. How much money have you got?"

In the presence of so many millions, Washington could not keep from blushing when he had to confess that he had but eighteen dollars in the world.

"Well, all right—don't despair. Other people have been obliged to begin with less. I have a small idea that may develop into something for us both, all in good time. Keep your money close and add to it. I'll make it breed. I've been experimenting (to pass away the time,) on a little preparation for curing sore eyes—a kind of decoction nine-tenths water and the other tenth drugs that don't cost more than a dollar a barrel; I'm still experimenting; there's one ingredient wanted yet to perfect the thing, and somehow I can't just manage to hit upon the thing that's necessary, and I don't dare talk with a chemist, of course. But I'm progressing, and before many weeks I wager the country will ring with the fame of Beriah Sellers' Infallible Imperial Oriental Optic Liniment and Salvation for Sore Eyes—the Medical Wonder of the Age! Small bottles fifty cents, large ones a dollar. Average cost, five and seven cents for the two sizes. The first year sell, say, ten thousand bottles in Missouri, seven thousand in Iowa, three thousand in Arkansas, four thousand in Kentucky, six thousand in Illinois, and say twenty-five thousand in the rest of the country. Total, fifty-five thousand bottles; profit clear of all expenses, twenty thousand dollars at the very lowest calculation. All the capital needed is to manufacture the first two thousand bottles—say a hundred and fifty dollars—then the money would begin to flow in. The second year, sales would reach 200,000 bottles—clear profit, say, $75,000—and in the meantime the great factory would be building in St. Louis, to cost, say, $100,000. The third year we could easily sell 1,000,000 bottles in the United States and————"

"O, splendid!" said Washington. "Let's commence right away—let's————"

"————1,000,000 bottles in the United States—profit at least $350,000—and *then* it would begin to be time to turn our attention toward the *real* idea of the business."

"The *real* idea of it! Ain't $350,000 a year a pretty real————"

"Stuff! Why what an infant you are, Washington—what a guileless, short-sighted, easily-contented innocent you are, my poor little country-bred know-nothing! Would I go to all that trouble and bother for the poor crumbs a body might pick up in *this* country? Now do I look like a man who—does my history suggest that I am a man who deals in trifles, contents himself with the narrow horizon that hems in the common herd, sees no further than the end of his nose? Now *you* know that that is not me—couldn't *be* me. *You* ought to know that if I throw my time and abilities into a patent medicine, it's a patent medicine whose field of operations is the solid earth! its clients the swarming nations that inhabit it! Why what is the republic of America for an eye-water country? Lord bless you, it is nothing but a barren highway that you've got to cross to get *to* the true eye-water market! Why, Washington, in the Oriental countries people swarm like the sands of the desert; every square mile of ground upholds its thousands upon thousands of struggling human creatures—and every separate and individual devil of them's got the ophthalmia! It's as natural to them as noses are—and sin. It's born with them, it stays with them, it's all that some of them have left when they die. Three years of introductory trade in the orient and what will be the result? Why, our headquarters would be in Constantinople and our hindquarters in Further India! Factories and warehouses in Cairo, Ispahan, Bagdad, Damascus, Jerusalem, Yedo,[21] Peking, Bangkok, Delhi, Bombay and Calcutta! Annual income—well, God only knows how many millions and millions apiece!"

Washington was so dazed, so bewildered—his heart and his eyes had wandered so far away among the strange lands beyond the seas, and such avalanches of coin and currency had fluttered and jingled confusedly down before him, that he was now as one who has been whirling round and round for a time, and, stopping all at once, finds his surroundings still whirling and all objects a dancing chaos. However, little by little the Sellers family cooled down and crystalized into shape, and the poor room lost its glitter and resumed its poverty. Then the youth found his voice and begged Sellers to drop everything and hurry up the eye-water; and he got his eighteen dollars and tried to force it upon the Colonel—pleaded with him to take it—implored him to do it. But the Colonel would not; said he would not need the capital (in his native magnificent way he called that eighteen dollars Capital) till the eye-water was an accomplished fact. He made Washington easy in his mind, though, by promising that he would call for it just as soon as the invention was finished, and he added the glad tidings that nobody but just they two should be admitted to a share in the speculation.

When Washington left the breakfast table he could have worshiped that man. Washington was one of that kind of people whose hopes are in the very clouds one day and in the gutter the next. He walked on air, now. The Colonel was ready to take him around and introduce him to the employment he had found for him, but Washington begged for a few moments in which to write home; with his kind of people, to ride to-day's new interest to death and put off yesterday's till another time, is nature itself. He ran up stairs and wrote glowingly, enthusiastically, to his mother about the hogs and the corn, the banks and the eye-water—and added a few inconsequential millions to each project. And he said that people little dreamed what a man Col. Sellers was, and that the world would open its eyes when it found out. And he closed his letter thus:

"So make yourself perfectly easy, mother—in a little while you shall have everything you want, and more. I am not likely to stint *you* in anything, I fancy. This money will not be for me, alone, but for all of us. I want all to share alike; and there is going to be far more for each than one person can spend. Break it to father cautiously—you understand the need of that—break it to him cautiously, for he has had such cruel hard fortune, and is so stricken by it that great good news might prostrate him more surely than even bad, for he is used to the bad but is grown sadly unaccustomed to the other. Tell Laura—tell all the children. And write to Clay about it if he is not with you yet. You may tell Clay that whatever I get he can freely share in—freely. He knows that that is true—there will be no need that I should swear to that to make him believe it. Good-bye—and mind what I say: Rest perfectly easy, one and all of you, for our troubles are nearly at an end."

Poor lad, he could not know that his mother would cry some loving, compassionate tears over his letter and put off the family with a synopsis of its contents which conveyed a deal of love to them but not much idea of his prospects or projects. And he never dreamed that such a joyful letter could sadden her and fill her night with sighs, and troubled thoughts, and bodings of the future, instead of filling it with peace and blessing it with restful sleep.

When the letter was done, Washington and the Colonel sallied forth, and as they walked along Washington learned what he was to be. He was to be a clerk in a real estate office. Instantly the fickle youth's dreams forsook the magic eye-water and flew back to the Tennessee Land. And the gorgeous possibilities of that great domain straightway began to occupy his imagination to such a degree that he could scarcely manage to keep even enough of his attention upon the Colonel's talk to retain the general run of what he was saying. He was glad it was a real estate office—he was a made man now, sure.

The Colonel said that General Boswell was a rich man and had a good and growing business; and that Washington's work would be light and he would get forty dollars a month and be boarded and lodged in the General's family—which was as good as ten dollars more; and even better, for he could not live as well even at the "City Hotel" as he would there, and yet the hotel charged fifteen dollars a month where a man had a good room.

General Boswell was in his office; a comfortable looking place, with plenty of outline maps hanging about the walls and in the windows, and a spectacled man was marking out another one on a long table. The office was in the principal street. The General received Washington with a kindly but reserved politeness. Washington rather liked his looks. He was about fifty years old, dignified, well preserved and well dressed. After the Colonel took his leave, the General talked a while with Washington—his talk consisting chiefly of instructions about the clerical duties of the place. He seemed satisfied as to Washington's ability to take care of the books, he was evidently a pretty fair theoretical book-keeper, and experience would soon harden theory into practice. By and by dinner-time came, and the two walked to the General's house; and now Washington noticed an instinct in himself that moved him to keep not in the General's rear, exactly, but yet not at his side— somehow the old gentleman's dignity and reserve did not inspire familiarity.

CHAPTER IX

Quando ti veddi per la prima volta,
Parse che mi s'aprisse il paradiso,
E venissano gli augioli a un per volta
Tutti ad apporsi sopra al tuo bel viso,
Tutti ad apporsi sopra il tuo bel volto,
M'incatenasti, e non mi so'anco sciolto—

Yʋmohmi hoka, himak a yakni ilʋppʋt immi ha chi ho—

—Tajma kittôrnaminut innèiziungnaerame, isikkaene sinikbingmun
illièj, annerningaerdlunilo siurdliminut piok.

Mos. Agl. Siurdl. 49.32.

WASHINGTON DREAMED HIS WAY along the street, his fancy flitting from grain to hogs, from hogs to banks, from banks to eyewater, from eye-water to Tennessee Land, and lingering but a feverish moment upon each of these fascinations. He was conscious of but one outward thing, to wit, the General, and he was really not vividly conscious of him.

Arrived at the finest dwelling in the town, they entered it and were at home. Washington was introduced to Mrs. Boswell, and his imagination was on the point of flitting into the vapory realms of speculation again, when a lovely girl of sixteen or seventeen came in. This vision swept Washington's mind clear of its chaos of glittering rubbish in an instant. Beauty had fascinated him before; many times he had been in love—even for weeks at a time with the same object—but his heart had never suffered so sudden and so fierce an assault as this, within his recollection.

Louise Boswell occupied his mind and drifted among his multiplication tables all the afternoon. He was constantly catching himself in a reverie—reveries made up of recalling how she looked when she first burst upon him; how her voice thrilled him when she first spoke; how charmed the very air seemed by her presence. Blissful as the afternoon was, delivered up to such a revel as this, it seemed an eternity, so impatient was he to see the girl again. Other afternoons like it followed. Washington plunged into this love affair as he plunged into everything else—upon impulse and without reflection. As the days went by it seemed plain that he was growing in favor with Louise,—not sweepingly so, but yet perceptibly, he fancied. His attentions to her troubled her father and mother a little, and they warned Louise, without stating particulars or making allusions to any special person, that a girl was sure to make a mistake who allowed herself to marry anybody but a man who could support her well.

Some instinct taught Washington that his present lack of money would be an obstruction, though possibly not a bar, to his hopes, and straightway his poverty became a torture to him which cast all his former sufferings under that head into the shade. He longed for riches now as he had never longed for them before.

He had been once or twice to dine with Col. Sellers, and had been discouraged to note that the Colonel's bill of fare was falling off both in quantity and quality—a sign, he feared, that the lacking ingredient in the eye-water still remained undiscovered—though Sellers always explained that these changes in the family diet had been ordered by the doctor, or suggested by some new scientific work the Colonel had stumbled upon. But it always turned out that the lacking ingredient *was* still lacking—though it always appeared, at the same time, that the Colonel was right on its heels.

Every time the Colonel came into the real estate office Washington's heart bounded and his eyes lighted with hope, but it always turned out that the Colonel was merely on the scent of some vast, undefined landed speculation—although he was customarily able to say that he was nearer to the all-necessary ingredient than ever, and could almost name the hour when success would dawn. And then Washington's heart would sink again and a sigh would tell when it touched bottom.

About this time a letter came, saying that Judge Hawkins had been ailing for a fortnight, and was now considered to be seriously ill. It was thought best that Washington should come home. The news filled him with grief, for he loved and honored his father; the Boswells were touched by the youth's sorrow, and even the General unbent and said encouraging things to him.—There was balm in this; but when Louise bade him good-bye, and shook his hand and said, "Don't be cast down—it will all come out right—I *know* it will all come out right," it seemed a blessed thing to be in misfortune, and the tears that welled up to his eyes were the messengers of an adoring and a grateful heart; and when the girl saw them and answering tears came into her own eyes, Washington could hardly contain the excess of happiness that poured into the cavities of his breast that were so lately stored to the roof with grief.

All the way home he nursed his woe and exalted it. He pictured himself as *she* must be picturing him: a noble, struggling young spirit persecuted by misfortune, but bravely and patiently waiting in the shadow of a dread calamity and preparing to meet the blow as became one who was all too used to hard fortune and the pitiless buffetings of fate. These thoughts made him weep, and weep more broken-heartedly than ever; and he wished that she could see his sufferings *now*.

There was nothing significant in the fact that Louise, dreamy and distraught, stood at her bedroom bureau that night, scribbling "Washington" here and there over a sheet of paper. But there was something significant in the fact that she scratched the word out every time she wrote it; examined the erasure critically to see if anybody could guess at what the word had been; then buried it under a maze of obliterating lines; and finally, as if still unsatisfied, burned the paper.

When Washington reached home, he recognized at once how serious his father's case was. The darkened room, the labored breathing and occasional moanings of the patient, the tip-toeing of the attendants and their whispered consultations, were full of sad meaning. For three or four nights Mrs. Hawkins and Laura had been watching by the bedside; Clay had arrived, preceding Washington by one day, and he was now added to the corps of watchers. Mr. Hawkins would have none but these three, though neighborly assistance was offered by old friends. From this time forth three-hour watches were instituted, and day and night the watchers kept their vigils. By degrees Laura and her mother began to show wear, but neither of them would yield a minute of their tasks to Clay.—He ventured once to let the midnight hour pass without calling Laura, but he ventured no more; there was that about her rebuke when he tried to explain, that taught him that to let her sleep when she might be ministering to her father's needs, was to rob her of moments that were priceless in her eyes; he perceived that she regarded it as a privilege to watch, not a burden. And he had noticed, also, that when midnight struck, the patient turned his eyes toward the door, with an expectancy in them which presently grew into a longing but brightened into contentment as soon as the door opened and Laura appeared. And he did not need Laura's rebuke when he heard his father say:

"Clay is good, and you are tired, poor child; but I wanted you so."

"Clay is not good, father—he did not call me. I would not have treated *him* so. How could you do it, Clay?"

Clay begged forgiveness and promised not to break faith again; and as he betook him to his bed, he said to himself, "It's a steadfast little soul; whoever thinks he is doing the Duchess a kindness by intimating that she is not sufficient for any undertaking she puts her hand to, makes a mistake; and if I did not know it before, I know now that there are surer ways of pleasing her than by trying to lighten her labor when that labor consists in wearing herself out for the sake of a person she loves."

A week drifted by, and all the while the patient sank lower and lower. The night drew on that was to end all suspense. It was a wintry one. The darkness gathered, the snow was falling, the wind wailed plaintively about the house or shook it with fitful gusts. The doctor had paid his last visit and gone away with that dismal remark to the nearest friend of the family that he "believed there was nothing more that he could do"—a remark which is always overheard by some one it is not meant for and strikes a lingering half-conscious hope dead with a withering shock; the medicine phials had been removed from the bedside and put out of sight, and all things made orderly and meet for the solemn event that was impending; the patient, with closed eyes, lay scarcely breathing; the watchers sat by and wiped the gathering damps from his forehead while the silent tears flowed down their faces; the deep hush was only interrupted by sobs from the children, grouped about the bed.

After a time,—it was toward midnight now—Mr. Hawkins roused out of a doze, looked about him and was evidently trying to speak. Instantly Laura lifted his head and in a failing voice he said, while something of the old light shone in his eyes:

"Wife—children—come nearer—nearer. The darkness grows. Let me see you all, once more."

The group closed together at the bedside, and their tears and sobs came now without restraint.

"I am leaving you in cruel poverty. I have been—so foolish—so short-sighted. But courage! A better day is—is coming. Never lose sight of the Tennessee Land! Be wary. There is wealth stored up for you there—wealth that is boundless! The children shall hold up their heads with the best in the land, yet. Where are the papers?—Have you got the papers safe? Show them—show them to me!"

Under his strong excitement his voice had gathered power and his last sentences were spoken with scarcely a perceptible halt or hindrance. With an effort he had raised himself almost without assistance to a sitting posture. But now the fire faded out of his eyes and he fell back exhausted. The papers were brought and held before him, and the answering smile that flitted across his face showed that he was satisfied. He closed his eyes, and the signs of approaching dissolution multiplied rapidly. He lay almost motionless for a little while, then suddenly partly raised his head and looked about him as one who peers into a dim uncertain light. He muttered:

"Gone? No—I see you—still. It is—it is—over. But you are—safe. Safe. The Ten———"

The voice died out in a whisper; the sentence was never finished. The emaciated fingers began to pick at the coverlet, a fatal sign. After a time there were no sounds but the cries of the mourners within and the gusty turmoil of the wind without. Laura had bent down and kissed her father's lips as the spirit left the body; but she did not sob, or utter any ejaculation; her tears flowed silently. Then she closed the dead eyes, and crossed the hands upon the breast; after a season, she kissed the forehead reverently, drew the sheet up over the face, and then walked apart and sat down with the look of one who is done with life and has no further interest in its joys and sorrows, its hopes or its ambitions. Clay buried his face in the coverlet of the bed; when the other children and the mother realized that death was indeed come at last, they threw themselves into each other's arms and gave way to a frenzy of grief.

CHAPTER X

—Okarbigàlo: "Kia pannigátit? Assarsara! uamnut nevsoïngoarna"—
Mo. Agleg. Siurdl. 24. 23.

Nootah nuttaunes, natwontash
Kukkeihtash, wonk yeuyeu
Wannaanum kummissinninnumog
Kak Koosh week pannuppu.

—La Giannetta rispose: Madama voi dalla povertà di mio padre
togliendomi, come figliuola cresciuta m'avete, e per questo agni vostro
piacer far dovrei—
Boccacio, Decam. Giom. 2, Nov. 6.

ONLY TWO OR THREE DAYS had elapsed since the funeral, when something happened which was to change the drift of Laura's life somewhat, and influence in a greater or lesser degree the formation of her character.

Major Lackland had once been a man of note in the State—a man of extraordinary natural ability and as extraordinary learning. He had been universally trusted and honored in his day, but had finally fallen into misfortune; while serving his third term in Congress, and while upon the point of being elevated to the Senate—which was considered the summit of earthly aggrandizement in those days—he had yielded to temptation, when in distress for money wherewith to save his estate, and sold his vote. His crime was discovered, and his fall followed instantly. Nothing could reinstate him in the confidence of the people, his ruin was irretrievable—his disgrace complete. All doors were closed against him, all men avoided him. After years of sulking retirement and dissipation, death had relieved him of his troubles at last, and his funeral followed close upon that of Mr. Hawkins. He died as he had latterly lived—wholly alone and friendless. He had no relatives—or if he had they did not acknowledge him. The coroner's jury found certain memoranda upon his body and about the premises which revealed a fact not suspected by the villagers before—viz., that Laura was not the child of Mr. and Mrs. Hawkins.

The gossips were soon at work. They were but little hampered by the fact that the memoranda referred to betrayed nothing but the bare circumstance that Laura's real parents were unknown, and stopped there. So far from being hampered by this, the gossips seemed to gain all the more freedom from it. They supplied all the missing information themselves, they filled up all the blanks. The town soon teemed with histories of Laura's origin and secret history, no two versions precisely alike, but all elaborate, exhaustive, mysterious and interesting, and all agreeing in one vital particular—to wit, that there was a suspicious cloud about her birth, not to say a disreputable one.

Laura began to encounter cold looks, averted eyes and peculiar nods and gestures which perplexed her beyond measure; but presently the pervading gossip found its way to her, and she understood them then. Her pride was stung. She was astonished, and at first incredulous. She was about to ask her mother if there was any truth in these reports, but upon second thought held her peace. She soon gathered that Major Lackland's memoranda seemed to refer to letters which had passed between himself and Judge Hawkins. She shaped her course without difficulty the day that that hint reached her.

That night she sat in her room till all was still, and then she stole into the garret and began a search. She rummaged long among boxes of musty papers relating to business matters of no interest to her, but at last she found several bundles of letters. One bundle was marked "private," and in that she found what she wanted. She selected six or eight letters from the package and began to devour their contents, heedless of the cold.

By the dates, these letters were from five to seven years old. They were all from Major Lackland to Mr. Hawkins. The substance of them was, that some one in the east had been inquiring of Major Lackland about a lost child and its parents, and that it was conjectured that the child might be Laura.

Evidently some of the letters were missing, for the name of the inquirer was not mentioned; there was a casual reference to "this handsome-featured aristocratic gentleman," as if the reader and the writer were accustomed to speak of him and knew who was meant.

In one letter the Major said he agreed with Mr. Hawkins that the inquirer seemed not altogether on the wrong track; but he also agreed that it would be best to keep quiet until more convincing developments were forthcoming.

Another letter said that "the poor soul broke completely down when he saw Laura's picture, and declared it must be she."

Still another said,

"He seems entirely alone in the world, and his heart is so wrapped up in this thing that I believe that if it proved a false hope, it would kill him; I have persuaded him to wait a little while and go west when I go."

Another letter had this paragraph in it:

"He is better one day and worse the next, and is out of his mind a good deal of the time. Lately his case has developed a something which is a wonder to the hired nurses, but which will not be much of a marvel to you if you have read medical philosophy much. It is this: his lost memory returns to him when he is delirious, and goes away again when he is himself—just as old Canada Joe used to talk the French *patois* of his boyhood in the delirium of typhus fever, though he could not do it when his mind was clear. Now this poor gentleman's memory has always broken down before he reached the explosion of the steamer; he could only remember starting up the river with his wife and child, and he had an idea that there was a race, but he was not certain; he could not name the boat he was on; there was a dead blank of a month or more that supplied not an item to his recollection. It was not for me to assist him, of course. But now in his delirium *it all comes out:* the names of the boats, every incident of the explosion, and likewise the details of his astonishing escape—that is, up to where, just as a yawl-boat was approaching him (he was clinging to the starboard wheel of the burning wreck at the time), a falling timber struck him on the head. But I will write out his wonderful escape in full to-morrow or next day. Of course the physicians will not let me tell him now that our Laura is indeed his child—that must come later, when his health is thoroughly restored. His case is not considered dangerous at all; he will recover presently, the doctors say. But they insist that he must travel a little when he gets well—they recommend a short sea voyage, and they say he can be persuaded to try it if we continue to keep him in ignorance and promise to let him see L. as soon as he returns."

The letter that bore the latest date of all, contained this clause:

"It is the most unaccountable thing in the world; the mystery remains as impenetrable as ever; I have hunted high and low for him, and inquired of everybody, but in vain; all trace of him ends at that hotel in New York; I never have seen or heard of him since, up to this day; he could hardly have sailed, for his name does not appear upon the books of any shipping office in New York or Boston or Baltimore. How fortunate it seems, now, that we kept this thing to ourselves; Laura still has a father in you, and it is better for her that we drop this subject here forever."

That was all. Random remarks here and there, being pieced together gave Laura a vague impression of a man of fine presence, about forty-three or forty-five years of age, with dark hair and eyes, and a slight limp in his walk—it was not stated which leg was defective. And this indistinct shadow represented her father. She made an exhaustive search for the missing letters, but found none. They had probably been burned; and she doubted not that the ones she had ferreted out would have shared the same fate if Mr. Hawkins had not been a dreamer, void of method, whose mind was perhaps in a state of conflagration over some bright new speculation when he received them.

She sat long, with the letters in her lap, thinking—and unconsciously freezing. She felt like a lost person who has traveled down a long lane in good hope of escape, and, just as the night descends finds his progress barred by a bridgeless river whose further shore, if it has one, is lost in the darkness. If she could only have found these letters a month sooner! That was her thought. But now the dead had carried their secrets with them. A dreary melancholy settled down upon her. An undefined sense of injury crept into her heart. She grew very miserable.

She had just reached the romantic age—the age when there is a sad sweetness, a dismal comfort to a girl to find out that there is a mystery connected with her birth, which no other piece of good luck can afford. She had more than her rightful share of practical good sense, but still she was human; and to be human is to have one's little modicum of romance secreted away in one's composition. One never ceases to make a hero of one's self, (in private), during life, but only alters the style of his heroism from time to time as the drifting years belittle certain gods of his admiration and raise up others in their stead that seem greater.

The recent wearing days and nights of watching, and the wasting grief that had possessed her, combined with the profound depression that naturally came with the reaction of idleness, made Laura peculiarly susceptible at this time to romantic impressions. She was a heroine, now, with a mysterious father somewhere. She could not really tell whether she wanted to find him and spoil it all or not; but still all the traditions of romance pointed to the making the attempt as the usual and necessary course to follow; therefore she would some day begin the search when opportunity should offer.

Now a former thought struck her—she would speak to Mrs. Hawkins. And naturally enough Mrs. Hawkins appeared on the stage at that moment.

She said she knew all—she knew that Laura had discovered the secret that Mr. Hawkins, the elder children, Col. Sellers and herself had kept so long and so faithfully; and she cried and said that now that troubles had begun they would never end; her daughter's love would wean itself away from her and her heart would break. Her grief so wrought upon Laura that the girl almost forgot her own troubles for the moment in her compassion for her mother's distress. Finally Mrs. Hawkins said:

"Speak to me, child—do not forsake me. Forget all this miserable talk. Say I am your mother!—I have loved you so long, and there is no other. I *am* your mother, in the sight of God, and nothing shall ever take you from me!"

All barriers fell, before this appeal. Laura put her arms about her mother's neck and said:

"You *are* my mother, and always shall be. We will be as we have always been; and neither this foolish talk nor any other thing shall part us or make us less to each other than we are this hour."

There was no longer any sense of separation or estrangement between them. Indeed their love seemed more perfect now than it had ever been before. By and by they went down stairs and sat by the fire and talked long and earnestly about Laura's history and the letters. But it transpired that Mrs. Hawkins had never known of this correspondence between her husband and Major Lackland. With his usual consideration for his wife, Mr. Hawkins had shielded her from the worry the matter would have caused her.

Laura went to bed at last with a mind that had gained largely in tranquility and had lost correspondingly in morbid romantic exaltation. She was pensive, the next day, and subdued; but that was not matter for remark, for she did not differ from the mournful friends about her in that respect. Clay and Washington were the same loving and admiring brothers now that they had always been. The great secret was new to some of the younger children, but their love suffered no change under the wonderful revelation.

It is barely possible that things might have presently settled down into their old rut and the mystery have lost the bulk of its romantic sublimity in Laura's eyes, if the village gossips could have quieted down. But they could not quiet down and they did not. Day after day they called at the house, ostensibly upon visits of condolence, and they pumped away at the mother and the children without seeming to know that their questionings were in bad taste. They meant no harm—they only wanted to know. Villagers always want to know.

The family fought shy of the questionings, and of course that was high testimony—"if the Duchess was respectably born, why didn't they come out and prove it?—why did they stick to that poor thin story about picking her up out of a steamboat explosion?"

Under this ceaseless persecution, Laura's morbid self-communing was renewed. At night the day's contribution of detraction, innuendo and malicious conjecture would be canvassed in her mind, and then she would drift into a course of thinking. As her thoughts ran on, the indignant tears would spring to her eyes, and she would spit out fierce little ejaculations at intervals. But finally she would grow calmer and say some comforting disdainful thing—something like this:

"But who are they?—Animals! What are their opinions to me? Let them talk—I will not stoop to be affected by it. I could hate————. Nonsense—nobody I care for or in any way respect is changed toward me, I fancy."

She may have supposed she was thinking of many individuals, but it was not so—she was thinking of only one. And her heart warmed somewhat, too, the while. One day a friend overheard a conversation like this:—and naturally came and told her all about it:

"Ned, they say you don't go there any more. How is that?"

"Well, I don't; but I tell you it's not because I don't want to and it's not because *I* think it is any matter who her father was or who he wasn't, either; it's only on account of this talk, talk, talk. I think she is a fine girl every way, and so would you if you knew her as well as I do; but you know how it is when a girl once gets talked about—it's all up with her—the world won't ever let her alone, after that."

The only comment Laura made upon this revelation, was:

"Then it appears that if this trouble had not occurred I could have had the happiness of Mr. Ned Thurston's serious attentions. He is well favored in person, and well liked, too, I believe, and comes of one of the first families of the village. He is prosperous, too, I hear; has been a doctor a year, now, and has had two patients—no, three, I think; yes, it *was* three. I attended their funerals. Well, other people have hoped and been disappointed; I am not alone in that. I wish you could stay to dinner, Maria—we are going to have sausages; and besides, I wanted to talk to you about Hawkeye and make you promise to come and see us when we are settled there."

But Maria could not stay. She had come to mingle romantic tears with Laura's over the lover's defection and had found herself dealing with a heart that could not rise to an appreciation of affliction because its interest was all centered in sausages.

But as soon as Maria was gone, Laura stamped her expressive foot and said:

"The coward! Are all books lies? I thought he would fly to the front, and be brave and noble, and stand up for me against all the world, and defy my enemies, and wither these gossips with his scorn! Poor crawling thing, let him go. I *do* begin to despise this world!"

She lapsed into thought. Presently she said:

"If the time ever comes, and I get a chance, Oh, I'll————"

She could not find a word that was strong enough, perhaps. By and by she said:

"Well, I am glad of it—I'm glad of it. I never cared anything for him anyway!"

And then, with small consistency, she cried a little, and patted her foot more indignantly than ever.

CHAPTER XI

ずらゐぞあもどへらく

Two months had gone by and the Hawkins family were domiciled in Hawkeye. Washington was at work in the real estate office again, and was alternately in paradise or the other place just as it happened that Louise was gracious to him or seemingly indifferent—because indifference or preoccupation could mean nothing else than that she was thinking of some other young person. Col. Sellers had asked him several times, to dine with him, when he first returned to Hawkeye, but Washington, for no particular reason, had not accepted. No particular reason except one which he preferred to keep to himself—viz. that he could not bear to be away from Louise. It occurred to him, now, that the Colonel had not invited him lately—could he be offended? He resolved to go that very day, and give the Colonel a pleasant surprise. It was a good idea; especially as Louise had absented herself from breakfast that morning, and torn his heart; he would tear hers, now, and let her see how it felt.

The Sellers family were just starting to dinner when Washington burst upon them with his surprise. For an instant the Colonel looked nonplussed, and just a bit uncomfortable; and Mrs. Sellers looked actually distressed; but the next moment the head of the house was himself again, and exclaimed:

"All right, my boy, all right—always glad to see you—always glad to hear your voice and take you by the hand. Don't wait for special invitations—that's all nonsense among friends. Just come whenever you can, and come as often as you can—the oftener the better. You can't please us any better than that, Washington; the little woman will tell you so herself. We don't pretend to style. Plain folks, you know—plain folks. Just a plain family dinner, but such as it is, our friends are *always* welcome, I reckon you know that yourself, Washington. Run along, children, run along;

Lafayette,* stand off the cat's tail, child, can't you see what you're doing?—Come, come, come, Roderick Dhu,[22] it isn't nice for little boys to hang onto young gentlemen's coat tails—but never mind him, Washington, he's full of spirits and don't mean any harm. Children will be children, you know. Take the chair next to Mrs. Sellers, Washington,—tut, tut, Marie Antoinette, let your brother have the fork if he wants it, you are bigger than he is."

Washington contemplated the banquet, and wondered if he were in his right mind. Was this the plain family dinner? And was it all present? It was soon apparent that this was indeed the dinner: it was all on the table: it consisted of abundance of clear, fresh water, and a basin of raw turnips—nothing more.

Washington stole a glance at Mrs. Sellers's face, and would have given the world, the next moment, if he could have spared her that. The poor woman's face was crimson, and the tears stood in her eyes. Washington did not know what to do. He wished he had never come there and spied out this cruel poverty and brought pain to that poor little lady's heart and shame to her cheek; but he was there, and there was no escape. Col. Sellers hitched back his coat sleeves airly from his wrists as who should say "*Now* for solid enjoyment!" seized a fork, flourished it and began to harpoon turnips and deposit them in the plates before him:

"Let me help you, Washington—Lafayette pass this plate to Washington—ah, well, well, my boy, things are looking pretty bright, now, *I* tell you. Speculation—my! the whole atmosphere's full of money. I wouldn't take three fortunes for one little operation I've got on hand now—have anything from the casters?[23] Well, you're right, you're right. Some people like mustard with turnips, but—now there was Baron Poniatowski[24]—Lord, but

---

* In those old days the average man called his children after his most revered literary and historical idols; consequently there was hardly a family, at least in the West, but had a Washington in it—and also a Lafayette, a Franklin, and six or eight sounding names from Byron, Scott, and the Bible, if the offspring held out. To visit such a family, was to find one's self confronted by a congress made up of representatives of the imperial myths and the majestic dead of all the ages. There was something thrilling about it, to a stranger, not to say awe inspiring.

that man did know how to live!—true Russian you know, Russian to the back bone; I say to my wife, give me a Russian every time, for a table comrade. The Baron used to say, 'Take mustard, Sellers, try the mustard,—a man *can't* know what turnips are in perfection without mustard,' but I always said, 'No, Baron, I'm a plain man, and I want my food plain—none of your embellishments for Beriah Sellers—no made dishes for me! And it's the best way—high living kills more than it cures in this world, you can rest assured of that.—Yes indeed, Washington, I've got one little operation on hand that—take some more water—help yourself, won't you?—help yourself, there's plenty of it.—You'll find it pretty good, I guess. How does that fruit strike you?"

Washington said he did not know that he had ever tasted better. He did not add that he detested turnips even when they were cooked—loathed them in their natural state. No, he kept this to himself, and praised the turnips to the peril of his soul.

"I thought you'd like them. Examine them—examine them—they'll bear it. See how perfectly firm and juicy they are—they can't start any like them in this part of the country, I tell you. These are from New Jersey—I imported them myself. They cost like sin, too; but lord bless me, I go in for having the best of a thing, even if it does cost a little more—it's the best economy, in the long run. These are the Early Malcolm—it's a turnip that can't be produced except in just one orchard, and the supply never is up to the demand. Take some more water, Washington—you can't drink too much water with fruit—all the doctors say that. The plague can't come where this article is, my boy!"

"Plague? What plague?"

"What plague, indeed? Why the Asiatic plague that nearly depopulated London a couple of centuries ago."

"But how does that concern us? There is no plague here, I reckon."

"Sh! I've let it out! Well, never mind—just keep it to yourself. Perhaps I oughtn't said anything, but it's *bound* to come out sooner or later, so what is the odds? Old McDowells wouldn't like me to—to—bother it all, I'll just tell the whole thing and let it go. You see, I've been down to St. Louis, and I happened to run across old Dr. McDowells—thinks the world of me, does the doctor. He's a man that keeps himself to himself, and well he may, for he knows that he's got a reputation that covers the whole earth—he won't condescend to open himself out to many people, but lord bless you, he and I are just like brothers; he won't let me go to a hotel when I'm in the city—says I'm the only man that's company to him, and I don't know but there's some truth in it, too, because although I never like to glorify myself and make a great to-do over what I am or what I can do or what I know, I don't mind saying here among friends that I *am* better read up in most sciences, maybe, than the general run of professional men in these days. Well, the other day he let me into a little secret, strictly on the quiet, about this matter of the plague.

"You see it's booming right along in our direction—follows the Gulf Stream, you know, just as all those epidemics do,—and within three months it will be just waltzing through this land like a whirlwind! And whoever it touches can make his will and contract for the funeral. Well you can't *cure* it, you know, but you can prevent it. How? Turnips! that's it! Turnips and water! Nothing like it in the world, old McDowells says, just fill yourself up two or three times a day, and you can snap your fingers at the plague. Sh!—keep mum, but just you confine yourself to that diet and you're all right. I wouldn't have old McDowells know that I told about it for anything—he never would speak to me again. Take some more water, Washington—the more water you drink, the better. Here, let me give you some more of the turnips. No, no, no, now, I insist. There, now. Absorb those. They're mighty sustaining—brim full of nutriment—all the medical books say so. Just eat from four to seven good-sized turnips at a meal, and drink from a pint and a half to a quart of water, and then just sit around a couple of hours and let them ferment. You'll feel like a fighting cock next day."

Fifteen or twenty minutes later the Colonel's tongue was still chattering away—he had piled up several future fortunes out of several incipient "operations" which he had blundered into within the past week, and was now soaring along through some brilliant expectations born of late promising experiments upon the lacking ingredient of the eye-water. And at such a time Washington ought to have been a rapt and enthusiastic listener, but he was not, for two matters disturbed his mind and distracted his attention. One was, that he discovered, to his confusion and shame, that in allowing himself to be helped a second time to the turnips, he had robbed those hungry children. He had not needed the dreadful "fruit," and had not wanted it; and when he saw the pathetic sorrow in their faces when they asked for more and there was no more to give them, he hated himself for his stupidity and pitied the famishing young things with all his heart. The other matter that disturbed him was the dire inflation that had begun in his stomach. It grew and grew, it became more and more insupportable. Evidently the turnips were "fermenting." He forced himself to sit still as long as he could, but his anguish conquered him at last.

He rose in the midst of the Colonel's talk and excused himself on the plea of a previous engagement. The Colonel followed him to the door, promising over and over again that he would use his influence to get some of the Early Malcolms for him, and insisting that he should not be such a stranger but come and take pot-luck with him every chance he got. Washington was glad enough to get away and feel free again. He immediately bent his steps toward home.

In bed he passed an hour that threatened to turn his hair gray, and then a blessed calm settled down upon him that filled his heart with gratitude. Weak and languid, he made shift to turn himself about and seek rest and sleep; and as his soul hovered upon the brink of unconsciousness, he heaved a long, deep sigh, and said to himself that in his heart he had cursed the Colonel's preventive of rheumatism, before, and now *let* the plague come if it must—he was done with preventives; if ever any man beguiled him with turnips and water again, let him die the death.

If he dreamed at all that night, no gossiping spirit disturbed his visions to whisper in his ear of certain matters just then in bud in the East, more than a thousand miles away that after the lapse of a few years would develop influences which would profoundly affect the fate and fortunes of the Hawkins family.

CHAPTER XII

𓊖 𓏤 𓃭 𓏏𓏤 𓏥 𓏏𓏤

Todtenb. 141.17, 4.

"OH, IT'S EASY ENOUGH to make a fortune," Henry said.

"It seems to be easier than it is, I begin to think," replied Philip.

"Well, why don't you go into something? You'll never dig it out of the Astor Library."[25]

If there be any place and time in the world where and when it seems easy to "go into something" it is in Broadway on a spring morning, when one is walking city-ward, and has before him the long lines of palace-shops with an occasional spire seen through the soft haze that lies over the lower town, and hears the roar and hum of its multitudinous traffic.

To the young American, here or elsewhere, the paths to fortune are innumerable and all open; there is invitation in the air and success in all his wide horizon. He is embarrassed which to choose, and is not unlikely to waste years in dallying with his chances, before giving himself to the serious tug and strain of a single object. He has no traditions to bind him or guide him, and his impulse is to break away from the occupation his father has followed, and make a new way for himself.

Philip Sterling used to say that if he should seriously set himself for ten years to any one of the dozen projects that were in his brain, he felt that he could be a rich man. He wanted to be rich, he had a sincere desire for a fortune, but for some unaccountable reason he hesitated about addressing himself to the narrow work of getting it. He never walked Broadway, a part of its tide of abundant shifting life, without feeling something of the flush of wealth, and unconsciously taking the elastic step of one well-to-do in this prosperous world.

Especially at night in the crowded theatre—Philip was too

young to remember the old Chambers' Street box,[26] where the serious Burton[27] led his hilarious and pagan crew—in the intervals of the screaming comedy, when the orchestra scraped and grunted and tooted its dissolute tunes, the world seemed full of opportunities to Philip, and his heart exulted with a conscious ability to take any of its prizes he chose to pluck.

Perhaps it was the swimming ease of the acting on the stage, where virtue had its reward in three easy acts, perhaps it was the excessive light of the house, or the music, or the buzz of the excited talk between acts, perhaps it was youth which believed everything, but for some reason while Philip was at the theatre he had the utmost confidence in life and his ready victory in it.

Delightful illusion of paint and tinsel and silk attire, of cheap sentiment and high and mighty dialogue! Will there not always be rosin enough for the squeaking fiddle-bow? Do we not all like the maudlin hero, who is sneaking round the right entrance, in wait to steal the pretty wife of his rich and tyrannical neighbor from the paste-board cottage at the left entrance? and when he advances down to the foot-lights and defiantly informs the audience that, "he who lays his hand on a woman except in the way of kindness,"[28] do we not all applaud so as to drown the rest of the sentence?

Philip never was fortunate enough to hear what would become of a man who should lay his hand on a woman with the exception named; but he learned afterwards that the woman who lays her hand on a man, without any exception whatsoever, is always acquitted by the jury.

The fact was, though Philip Sterling did not know it, that he wanted several other things quite as much as he wanted wealth. The modest fellow would have liked fame thrust upon him[29] for some worthy achievement; it might be for a book, or for the skillful management of some great newspaper, or for some daring expedition like that of Lt. Strain[30] or Dr. Kane.[31] He was unable to decide exactly what it should be. Sometimes he thought he would like to stand in a conspicuous pulpit and humbly preach the gospel of repentance; and it even crossed his mind that it would be noble to give himself to a missionary life to some benighted region, where the date-palm grows, and the nightingale's voice is in tune, and the bul-bul[32] sings on the off nights. If he were good enough he would attach himself to that company of young men in the Theological Seminary, who were seeing New York life in preparation for the ministry.

Philip was a New England boy and had graduated at Yale; he had not carried off with him all the learning of that venerable institution, but he knew some things that were not in the regular course of study. A very good use of the English language and considerable knowledge of its literature was one of them; he could sing a song very well, not in tune to be sure, but with enthusiasm; he could make a magnetic speech at a moment's notice in the class room, the debating society, or upon any fence or dry-goods box that was convenient; he could lift himself by one arm, and do the giant swing[33] in the gymnasium; he could strike out from his left shoulder; he could handle an oar like a professional and pull stroke in a winning race. Philip had a good appetite, a sunny temper, and a clear hearty laugh. He had brown hair, hazel eyes set wide apart, a broad but not high forehead, and a fresh winning face. He was six feet high, with broad shoulders, long legs and a swinging gait; one of those loose-jointed, capable fellows, who saunter into the world with a free air and usually make a stir in whatever company they enter.

After he left college Philip took the advice of friends and read law. Law seemed to him well enough as a science, but he never could discover a practical case where it appeared to him worth while to go to law, and all the clients who stopped with this new clerk in the ante-room of the law office where he was writing, Philip invariably advised to settle—no matter how, but settle—greatly to the disgust of his employer, who knew that justice between man and man could only be attained by the recognized processes, with the attendant fees. Besides Philip hated the copying of pleadings, and he was certain that a life of "whereases" and "aforesaids" and whipping the devil round the stump,[34] would be intolerable.

His pen therefore, and whereas, and not as aforesaid, strayed off into other scribbling. In an unfortunate hour, he had two or three papers accepted by first-class magazines, at three dollars the printed page, and, behold, his vocation was open to him. He would make his mark in literature. Life has no moment so sweet as that in which a young man believes himself called into the immortal ranks of the masters of literature. It is such a noble ambition, that it is a pity it has usually such a shallow foundation.

At the time of this history, Philip had gone to New York for a career. With his talent he thought he should have little difficulty in getting an editorial position upon a metropolitan newspaper; not that he knew anything about newspaper work, or had the least idea of journalism; he knew he was not fitted for the technicalities of the subordinate departments, but he could write leaders with perfect ease, he was sure. The drudgery of the newspaper office was too distasteful, and besides it would be beneath the dignity of a graduate and a successful magazine writer. He wanted to begin at the top of the ladder.

To his surprise he found that every situation in the editorial department of the journals was full, always had been full, was always likely to be full. It seemed to him that the newspaper managers didn't want genius, but mere plodding and grubbing. Philip therefore read diligently in the Astor Library, planned literary works that should compel attention, and nursed his genius. He had no friend wise enough to tell him to step in to the Dorking Convention,[35] then in session, make a sketch of the men and women on the platform, and take it to the editor of the *Daily Grapevine*, and see what he could get a line for it.

One day he had an offer from some country friends, who believed in him, to take charge of a provincial daily newspaper, and he went to consult Mr. Gringo[36]—Gringo who years ago managed the *Atlas*[37]—about taking the situation.

"Take it of course," says Gringo, "take anything that offers, why not?"

"But they want me to make it an opposition paper."

"Well, make it that. That party is going to succeed, it's going to elect the next president."

"I don't believe it," said Philip, stoutly, "it's wrong in principle, and it ought not to succeed, but I don't see how I can go for a thing I don't believe in."

"O, very well," said Gringo, turning away with a shade of contempt, "you'll find if you are going into literature and newspaper work that you can't afford a conscience like that."

But Philip did afford it, and he wrote, thanking his friends, and declining because he said the political scheme would fail, and ought to fail. And he went back to his books and to his waiting for an opening large enough for his dignified entrance into the literary world.

It was in this time of rather impatient waiting that Philip was one morning walking down Broadway with Henry Brierly. He frequently accompanied Henry part way down town to what the latter called his office in Broad Street,[38] to which he went, or pretended to go, with regularity every day. It was evident to the most casual acquaintance that he was a man of affairs, and that his time was engrossed in the largest sort of operations, about which there was a mysterious air. His liability to be suddenly summoned to Washington, or Boston or Montreal or even to Liverpool was always imminent. He never was so summoned, but none of his acquaintances would have been surprised to hear any day that he had gone to Panama or Peoria, or to hear from him that he had bought the Bank of Commerce.[39]

The two were intimate at that time,—they had been classmates—and saw a great deal of each other. Indeed, they lived together in Ninth Street, in a boarding house there, which had the honor of lodging and partially feeding several other young fellows of like kidney, who have since gone their several ways into fame or into obscurity.

It was during the morning walk to which reference has been made that Henry Brierly suddenly said, "Philip, how would you like to go to St. Jo?"[40]

"I think I should like it of all things," replied Philip, with some hesitation, "but what for."

"Oh, it's a big operation. We are going, a lot of us, railroad men, engineers, contractors. You know my uncle is a great railroad man. I've no doubt I can get you a chance to go if you'll go."

"But in what capacity would I go?"

"Well, I'm going as an engineer. You can go as one."

"I don't know an engine from a coal cart."

"Field engineer, civil engineer. You can begin by carrying a rod, and putting down the figures. It's easy enough. I'll show you about that. We'll get Trautwine[41] and some of those books."

"Yes, but what is it for, what is it all about?"

"Why don't you see? We lay out a line, spot the good land, enter it up, know where the stations are to be, spot them, buy lots; there's heaps of money in it. We wouldn't engineer long."

"When do you go?" was Philip's next question, after some moments of silence.

"To-morrow. Is that too soon?"

"No, it's not too soon. I've been ready to go anywhere for six months. The fact is, Henry, that I'm about tired of trying to force myself into things, and am quite willing to try floating with the stream for a while, and see where I will land. This seems like a providential call; it's sudden enough."

The two young men who were by this time full of the adventure, went down to the Wall street office of Henry's uncle and had a talk with that wily operator. The uncle knew Philip very well, and was pleased with his frank enthusiasm, and willing enough to give him a trial in the western venture. It was settled therefore, in the prompt way in which things are settled in New York, that they would start with the rest of the company next morning for the west.

On the way up town these adventurers bought books on engineering, and suits of India rubber,[42] which they supposed they would need in a new and probably damp country, and many other things which nobody ever needed anywhere.

The night was spent in packing up and writing letters, for Philip would not take such an important step without informing his friends. If they disapprove, thought he, I've done my duty by letting them know. Happy youth, that is ready to pack its valise, and start for Cathay on an hour's notice.

"By the way," calls out Philip from his bed-room, to Henry, "where is St. Jo?"

"Why, it's in Missouri somewhere, on the frontier I think. We'll get a map."

"Never mind the map. We will find the place itself. I was afraid it was nearer home."

Philip wrote a long letter, first of all, to his mother, full of love and glowing anticipations of his new opening. He wouldn't bother her with business details, but he hoped that the day was not far off when she would see him return, with a moderate fortune, and something to add to the comfort of her advancing years.

To his uncle he said that he had made an arrangement with some New York capitalists to go to Missouri, in a land and railroad operation, which would at least give him a knowledge of the world and not unlikely offer him a business opening. He knew his uncle would be glad to hear that he had at last turned his thoughts to a practical matter.

It was to Ruth Bolton that Philip wrote last. He might never see her again; he went to seek his fortune. He well knew the perils of the frontier, the savage state of society, the lurking Indians and the dangers of fever. But there was no real danger to a person who took care of himself. Might he write to her often and tell her of his life. If he returned with a fortune, perhaps and perhaps. If he was unsuccessful, or if he never returned—perhaps it would be as well. No time or distance, however, would ever lessen his interest in her. He would say good-night, but not good-bye.

In the soft beginning of a Spring morning, long before New York had breakfasted, while yet the air of expectation hung about the wharves of the metropolis, our young adventurers made their way to the Jersey City railway station of the Erie road, to begin the long, swinging, crooked journey, over what a writer of a former day called a causeway of cracked rails and cows, to the West.

CHAPTER XIII

What ever to say he toke in his entente,
his language was so fayer & pertynante,
yt semeth vnto manys herying
not only the worde, but veryly the thyng.
Caxton's Book of Curtesye.

IN THE PARTY of which our travelers found themselves members, was Duff Brown, the great railroad contractor, and subsequently a well-known member of Congress; a bluff, jovial Bost'n man, thick-set, clean shaven, with a heavy jaw and a low forehead—a very pleasant man if you were not in his way. He had government contracts also, custom houses and dry docks, from Portland to New Orleans, and managed to get out of Congress, in appropriations, about weight for weight of gold for the stone furnished.

Associated with him, and also of this party, was Rodney Schaick, a sleek New York broker, a man as prominent in the church as in the stock exchange, dainty in his dress, smooth of speech, the necessary complement of Duff Brown in any enterprise that needed assurance and adroitness.

It would be difficult to find a pleasanter traveling party, one that shook off more readily the artificial restraints of Puritanic strictness, and took the world with good-natured allowance. Money was plenty for every attainable luxury, and there seemed to be no doubt that its supply would continue, and that fortunes were about to be made without a great deal of toil. Even Philip soon caught the prevailing spirit; Harry did not need any inoculation, he always talked in six figures. It was as natural for the dear boy to be rich as it is for most people to be poor.

The elders of the party were not long in discovering the fact, which almost all travelers to the west soon find out, that the water was poor. It must have been by a lucky premonition of this that they all had brandy flasks with which to qualify the water of the country; and it was no doubt from an uneasy feeling of the danger of being poisoned that they kept experimenting, mixing a little of the dangerous and changing fluid, as they passed along, with the contents of the flasks, thus saving their lives hour by hour. Philip learned afterwards that temperance and the strict observance of Sunday and a certain gravity of deportment are geographical habits, which people do not usually carry with them away from home.

Our travelers stopped in Chicago long enough to see that they could make their fortunes there in two weeks' time, but it did not seem worth while; the west was more attractive; the further one went the wider the opportunities opened. They took railroad to Alton and the steamboat from there to St. Louis, for the change and to have a glimpse of the river.

"Isn't this jolly?" cried Henry, dancing out of the barber's room, and coming down the deck with a one, two, three step, shaven, curled and perfumed after his usual exquisite fashion.

"What's jolly?" asked Philip, looking out upon the dreary and monotonous waste through which the shaking steamboat was coughing its way.

"Why, the whole thing: it's immense I can tell you. I wouldn't give *that* to be guaranteed a hundred thousand cold cash in a year's time."

"Where's Mr. Brown?"

"He is in the saloon, playing poker with Schaick, and that long haired party with the striped trousers, who scrambled aboard when the stage-plank was half hauled in, and the big Delegate to Congress from out west."

"That's a fine looking fellow, that delegate, with his glossy black whiskers; looks like a Washington man; I shouldn't think he'd be at poker."

"Oh, it's only five cent ante, just to make it interesting, the Delegate said."

"But I shouldn't think a representative of Congress would play poker any way in a public steamboat."

"Nonsense, you've got to pass the time. I tried a hand myself, but those old fellows are too many for me. The Delegate knows all the points. I'd bet a hundred dollars he will ante his way right into the United States Senate when his territory comes in. He's got the cheek for it."

"He has the grave and thoughtful manner of expectoration of a public man, for one thing," added Philip.

"Harry," said Philip, after a pause, "what have you got on those big boots for; do you expect to wade ashore?"

"I'm breaking 'em in."

The fact was Harry had got himself up in what he thought a proper costume for a new country, and was in appearance a sort of compromise between a dandy of Broadway and a backwoodsman. Harry, with blue eyes, fresh complexion, silken whiskers and curly chestnut hair, was as handsome as a fashion plate. He wore this morning a soft hat, a short cut-away coat, an open vest displaying immaculate linen, a leathern belt round his waist, and top-boots of soft leather, well polished, that came above his knees and required a string attached to his belt to keep them up. The light hearted fellow gloried in these shining encasements of his well shaped legs, and told Philip that they were a perfect protection against prairie rattlesnakes, which never strike above the knee.

The landscape still wore an almost wintry appearance when our travelers left Chicago. It was a genial spring day when they landed at St. Louis; the birds were singing, the blossoms of peach trees in city garden plots, made the air sweet, and in the roar and tumult on the long river levee they found an excitement that accorded with their own hopeful anticipations.

The party went to the Southern Hotel, where the great Duff Brown was very well known, and indeed was a man of so much importance that even the office clerk was respectful to him. He might have respected in him also a certain vulgar swagger and insolence of money, which the clerk greatly admired.

The young fellows liked the house and liked the city; it seemed to them a mighty free and hospitable town. Coming from the East they were struck with many peculiarities. Everybody smoked in the streets, for one thing, they noticed; everybody "took a drink" in an open manner whenever he wished to do so or was asked, as if the habit needed no concealment or apology. In the evening when they walked about they found people sitting on the door-steps of their dwellings, in a manner not usual in a northern city; in front of some of the hotels and saloons the side walks were filled with chairs and benches—Paris fashion, said Harry—upon which people lounged in these warm spring evenings, smoking, always smoking; and the clink of glasses and billiard balls was in the air. It was delightful.

Harry at once found on landing that his backwoods custom would not be needed in St. Louis, and that, in fact, he had need of all the resources of his wardrobe to keep even with the young swells of the town. But this did not much matter, for Harry was always superior to his clothes. As they were likely to be detained some time in the city, Harry told Philip that he was going to im-prove his time. And he did. It was an encouragement to any in-dustrious man to see this young fellow rise, carefully dress himself, eat his breakfast deliberately, smoke his cigar tranquilly, and then repair to his room, to what he called his work, with a grave and occupied manner, but with perfect cheerfulness.

Harry would take off his coat, remove his cravat, roll up his shirt-sleeves, give his curly hair the right touch before the glass, get out his book on engineering, his boxes of instruments, his drawing-paper, his profile paper,[43] open the book of logarithms, mix his India ink, sharpen his pencils, light a cigar, and sit down at the table to "lay out a line," with the most grave notion that he was mastering the details of engineering. He would spend half a day in these preparations without ever working out a problem or having the faintest conception of the use of lines or logarithms. And when he had finished, he had the most cheerful confidence that he had done a good day's work.

It made no difference, however, whether Harry was in his room in a hotel or in a tent, Philip soon found, he was just the same. In camp he would get himself up in the most elaborate toi-let at his command, polish his long boots to the top, lay out his work before him, and spend an hour or longer, if anybody was looking for him, humming airs, knitting his brows, and "work-ing" at engineering; and if a crowd of gaping rustics were looking on all the while it was perfectly satisfactory to him.

"You see," he says to Philip one morning at the hotel when he was thus engaged, "I want to get the theory of this thing, so that I can have a check on the engineers."

"I thought you were going to be an engineer yourself," queried Philip.

"Not many times, if the court knows herself. There's better game. Brown and Schaick have, or will have, the control for the whole time of the Salt Lick Pacific Extension, forty thousand dollars a mile over the prairie, with extra for hard-pan—and it'll be pretty much all hard-pan I can tell you; besides every alternate section of land on this line. There's millions in the job. I'm to have the sub-contract for the first fifty miles, and you can bet it's a soft thing.

"I'll tell you what to do, Philip," continued Harry, in a burst of generosity, "if I don't get you into my contract, you'll be with the engineers, and you just stick a stake at the first ground marked for a dêpot, buy the land of the farmer before he knows where the dêpot will be, and we'll turn a hundred or so on that. I'll advance the money for the payments, and you can sell the lots. Schaick is going to let me have ten thousand just for a flyer in such operations."

"But that's a good deal of money."

"Wait till you are used to handling money. I didn't come out here for a bagatelle. My uncle wanted me to stay East and go in on the Mobile custom house,[44] work up the Washington end of it; he said there was a fortune in it for a smart young fellow, but I preferred to take the chances out here. Did I tell you I had an offer from Bobbett and Fanshaw to go into their office as confidential clerk on a salary to ten thousand?"

"Why didn't you take it?" asked Philip, to whom a salary of two thousand would have seemed wealth, before he started on this journey.

"Take it? I'd rather operate on my own hook," said Harry, in his most airy manner.

A few evenings after their arrival at the Southern, Philip and Harry made the acquaintance of a very agreeable gentleman, whom they had frequently seen before about the hotel corridors, and passed a casual word with. He had the air of a man of business, and was evidently a person of importance.

The precipitating of this casual intercourse into the more substantial form of an acquaintanceship was the work of the gentleman himself, and occurred in this wise. Meeting the two friends in
the lobby one evening, he asked them to give him the time, and
added:

"Excuse me, gentlemen—strangers in St. Louis? Ah, yes—
yes. From the East, perhaps? Ah, just so, just so. Eastern born
myself—Virginia. Sellers is my name—Beriah Sellers. Ah—by the
way—New York, did you say? That reminds me; just met some
gentlemen from your State a week or two ago—very prominent
gentlemen—in public life they are; you must know them, without
doubt. Let me see—let me see. Curious those names have escaped
me. I know they were from your State, because I remember
afterward my old friend Governor Shackleby said to me—fine
man, is the Governor—one of the finest men our country has
produced—said he, 'Colonel, how did you like those New York
gentlemen?—not many such men in the world, Colonel Sellers,'
said the Governor—yes, it was New York he said—I remember
it distinctly. I *can't* recall those names, somehow. But no matter.
Stopping here, gentlemen—stopping at the Southern?"

In shaping their reply in their minds, the title "Mr." had a place
in it; but when their turn had arrived to speak, the title "Colonel"
came from their lips instead.

They said yes, they were abiding at the Southern, and thought
it a very good house.

"Yes, yes, the Southern is fair. I myself go to the Planter's, old,
aristocratic house. We Southern gentlemen don't change our
ways, you know. I always make it my home there when I run
down from Hawkeye—my plantation is in Hawkeye, a little up in
the country. You should know the Planter's."

Philip and Harry both said they should like to see a hotel that
had been so famous in its day—a cheerful hostelrie, Philip said it
must have been where duels were fought there across the dining-
room table.

"You may believe it, sir, an uncommonly pleasant lodging.
Shall we walk?"

And the three strolled along the streets, the Colonel talking all the way in the most liberal and friendly manner, and with a frank open-heartedness that inspired confidence.

"Yes, born East myself, raised all along, know the West—a great country, gentlemen. The place for a young fellow of spirit to pick up a fortune, simply pick it up, it's lying round loose here. Not a day that I don't put aside an opportunity, too busy to look into it. Management of my own property takes my time. First visit? Looking for an opening?"

"Yes, looking around," replied Harry.

"Ah, here we are. You'd rather sit here in front than go to my apartments? So had I. An opening, eh?"

The Colonel's eyes twinkled. "Ah, just so. The whole country is opening up, all we want is capital to develop it. Slap down the rails and bring the land into market. The richest land on God Almighty's footstool is lying right out there. If I had my capital free I could plant it for millions."

"I suppose your capital is largely in your plantation?" asked Philip.

"Well, partly, sir, partly. I'm down here now with reference to a little operation—a little side thing merely. By the way gentlemen, excuse the liberty, but it's about my usual time"—

The Colonel paused, but as no movement of his acquaintances followed this plain remark, he added, in an explanatory manner,

"I'm rather particular about the exact time—have to be in this climate."

Even this open declaration of his hospitable intention not being understood the Colonel politely said,

"Gentlemen, will you take something?"

Col. Sellers led the way to a saloon on Fourth street under the hotel, and the young gentlemen fell into the custom of the country.

"Not that," said the Colonel to the bar-keeper, who shoved along the counter a bottle of apparently corn-whiskey, as if he had done it before on the same order; "not that," with a wave of the hand. "That Otard[45] if you please. Yes. Never take an inferior liquor, gentlemen, not in the evening, in this climate. There. That's the stuff. My respects!"

The hospitable gentleman, having disposed of his liquor, remarking that it was not quite the thing—"when a man has his own cellar to go to, he is apt to get a little fastidious about his liquors"—called for cigars. But the brand offered did not suit him; he motioned the box away, and asked for some particular Havana's, those in separate wrappers.

"I always smoke this sort, gentlemen; they are a little more expensive, but you'll learn, in this climate, that you'd better not economize on poor cigars."

Having imparted this valuable piece of information, the Colonel lighted the fragrant cigar with satisfaction, and then carelessly put his fingers into his right vest pocket. That movement being without result, with a shade of disappointment on his face, he felt in his left vest pocket. Not finding anything there, he looked up with a serious and annoyed air, anxiously slapped his right pantaloon's pocket, and then his left, and exclaimed,

"By George, that's annoying. By George, that's mortifying. Never had anything of that kind happen to me before. I've left my pocket-book. Hold! Here's a bill, after all. No, thunder, it's a receipt."

"Allow me," said Philip, seeing how seriously the Colonel was annoyed, and taking out his purse.

The Colonel protested he couldn't think of it, and muttered something to the bar-keeper about "hanging it up,"[46] but the vender of exhilaration made no sign, and Philip had the privilege of paying the costly shot; Col. Sellers profusely apologizing and claiming the right "next time, next time."

As soon as Beriah Sellers had bade his friends good-night and seen them depart, he did not retire to apartments in the Planter's, but took his way to his lodgings with a friend in a distant part of the city.

CHAPTER XIV

Pulchra duos inter sita stat Philadelphia rivos;
  Inter quos duo sunt millia longa viae.
Delawar his major, Sculkil minor ille vocatur;
  Indis et Suevis notus uterque diu.
Hic plateas mensor spatiis delineat aequis,
  Et domui recto est ordine juncta domus.
                                        T. Makin.

Vergin era fra lor di già matura
  Verginità, d'alti pensieri e regi,
D'alta beltà; ma sua beltà non cura,
  O tanta sol, quant' onestà sen fregi.
                                        Tasso.

THE LETTER that Philip Sterling wrote to Ruth Bolton, on the evening of setting out to seek his fortune in the west, found that young lady in her own father's house in Philadelphia. It was one of the pleasantest of the many charming suburban houses in that hospitable city, which is territorially one of the largest cities in the world, and only prevented from becoming the convenient metropolis of the country by the intrusive strip of Camden and Amboy sand which shuts it off from the Atlantic ocean. It is a city of steady thrift, the arms of which might well be the deliberate but delicious terrapin that imparts such a royal flavor to its feasts.

It was a spring morning, and perhaps it was the influence of it that made Ruth a little restless, satisfied neither with the outdoors nor the in-doors. Her sisters had gone to the city to show some country visitors Independence Hall, Girard College[47] and Fairmount Water Works and Park,[48] four objects which Americans cannot die peacefully, even in Naples, without having seen. But Ruth confessed that she was tired of them, and also of the Mint. She was tired of other things. She tried this morning an air or two upon the piano, sang a simple song in a sweet, but slightly metallic voice, and then seating herself by the open window, read Philip's letter.

Was she thinking about Philip, as she gazed across the fresh lawn over the tree tops to the Chelton Hills, or of that world which his entrance into her tradition-bound life had been one of the means of opening to her? Whatever she thought, she was not idly musing, as one might see by the expression of her face. After a time she took up a book; it was a medical work, and to all appearance about as interesting to a girl of eighteen as the statutes at large; but her face was soon aglow over its pages, and she was so absorbed in it that she did not notice the entrance of her mother at the open door.

"Ruth?"

"Well, mother," said the young student, looking up, with a shade of impatience.

"I wanted to talk with thee a little about thy plans."

"Mother, thee knows I couldn't stand it at Westfield; the school stifled me, it's a place to turn young people into dried fruit."

"I know," said Margaret Bolton, with a half anxious smile, "thee chafes against all the ways of Friends, but what will thee do? Why is thee so discontented?"

"If I must say it, mother, I want to go away, and get out of this dead level."

With a look half of pain and half of pity, her mother answered, "I am sure thee is little interfered with; thee dresses as thee will, and goes where thee pleases, to any church thee likes, and thee has music. I had a visit yesterday from the society's committee by way of discipline, because we have a piano in the house, which is against the rules."

"I hope thee told the elders that father and I are responsible for the piano, and that, much as thee loves music, thee is never in the room when it is played. Fortunately father is already out of meeting, so they can't discipline him. I heard father tell cousin Abner that he was whipped so often for whistling when he was a boy that he was determined to have what compensation he could get now."

"Thy ways greatly try me, Ruth, and all thy relations. I desire thy happiness first of all, but thee is starting out on a dangerous path. Is thy father willing thee should go away to a school of the world's people?"

"I have not asked him," Ruth replied with a look that might imply that she was one of those determined little bodies who first made up her own mind and then compelled others to make up theirs in accordance with hers.

"And when thee has got the education thee wants, and lost all relish for the society of thy friends and the ways of thy ancestors, what then?"

Ruth turned square round to her mother, and with an impassive face and not the slightest change of tone, said,

"Mother, I'm going to study medicine?"

Margaret Bolton almost lost for a moment her habitual placidity.

"Thee study medicine! A slight frail girl like thee, study medicine! Does thee think thee could stand it six months? And the lectures, and the dissecting rooms, has thee thought of the dissecting rooms?"

"Mother," said Ruth calmly, "I have thought it all over. I know I can go through the whole, clinics, dissecting room and all. Does thee think I lack nerve? What is there to fear in a person dead more than in a person living?"

"But thy health and strength, child; thee can never stand the severe application. And, besides, suppose thee does learn medicine?"

"I will practice it."

"Here?"

"Here."

"Where thee and thy family are known?"

"If I can get patients."

"I hope at least, Ruth, thee will let us know when thee opens an office," said her mother, with an approach to sarcasm that she rarely indulged in, as she rose and left the room.

Ruth sat quite still for a time, with face intent and flushed. It was out now. She had begun her open battle.

The sight-seers returned in high spirits from the city. Was there any building in Greece to compare with Girard College, was there ever such a magnificent pile of stone devised for the shelter of poor orphans? Think of the stone shingles of the roof eight inches thick! Ruth asked the enthusiasts if they would like to live in such a sounding mausoleum, with its great halls and echoing rooms, and no comfortable place in it for the accommodation of any body? If they were orphans, would they like to be brought up in a Grecian temple?

And then there was Broad street! Wasn't it the broadest and the longest street in the world? There certainly was no end to it, and even Ruth was Philadelphian enough to believe that a street ought not to have any end, or architectural point upon which the weary eye could rest.

But neither St. Girard,[49] nor Broad street, neither wonders of the Mint[50] nor the glories of the Hall where the ghosts of our fathers sit always signing the Declaration, impressed the visitors so much as the splendors of the Chestnut street windows, and the bargains on Eighth street. The truth is that the country cousins had come to town to attend the Yearly Meeting, and the amount of shopping that preceded that religious event was scarcely exceeded by the preparations for the opera in more worldly circles.

"Is thee going to the Yearly Meeting, Ruth?" asked one of the girls.

"I have nothing to wear," replied that demure person. "If thee wants to see new bonnets, orthodox to a shade and conformed to the letter of the true form, thee must go to the Arch Street Meeting.[51] Any departure from either color or shape would be instantly taken note of. It has occupied mother a long time, to find at the shops the exact shade for her new bonnet. Oh, thee must go by all means. But thee won't see there a sweeter woman than mother."

"And thee won't go?"

"Why should I? I've been again and again. If I go to Meeting at all I like best to sit in the quiet old house in Germantown, where the windows are all open and I can see the trees, and hear the stir of the leaves. It's such a crush at the Yearly Meeting at Arch Street, and then there's the row of sleek-looking young men who line the curbstone and stare at us as we come out. No, I don't feel at home there."

That evening Ruth and her father sat late by the drawing-room fire, as they were quite apt to do at night. It was always a time of confidences.

"Thee has another letter from young Sterling," said Eli Bolton.

"Yes. Philip has gone to the far west."

"How far?"

"He doesn't say, but it's on the frontier, and on the map everything beyond it is marked 'Indians' and 'desert,' and looks as desolate as a Wednesday Meeting."

"Humph. It was time for him to do something. Is he going to start a daily newspaper among the Kick-a-poos?"[52]

"Father, thee's unjust to Philip. He's going into business."

"What sort of business can a young man go into without capital?"

"He doesn't say exactly what it is," said Ruth a little dubiously, "but it's something about land and railroads, and thee knows, father, that fortunes are made nobody knows exactly how, in a new country."

"I should think so, you innocent puss, and in an old one too. But Philip is honest, and he has talent enough, if he will stop scribbling, to make his way. But thee may as well take care of theeself, Ruth, and not go dawdling along with a young man in his adventures, until thy own mind is a little more settled what thee wants."

This excellent advice did not seem to impress Ruth greatly, for she was looking away with that abstraction of vision which often came into her gray eyes, and at length she exclaimed, with a sort of impatience,

"I wish I could go west, or south, or somewhere. What a box women are put into, measured for it, and put in young; if we go anywhere it's in a box, veiled and pinioned and shut in by disabilities. Father, I should like to break things and get loose."

What a sweet-voiced little innocent, it was to be sure.

"Thee will no doubt break things enough when thy time comes, child; women always have; but what does thee want now that thee hasn't?"

"I want to be something, to make myself something, to do something. Why should I rust, and be stupid, and sit in inaction because I am a girl? What would happen to me if thee should lose thy property and die? What one useful thing could I do for a living, for the support of mother and the children? And if I had a fortune, would thee want me to lead a useless life?"

"Has thy mother led a useless life?"

"Somewhat that depends upon whether her children amount to anything," retorted the sharp little disputant. "What's the good, father, of a series of human beings who don't advance any?"

Friend Eli, who had long ago laid aside the Quaker dress, and was out of Meeting, and who in fact after a youth of doubt could not yet define his belief, nevertheless looked with some wonder at this fierce young eagle of his, hatched in a Friend's dove-cote. But he only said,

"Has thee consulted thy mother about a career, I suppose it is a career thee wants?"

Ruth did not reply directly; she complained that her mother didn't understand her. But that wise and placid woman understood the sweet rebel a great deal better than Ruth understood herself. She also had a history, possibly, and had sometime beaten her young wings against the cage of custom, and indulged in dreams of a new social order, and had passed through that fiery period when it seems possible for one mind, which has not yet tried its limits, to break up and re-arrange the world.

Ruth replied to Philip's letter in due time and in the most cordial and unsentimental manner. Philip liked the letter, as he did everything she did; but he had a dim notion that there was more about herself in the letter than about him. He took it with him from the Southern Hotel, when he went to walk, and read it over and again in an unfrequented street as he stumbled along. The rather common-place and unformed hand-writing seemed to him peculiar and characteristic, different from that of any other woman.

Ruth was glad to hear that Philip had made a push into the world, and she was sure that his talent and courage would make a way for him. She should pray for his success at any rate, and especially that the Indians, in St. Louis, would not take his scalp.

Philip looked rather dubious at this sentence, and wished that he had written nothing about Indians.

CHAPTER XV

—Rationalem quidem puto medicinam esse debere: instrui vero ab evidentibus causis, obscuris omnibus non à cogitatione artificis, sed ab ipsa arte rejectis. Incidere autem vivorum corpora, et crudele, et supervacuum est: mortuorum corpora discentibus necessarium.

Celsus.

ELI BOLTON and his wife talked over Ruth's case, as they had often done before, with no little anxiety. Alone of all their children she was impatient of the restraints and monotony of the Friends' Society, and wholly indisposed to accept the "inner light" as a guide into a life of acceptance and inaction. When Margaret told her husband of Ruth's newest project, he did not exhibit so much surprise as she looked for. In fact he said that he did not see why a woman should not enter the medical profession if she felt a call to it.

"But," said Margaret, "consider her total inexperience of the world, and her frail health. Can such a slight little body endure the ordeal of the preparation for, or the strain of, the practice of the profession?"

"Did thee ever think, Margaret, whether she can endure being thwarted in an object on which she has so set her heart, as she has on this? Thee has trained her thyself at home, in her enfeebled childhood, and thee knows how strong her will is, and what she has been able to accomplish in self-culture by the simple force of her determination. She never will be satisfied until she has tried her own strength."

"I wish," said Margaret, with an inconsequence that is not exclusively feminine, "that she were in the way to fall in love and marry by and by. I think that would cure her of some of her notions. I am not sure but if she went away to some distant school, into an entirely new life, her thoughts would be diverted."

Eli Bolton almost laughed as he regarded his wife, with eyes that never looked at her except fondly, and replied,

"Perhaps thee remembers that thee had notions also, before we were married, and before thee became a member of Meeting. I think Ruth comes honestly by certain tendencies which thee has hidden under the Friends' dress."

Margaret could not say no to this, and while she paused, it was evident that memory was busy with suggestions to shake her present opinions.

"Why not let Ruth try the study for a time," suggested Eli; "there is a fair beginning of a Woman's Medical College[53] in the city. Quite likely she will soon find that she needs first a more general culture, and fall in with thy wish that she should see more of the world at some large school."

There really seemed to be nothing else to be done, and Margaret consented at length without approving. And it was agreed that Ruth, in order to spare her fatigue, should take lodgings with friends near the college and make a trial in the pursuit of that science to which we all owe our lives, and sometimes as by a miracle of escape.

That day Mr. Bolton brought home a stranger to dinner, Mr. Bigler of the great firm of Pennybacker, Bigler & Small, railroad contractors. He was always bringing home somebody, who had a scheme; to build a road, or open a mine, or plant a swamp with cane to grow paper-stock, or found a hospital, or invest in a patent shad-bone separator, or start a college somewhere on the frontier, contiguous to a land speculation.

The Bolton house was a sort of hotel for this kind of people. They were always coming. Ruth had known them from childhood, and she used to say that her father attracted them as naturally as a sugar hogshead does flies. Ruth had an idea that a large portion of the world lived by getting the rest of the world into schemes. Mr. Bolton never could say "no" to any of them, not even, said Ruth again, to the society for stamping oyster shells with scripture texts before they were sold at retail.

Mr. Bigler's plan this time, about which he talked loudly, with his mouth full, all dinner time, was the building of the Tunkhannock, Rattlesnake and Youngwomanstown railroad,[54] which would not only be a great highway to the west, but would open to market inexhaustible coal-fields and untold millions of lumber. The plan of operations was very simple.

"We'll buy the lands," explained he, "on long time, backed by the notes of good men; and then mortgage them for money enough to get the road well on. Then get the towns on the line to issue their bonds for stock, and sell their bonds for enough to complete the road, and partly stock it, especially if we mortgage each section as we complete it. We can then sell the rest of the stock on the prospect of the business of the road through an improved country, and also sell the lands at a big advance, on the strength of the road. All we want," continued Mr. Bigler in his frank manner, "is a few thousand dollars to start the surveys, and arrange things in the legislature. There is some parties will have to be seen, who might make us trouble."

"It will take a good deal of money to start the enterprise," remarked Mr. Bolton, who knew very well what "seeing" a Pennsylvania Legislature meant, but was too polite to tell Mr. Bigler what he thought of him, while he was his guest; "what security would one have for it?"

Mr. Bigler smiled a hard kind of smile, and said, "You'd be inside, Mr. Bolton, and you'd have the first chance in the deal."

This was rather unintelligible to Ruth, who was nevertheless somewhat amused by the study of a type of character she had seen before. At length she interrupted the conversation by asking,

"You'd sell the stock, I suppose, Mr. Bigler, to anybody who was attracted by the prospectus?"

"O, certainly, serve all alike," said Mr. Bigler, now noticing Ruth for the first time, and a little puzzled by the serene, intelligent face that was turned towards him.

"Well, what would become of the poor people who had been led to put their little money into the speculation, when you got out of it and left it half way?"

It would be no more true to say of Mr. Bigler that he was or could be embarrassed, than to say that a brass counterfeit dollar-piece would change color when refused; the question annoyed him a little, in Mr. Bolton's presence.

"Why, yes, Miss, of course, in a great enterprise for the benefit of the community there will little things occur, which, which— and, of course, the poor ought to be looked to; I tell my wife, that the poor must *be* looked to; if you can tell who are poor—there's

so many impostors. And then, there's so many poor in the legislature to be looked after," said the contractor with a sort of a
chuckle, "isn't that so, Mr. Bolton?"

Eli Bolton replied the he never had much to do with the legislature.

"Yes," continued this public benefactor, "an uncommon poor
lot this year, uncommon. Consequently an expensive lot. The fact
is, Mr. Bolton, that the price is raised so high on United States
Senator now, that it affects the whole market; you can't get any
public improvement through on reasonable terms. Simony[55] is
what I call it, Simony," repeated Mr. Bigler, as if he had said a
good thing.

Mr. Bigler went on and gave some very interesting details of
the intimate connection between railroads and politics, and thoroughly entertained himself all dinner time, and as much disgusted
Ruth, who asked no more questions, and her father who replied
in monosyllables.

"I wish," said Ruth to her father, after the guest had gone, "that
you wouldn't bring home any more such horrid men. Do all men
who wear big diamond breast-pins, flourish their knives at the
table, and use bad grammar, and cheat?"

"O, child, thee mustn't be too observing. Mr. Bigler is one of
the most important men in the state; nobody has more influence
at Harrisburg. I don't like him any more than thee does, but I'd
better lend him a little money than to have his ill-will."

"Father, I think thee'd better have his ill-will than his company. Is it true that he gave money to help build the pretty little
church of St. James the Less,[56] and that he is one of the vestry-
men?"

"Yes. He is not such a bad fellow. One of the men in Third
street asked him the other day, whether his was a high church or a
low church? Bigler said he didn't know; he'd been in it once, and
he could touch the ceiling in the side aisle with his hand."

"I think he's just horrid," was Ruth's final summary of him, after the manner of the swift judgment of women, with no consideration of the extenuating circumstances. Mr. Bigler had no idea
that he had not made a good impression on the whole family; he
certainly intended to be agreeable. Margaret agreed with her

daughter, and though she never said anything to such people, she was grateful to Ruth for sticking at least one pin into him.

Such was the serenity of the Bolton household that a stranger in it would never have suspected there was any opposition to Ruth's going to the Medical School. And she went quietly to take her residence in town, and began her attendance of the lectures, as if it were the most natural thing in the world. She did not heed, if she heard, the busy and wondering gossip of relations and acquaintances, gossip that has no less currency among the Friends than elsewhere because it is whispered slyly and creeps about in an undertone.

Ruth was absorbed, and for the first time in her life thoroughly happy; happy in the freedom of her life, and in the keen enjoyment of the investigation that broadened its field day by day. She was in high spirits when she came home to spend First Days; the house was full of her gaiety and her merry laugh, and the children wished that Ruth would never go away again. But her mother noticed, with a little anxiety, the sometimes flushed face, and the sign of an eager spirit in the kindling eyes, and, as well, the serious air of determination and endurance in her face at unguarded moments.

The college was a small one and it sustained itself not without difficulty in this city, which is so conservative, and is yet the origin of so many radical movements. There were not more than a dozen attendants on the lectures all together, so that the enterprise had the air of an experiment, and the fascination of pioneering for those engaged in it. There was one woman physician driving about town in her carriage, attacking the most violent diseases in all quarters with persistent courage, like a modern Bellona in her war chariot, who was popularly supposed to gather in fees to the amount of ten to twenty thousand dollars a year. Perhaps some of these students looked forward to the near day when they would support such a practice and a husband besides, but it is unknown that any of them ever went further than practice in hospitals and in their own nurseries, and it is feared that some of them were quite as ready as their sisters, in emergencies, to "call a man."

If Ruth had any exaggerated expectations of a professional life, she kept them to herself, and was known to her fellows of the class simply as a cheerful, sincere student, eager in her investigations, and never impatient at anything, except an insinuation that women had not as much mental capacity for science as men.

"They really say," said one young Quaker sprig to another youth of his age, "that Ruth Bolton is really going to be a sawbones, attends lectures, cuts up bodies, and all that. She's cool enough for a surgeon, anyway." He spoke feelingly, for he had very likely been weighed in Ruth's calm eyes sometime, and thoroughly scared by the little laugh that accompanied a puzzling reply to one of his conversational nothings. Such young gentlemen, at this time, did not come very distinctly into Ruth's horizon, except as amusing circumstances.

About the details of her student life, Ruth said very little to her friends, but they had reason to know, afterwards, that it required all her nerve and the almost complete exhaustion of her physical strength, to carry her through. She began her anatomical practice upon detached portions of the human frame, which were brought into the demonstrating room—dissecting the eye, the ear, and a small tangle of muscles and nerves—an occupation which had not much more savor of death in it than the analysis of a portion of a plant out of which the life went when it was plucked up by the roots. Custom inures the most sensitive persons to that which is at first most repellant; and in the late war we saw the most delicate women, who could not at home endure the sight of blood, become so used to scenes of carnage, that they walked the hospitals and the margins of battle-fields, amid the poor remnants of torn humanity, with as perfect self-possession as if they were strolling in a flower garden.

It happened that Ruth was one evening deep in a line of investigation which she could not finish or understand without demonstration, and so eager was she in it, that it seemed as if she could not wait till the next day. She, therefore, persuaded a fellow student, who was reading that evening with her, to go down to the dissecting room of the college, and ascertain what they wanted to know by an hour's work there. Perhaps, also, Ruth wanted to test her own nerve, and to see whether the power of association was stronger in her mind than her own will.

The janitor of the shabby and comfortless old building admitted the girls, not without suspicion, and gave them lighted candles, which they would need, without other remark than "there's a new one, Miss," as the girls went up the broad stairs.

They climbed to the third story, and paused before a door, which they unlocked, and which admitted them into a long apartment, with a row of windows on one side and one at the end. The room was without light, save from the stars and the candles the girls carried, which revealed to them dimly two long and several small tables, a few benches and chairs, a couple of skeletons hanging on the wall, a sink, and cloth-covered heaps of something upon the tables here and there.

The windows were open, and the cool night wind came in strong enough to flutter a white covering now and then, and to shake the loose casements. But all the sweet odors of the night could not take from the room a faint suggestion of mortality.

The young ladies paused a moment. The room itself was familiar enough, but night makes almost any chamber eerie, and especially such a room of detention as this where the mortal parts of the unburied might almost be supposed to be visited, on the sighing night winds, by the wandering spirits of their late tenants.

Opposite and at some distance across the roofs of lower buildings, the girls saw a tall edifice, the long upper story of which seemed to be a dancing hall. The windows of that were also open, and through them they heard the scream of the jiggered and tortured violin, and the pump, pump of the oboe, and saw the moving shapes of men and women in quick transition, and heard the prompter's drawl.[57]

"I wonder," said Ruth, "what the girls dancing there would think if they saw us, or knew that there was such a room as this so near them."

She did not speak very loud, and, perhaps unconsciously, the girls drew near to each other as they approached the long table in the centre of the room. A straight object lay upon it, covered with a sheet. This was doubtless "the new one" of which the janitor spoke. Ruth advanced, and with a not very steady hand lifted the white covering from the upper part of the figure and turned it down. Both the girls started. It was a negro. The black face seemed to defy the pallor of death, and asserted an ugly life-likeness that was frightful. Ruth was as pale as the white sheet, and her comrade whispered, "Come away, Ruth, it is awful."

Perhaps it was the wavering light of the candles, perhaps it was only the agony from a death of pain, but the repulsive black face seemed to wear a scowl that said, "Haven't you yet done with the outcast, persecuted black man, but you must now haul him from his grave, and send even your women to dismember his body?"

Who is this dead man, one of thousands who died yesterday, and will be dust anon, to protest that science shall not turn his worthless carcass to some account?

Ruth could have had no such thought, for with a pity in her sweet face, that for the moment overcame fear and disgust, she reverently replaced the covering, and went away to her own table, as her companion did to hers. And there for an hour they worked at their several problems, without speaking, but not without an awe of the presence there, "the new one," and not without an awful sense of life itself, as they heard the pulsations of the music and the light laughter from the dancing hall.

When, at length, they went away, and locked the dreadful room behind them, and came out into the street, where people were passing, they, for the first time, realized, in the relief they felt, what a nervous strain they had been under.

CHAPTER XVI

Todtenb. 117. 1.3.

WHILE RUTH WAS THUS ABSORBED in her new occupation, and the spring was wearing away, Philip and his friends were still detained at the Southern Hotel. The great contractors had concluded their business with the state and railroad officials and with the lesser contractors, and departed for the East. But the serious illness of one of the engineers kept Philip and Henry in the city and occupied in alternate watchings.

Philip wrote to Ruth of the new acquaintance they had made, Col. Sellers, an enthusiastic and hospitable gentleman, very much interested in the development of the country, and in their success. They had not had an opportunity to visit at his place "up in the country" yet, but the Colonel often dined with them, and in confidence, confided to them his projects, and seemed to take a great liking to them, especially to his friend Harry. It was true that he never seemed to have ready money, but he was engaged in very large operations.

The correspondence was not very brisk between these two young persons, so differently occupied; for though Philip wrote long letters, he got brief ones in reply, full of sharp little observations however, such as one concerning Col. Sellers, namely, that such men dined at their house every week.

Ruth's proposed occupation astonished Philip immensely, but while he argued it and discussed it, he did not dare hint to her his fear that it would interfere with his most cherished plans. He too sincerely respected Ruth's judgment to make any protest, however, and he would have defended her course against the world.

This enforced waiting at St. Louis was very irksome to Philip. His money was running away, for one thing, and he longed to get into the field, and see for himself what chance there was for a fortune or even an occupation. The contractors had given the young men leave to join the engineer corps as soon as they could, but otherwise had made no provision for them, and in fact had left them with only the most indefinite expectations of something large in the future.

Harry was entirely happy, in his circumstances. He very soon knew everybody, from the governor of the state down to the waiters at the hotel. He had the Wall street slang at his tongue's end; he always talked like a capitalist, and entered with enthusiasm into all the land and railway schemes with which the air was thick.

Col. Sellers and Harry talked together by the hour and by the day. Harry informed his new friend that he was going out with the engineer corps of the Salt Lick Pacific Extension, but that wasn't his real business.

"I'm to have, with another party," said Harry, "a big contract in the road, as soon as it is let; and, meantime, I'm with the engineers to spy out the best land and the dêpot sites."

"It's everything," suggested the Colonel, "in knowing where to invest. I've known people throw away their money because they were too consequential to take Sellers's advice. Others, again, have made their pile on taking it. I've looked over the ground, I've been studying it for twenty years. You can't put your finger on a spot in the map of Missouri that I don't know as if I'd made it. When you want to place anything," continued the Colonel, confidently, "just let Beriah Sellers know. That's all."

"Oh, I haven't got much in ready money I can lay my hands on now, but if a fellow could do anything with fifteen or twenty thousand dollars, as a beginning, I shall draw for that when I see the right opening."

"Well, that's something, that's something, fifteen or twenty thousand dollars, say twenty—as an advance," said the Colonel reflectively, as if turning over in his mind for a project that could be entered on with such a trifling sum.

"I'll tell you what it is—but only to you Mr. Brierly, only to you, mind; I've got a little project that I've been keeping. It looks small, looks small on paper, but it's got a big future. What should you say, sir, to a city, built up like the rod of Aladdin had touched it, built up in two years, where now you wouldn't expect it any more than you'd expect a light-house on the top of Pilot Knob?[58] and you could own the land! It can be done, sir. It can be done!"

The Colonel hitched up his chair close to Harry, laid his hand on his knee, and, first looking about him, said in a low voice, "The Salt Lick Pacific Extension is going to run through Stone's Landing! The Almighty never laid out a cleaner piece of level prairie for a city; and it's the natural center of all that region of hemp and tobacco."

"What makes you think the road will go there? It's twenty miles, on the map, off the straight line of the road?"

"You can't tell what is the straight line till the engineers have been over it. Between us, I have talked with Jeff Thompson, the division engineer. He understands the wants of Stone's Landing, and the claims of the inhabitants—who are to be there. Jeff says that a railroad is for the accommodation of the people and not for the benefit of gophers; and if he don't run this to Stone's Landing he'll be damned! You ought to know Jeff; he's one of the most enthusiastic engineers in this western country, and one of the best fellows that ever looked through the bottom of a glass."

The recommendation was not undeserved. There was nothing that Jeff wouldn't do, to accommodate a friend, from sharing his last dollar with him, to winging him in a duel. When he understood from Col. Sellers how the land lay at Stone's Landing, he cordially shook hands with that gentleman, asked him to drink, and fairly roared out, "Why, God bless my soul, Colonel, a word from one Virginia gentleman to another is 'nuff ced.' There's Stone's Landing been waiting for a railroad more than four thousand years, and damme if she shan't have it."

Philip had not so much faith as Harry in Stone's Landing, when the latter opened the project to him, but Harry talked about it as if he already owned that incipient city.

Harry thoroughly believed in all his projects and inventions, and lived day by day in their golden atmosphere. Everybody liked the young fellow, for how could they help liking one of such engaging manners and large fortune? The waiters at the hotel would do more for him than for any other guest, and he made a great many acquaintances among the people of St. Louis, who liked his sensible and liberal views about the development of the western country, and about St. Louis. He said it ought to be the national capital. Harry made partial arrangements with several of the merchants for furnishing supplies for his contract on the Salt Lick Pacific Extension; consulted the maps with the engineers, and went over the profiles with the contractors, figuring out estimates for bids. He was exceedingly busy with those things when he was not at the bedside of his sick acquaintance, or arranging the details of his speculation with Col. Sellers.

Meantime the days went along and the weeks, and the money in Harry's pocket got lower and lower. He was just as liberal with what he had as before, indeed it was his nature to be free with his money or with that of others, and he could lend or spend a dollar with an air that made it seem like ten. At length, at the end of one week, when his hotel bill was presented, Harry found not a cent in his pocket to meet it. He carelessly remarked to the landlord that he was not that day in funds, but he would draw on New York, and he sat down and wrote to the contractors in that city a glowing letter about the prospects of the road, and asked them to advance a hundred or two, until he got at work. No reply came. He wrote again, in an unoffended business like tone, suggesting that he had better draw at three days. A short answer came to this, simply saying that money was very tight in Wall street just then, and that he had better join the engineer corps as soon as he could.

But the bill had to be paid, and Harry took it to Philip, and asked him if he thought he hadn't better draw on his uncle. Philip had not much faith in Harry's power of "drawing," and told him that he would pay the bill himself. Whereupon Harry dismissed the matter then and thereafter from his thoughts, and, like a light-hearted good fellow as he was, gave himself no more trouble about his board-bills. Philip paid them, swollen as they were with a monstrous list of extras; but he seriously counted the diminishing bulk of his own hoard, which was all the money he had in the world. Had he not tacitly agreed to share with Harry to the last in this adventure, and would not the generous fellow divide with him if he, Philip, were in want and Harry had anything?

The fever at length got tired of tormenting the stout young engineer, who lay sick at the hotel, and left him, very thin, a little sallow but an "acclimated" man. Everybody said he was "acclimated" now, and said it cheerfully. What it is to be acclimated to western fevers no two persons exactly agree. Some say it is a sort of vaccination that renders death by some malignant type of fever less probable. Some regard it as a sort of initiation, like that into the Odd Fellows, which renders one liable to his regular dues thereafter. Others consider it merely the acquisition of a habit of taking every morning before breakfast a dose of bitters, composed of whiskey and assafoetida, out of the acclimation jug.

Jeff Thompson afterwards told Philip that he once asked Senator Atchison,[59] then acting Vice-President of the United States, about the possibility of acclimation; he thought the opinion of the second officer of our great government would be valuable on this point. They were sitting together on a bench before a country tavern, in the free converse permitted by our democratic habits.

"I suppose, Senator, that you have become acclimated to this country?"

"Well," said the Vice-President, crossing his legs, pulling his wide-awake[60] down over his forehead, causing a passing chicken to hop quickly one side by the accuracy of his aim, and speaking with senatorial deliberation, "I think I have. I've been here twenty-five years, and dash, dash my dash to dash, if I haven't entertained twenty-five separate and distinct earthquakes, one a year. The niggro is the only person who can stand the fever and ague of this region."

The convalescence of the engineer was the signal for breaking up quarters at St. Louis, and the young fortune-hunters started up the river in good spirits. It was only the second time either of them had been upon a Mississippi steamboat, and nearly everything they saw had the charm of novelty. Col. Sellers was at the landing to bid them good-bye.

"I shall send you up that basket of champagne by the next boat; no, no; no thanks; you'll find it not bad in camp," he cried out as the plank was hauled in. "My respects to Thompson. Tell him to sight for Stone's. Let me know, Mr. Brierly, when you are ready to locate; I'll come over from Hawkeye. Good-bye."

And the last the young fellows saw of the Colonel, he was waving his hat, and beaming prosperity and good luck.

The voyage was delightful, and was not long enough to become monotonous. The travelers scarcely had time indeed to get accustomed to the splendors of the great saloon where the tables were spread for meals, a marvel of paint and gilding, its ceiling hung with fancifully cut tissue-paper of many colors, festooned and arranged in endless patterns. The whole was more beautiful than a barber's shop. The printed bill of fare at dinner was longer and more varied, the proprietors justly boasted, than that of any hotel in New York. It must have been the work of an author of talent and imagination, and it surely was not his fault if the dinner itself was to a certain extent a delusion, and if the guests got something that tasted pretty much the same whatever dish they ordered; nor was it his fault if a general flavor of rose[61] in all the dessert dishes suggested that they had passed through the barber's saloon on their way from the kitchen.

The travelers landed at a little settlement on the left bank, and at once took horses for the camp in the interior, carrying their clothes and blankets strapped behind the saddles. Harry was dressed as we have seen him once before, and his long and shining boots attracted not a little the attention of the few persons they met on the road, and especially of the bright faced wenches who lightly stepped along the highway, picturesque in their colored kerchiefs, carrying light baskets, or riding upon mules and balancing before them a heavier load.

Harry sang fragments of operas and talked about their fortune. Philip even was excited by the sense of freedom and adventure, and the beauty of the landscape. The prairie, with its new grass and unending acres of brilliant flowers—chiefly the innumerable varieties of phlox—bore the look of years of cultivation, and the occasional open groves of white oaks gave it a park-like appearance. It was hardly unreasonable to expect to see at any moment, the gables and square windows of an Elizabethan mansion in one of the well kept groves.

Towards sunset of the third day, when the young gentlemen thought they ought to be near the town of Magnolia, near which they had been directed to find the engineers' camp, they descried a log house and drew up before it to enquire the way. Half the building was store, and half was dwelling house. At the door of the latter stood a negress with a bright turban on her head, to whom Philip called,

"Can you tell me, auntie, how far it is to the town of Magnolia?"

"Why, bress you chile," laughed the woman, "you's dere now."

It was true. This log house was the compactly built town, and all creation was its suburbs. The engineers' camp was only two or three miles distant.

"You's boun' to find it," directed auntie, "if you don't keah nuffin 'bout de road, and go fo' de sundown."

A brisk gallop brought the riders in sight of the twinkling light of the camp, just as the stars came out. It lay in a little hollow, where a small stream ran through a sparse grove of young white oaks. A half dozen tents were pitched under the trees, horses and oxen were corraled at a little distance, and a group of men sat on camp stools or lay on blankets about a bright fire. The twang of a banjo became audible as they drew nearer, and they saw a couple of negroes, from some neighboring plantation, "breaking down"[62] a juba[63] in approved style, amid the "hi, hi's" of the spectators.

Mr. Jeff Thompson, for it was the camp of this redoubtable engineer, gave the travelers a hearty welcome, offered them ground room in his own tent, ordered supper, and set out a small jug, a drop from which he declared necessary on account of the chill of the evening.

"I never saw an Eastern man," said Jeff, "who knew how to drink from a jug with one hand. It's as easy as lying. So." He grasped the handle with the right hand, threw the jug back upon his arm, and applied his lips to the nozzle. It was an act as graceful as it was simple. "Besides," said Mr. Thompson, setting it down, "it puts every man on his honor as to quantity."

Early to turn in was the rule of the camp, and by nine o'clock everybody was under his blanket, except Jeff himself, who worked awhile at his table over his field-book, and then arose, stepped outside the tent door and sang, in a strong and not unmelodious tenor, the Star Spangled Banner from beginning to end. It proved to be his nightly practice to let off the unexpended steam of his conversational powers, in the words of his stirring song.

It was a long time before Philip got to sleep. He saw the fire light, he saw the clear stars through the tree-tops, he heard the gurgle of the stream, the stamp of the horses, the occasional barking of the dog which followed the cook's wagon, the hooting of an owl; and when these failed he saw Jeff, standing on a battlement, mid the rocket's red glare, and heard him sing, "Oh, say, can you see?" It was the first time he had ever slept on the ground.

CHAPTER XVII

—"We have view'd it,
And measur'd it within all, by the scale:
The richest tract of land, love, in the kingdom!
There will be made seventeen or eighteen millions,
Or more, as't may be handled!"
The Devil Is an Ass.

NOBODY DRESSED more like an engineer than Mr. Henry Brierly. The completeness of his appointments was the envy of the corps, and the gay fellow himself was the admiration of the camp servants, axemen, teamsters and cooks.

"I reckon you didn't git them boots no wher's this side o' Sent Louis?" queried the tall Missouri youth who acted as commissary's assistant.

"No, New York."

"Yas, I've heern o' New York," continued the butternut lad, attentively studying each item of Harry's dress, and endeavoring to cover his design with interesting conversation. "'N there's Massachusetts."

"It's not far off."

"I've heern Massachusetts was a ———— of a place. Les' see, what state's Massachusetts in?"

"Massachusetts," kindly replied Harry, "is in the state of Boston."

"Abolish'n wasn't it? They must a cost right smart," referring to the boots.

Harry shouldered his rod and went to the field, tramped over the prairie by day, and figured up results at night, with the utmost cheerfulness and industry, and plotted the line on the profile paper, without, however, the least idea of engineering practical or theoretical. Perhaps there was not a great deal of scientific knowledge in the entire corps, nor was very much needed. They were making what is called a preliminary survey, and the chief object of a preliminary survey was to get up an excitement about the road, to interest every town in that part of the state in it, under the belief that the road would run through it, and to get the aid of every planter upon the prospect that a station would be on his land.

Mr. Jeff Thompson was the most popular engineer who could be found for this work. He did not bother himself much about details or practicabilities of location, but ran merrily along, sighting from the top of one divide to the top of another, and striking "plumb" every town site and big plantation within twenty or thirty miles of his route. In his own language he "just went booming."

This course gave Harry an opportunity, as he said, to learn the practical details of engineering, and it gave Philip a chance to see the country, and to judge for himself what prospect of a fortune it offered. Both he and Harry got the "refusal" of more than one plantation as they went along, and wrote urgent letters to their eastern correspondents, upon the beauty of the land and the certainty that it would quadruple in value as soon as the road was finally located. It seemed strange to them that capitalists did not flock out there and secure this land.

They had not been in the field over two weeks when Harry wrote to his friend Col. Sellers that he'd better be on the move, for the line was certain to go to Stone's Landing. Any one who looked at the line on the map, as it was laid down from day to day, would have been uncertain which way it was going; but Jeff had declared that in his judgment the only practicable route from the point they then stood on was to follow the divide to Stone's Landing, and it was generally understood that that town would be the next one hit.

"We'll make it, boys," said the chief, "if we have to go in a balloon."

And make it they did. In less than a week, this indomitable engineer had carried his moving caravan over slues and branches, across bottoms and along divides, and pitched his tents in the very heart of the city of Stone's Landing.

"Well, I'll be dashed," was heard the cheery voice of Mr. Thompson, as he stepped outside the tent door at sunrise next morning. "If this don't get me. I say, you, Grayson, get out your sighting iron and see if you can find old Sellers's town. Blame me if we wouldn't have run plumb by it if twilight had held on a little longer. Oh! Sterling, Brierly, get up and see the city. There's a steamboat just coming round the bend." And Jeff roared with laughter. "The mayor'll be round here to breakfast."

The fellows turned out of the tents, rubbing their eyes, and stared about them. They were camped on the second bench of the narrow bottom of a crooked, sluggish stream, that was some five rods wide in the present good stage of water. Before them were a dozen log cabins, with stick and mud chimneys, irregularly disposed on either side of a not very well defined road, which did not seem to know its own mind exactly, and, after straggling through the town, wandered off over the rolling prairie in an uncertain way, as if it had started for nowhere and was quite likely to reach its destination. Just as it left the town, however, it was cheered and assisted by a guide-board, upon which was the legend "10 Mils to Hawkeye."

The road had never been made except by the travel over it, and at this season—the rainy June—it was a way of ruts cut in the black soil, and of fathomless mud-holes. In the principal street of the city, it had received more attention; for hogs, great and small, rooted about in it and wallowed in it, turning the street into a liquid quagmire which could only be crossed on pieces of plank thrown here and there.

About the chief cabin, which was the store and grocery of this mart of trade, the mud was more liquid than elsewhere, and the rude platform in front of it and the dry-goods boxes mounted thereon were places of refuge for all the loafers of the place. Down by the stream was a dilapidated building which served for a hemp warehouse, and a shaky wharf extended out from it into the water. In fact a flat-boat was there moored by it, its setting poles[64] lying across the gunwales. Above the town the stream was crossed by a crazy wooden bridge, the supports of which leaned all ways in the soggy soil; the absence of a plank here and there in the flooring made the crossing of the bridge faster than a walk an offense not necessary to be prohibited by law.

"This, gentlemen," said Jeff, "is Columbus River, *alias* Goose Run. If it was widened, and deepened, and straightened, and made long enough, it would be one of the finest rivers in the western country."

As the sun rose and sent his level beams along the stream, the thin stratum of mist, or malaria, rose also and dispersed, but the light was not able to enliven the dull water nor give any hint of its apparently fathomless depth. Venerable mud-turtles crawled up and roosted upon the old logs in the stream, their backs glistening in the sun, the first inhabitants of the metropolis to begin the active business of the day.

It was not long, however, before smoke began to issue from the city chimneys; and before the engineers had finished their breakfast they were the object of the curious inspection of six or eight boys and men, who lounged into the camp and gazed about them with languid interest, their hands in their pockets every one.

"Good morning, gentlemen," called out the chief engineer, from the table.

"Good mawning," drawled out the spokesman of the party. "I allow thish-yers the railroad, I heern it was a-comin'."

"Yes, this is the railroad, all but the rails and the iron-horse."

"I reckon you kin git all the rails you want outen my white oak timber over thar," replied the first speaker, who appeared to be a man of property and willing to strike up a trade.

"You'll have to negotiate with the contractors about the rails, sir," said Jeff; "here's Mr. Brierly, I've no doubt would like buy your rails when the time comes."

"O," said the man, "I thought maybe you'd fetch the whole bilin[65] along with you. But if you want rails, I've got 'em, haint I Eph."

"Heaps," said Eph, without taking his eyes off the group at the table.

"Well," said Mr. Thompson, rising from his seat and moving towards his tent, "the railroad has come to Stone's Landing, sure; I move we take a drink on it all round."

The proposal met with universal favor. Jeff gave prosperity to Stone's Landing and navigation to Goose Run, and the toast was washed down with gusto, in the simple fluid of corn, and with the return compliment that a railroad was a good thing, and that Jeff Thompson was no slouch.

About ten o'clock a horse and wagon was descried making a

slow approach to the camp over the prairie. As it drew near, the wagon was seen to contain a portly gentleman, who hitched impatiently forward on his seat, shook the reins and gently touched up his horse, in the vain attempt to communicate his own energy to that dull beast, and looked eagerly at the tents. When the conveyance at length drew up to Mr. Thompson's door, the gentleman descended with great deliberation, straightened himself up, rubbed his hands, and beaming satisfaction from every part of his radiant frame, advanced to the group that was gathered to welcome him, and which had saluted him by name as soon as he came within hearing.

"Welcome to Napoleon, gentlemen, welcome. I am proud to see you here Mr. Thompson. You are looking well Mr. Sterling. This is the country, sir. Right glad to see you Mr. Brierly. You got that basket of champagne? No? Those blasted river thieves! I'll never send anything more by 'em. The best brand, Roederer.[66] The last I had in my cellar, from a lot sent me by Sir George Gore[67]—took him out on a buffalo hunt, when he visited our country. Is always sending me some trifle. You haven't looked about any yet, gentlemen? It's in the rough yet, in the rough. Those buildings will all have to come down. That's the place for the public square, Court House, hotels, churches, jail—all that sort of thing. About where we stand, the deepo. How does that strike your engineering eye, Mr. Thompson? Down yonder the business streets, running to the wharves. The University up there, on rising ground, sightly place, see the river for miles. That's Columbus river, only forty-nine miles to the Missouri. You see what it is, placid, steady, no current to interfere with navigation, wants widening in places and dredging, dredge out the harbor and raise a levee in front of the town; made by nature on purpose for a mart. Look at all this country, not another building within ten miles, no other navigable stream, lay of the land points right here; hemp, tobacco, corn, must come here. The railroad will do it, Napoleon won't know itself in a year."

"Don't now evidently," said Philip aside to Harry. "Have you breakfasted Colonel?"

"Hastily. Cup of coffee. Can't trust any coffee I don't import myself. But I put up a basket of provisions, wife would put in a few delicacies, women always will, and a half dozen of that Burgundy, I was telling you of Mr. Brierly. By the way, you never got to dine with me." And the Colonel strode away to the wagon and looked under the seat for the basket.

Apparently it was not there. For the Colonel raised up the flap, looked in front and behind, and then exclaimed,

"Confound it. That comes of not doing a thing yourself. I trusted to the women folks to set that basket in the wagon, and it ain't there."

The camp cook speedily prepared a savory breakfast for the Colonel, broiled chicken, eggs, corn-bread, and coffee, to which he did ample justice, and topped off with a drop of Old Bourbon, from Mr. Thompson's private store, a brand which he said he knew well, he should think it came from his own side-board.

While the engineer corps went to the field, to run back a couple of miles and ascertain, approximately, if a road could ever get down to the Landing, and to sight ahead across the Run, and see if it could ever get out again, Col. Sellers and Harry sat down and began to roughly map out the city of Napoleon on a large piece of drawing paper.

"I've got the refusal of a mile square here," said the Colonel, "in our names, for a year, with a quarter interest reserved for the four owners."

They laid out the town liberally, not lacking room, leaving space for the railroad to come in, and for the river as it was to be when improved.

The engineers reported that the railroad could come in, by taking a little sweep and crossing the stream on a high bridge, but the grades would be steep. Col. Sellers said he didn't care so much about the grades, if the road could only be made to reach the elevators on the river. The next day Mr. Thompson made a hasty survey of the stream for a mile or two, so that the Colonel and Harry were enabled to show on their map how nobly that would accommodate the city. Jeff took a little writing from the Colonel and Harry for a prospective share but Philip declined to join in, saying that he had no money, and didn't want to make engagements he couldn't fulfill.

The next morning the camp moved on, followed till it was out of sight by the listless eyes of the group in front of the store, one of whom remarked that, "he'd be doggoned if he ever expected to see *that* railroad any mo'."

Harry went with the Colonel to Hawkeye to complete their arrangements, a part of which was the preparation of a petition to Congress for the improvement of the navigation of Columbus River.

CHAPTER XVIII

·OI+/II·:⊙Ǝⅅ⋈+⊡I
···:++IO:⊙II⅃···ƐO:

Bedda ag Idda.

—"Eve us lo convintz qals er,
Que voill que m prendats a moiler.
—Qu'en aissi l'a Dieus establida
Per que not pot esser partida."
    Roman de Jaufre.

EIGHT YEARS HAVE PASSED since the death of Mr. Hawkins.
Eight years are not many in the life of a nation or the history of a
state, but they may be years of destiny that shall fix the current of
the century following. Such years were those that followed the
little scrimmage on Lexington Common. Such years were those
that followed the double-shotted demand for the surrender of
Fort Sumter. History is never done with inquiring of these years,
and summoning witnesses about them, and trying to understand
their significance.

The eight years in America from 1860 to 1868 uprooted institutions that were centuries old, changed the politics of a people,
transformed the social life of half the country, and wrought so
profoundly upon the entire national character that the influence
cannot be measured short of two or three generations.

As we are accustomed to interpret the economy of providence,
the life of the individual is as nothing to that of the nation or the
race; but who can say, in the broader view and the more intelligent
weight of values, that the life of one man is not more than that of
a nationality, and that there is not a tribunal where the tragedy of
one human soul shall not seem more significant than the over-
turning of any human institution whatever?

When one thinks of the tremendous forces of the upper and the
nether world which play for the mastery of the soul of a woman
during the few years in which she passes from plastic girlhood to

130

the ripe maturity of womanhood, he may well stand in awe before the momentous drama.

What capacities she has of purity, tenderness, goodness; what capacities of vileness, bitterness and evil. Nature must needs be lavish with the mother and creator of men, and center in her all the possibilities of life. And a few critical years can decide whether her life is to be full of sweetness and light, whether she is to be the vestal of a holy temple, or whether she will be the fallen priestess of a desecrated shrine. There are women, it is true, who seem to be capable neither of rising much nor of falling much, and whom a conventional life saves from any special development of character.

But Laura was not one of them. She had the fatal gift of beauty, and that more fatal gift which does not always accompany mere beauty, the power of fascination, and a power that may, indeed, exist without beauty. She had will, and pride and courage and ambition, and she was left to be very much her own guide at the age when romance comes to the aid of passion, and when the awakening powers of her vigorous mind had little object on which to discipline themselves.

The tremendous conflict that was fought in this girl's soul none of those about her knew, and very few knew that her life had in it anything unusual or romantic or strange.

Those were troublous days in Hawkeye as well as in most other Missouri towns, days of confusion, when between Unionist and Confederate occupations, sudden maraudings and bushwhackings and raids, individuals escaped observation or comment in actions that would have filled the town with scandal in quiet times.

Fortunately we only need to deal with Laura's life at this period historically, and look back upon such portions of it as will serve to reveal the woman as she was at the time of the arrival of Mr. Harry Brierly in Hawkeye.

The Hawkins family were settled there, and had a hard enough struggle with poverty and the necessity of keeping up appearances in accord with their own family pride and the large expectations they secretly cherished of a fortune in the Knobs of East Tennessee. How pinched they were perhaps no one knew but

Clay, to whom they looked for almost their whole support. Washington had been in Hawkeye off and on, attracted away occasionally by some tremendous speculation, from which he invariably returned to Gen. Boswell's office as poor as he went. He was the inventor of no one knew how many useless contrivances, which were not worth patenting, and his years had been passed in dreaming and planning to no purpose; until he was now a man of about thirty, without a profession or a permanent occupation, a tall, brown-haired, dreamy person of the best intentions and the frailest resolution. Probably however the eight years had been happier to him than to any others in his circle, for the time had been mostly spent in a blissful dream of the coming of enormous wealth.

He went out with a company from Hawkeye to the war, and was not wanting in courage, but he would have been a better soldier if he had been less engaged in contrivances for circumventing the enemy by strategy unknown to the books.

It happened to him to be captured in one of his self-appointed expeditions, but the federal colonel released him, after a short examination, satisfied that he could most injure the confederate forces opposed to the Unionists by returning him to his regiment.

Col. Sellers was of course a prominent man during the war. He was captain of the home guards in Hawkeye, and he never left home except upon one occasion, when on the strength of a rumor, he executed a flank movement and fortified Stone's Landing, a place which no one unacquainted with the country would be likely to find.

"Gad," said the Colonel afterwards, "the Landing is the key to upper Missouri, and it is the only place the enemy never captured. If other places had been defended as well as that was, the result would have been different, sir."

The Colonel had his own theories about war as he had in other things. If everybody had stayed at home as he did, he said, the South never would have been conquered. For what would there have been to conquer? Mr. Jeff Davis was constantly writing him to take command of a corps in the confederate army, but Col. Sellers said, no, his duty was at home. And he was by no means idle. He was the inventor of the famous air torpedo, which came very near destroying the Union armies in Missouri, and the city of St. Louis itself.

His plan was to fill a torpedo with Greek fire and poisonous and deadly missiles, attach it to a balloon, and then let it sail away over the hostile camp and explode at the right moment, when the time-fuse burned out. He intended to use this invention in the capture of St. Louis, exploding his torpedoes over the city, and raining destruction upon it until the army of occupation would gladly capitulate. He was unable to procure the Greek fire, but he constructed a vicious torpedo which would have answered the purpose, but the first one prematurely exploded in his wood-house, blowing it clean away, and setting fire to his house. The neighbors helped him put out the conflagration, but they discouraged any more experiments of that sort.

The patriotic old gentleman, however, planted so much powder and so many explosive contrivances in the roads leading into Hawkeye, and then forgot the exact spots of danger, that people were afraid to travel the highways, and used to come to town across the fields. The Colonel's motto was, "Millions for defence but not one cent for tribute."[68]

When Laura came to Hawkeye she might have forgotten the annoyances of the gossips of Murpheysburg and have outlived the bitterness that was growing in her heart, if she had been thrown less upon herself, or if the surroundings of her life had been more congenial and helpful. But she had little society, less and less as she grew older that was congenial to her, and her mind preyed upon itself, and the mystery of her birth at once chagrined her and raised in her the most extravagant expectations.

She was proud and she felt the sting of poverty. She could not but be conscious of her beauty also, and she was vain of that, and came to take a sort of delight in the exercise of her fascinations upon the rather loutish young men who came in her way and whom she despised.

There was another world opened to her—a world of books. But it was not the best world of that sort, for the small libraries she had access to in Hawkeye were decidedly miscellaneous, and largely made up of romances and fictions which fed her imagination with the most exaggerated notions of life, and showed her

men and women in a very false sort of heroism. From these stories she learned what a woman of keen intellect and some culture
joined to beauty and fascination of manner, might expect to accomplish in society as she read of it; and along with these ideas
she imbibed other very crude ones in regard to the emancipation
of woman.

There were also other books—histories, biographies of distinguished people, travels in far lands, poems, especially those of Byron, Scott and Shelley and Moore, which she eagerly absorbed,
and appropriated therefrom what was to her liking. Nobody in
Hawkeye had read so much or, after a fashion, studied so diligently as Laura. She passed for an accomplished girl, and no
doubt thought herself one, as she was, judged by any standard
near her.

During the war there came to Hawkeye a confederate officer,
Col. Selby, who was stationed there for a time, in command of
that district. He was a handsome, soldierly man of thirty years, a
graduate of the University of Virginia, and of distinguished family, if his story might be believed, and, it was evident, a man of the
world and of extensive travel and adventure.

To find in such an out of the way country place a woman like
Laura was a piece of good luck upon which Col. Selby congratu-
lated himself. He was studiously polite to her and treated her with
a consideration to which she was unaccustomed. She had read of
such men, but she had never seen one before, one so high-bred, so
noble in sentiment, so entertaining in conversation, so engaging in
manner.

It is a long story; unfortunately it is an old story, and it need
not be dwelt on. Laura loved him, and believed that his love for
her was as pure and deep as her own. She worshiped him and
would have counted her life a little thing to give him, if he would
only love her and let her feed the hunger of her heart upon him.

The passion possessed her whole being, and lifted her up, till
she seemed to walk on air. It was all true, then, the romances she
had read, the bliss of love she had dreamed of. Why had she never
noticed before how blithesome the world was, how jocund with
love; the birds sang it, the trees whispered it to her as she passed,

the very flowers beneath her feet strewed the way as for a bridal march.

When the colonel went away they were engaged to be married, as soon as he could make certain arrangements which he represented to be necessary, and quit the army.

He wrote to her from Harding, a small town in the southwest corner of the state, saying that he should be held in the service longer than he had expected, but that it would not be more than a few months, then he should be at liberty to take her to Chicago where he had property, and should have business, either now or as soon as the war was over, which he thought could not last long. Meantime why should they be separated? He was established in comfortable quarters, and if she could find company and join him, they would be married, and gain so many more months of happiness.

Was woman ever prudent when she loved? Laura went to Harding, the neighbors supposed to nurse Washington who had fallen ill there.

Her engagement was, of course, known in Hawkeye, and was indeed a matter of pride to her family. Mrs. Hawkins would have told the first inquirer that Laura had gone to be married; but Laura had cautioned her; she did not want to be thought of, she said, as going in search of a husband; let the news come back after she was married.

So she traveled to Harding on the pretence we have mentioned, and was married. She was married, but something must have happened on that very day or the next that alarmed her. Washington did not know then or after what it was, but Laura bound him not to send news of her marriage to Hawkeye yet, and to enjoin her mother not to speak of it. Whatever cruel suspicion or nameless dread this was, Laura tried bravely to put it away, and not let it cloud her happiness.

Communication that summer, as may be imagined, was neither regular nor frequent between the remote confederate camp at Harding and Hawkeye, and Laura was in a measure lost sight of—indeed, everyone had troubles enough of his own without borrowing from his neighbors.

Laura had given herself utterly to her husband, and if he had faults, if he was selfish, if he was sometimes coarse, if he was dissipated, she did not or would not see it. It was the passion of her life, the time when her whole nature went to flood tide and swept away all barriers. Was her husband ever cold or indifferent? She shut her eyes to everything but her sense of possession of her idol.

Three months passed. One morning her husband informed her that he had been ordered South, and must go within two hours.

"I can be ready," said Laura, cheerfully.

"But I can't take you. You must go back to Hawkeye."

"Can't—take—me?" Laura asked, with wonder in her eyes. "I can't live without you. You said"—

"O bother what I said"—and the Colonel took up his sword to buckle it on, and then continued coolly, "the fact is Laura, our romance is played out."

Laura heard, but she did not comprehend. She caught his arm and cried, "George, how can you joke so cruelly? I will go any where with you. I will wait any where. I can't go back to Hawkeye."

"Well, go where you like. Perhaps," continued he with a sneer, "you would do as well to wait here, for another colonel."

Laura's brain whirled. She did not yet comprehend. "What does this mean? Where are you going?"

"It means," said the officer, in measured words, "that you haven't anything to show for a legal marriage, and that I am going to New Orleans."

"It's a lie, George, it's a lie. I am your wife. I shall go. I shall follow you to New Orleans."

"Perhaps my wife might not like it!"

Laura raised her head, her eyes flamed with fire, she tried to utter a cry, and fell senseless on the floor.

When she came to herself the Colonel was gone. Washington Hawkins stood at her bedside. Did she come to herself? Was there anything left in her heart but hate and bitterness, a sense of an infamous wrong at the hands of the only man she had ever loved?

She returned to Hawkeye. With the exception of Washington and his mother, no one knew what had happened. The neighbors supposed that the engagement with Col. Selby had fallen through.

Laura was ill for a long time, but she recovered; she had that resolution in her that could conquer death almost. And with her
health came back her beauty, and an added fascination, a something that might be mistaken for sadness. Is there a beauty in the
knowledge of evil, a beauty that shines out in the face of a person
whose inward life is transformed by some terrible experience? Is
the pathos in the eyes of the Beatrice Cenci[69] from her guilt or her
innocence?

Laura was not much changed. The lovely woman had a devil in
her heart. That was all.

CHAPTER XIX

Wie entwickeln sich doch schnelle
Aus der flüchtigsten Empfindung
Leidenschaften ohne Grenzen
Und die zärtlichste Verbindung?
Täglich wächst zu dieser Dame
Meines Herzens tiefste Neigung,
Und dass ich in sie verliebt sei,
Wird mir fast zür Ueberzeugung.

Heine.

MR. HARRY BRIERLY drew his pay as an engineer while he was living at the City Hotel in Hawkeye. Mr. Thompson had been kind enough to say that it didn't make any difference whether he was with the corps or not; and although Harry protested to the Colonel daily and to Washington Hawkins that he must go back at once to the line and superintend the lay-out with reference to his contract, yet he did not go, but wrote instead long letters to Philip, instructing him to keep his eye out, and to let him know when any difficulty occurred that required his presence.

Meantime Harry blossomed out in the society of Hawkeye, as he did in any society where fortune cast him and he had the slightest opportunity to expand. Indeed the talents of a rich and accomplished young fellow like Harry were not likely to go unappreciated in such a place. A land operator, engaged in vast speculations, a favorite in the select circles of New York, in correspondence with brokers and bankers, intimate with public men at Washington, one who could play the guitar and touch the banjo lightly, and who had an eye for a pretty girl, and knew the language of flattery, was welcome everywhere in Hawkeye. Even Miss Laura Hawkins thought it worth while to use her fascinations upon him, and to endeavor to entangle the volatile fellow in the meshes of her attractions.

"Gad," says Harry to the Colonel, "she's a superb creature, she'd make a stir in New York, money or no money. There are men I know would give her a railroad or an opera house,[70] or whatever she wanted—at least they'd promise."

Harry had a way of looking at women as he looked at anything else in the world he wanted, and he half resolved to appropriate Miss Laura, during his stay in Hawkeye. Perhaps the colonel divined his thoughts, or was offended at Harry's talk, for he replied,

"No nonsense, Mr. Brierly. Nonsense won't do in Hawkeye, not with my friends. The Hawkinses' blood is good blood, all the way from Tennessee. The Hawkinses are under the weather now, but their Tennessee property is millions when it comes into market."

"Of course, Colonel. Not the least offense intended. But you can see she is a fascinating woman. I was only thinking, as to this appropriation, now, what such a woman could do in Washington. All correct, too, all correct. Common thing, I assure you in Washington; the wives of senators, representatives, cabinet officers, all sorts of wives, and some who are not wives, use their influence. You want an appointment? Do you go to Senator X? Not much. You get on the right side of his wife. Is it an appropriation? You'd go straight to the Committee, or to the Interior office, I suppose? You'd learn better than that. It takes a woman to get any thing through the Land Office. I tell you, Miss Laura would fascinate an appropriation right through the Senate and the House of Representatives in one session, if she was in Washington, as your friend, Colonel, of course as your friend."

"Would you have her sign our petition?" asked the Colonel, innocently.

Harry laughed. "Women don't get anything by petitioning Congress; nobody does, that's for form. Petitions are referred somewhere, and that's the last of them; you can't refer a handsome woman so easily, when she is present. They prefer 'em mostly."

The petition however was elaborately drawn up, with a glowing description of Napoleon and the adjacent country, and a statement of the absolute necessity to the prosperity of that region and of one of the stations on the great through route to the Pacific, of the immediate improvement of Columbus River; to this was appended a map of the city and a survey of the river. It was signed by all the people at Stone's Landing who could write their names, by Col. Beriah Sellers, and the Colonel agreed to have the names headed by all the senators and representatives from the state and by a sprinkling of ex-governors and ex-members of congress. When completed it was a formidable document. Its preparation and that of more minute plots of the new city consumed the valuable time of Sellers and Harry for many weeks, and served to keep them both in the highest spirits.

In the eyes of Washington Hawkins, Harry was a superior being, a man who was able to bring things to pass in a way that excited his enthusiasm. He never tired of listening to his stories of what he had done and of what he was going to do. As for Washington, Harry thought he was a man of ability and comprehension, but "too visionary," he told the Colonel. The Colonel said he might be right, but he had never noticed anything visionary about him.

"He's got his plans, sir. God bless my soul, at his age, I was full of plans. But experience sobers a man, I never touch any thing now that hasn't been weighed in my judgment; and when Beriah Sellers puts his judgment on a thing, there it is."

Whatever might have been Harry's intentions with regard to Laura, he saw more and more of her every day, until he got to be restless and nervous when he was not with her. That consummate artist in passion allowed him to believe that the fascination was mainly on his side, and so worked upon his vanity, while inflaming his ardor, that he scarcely knew what he was about. Her coolness and coyness were even made to appear the simple precautions of a modest timidity, and attracted him even more than the little tendernesses into which she was occasionally surprised. He could never be away from her long, day or evening; and in a short time their intimacy was the town talk. She played with him so adroitly that Harry thought she was absorbed in love for him, and yet he was amazed that he did not get on faster in his conquest.

And when he thought of it, he was piqued as well. A country girl, poor enough, that was evident; living with her family in a cheap and most unattractive frame house, such as carpenters build in America, scantily furnished and unadorned; without the adventitious aids of dress or jewels or the fine manners of society— Harry couldn't understand it. But she fascinated him, and held him just beyond the line of absolute familiarity at the same time. While he was with her she made him forget that the Hawkinses' house was nothing but a wooden tenement, with four small square rooms on the ground floor and a half story; it might have been a palace for aught he knew.

Perhaps Laura was older than Harry. She was, at any rate, at that ripe age when beauty in woman seems more solid than in the budding period of girlhood, and she had come to understand her powers perfectly, and to know exactly how much of the suscepti- bility and archness of the girl it was profitable to retain. She saw that many women, with the best intentions, make a mistake of carrying too much girlishness into womanhood. Such a woman would have attracted Harry at any time, but only a woman with a cool brain and exquisite art could have made him lose his head in this way; for Harry thought himself a man of the world. The young fellow never dreamed that he was merely being experi- mented on; he was to her a man of another society and another culture, different from that she had any knowledge of except in books, and she was not unwilling to try on him the fascinations of her mind and person.

For Laura had her dreams. She detested the narrow limits in which her lot was cast, she hated poverty. Much of her reading had been of modern works of fiction, written by her own sex, which had revealed to her something of her own powers and given her indeed, an exaggerated notion of the influence, the wealth, the position a woman may attain who has beauty and tal- ent and ambition and a little culture, and is not too scrupulous in the use of them. She wanted to be rich, she wanted luxury, she wanted men at her feet, her slaves, and she had not—thanks to some of the novels she had read—the nicest discrimination be- tween notoriety and reputation; perhaps she did not know how fatal notoriety usually is to the bloom of womanhood.

With the other Hawkins children Laura had been brought up in the belief that they had inherited a fortune in the Tennessee Lands. She did not by any means share all the delusion of the fam- ily; but her brain was not seldom busy with schemes about it. Washington seemed to her only to dream of it and to be willing to wait for its riches to fall upon him in a golden shower; but she was impatient, and wished she were a man to take hold of the business.

"You men must enjoy your schemes and your activity and liberty to go about the world," she said to Harry one day, when he had been talking of New York and Washington and his incessant engagements.

"Oh, yes," replied that martyr to business, "it's all well enough, if you don't have too much of it, but it only has one object."

"What is that?"

"If a woman doesn't know, it's useless to tell her. What do you suppose I am staying in Hawkeye for, week after week, when I ought to be with my corps?"

"I suppose it's your business with Col. Sellers about Napoleon, you've always told me so," answered Laura, with a look intended to contradict her words.

"And now I tell you that is all arranged, I suppose you'll tell me I ought to go?"

"Harry!" exclaimed Laura, touching his arm and letting her pretty hand rest there a moment. "Why should I want you to go away? The only person in Hawkeye who understands me."

"But you refuse to understand *me*," replied Harry, flattered but still petulant. "You are like an iceberg, when we are alone."

Laura looked up with wonder in her great eyes, and something like a blush suffusing her face, followed by a look of languor that penetrated Harry's heart as if it had been longing. "Did I ever show any want of confidence in you, Harry?" And she gave him her hand, which Harry pressed with effusion—something in her manner told him that he must be content with that favor.

It was always so. She excited his hopes and denied him, inflamed his passion and restrained it, and wound him in her toils day by day. To what purpose? It was keen delight to Laura to prove that she had power over men.

Laura liked to hear about life at the east, and especially about the luxurious society in which Mr. Brierly moved when he was at home. It pleased her imagination to fancy herself a queen in it.

"You should be a winter in Washington," Harry said.

"But I have no acquaintances there."

"Don't know any of the families of the congressmen? They like to have a pretty woman staying with them."

"Not one."

"Suppose Col. Sellers should have business there; say, about this Columbus River appropriation?"

"Sellers!" and Laura laughed.

"You needn't laugh. Queerer things have happened. Sellers knows everybody from Missouri, and from the West, too, for that matter. He'd introduce you to Washington life quick enough. It doesn't need a crowbar to break your way into society there as it does in Philadelphia. It's democratic, Washington is. Money or beauty will open any door. If I were a handsome woman, I shouldn't want any better place than the capital to pick up a prince or a fortune."

"Thank you," replied Laura. "But I prefer the quiet of home, and the love of those I know;" and her face wore a look of sweet contentment and unworldliness that finished Mr. Harry Brierly for the day.

Nevertheless, the hint that Harry had dropped fell upon good ground, and bore fruit an hundred fold; it worked in her mind until she had built up a plan on it, and almost a career for herself. Why not, she said, why shouldn't I do as other women have done? She took the first opportunity to see Col. Sellers, and to sound him about the Washington visit. How was he getting on with his navigation scheme, would it be likely to take him from home to Jefferson City;[71] or to Washington, perhaps?

"Well, maybe. If the people of Napoleon want me to go to Washington, and look after that matter, I might tear myself from my home. It's been suggested to me, but—not a word of it to Mrs. Sellers and the children. Maybe they wouldn't like to think of their father in Washington. But Dilworthy, Senator Dilworthy, says to me, 'Colonel, you are the man, you could influence more votes than any one else on such a measure, an old settler, a man of the people, you know the wants of Missouri; you've a respect for religion too,' says he, 'and know how the cause of the gospel goes with improvements,' Which is true enough, Miss Laura, and hasn't been enough thought of in connection with Napoleon.

He's an able man, Dilworthy, and a good man. A man has got to be good to succeed as he has. He's only been in Congress a few years, and he must be worth a million. First thing in the morning when he stayed with me he asked about family prayers, whether we had 'em before or after breakfast. I hated to disappoint the Senator, but I had to out with it, tell him we didn't have 'em, not steady. He said he understood, business interruptions and all that, some men were well enough without, but as for him he never neglected the ordinances of religion. He doubted if the Columbus River appropriation would succeed if we did not invoke the Divine Blessing on it."

Perhaps it is unnecessary to say to the reader that Senator Dilworthy had not stayed with Col. Sellers while he was in Hawkeye; this visit to his house being only one of the Colonel's hallucinations—one of those instant creations of his fertile fancy, which were always flashing into his brain and out of his mouth in the course of any conversation and without interrupting the flow of it.

During the summer Philip rode across the country and made a short visit in Hawkeye, giving Harry an opportunity to show him the progress that he and the Colonel had made in their operation at Stone's Landing, to introduce him also to Laura, and to borrow a little money when he departed. Harry bragged about his conquest, as was his habit, and took Philip round to see his western prize.

Laura received Mr. Philip with a courtesy and a slight hauteur that rather surprised and not a little interested him. He saw at once that she was older than Harry, and soon made up his mind that she was leading his friend a country dance[72] to which he was unaccustomed. At least he thought he saw that, and half hinted as much to Harry, who flared up at once; but on a second visit Philip was not so sure, the young lady was certainly kind and friendly and almost confiding with Harry, and treated Philip with the greatest consideration. She deferred to his opinions, and listened attentively when he talked, and in time met his frank manner with an equal frankness, so that he was quite convinced that whatever she might feel towards Harry, she was sincere with him. Perhaps his manly way did win her liking. Perhaps in her mind, she compared him with Harry, and recognized in him a man to whom a woman might give her whole soul, recklessly and with little care if she lost it. Philip was not invincible to her beauty nor to the intellectual charm of her presence.

The week seemed very short that he passed in Hawkeye, and when he bade Laura good by, he seemed to have known her a year.

"We shall see you again, Mr. Sterling," she said as she gave him her hand, with just a shade of sadness in her handsome eyes.

And when he turned away she followed him with a look that might have disturbed his serenity, if he had not at the moment had a little square letter in his breast pocket, dated at Philadelphia, and signed "Ruth."

CHAPTER XX

—ꝺꙋaꙋall bꙺoꙺꙺꙅloꙺaꙅ ꙅo ꙿbꙋaꙺꙍ ꙺꙺꙺꙅcꙺe ⁊ ꙺꙋꙺlaꙋꙺa ceꙺlle, ⁊ coꙿaꙺꙺle, ꙅo ꙅꙅaꙺꙍꙋꙺꙍ ꙅeꙺꙺceꙺ ꙺꙺa ꙍꙺeꙺꙍ aꙅꙅaꙺ la ꙅaꙍ aeꙺ aꙅ aꙅ cꙺoꙍ—

THE VISIT OF Senator Abner Dilworthy was an event in Hawkeye. When a Senator, whose place is in Washington moving among the Great and guiding the destinies of the nation, condescends to mingle among the people and accept the hospitalities of such a place as Hawkeye, the honor is not considered a light one. All parties are flattered by it and politics are forgotten in the presence of one so distinguished among his fellows.

Senator Dilworthy, who was from a neighboring state, had been a Unionist in the darkest days of his country, and had thriven by it, but was that any reason why Col. Sellers, who had been a confederate and had not thriven by it, should give him the cold shoulder?

The Senator was the guest of his old friend Gen. Boswell, but it almost appeared that he was indebted to Col. Sellers for the unreserved hospitalities of the town. It was the large hearted Colonel who, in a manner, gave him the freedom of the city.

"You are known here, sir," said the Colonel, "and Hawkeye is proud of you. You will find every door open, and a welcome at every hearthstone. I should insist upon your going to my house, if you were not claimed by your older friend Gen. Boswell. But you will mingle with our people, and you will see here developments that will surprise you."

The Colonel was so profuse in his hospitality that he must have made the impression upon himself that he had entertained the Senator at his own mansion during his stay; at any rate, he afterwards always spoke of him as his guest, and not seldom referred to the Senator's relish of certain viands on his table. He did, in fact, press him to dine upon the morning of the day the Senator was going away.

Senator Dilworthy was large and portly, though not tall—a pleasant spoken man, a popular man with the people.

He took a lively interest in the town and all the surrounding country, and made many inquiries as to the progress of agriculture, of education, and of religion, and especially as to the condition of the emancipated race.

"Providence," he said, "has placed them in our hands, and although you and I, General, might have chosen a different destiny for them, under the Constitution, yet Providence knows best."

"You can't do much with 'em," interrupted Col. Sellers. "They are a speculating race, sir, disinclined to work for white folks without security, planning how to live by only working for themselves. Idle, sir, there's my garden just a ruin of weeds. Nothing practical in 'em."

"There is some truth in your observation, Colonel, but you must educate them."

"You educate the niggro and you make him more speculating than he was before. If he won't stick to any industry except for himself now, what will he do then?"

"But, Colonel, the negro when educated will be more able to make his speculations fruitful."

"Never, sir, never. He would only have a wider scope to injure himself. A niggro has no grasp, sir. Now, a white man can conceive great operations, and carry them out; a niggro can't."

"Still," replied the Senator, "granting that he might injure himself in a worldly point of view, his elevation through education would multiply his chances for the hereafter—which is the important thing after all, Colonel. And no matter what the result is, we must fulfill our duty by this being."

"I'd elevate his soul," promptly responded the Colonel; "that's just it; you can't make his soul too immortal, but I wouldn't touch *him*, himself. Yes, sir! Make his soul immortal, but don't disturb the niggro as he is."

Of course one of the entertainments offered the Senator was a public reception, held in the court house, at which he made a speech to his fellow citizens. Col. Sellers was master of ceremonies. He escorted the band from the city hotel to Gen. Boswell's; he marshalled the procession of Masons, of Odd Fellows, and of

Firemen, the Good Templars, the Sons of Temperance, the Cadets of Temperance, the Daughters of Rebecca,[73] the Sunday School children, and citizens generally, which followed the senator to the court house; he bustled about the room long after every one else was seated, and loudly cried "order!" in the dead silence which preceded the introduction of the Senator by Gen. Boswell. The occasion was one to call out his finest powers of personal appearance, and one he long dwelt on with pleasure.

This not being an edition of the *Congressional Globe* it is impossible to give Senator Dilworthy's speech in full. He began somewhat as follows:—

"Fellow citizens: It gives me great pleasure to thus meet and mingle with you, to lay aside for a moment the heavy duties of an official and burdensome station, and confer in familiar converse with my friends in your great state. The good opinion of my fellow citizens of all sections is the sweetest solace in all my anxieties. I look forward with longing to the time when I can lay aside the cares of office—" ["dam sight," shouted a tipsy fellow near the door. Cries of "put him out."]

"My friends, do not remove him. Let the misguided man stay. I see that he is a victim of that evil which is swallowing up public virtue and sapping the foundation of society. As I was saying, when I can lay down the cares of office and retire to the sweets of private life in some such sweet, peaceful, intelligent, wide-awake and patriotic place as Hawkeye (applause). I have traveled much, I have seen all parts of our glorious union, but I have never seen a lovelier village than yours, or one that has more signs of commercial and industrial and religious prosperity—(more applause)."

The Senator then launched into a sketch of our great country, and dwelt for an hour or more upon its prosperity and the dangers which threatened it.

He then touched reverently upon the institutions of religion, and upon the necessity of private purity, if we were to have any public morality. "I trust," he said, "that there are children within the sound of my voice," and after some remarks to them, the Senator closed with an apostrophe to "the genius of American Liberty, walking with the Sunday School in one hand and Temperance in the other up the glorified steps of the National Capitol."

Col. Sellers did not of course lose the opportunity to impress upon so influential a person as the Senator the desirability of improving the navigation of Columbus river. He and Mr. Brierly took the Senator over to Napoleon and opened to him their plan. It was a plan that the Senator could understand without a great deal of explanation, for he seemed to be familiar with the like improvements elsewhere. When, however, they reached Stone's Landing the Senator looked about him and inquired,

"Is this Napoleon?"

"This is the nucleus, the nucleus," said the Colonel, unrolling his map. "Here is the deepo, the church, the City Hall and so on."

"Ah, I see. How far from here is Columbus River? Does that stream empty—"

"That, why, that's Goose Run. Thar ain't no Columbus, thout'n it's over to Hawkeye," interrupted one of the citizens, who had come out to stare at the strangers. "A railroad come here last summer, but it haint been here no mo'."

"Yes, sir," the Colonel hastened to explain, "in the old records Columbus River is called Goose Run. You see how it sweeps round the town—forty-nine miles to the Missouri; sloop navigation all the way pretty much, drains this whole country; when it's improved steamboats will run right up here. It's got to be enlarged, deepened. You see by the map, Columbus River. This country must have water communication!"

"You'll want a considerable appropriation, Col. Sellers."

"I should say a million; is that your figure Mr. Brierly?"

"According to our surveys," said Harry, "a million would do it; a million spent on the river would make Napoleon worth two millions at least."

"I see," nodded the Senator. "But you'd better begin by asking only for two or three hundred thousand, the usual way. You can begin to sell town lots on that appropriation you know."

The Senator, himself, to do him justice, was not very much interested in the country or the stream, but he favored the appropriation, and he gave the Colonel and Mr. Brierly to understand that he would endeavor to get it through. Harry, who thought he was shrewd and understood Washington, suggested an interest. But he saw that the Senator was wounded by the suggestion.

"You will offend me by repeating such an observation," he said. "Whatever I do will be for the public interest. It will require a portion of the appropriation for necessary expenses, and I am sorry to say that there are members who will have to be seen. But you can reckon upon my humble services."

This aspect of the subject was not again alluded to. The Senator possessed himself of the facts, not from his observation of the ground, but from the lips of Col. Sellers, and laid the appropriation scheme away among his other plans for benefiting the public.

It was on this visit also that the Senator made the acquaintance of Mr. Washington Hawkins, and was greatly taken with his innocence, his guileless manner and perhaps with his ready adaptability to enter upon any plan proposed.

Col. Sellers was pleased to see this interest that Washington had awakened, especially since it was likely to further his expectations with regard to the Tennessee lands; the Senator having remarked to the Colonel, that he delighted to help any deserving young man, when the promotion of a private advantage could at the same time be made to contribute to the general good. And he did not doubt that this was an opportunity of that kind.

The result of several conferences with Washington was that the Senator proposed that he should go to Washington with him and become his private secretary and the secretary of his committee; a proposal which was eagerly accepted.

The Senator spent Sunday in Hawkeye and attended church. He cheered the heart of the worthy and zealous minister by an expression of his sympathy in his labors, and by many inquiries in regard to the religious state of the region. It was not a very promising state, and the good man felt how much lighter his task would be, if he had the aid of such a man as Senator Dilworthy.

"I am glad to see, my dear sir," said the Senator, "that you give them the doctrines. It is owing to a neglect of the doctrines, that there is such a fearful falling away in the country. I wish that we might have you in Washington—as chaplain, now, in the senate."

The good man could not but be a little flattered, and if sometimes, thereafter, in his discouraging work, he allowed the thought that he might perhaps be called to Washington as chaplain of the Senate, to cheer him, who can wonder. The Senator's commendation at least did one service for him, it elevated him in the opinion of Hawkeye.

Laura was at church alone that day, and Mr. Brierly walked home with her. A part of their way lay with that of General Boswell and Senator Dilworthy, and introductions were made. Laura had her own reasons for wishing to know the Senator, and the Senator was not a man who could be called indifferent to charms such as hers. That meek young lady so commended herself to him in the short walk, that he announced his intentions of paying his respects to her the next day, an intention which Harry received glumly; and when the Senator was out of hearing he called him "an old fool."

"Fie," said Laura, "I do believe you are jealous, Harry. He is a very pleasant man. He said you were a young man of great promise."

The Senator did call next day, and the result of his visit was that he was confirmed in his impression that there was something about him very attractive to ladies. He saw Laura again and again during his stay, and felt more and more the subtle influence of her feminine beauty, which every man felt who came near her.

Harry was beside himself with rage while the Senator remained in town; he declared that women were always ready to drop any man for higher game; and he attributed his own ill-luck to the Senator's appearance. The fellow was in fact crazy about her beauty and ready to beat his brains out in chagrin. Perhaps Laura enjoyed his torment, but she soothed him with blandishments that increased his ardor, and she smiled to herself to think that he had, with all his protestations of love, never spoken of marriage. Probably the vivacious fellow never had thought of it. At any rate when he at length went away from Hawkeye he was no nearer it. But there was no telling to what desperate lengths his passion might not carry him.

Laura bade him good-bye with tender regret, which, however, did not disturb her peace or interfere with her plans. The visit of Senator Dilworthy had become of more importance to her, and it by and by bore the fruit she longed for, in an invitation to visit his family in the National Capital during the winter session of Congress.

CHAPTER XXI

Unusquisque sua noverit ire via.—
Propert. Eleg. 25.

O lift your natures up:
Embrace our aims: work out your freedom. Girls,
Knowledge is now no more a fountain sealed;
Drink deep until the habits of the slave,
The sins of emptiness, gossip and spite
And slander, die.

The Princess.

WHETHER MEDICINE IS A SCIENCE, or only an empirical method of getting a living out of the ignorance of the human race, Ruth found before her first term was over at the medical school that there were other things she needed to know quite as much as that which is taught in medical books, and that she could never satisfy her aspirations without more general culture.

"Does your doctor know any thing—I don't mean about medicine, but about things in general, is he a man of information and good sense?" once asked an old practitioner. "If he doesn't know any thing but medicine the chance is he doesn't know that."

The close application to her special study was beginning to tell upon Ruth's delicate health also, and the summer brought with it only weariness and indisposition for any mental effort.

In this condition of mind and body the quiet of her home and the unexciting companionship of those about her were more than ever tiresome.

She followed with more interest Philip's sparkling account of his life in the west, and longed for his experiences, and to know some of those people of a world so different from hers, who alternately amused and displeased him. He at least was learning the world, the good and the bad of it, as must happen to every one who accomplishes anything in it.

But what, Ruth wrote, could a woman do, tied up by custom, and cast into particular circumstances out of which it was almost impossible to extricate herself? Philip thought that he would go some day and extricate Ruth, but he did not write that, for he had the instinct to know that this was not the extrication she dreamed of, and that she must find out by her own experience what her heart really wanted.

Philip was not a philosopher, to be sure, but he had the old fashioned notion, that whatever a woman's theories of life might be, she would come round to matrimony, only give her time. He could indeed recall to mind one woman—and he never knew a nobler—whose whole soul was devoted and who believed that her life was consecrated to a certain benevolent project in single-ness of life, who yielded to the touch of matrimony, as an icicle yields to a sunbeam.

Neither at home nor elsewhere did Ruth utter any complaint, or admit any weariness or doubt of her ability to pursue the path she had marked out for herself. But her mother saw clearly enough her struggle with infirmity, and was not deceived by either her gaiety or by the cheerful composure which she carried into all the ordinary duties that fell to her. She saw plainly enough that Ruth needed an entire change of scene and of occupation, and perhaps she believed that such a change, with the knowledge of the world it would bring, would divert Ruth from a course for which she felt she was physically entirely unfitted.

It therefore suited the wishes of all concerned, when autumn came, that Ruth should go away to school. She selected a large New England Seminary, of which she had often heard Philip speak, which was attended by both sexes and offered almost collegiate advantages of education. Thither she went in September, and began for the second time in the year a life new to her.

The Seminary was the chief feature of Fallkill, a village of two to three thousand inhabitants. It was a prosperous school, with three hundred students, a large corps of teachers, men and women, and with a venerable rusty row of academic buildings on the shaded square of the town. The students lodged and boarded in private families in the place, and so it came about that while the school did a great deal to support the town, the town gave the students society and the sweet influences of home life. It is at least respectful to say that the influences of home life are sweet.

Ruth's home, by the intervention of Philip, was in a family—one of the rare exceptions in life or in fiction—that had never known better days. The Montagues, it is perhaps well to say, had intended to come over in the Mayflower, but were detained at Delft Haven by the illness of a child. They came over to Massachusetts Bay in another vessel, and thus escaped the onus of that brevet nobility under which the successors of the Mayflower Pilgrims have descended. Having no factitious weight of dignity to carry, the Montagues steadily improved their condition from the day they landed, and they were never more vigorous or prosperous than at the date of this narrative. With character compacted by the rigid Puritan discipline of more than two centuries, they had retained its strength and purity and thrown off its narrowness, and were now blossoming under the generous modern influences. Squire Oliver Montague, a lawyer who had retired from the practice of his profession except in rare cases, dwelt in a square old fashioned New England mansion a quarter of a mile away from the green. It was called a mansion because it stood alone with ample fields about it, and had an avenue of trees leading to it from the road, and on the west commanded a view of a pretty little lake with gentle slopes and nodding groves. But it was just a plain, roomy house, capable of extending to many guests an unpretending hospitality.

The family consisted of the Squire and his wife, a son and a daughter married and not at home, a son in college at Cambridge, another son at the Seminary, and a daughter Alice, who was a year or more older than Ruth. Having only riches enough to be able to gratify reasonable desires, and yet make their gratifications always a novelty and a pleasure, the family occupied that just mean in life, which is so rarely attained, and still more rarely enjoyed without discontent.

If Ruth did not find so much luxury in the house as in her own home, there were evidences of culture, of intellectual activity and of a zest in the affairs of all the world, which greatly impressed her. Every room had its book-cases or book-shelves, and was more or less a library; upon every table was liable to be a litter of new books, fresh periodicals and daily newspapers. There were plants in the sunny windows and some choice engravings on the walls, with bits of color in oil or water-colors; the piano was sure to be open and strewn with music; and there were photographs and little souvenirs here and there of foreign travel. An absence of any "what-nots" in the corners with rows of cheerful shells, and Hindoo gods, and Chinese idols, and nests of useless boxes of lacquered wood, might be taken as denoting a languidness in the family concerning foreign missions, but perhaps unjustly.

At any rate the life of the world flowed freely into this hospitable house, and there was always so much talk there of the news of the day, of the new books and of authors, of Boston radicalism and New York civilization, and the virtue of Congress, that small gossip stood a very poor chance.

All this was in many ways so new to Ruth that she seemed to have passed into another world, in which she experienced a freedom and a mental exhilaration unknown to her before. Under this influence she entered upon her studies with keen enjoyment, finding for a time all the relaxation she needed, in the charming social life at the Montague house.

It is strange, she wrote to Philip, in one of her occasional letters, that you never told me more about this delightful family, and scarcely mentioned Alice who is the life of it, *just the noblest* girl, unselfish, knows how to do so many things, with lots of talent, with a dry humor, and an odd way of looking at things, and yet quiet and even serious often—one of your "capable" New England girls. We shall be great friends. It had never occurred to Philip that there was any thing extraordinary about the family that needed mention. He knew dozens of girls like Alice, he thought to himself, but only one like Ruth.

Good friends the two girls were from the beginning. Ruth was a study to Alice, the product of a culture entirely foreign to her experience, so much a child in some things, so much a woman in others; and Ruth in turn, it must be confessed, probing Alice sometimes with her serious gray eyes, wondered what her object in life was, and whether she had any purpose beyond living as she now saw her. For she could scarcely conceive of a life that should not be devoted to the accomplishment of some definite work, and she had no doubt that in her own case everything else would yield to the professional career she had marked out.

"So you know Philip Sterling," said Ruth one day as the girls sat at their sewing. Ruth never embroidered, and never sewed when she could avoid it. Bless her.

"Oh yes we are old friends. Philip used to come to Fallkill often while he was in college. He was once rusticated here for a term."

"Rusticated?"

"Suspended for some College scrape. He was a great favorite here. Father and he were famous friends. Father said that Philip had no end of nonsense in him and was always blundering into something, but he was a royal good fellow and would come out all right."

"Did you think he was fickle?"

"Why, I never thought whether he was or not," replied Alice looking up. "I suppose he was always in love with some girl or another, as college boys are. He used to make me his confidant now and then, and be terribly in the dumps."

"Why did he come to you?" pursued Ruth; "you were younger than he."

"I'm sure I don't know. He was at our house a good deal. Once at a picnic by the lake, at the risk of his own life, he saved sister Millie from drowning, and we all liked to have him here. Perhaps he thought as he had saved one sister, the other ought to help him when he was in trouble. I don't know."

The fact was that Alice was a person who invited confidences, because she never betrayed them, and gave abundant sympathy in return. There are persons, whom we all know, to whom human confidences, troubles and heartaches flow as naturally as streams to a placid lake.

This is not a history of Fallkill, nor of the Montague family, worthy as both are of that honor, and this narrative cannot be diverted into long loitering with them. If the reader visits the village to-day, he will doubtless be pointed out the Montague dwelling, where Ruth lived, the cross-lots path she traversed to the Seminary, and the venerable chapel with its cracked bell.

In the little society of the place, the Quaker girl was a favorite, and no considerable social gathering or pleasure party was thought complete without her. There was something in this seemingly transparent and yet deep character, in her childlike gaiety and enjoyment of the society about her, and in her not seldom absorption in herself, that would have made her long remembered there if no events had subsequently occurred to recall her to mind.

To the surprise of Alice, Ruth took to the small gaieties of the village with a zest of enjoyment that seemed foreign to one who had devoted her life to a serious profession from the highest motives. Alice liked society well enough, she thought, but there was nothing exciting in that of Fallkill, nor anything novel in the attentions of the well-bred young gentlemen one met in it. It must have worn a different aspect to Ruth, for she entered into its pleasures at first with curiosity, and then with interest and finally with a kind of staid abandon that no one would have deemed possible for her. Parties, picnics, rowing-matches, moonlight strolls, nutting-expeditions in the October woods,—Alice declared that it was a whirl of dissipation. The fondness of Ruth, which was scarcely disguised, for the company of agreeable young fellows, who talked nothings, gave Alice opportunity for no end of banter.

"Do you look upon them as 'subjects,' dear?" she would ask.

And Ruth laughed her merriest laugh, and then looked sober again. Perhaps she was thinking, after all, whether she knew herself.

If you should rear a duck in the heart of the Sahara, no doubt it would swim if you brought it to the Nile.

Surely no one would have predicted when Ruth left Philadelphia that she would become absorbed to this extent, and so happy, in a life so unlike that she thought she desired. But no one can tell how a woman will act under any circumstances. The reason novelists nearly always fail in depicting women when they make them act, is that they let them do what they have observed some woman has done at sometime or another. And that is where they make a mistake; for a woman will never do again what has been done before. It is this uncertainty that causes women, considered as materials for fiction, to be so interesting to themselves and to others.

As the fall went on and the winter, Ruth did not distinguish herself greatly at the Fallkill Seminary as a student, a fact that apparently gave her no anxiety, and did not diminish her enjoyment of a new sort of power which had awakened within her.

CHAPTER XXII

Wohl giebt es im Leben kein süsseres Glück,
Als der Liebe Geständniss im Liebchen's Blick;
Wohl giebt es im Leben nicht höhere Lust,
Als Freuden der Liebe an liebender Brust.
Dem hat nie das Leben freundlich begegnet,
Den nicht die Weihe der Liebe gesegnet.
Doch der Liebe Glück, so himmlisch, so schön,
Kann nie ohne Glauben an Tugend bestehn.

Körner.

O ke aloha ka mea I oi aku ka maikai mamua o ka umeki poi a me ka ipukaia.

IN MID-WINTER, an event occurred of unusual interest to the inhabitants of the Montague house, and to the friends of the young ladies who sought their society.

This was the arrival at the Sassacus Hotel of two young gentlemen from the west.

It is the fashion in New England to give Indian names to the public houses, not that the late lamented savage knew how to keep a hotel, but that his warlike name may impress the traveler who humbly craves shelter there, and make him grateful to the noble and gentlemanly clerk if he is allowed to depart with his scalp safe.

The two young gentlemen were neither students for the Fallkill Seminary, nor lecturers on physiology, nor yet life assurance solicitors, three suppositions that almost exhausted the guessing power of the people at the hotel in respect to the names of "Philip Sterling and Henry Brierly, Missouri," on the register. They were handsome enough fellows, that was evident, browned by outdoor exposure, and with a free and lordly way about them that almost awed the hotel clerk himself. Indeed, he very soon set down Mr. Brierly as a gentleman of large fortune, with enormous interests on his shoulders. Harry had a way of casually mentioning western investments, through lines, the freighting business, and the route through the Indian territory to Lower California, which was calculated to give an importance to his lightest word.

"You've a pleasant town here, sir, and the most comfortable looking hotel I've seen out of New York," said Harry to the clerk; "we shall stay here a few days if you can give us a roomy suite of apartments."

Harry usually had the best of everything, wherever he went, as such fellows always do have in this accommodating world. Philip would have been quite content with less expensive quarters, but there was no resisting Harry's generosity in such matters.

Railroad surveying and real-estate operations were at a standstill during the winter in Missouri, and the young men had taken advantage of the lull to come east, Philip to see if there was any disposition in his friends, the railway contractors, to give him a share in the Salt Lick Union Pacific Extension, and Harry to open out to his uncle the prospects of the new city at Stone's Landing, and to procure congressional appropriations for the harbor and for making Goose Run navigable. Harry had with him a map of that noble stream and of the harbor, with a perfect net-work of railroads centering in it, pictures of wharves, crowded with steamboats, and of huge grain-elevators on the bank, all of which grew out of the combined imaginations of Col. Sellers and Mr. Brierly. The Colonel had entire confidence in Harry's influence with Wall street, and with congressmen, to bring about the consummation of their scheme, and he waited his return in the empty house at Hawkeye, feeding his pinched family upon the most gorgeous expectations with a reckless prodigality.

"Don't let 'em into the thing more than is necessary," says the Colonel to Harry: "give 'em a small interest; a lot apiece in the suburbs of the Landing ought to do a congressman, but I reckon you'll have to mortgage a part of the city itself to the brokers."

Harry did not find that eagerness to lend money on Stone's Landing in Wall street which Col. Sellers had expected, (it had seen too many such maps as he exhibited), although his uncle and some of the brokers looked with more favor on the appropriation for improving the navigation of Columbus River, and were not disinclined to form a company for that purpose. An appropriation was a tangible thing, if you could get hold of it, and it made little difference what it was appropriated for, so long as you got hold of it.

Pending these weighty negotiations, Philip has persuaded Harry to take a little run up to Fallkill, a not difficult task, for that young man would at any time have turned his back upon all the land in the west at sight of a new and pretty face, and he had, it must be confessed, a facility in love making which made it not at all an interference with the more serious business of life. He could not, to be sure, conceive how Philip could be interested in a young lady who was studying medicine, but he had no objection to going, for he did not doubt that there were other girls in Fallkill who were worth a week's attention.

The young men were received at the house of the Montagues with the hospitality which never failed there.

"We are glad to see you again," exclaimed the Squire heartily; "you are welcome Mr. Brierly, any friend of Phil's is welcome at our house."

"It's more like home to me, than any place except my own home," cried Philip, as he looked about the cheerful house and went through a general hand-shaking.

"It's a long time, though, since you have been here to say so," Alice said, with her father's frankness of manner; "and I suspect we owe the visit now to your sudden interest in the Fallkill Seminary."

Philip's color came, as it had an awkward way of doing in his tell-tale face, but before he could stammer a reply, Harry came in with,

"That accounts for Phil's wish to build a Seminary at Stone's Landing, our place in Missouri, when Col. Sellers insisted it should be a University. Phil appears to have a weakness for Seminaries."

"It would have been better for your friend Sellers," retorted Philip, "if he had had a weakness for district schools. Col. Sellers, Miss Alice, is a great friend of Harry's, who is always trying to build a house by beginning at the top."

"I suppose it's as easy to build a University on paper as a Seminary, and it looks better," was Harry's reflection; at which the Squire laughed, and said he quite agreed with him. The old gentleman understood Stone's Landing a good deal better than he would have done after an hour's talk with either of its expectant proprietors.

At this moment, and while Philip was trying to frame a question that he found it exceedingly difficult to put into words, the door opened quietly, and Ruth entered. Taking in the group with a quick glance, her eye lighted up, and with a merry smile she advanced and shook hands with Philip. She was so unconstrained and sincerely cordial, that it made that hero of the west feel somehow young, and very ill at ease.

For months and months he had thought of this meeting and pictured it to himself a hundred times, but he had never imagined it would be like this. He should meet Ruth unexpectedly, as she was walking alone from the school, perhaps, or entering the room where he was waiting for her, and she would cry "Oh! Phil," and then check herself, and perhaps blush, and Philip calm but eager and enthusiastic, would reassure her by his warm manner, and he would take her hand impressively, and she would look up timidly, and, after his long absence, perhaps he would be permitted to ———. Good heavens, how many times he had come to this point, and wondered if it could happen so. Well, well; he had never supposed that he should be the one embarrassed, and above all by a sincere and cordial welcome.

"We heard you were at the Sassacus House," were Ruth's first words; "and this I suppose is your friend?"

"I beg your pardon," Philip at length blundered out, "this is Mr. Brierly of whom I have written you."

And Ruth welcomed Harry with a friendliness that Philip thought was due to his friend, to be sure, but which seemed to him too level with her reception of himself, but which Harry received as his due from the other sex.

Questions were asked about the journey and about the West, and the conversation became a general one, until Philip at length found himself talking with the Squire in relation to land and railroads and things he couldn't keep his mind on; especially as he heard Ruth and Harry in an animated discourse, and caught the words "New York," and "opera," and "reception," and knew that Harry was giving his imagination full range in the world of fashion.

Harry knew all about the opera, green room and all (at least he said so) and knew a good many of the operas and could make very entertaining stories of their plots, telling how the soprano came in here, and the basso here, humming the beginning of their airs—tum-ti-tum-ti-ti—suggesting the profound dissatisfaction of the basso recitative—down-among-the-dead-men—and touching off the whole with an airy grace quite captivating; though he couldn't have sung a single air through to save himself, and he hadn't an ear to know whether it was sung correctly. All the same he doted on the opera, and kept a box there, into which he lounged occasionally to hear a favorite scene and meet his society friends. If Ruth was ever in the city he should be happy to place his box at the disposal of Ruth and her friends. Needless to say that she was delighted with the offer.

When she told Philip of it, that discreet young fellow only smiled, and said that he hoped she would be fortunate enough to be in New York some evening when Harry had not already given the use of his private box to some other friend.

The Squire pressed the visitors to let him send for their trunks and urged them to stay at his house, and Alice joined in the invitation, but Philip had reasons for declining. They staid to supper, however, and in the evening Philip had a long talk apart with Ruth, a delightful hour to him, in which she spoke freely of herself as of old, of her studies at Philadelphia and of her plans, and she entered into his adventures and prospects in the West with a genuine and almost sisterly interest; an interest, however, which did not exactly satisfy Philip—it was too general and not personal enough to suit him. And with all her freedom in speaking of her own hopes, Philip could not detect any reference to himself in them; whereas he never undertook anything that he did not think of Ruth in connection with it, he never made a plan that had not reference to her, and he never thought of anything as complete if she could not share it. Fortune, reputation—these had no value to him except in Ruth's eyes, and there were times when it seemed to him that if Ruth was not on this earth, he should plunge off into some remote wilderness and live in a purposeless seclusion.

"I hoped," said Philip, "to get a little start in connection with this new railroad, and make a little money, so that I could come east and engage in something more suited to my tastes. I shouldn't like to live in the West. Would you?"

"It never occurred to me whether I would or not," was the unembarrassed reply. "One of our graduates went to Chicago, and has a nice practice there. I don't know where I shall go. It would mortify mother dreadfully to have me driving about Philadelphia in a doctor's gig."

Philip laughed at the idea of it. "And does it seem as necessary to you to do it as it did before you came to Fallkill?"

It was a home question, and went deeper than Philip knew, for Ruth at once thought of practicing her profession among the young gentlemen and ladies of her acquaintance in the village; but she was reluctant to admit to herself that her notions of a career had undergone any change.

"Oh, I don't think I should come to Fallkill to practice, but I must do something when I am through school; and why not medicine?"

Philip would like to have explained why not, but the explanation would be of no use if it were not already obvious to Ruth.

Harry was equally in his element whether instructing Squire Montague about the investment of capital in Missouri, the improvement of Columbus River, the project he and some gentlemen in New York had for making a shorter Pacific connection with the Mississippi than the present one; or diverting Mrs. Montague with his experience in cooking in camp; or drawing for Miss Alice an amusing picture of the social contrasts of New England and the border where he had been.

Harry was a very entertaining fellow, having his imagination to help his memory, and telling his stories as if he believed them—as perhaps he did. Alice was greatly amused with Harry and listened so seriously to his romancing that he exceeded his usual limits. Chance allusions to his bachelor establishment in town and the place of his family on the Hudson, could not have been made by a millionaire more naturally.

"I should think," queried Alice, "you would rather stay in New York than to try the rough life at the West you have been speaking of."

"Oh, adventure," says Harry, "I get tired of New York. And

besides I got involved in some operations that I had to see through. Parties in New York only last week wanted me to go down into Arizona in a big diamond interest. I told them, no, no speculation for me. I've got my interests in Missouri; and I wouldn't leave Philip, as long as he stays there."

When the young gentlemen were on their way back to the hotel, Mr. Philip, who was not in very good humor, broke out,

"What the deuce, Harry, did you go on in that style to the Montagues for?"

"Go on?" cried Harry. "Why shouldn't I try to make a pleasant evening? And besides, ain't I going to do those things? What difference does it make about the mood and tense of a mere verb? Didn't uncle tell me only last Saturday, that I might as well go down to Arizona and hunt for diamonds? A fellow might as well make a good impression as a poor one."

"Nonsense. You'll get to believing your own romancing by and by."

"Well, you'll see. When Sellers and I get that appropriation, I'll show you an establishment in town and another on the Hudson and a box at the opera."

"Yes, it will be like Col. Sellers's plantation at Hawkeye. Did you ever see that?"

"Now, don't be cross, Phil. She's just superb, that little woman. You never told me."

"Who's just superb?" growled Philip, fancying this turn of the conversation less than the other.

"Well, Mrs. Montague, if you must know." And Harry stopped to light a cigar, and then puffed on in silence.

The little quarrel didn't last over night, for Harry never appeared to cherish any ill-will half a second, and Philip was too sensible to continue a row about nothing; and he had invited Harry to come with him.

The young gentlemen stayed in Fallkill a week, and were every day at the Montagues, and took part in the winter gaieties of the village. There were parties here and there to which the friends of Ruth and the Montagues were of course invited, and Harry in the generosity of his nature, gave in return a little supper at the hotel, very simple indeed, with dancing in the hall, and some refreshments passed round. And Philip found the whole thing in the bill when he came to pay it.

Before the week was over Philip thought he had a new light on the character of Ruth. Her absorption in the small gaieties of the society there surprised him. He had few opportunities for serious conversation with her. There was always some butterfly or another flitting about, and when Philip showed by his manner that he was not pleased, Ruth laughed merrily enough and rallied him on his soberness—she declared he was getting to be grim and unsocial. He talked indeed more with Alice than with Ruth, and scarcely concealed from her the trouble that was in his mind. It needed, in fact, no word from him, for she saw clearly enough what was going forward, and knew her sex well enough to know there was no remedy for it but time.

"Ruth is a dear girl, Philip, and has as much firmness of purpose as ever, but don't you see she has just discovered that she is fond of society? Don't you let her see you are selfish about it, is my advice."

The last evening they were to spend in Fallkill, they were at the Montagues, and Philip hoped that he would find Ruth in a different mood. But she was never more gay, and there was a spice of mischief in her eyes and in her laugh. "Confound it," said Philip to himself, "she's in a perfect twitter." He would have liked to quarrel with her, and fling himself out of the house in tragedy style, going perhaps so far as to blindly wander off miles into the country and bathe his throbbing brow in the chilling rain of the stars, as people do in novels; but he had no opportunity. For Ruth was as serenely unconscious of mischief as women can be at times, and fascinated him more than ever with her little demurenesses and half-confidences. She even said "Thee" to him once in reproach for a cutting speech he began. And this sweet little word made his heart beat like a trip-hammer, for never in all her life had she said "thee" to him before.

Was she fascinated with Harry's careless *bon homie* and gay assurance? Both chatted away in high spirits, and made the evening whirl along in the most mirthful manner. Ruth sang for Harry, and that young gentleman turned the leaves for her at the piano, and put in a bass note now and then where he thought it would tell.

Yes, it was a merry evening, and Philip was heartily glad when it was over, and the long leave-taking with the family was through with.

"Farewell Philip. Good-night Mr. Brierly," Ruth's clear voice sounded after them as they went down the walk.

And she spoke Harry's name last, thought Philip.

CHAPTER XXIII

"O see ye not yon narrow road
  So thick beset wi' thorns and briers?
That is the Path of Righteousness,
  Though after it but few inquires.

"And see ye not yon braid, braid road,
  That lies across the lily leven?
That is the Path of Wickedness,
  Though some call it the road to Heaven."
                        Thomas the Rhymer.

PHILIP AND HARRY reached New York in very different states of mind. Harry was buoyant. He found a letter from Col. Sellers urging him to go to Washington and confer with Senator Dilworthy. The petition was in his hands. It had been signed by everybody of any importance in Missouri, and would be presented immediately.

"I should go on myself," wrote the Colonel, "but I am engaged in the invention of a process for lighting such a city as St. Louis by means of water; just attach my machine to the water-pipes anywhere and the decomposition of the fluid begins, and you will have floods of light for the mere cost of the machine. I've nearly got the lighting part, but I want to attach to it a heating, cooking, washing and ironing apparatus. It's going to be the great thing, but we'd better keep this appropriation going while I am perfecting it."

Harry took letters to several congressmen from his uncle and from Mr. Duff Brown, each of whom had an extensive acquaintance in both houses where they were well known as men engaged in large private operations for the public good, and men, besides, who, in the slang of the day, understood the virtues of "addition, division and silence."

Senator Dilworthy introduced the petition into the Senate with the remark that he knew, personally, the signers of it, that they were men interested, it was true, in the improvement of the country, but he believed without any selfish motive, and that so far as he knew the signers were loyal. It pleased him to see upon the roll the names of many colored citizens, and it must rejoice every friend of humanity to know that this lately emancipated race were intelligently taking part in the development of the resources of their native land. He moved the reference of the petition to the proper committee.

Senator Dilworthy introduced his young friend to influential members, as a person who was very well informed about the Salt Lick Extension of the Pacific, and was one of the Engineers who had made a careful survey of Columbus River; and left him to exhibit his maps and plans and to show the connection between the public treasury, the city of Napoleon and legislation for the benefit of the whole country.

Harry was the guest of Senator Dilworthy. There was scarcely any good movement in which the Senator was not interested. His house was open to all the laborers in the field of total abstinence, and much of his time was taken up in attending the meetings of this cause. He had a Bible class in the Sunday school of the church which he attended, and he suggested to Harry that he might take a class during the time he remained in Washington; Mr. Washington Hawkins had a class. Harry asked the Senator if there was a class of young ladies for him to teach, and after that the Senator did not press the subject.

Philip, if the truth must be told, was not well satisfied with his western prospects, nor altogether with the people he had fallen in with. The railroad contractors held out large but rather indefinite promises. Opportunities for a fortune he did not doubt existed in Missouri, but for himself he saw no better means for livelihood than the mastery of the profession he had rather thoughtlessly entered upon. During the summer he had made considerable practical advance in the science of engineering; he had been diligent, and made himself to a certain extent necessary to the work he was engaged on. The contractors called him into their consultations frequently, as to the character of the country he had been over, and the cost of constructing the road, the nature of the work, etc.

Still Philip felt that if he was going to make either reputation or money as an engineer, he had a great deal of hard study before him, and it is to his credit that he did not shrink from it. While Harry was in Washington dancing attendance upon the national legislature and making the acquaintance of the vast lobby that encircled it, Philip devoted himself day and night, with an energy and a concentration he was capable of, to the learning and theory of his profession, and to the science of railroad-building. He wrote some papers at this time for the "Plow, the Loom and the Anvil,"[74] upon the strength of materials, and especially upon bridge-building, which attracted considerable attention, and were copied into the English "Practical Magazine."[75] They served at any rate to raise Philip in the opinion of his friends the contractors, for practical men have a certain superstitious estimation of ability with the pen, and though they may a little despise the talent, they are quite ready to make use of it.

Philip sent copies of his performances to Ruth's father and to other gentlemen whose good opinion he coveted, but he did not rest upon his laurels. Indeed, so diligently had he applied himself, that when it came time for him to return to the West, he felt himself, at least in theory, competent to take charge of a division in the field.

CHAPTER XXIV

Cante-teca. Iapi-Waxte otonwe kin he cajeyatapi nawahon; otonwe wijice hinca keyape se wacanmi.
Toketu-kaxta. Han, hecetu; takuwicawaye wijicapi ota hen tipi.

Mahp. Ekta Oicim. ya.

THE CAPITAL of the Great Republic was a new world to country-bred Washington Hawkins. St. Louis was a greater city, but its floating population did not hail from great distances, and so it had the general family aspect of the permanent population; but Washington gathered its people from the four winds of heaven, and so the manners, the faces and the fashions there, presented a variety that was infinite. Washington had never been in "society" in St. Louis, and he knew nothing of the ways of its wealthier citizens and had never inspected one of their dwellings. Consequently, everything in the nature of modern fashion and grandeur was a new and wonderful revelation to him.

Washington is an interesting city to any of us. It seems to become more and more interesting the oftener we visit it. Perhaps the reader has never been there? Very well. You arrive either at night, rather too late to do anything or see anything until morning, or you arrive so early in the morning that you consider it best to go to your hotel and sleep an hour or two while the sun bothers along over the Atlantic. You cannot well arrive at a pleasant intermediate hour, because the railway corporation that keeps the keys of the only door that leads into the town or out of it takes care of that. You arrive in tolerably good spirits, because it is only thirty-eight miles from Baltimore to the capital, and so you have only been insulted three times (provided you are not in a sleeping car—the average is higher, there): once when you renewed your ticket after stopping over in Baltimore, once when you were about to enter the "ladies' car" without knowing it *was* a lady's car, and once when you asked the conductor at what hour you would reach Washington.

You are assailed by a long rank of hackmen who shake their

whips in your face as you step out upon the sidewalk; you enter what they regard as a "carriage," in the capital, and you wonder why they do not take it out of service and put it in the museum: we have few enough antiquities, and it is little to our credit that we make scarcely any effort to preserve the few we have. You reach your hotel, presently—and here let us draw the curtain of charity—because of course you have gone to the wrong one. You being a stranger, how could you do otherwise? There are a hundred and eighteen bad hotels, and only one good one. The most renowned and popular hotel of them all is perhaps the worst one known to history.

It is winter, and night. When you arrived, it was snowing. When you reached the hotel, it was sleeting. When you went to bed, it was raining. During the night it froze hard, and the wind blew some chimneys down. When you got up in the morning, it was foggy. When you finished your breakfast at ten o'clock and went out, the sunshine was brilliant, the weather balmy and delicious, and the mud and slush deep and all-pervading. You will like the climate—when you get used to it.

You naturally wish to view the city; so you take an umbrella, an overcoat, and a fan, and go forth. The prominent features you soon locate and get familiar with; first you glimpse the ornamental upper works of a long, snowy palace projecting above a grove of trees, and a tall, graceful white dome with a statue on it surmounting the palace and pleasantly contrasting with the background of the blue sky. That building is the capitol; gossips will tell you that by the original estimates it was to cost $12,000,000 and that the government did come within $27,200,000 of building it for that sum.

You stand at the back of the capitol to treat yourself to a view, and it is a very noble one. You understand, the capitol stands upon the verge of a high piece of table land, a fine commanding position, and its front looks out over this noble situation for a city—but it don't see it, for the reason that when the capitol extension was decided upon, the property owners at once advanced their prices to such inhuman figures that the people went down and built the city in the muddy low marsh *behind* the temple of liberty; so now the lordly front of the building, with its imposing colonades, its projecting, graceful wings, its picturesque groups of statuary, and its long terraced ranges of steps, flowing down in white marble waves to the ground, merely looks out upon a sorrowful little desert of cheap boarding houses.

So you observe, that you take your view from the back of the capitol. And yet not from the airy outlooks of the dome, by the way, because to get there you must pass through the great rotunda: and to do that, you would have to see the marvelous Historical Paintings that hang there, and the bas-reliefs—and what have you done that you should suffer thus? And besides, you might have to pass through the old part of the building, and you could not help seeing Mr. Lincoln, as petrified by a young lady artist[76] for $10,000—and you might take his marble emancipation proclamation, which he holds out in his hand and contemplates, for a folded napkin; and you might conceive from his expression and his attitude, that he is finding fault with the washing. Which is not the case. Nobody knows what *is* the matter with him; but everybody feels for him. Well, you ought not to go into the dome any how, because it would be utterly impossible to go up there without seeing the frescoes in it—and why should you be interested in the delirium tremens of art?

The capitol is a very noble and a very beautiful building, both within and without, but you need not examine it now. Still, if you greatly prefer going into the dome, go. Now your general glance gives you picturesque stretches of gleaming water, on your left, with a sail here and there and a lunatic asylum on shore; over beyond the water, on a distant elevation, you see a squat yellow temple which your eye dwells upon lovingly through a blur of unmanly moisture, for it recalls your lost boyhood and the Parthenons done in molasses candy which made it blest and beautiful. Still in the distance, but on this side of the water and close to its edge, the Monument to the Father of his Country towers out of the mud—sacred soil is the customary term. It has the aspect of a factory chimney with the top broken off. The skeleton of a decaying scaffolding lingers about its summit, and tradition says that the spirit of Washington often comes down and sits on those rafters to enjoy this tribute of respect which the nation has reared as the symbol of its unappeasable gratitude. The Monument is to be finished, some day, and at that time our Washington will have risen still higher in the nation's veneration, and will be known as the Great-Great-Grandfather of his Country. The memorial Chimney stands in a quiet pastoral locality that is full of reposeful expression. With a glass you can see the cow-sheds about its base, and the contented sheep nibbling pebbles in the desert solitudes that surround it, and the tired pigs dozing in the holy calm of its protecting shadow.

Now you wrench your gaze loose and you look down in front of you and see the broad Pennsylvania Avenue stretching straight ahead for a mile or more till it brings up against the iron fence in front of a pillared granite pile, the Treasury building—an edifice that would command respect in any capital. The stores and hotels that wall in this broad avenue are mean, and cheap, and dingy, and are better left without comment. Beyond the Treasury is a fine large white barn, with wide unhandsome grounds about it. The President lives there. It is ugly enough outside, but that is nothing to what it is inside. Dreariness, flimsiness, bad taste reduced to mathematical completeness is what the inside offers to the eye, if it remains yet what it always has been.

The front and right hand views give you the city at large. It is a wide stretch of cheap little brick houses, with here and there a noble architectural pile lifting itself out of the midst—government buildings, these. If the thaw is still going on when you come down and go about town, you will wonder at the shortsightedness of the city fathers, when you come to inspect the streets, in that they do not dilute the mud a little more and use them for canals.

If you inquire around a little, you will find that there are more boarding houses to the square acre in Washington than there are in any other city in the land, perhaps. If you apply for a home in one of them, it will seem odd to you to have the landlady inspect you with a severe eye and then ask you if you are a member of Congress. Perhaps, just as a pleasantry, you will say yes. And then she will tell you that she is "full." Then you show her her advertisement in the morning paper, and there she stands, convicted and ashamed. She will try to blush, and it will be only polite in you to take the effort for the deed. She shows you her rooms,

now, and lets you take one—but she makes you pay in advance
for it. That is what you will get for pretending to be a member of
Congress. If you had been content to be merely a private citizen,
your trunk would have been sufficient security for your board.
If you are curious and inquire into this thing, the chances are that
your landlady will be ill-natured enough to say that the person
and property of a Congressman are exempt from arrest or detention, and that with the tears in her eyes she has seen several of the
people's representatives walk off to their several States and Territories carrying her unreceipted board bills in their pockets for
keepsakes. And before you have been in Washington many weeks
you will be mean enough to believe her, too.

Of course you contrive to see everything and find out everything. And one of the first and most startling things you find out
is, that every individual you encounter in the City of Washington
almost—and certainly every separate and distinct individual in
the public employment, from the highest bureau chief, clear
down to the maid who scrubs Department halls, the night watch-
men of the public buildings and the darkey boy who purifies the
Department spittoons—represents Political Influence. Unless
you can get the ear of a Senator, or a Congressman, or a Chief of
a Bureau or Department, and persuade him to use his "influence"
in your behalf, you cannot get an employment of the most trivial
nature in Washington. Mere merit, fitness and capability, are useless baggage to you without "influence." The population of
Washington consists pretty much entirely of government employés and the people who board them. There are thousands of
these employés, and they have gathered there from every corner
of the Union and got their berths through the intercession (command is nearer the word) of the Senators and Representatives of
their respective States. It would be an odd circumstance to see a
girl get employment at three or four dollars a week in one of the
great public cribs[77] without any political grandee to back her, but
merely because she was worthy, and competent, and a good citizen of a free country that "treats all persons alike." Washington
would be mildly thunderstruck at such a thing as that. If you are
a member of Congress, (no offence,) and one of your constituents
who doesn't know anything, and does not want to go into the

bother of learning something, and has no money, and no employment, and can't earn a living, comes besieging you for help, do
you say, "Come, my friend, if your services were valuable you
could get employment elsewhere—don't want you here?" Oh,
no. You take him to a Department and say, "Here, give this person something to pass away the time at—and a salary"—and the
thing is done. You throw him on his country. He is his country's
child, let his country support him. There is something good and
motherly about Washington, the grand old benevolent National
Asylum for the Helpless.

The wages received by this great hive of employés are placed at
the liberal figure meet and just for skilled and competent labor.
Such of them as are immediately employed about the two Houses
of Congress, are not only liberally paid also, but are remembered
in the customary Extra Compensation bill which slides neatly
through, annually, with the general grab that signalizes the last
night of a session, and thus twenty per cent. is added to their
wages, for—for fun, no doubt.

Washington Hawkins's new life was an unceasing delight to
him. Senator Dilworthy lived sumptuously, and Washington's
quarters were charming—gas; running water, hot and cold; bath-
room, coal fires, rich carpets, beautiful pictures on the walls;
books on religion, temperance, public charities and financial
schemes; trim colored servants, dainty food—everything a body
could wish for. And as for stationery, there was no end to it; the
government furnished it; postage stamps were not needed—the
Senator's frank could convey a horse through the mails, if necessary.

And then he saw such dazzling company. Renowned generals
and admirals who had seemed but colossal myths when he was in
the far west, went in and out before him or sat at the Senator's
table, solidified into palpable flesh and blood; famous statesmen
crossed his path daily; that once rare and awe-inspiring being, a
Congressman, was become a common spectacle—a spectacle so
common, indeed, that he could contemplate it without excitement, even without embarrassment; foreign ministers were visible
to the naked eye at happy intervals; he had looked upon the President himself, and lived. And more, this world of enchantment

teemed with speculation—the whole atmosphere was thick with it—and that indeed was Washington Hawkins's native air; none other refreshed his lungs so gratefully. He had found paradise at last.

The more he saw of his chief the Senator, the more he honored him, and the more conspicuously the moral grandeur of his character appeared to stand out. To possess the friendship and the kindly interest of such a man, Washington said in a letter to Louise, was a happy fortune for a young man whose career had been so impeded and so clouded as his.

The weeks drifted by; Harry Brierly flirted, danced, added luster to the brilliant Senatorial receptions, and diligently "buzzed" and "button-holed" Congressmen in the interest of the Columbus River scheme; meantime Senator Dilworthy labored hard in the same interest—and in others of equal national importance. Harry wrote frequently to Sellers, and always encouragingly; and from these letters it was easy to see that Harry was a pet with all Washington, and was likely to carry the thing through; that the assistance rendered him by "old Dilworthy" was pretty fair— pretty fair; "and every little helps, you know," said Harry.

Washington wrote Sellers officially, now and then. In one of his letters it appeared that whereas no member of the House committee favored the scheme at first, there was now needed but one more vote to compass a majority report. Closing sentence:

"Providence seems to further our efforts."
      (Signed,)   "ABNER DILWORTHY, U. S. S.,
          per WASHINGTON HAWKINS, P. S."[78]

At the end of a week, Washington was able to send the happy news,—officially, as usual,—that the needed vote had been added and the bill favorably reported from the Committee. Other letters recorded its perils in Committee of the whole, and by and by its victory, by just the skin of its teeth, on third reading and final passage. Then came letters telling of Mr. Dilworthy's struggles with a stubborn majority in his own Committee in the Senate; of how these gentlemen succumbed, one by one, till a majority was secured.

Then there was a hiatus. Washington watched every move on the board, and he was in a good position to do this, for he was clerk of this committee, and also one other. He received no salary as private secretary, but these two clerkships, procured by his benefactor, paid him an aggregate of twelve dollars a day, without counting the twenty per cent. extra compensation which would of course be voted to him on the last night of the session.

He saw the bill go into Committee of the whole and struggle for its life again, and finally worry through. In the fullness of time he noted its second reading, and by and by the day arrived when the grand ordeal came, and it was put upon its final passage. Washington listened with bated breath to the "Aye!" "No!" "No!" "Aye!" of the voters, for a few dread minutes, and then could bear the suspense no longer. He ran down from the gallery and hurried home to wait.

At the end of two or three hours the Senator arrived in the bosom of his family, and dinner was waiting. Washington sprang forward, with the eager question on his lips, and the Senator said:

"We may rejoice freely, now, my son—Providence has crowned our efforts with success."

CHAPTER XXV

𒀸 𒂊𒄩 𒄡 𒅖 𒅋 𒀝

WASHINGTON SENT grand good news to Col. Sellers that night. To Louise he wrote:

"It is beautiful to hear him talk when his heart is full of thankfulness for some manifestation of the Divine favor. You shall know him, some day my Louise, and knowing him you will honor him, as I do."

Harry wrote:

"I pulled it through, Colonel, but it was a tough job, there is no question about that. There was not a friend to the measure in the House committee when I began, and not a friend in the Senate committee except old Dil himself, but they were all fixed for a majority report when I hauled off my forces. Everybody here says you *can't* get a thing like this through Congress without buying committees for straight-out cash on delivery, but I think I've taught them a thing or two—if I could only make them believe it. When I tell the old residenters that this thing went through without buying a vote or making a promise, they say, 'That's rather too thin.' And when I say thin or not thin it's a fact, anyway, they say 'Come, now, but do you really believe that?' and when I say I don't believe anything about it, I *know* it, they smile and say, 'Well, you are pretty innocent, or pretty blind, one or the other—there's no getting around that.' Why they really do believe that votes *have* been bought—they do indeed. But let them keep on thinking so. I have found out that if a man knows how to talk to women, and has a little gift in the way of argument with men, he can afford to play for an appropriation against a money bag and give the money bag odds in the game. We've raked in $200,000 of Uncle Sam's money, say what they will—and there is more where this came from, when we want it, and I rather fancy I am the person that can go in and occupy it, too, if I do say it myself, that shouldn't, perhaps. I'll be with you within a week. Scare up all the men you can, and put them to work at once. When I get there I propose to make things hum."

The great news lifted Sellers into the clouds. He went to work on the instant. He flew hither and thither making contracts, engaging men, and steeping his soul in the ecstasies of business. He was the happiest man in Missouri. And Louise was the happiest woman; for presently came a letter from Washington which said:

"Rejoice with me for the long agony is over! We have waited patiently and faithfully, all these years, and now at last the reward is at hand. A man is to pay our family $40,000 for the Tennessee Land! It is but a little sum compared to what we could get by waiting, but I do so long to see the day when I can call you my own, that I have said to myself, better take this and enjoy life in a humble way than wear out our best days in this miserable separation. Besides, I can put this money into operations here that will increase it a hundred fold, yes, a thousand fold, in a few months. The air is full of such chances, and I know our family would consent in a moment that I should put in their shares with mine. Without a doubt we shall be worth half a million dollars in a year from this time—I put it at the very lowest figure, because it is always best to be on the safe side—half a million at the very lowest calculation, and then your father will give his consent and we can marry at last. Oh, that will be a glorious day. Tell our friends the good news—I want all to share it."

And she did tell her father and mother, but they said, let it be kept still for the present. The careful father also told her to write Washington and warn him not to speculate with the money, but to wait a little and advise with one or two wise old heads. She did this. And she managed to keep the good news to herself, though it would seem that the most careless observer might have seen by her springing step and her radiant countenance that some fine piece of good fortune had descended upon her.

Harry joined the Colonel at Stone's Landing, and that dead place sprang into sudden life. A swarm of men were hard at work, and the dull air was filled with the cheery music of labor. Harry had been constituted engineer-in-general, and he threw the full strength of his powers into his work. He moved among his hirelings like a king. Authority seemed to invest him with a new splendor. Col. Sellers, as general superintendent of a great public enterprise, was all that a mere human being could be—and more. These two grandees went at their imposing "improvement" with the air of men who had been charged with the work of altering the foundations of the globe.

They turned their first attention to straightening the river just above the Landing, where it made a deep bend, and where the maps and plans showed that the process of straightening would not only shorten distance but increase the "fall." They started a cut-off canal across the peninsula formed by the bend, and such another tearing up of the earth and slopping around in the mud as followed the order to the men, had never been seen in that region before. There was such a panic among the turtles that at the end of six hours there was not one to be found within three miles of Stone's Landing. They took the young and the aged, the decrepit and the sick upon their backs and left for tide-water in disorderly procession, the tadpoles following and the bull-frogs bringing up the rear.

Saturday night came, but the men were obliged to wait, because the appropriation had not come. Harry said he had written to hurry up the money and it would be along presently. So the work continued, on Monday. Stone's Landing was making quite a stir in the vicinity, by this time. Sellers threw a lot or two on the market, "as a feeler," and they sold well. He re-clothed his family, laid in a good stock of provisions, and still had money left. He started a bank account, in a small way—and mentioned the deposit casually to friends; and to strangers, too; to everybody, in fact; but not as a new thing—on the contrary, as a matter of life-long standing. He could not keep from buying trifles every day that were not wholly necessary, it was such a gaudy thing to get out his bank-book and draw a check, instead of using his old customary formula, "Charge it." Harry sold a lot or two, also—and had a dinner party or two at Hawkeye and a general good time with the money. Both men held on pretty strenuously for the coming big prices, however.

At the end of a month things were looking bad. Harry had besieged the New York headquarters of the Columbus River Slackwater Navigation Company with demands, then commands, and finally appeals, but to no purpose; the appropriation did not come; the letters were not even answered. The workmen were clamorous, now. The Colonel and Harry retired to consult.

"What's to be done?" said the Colonel.

"Hang'd if I know."

"Company say anything?"

"Not a word."

"You telegraphed yesterday?"

"Yes, and the day before, too."

"No answer?"

"No—confound them!"

Then there was a long pause. Finally both spoke at once:

"I've got it!"

"*I've* got it!"

"What's yours?" said Harry.

"Give the boys thirty-day orders on the Company for the back pay."

"That's it—that's my own idea to a dot. But then—but then———"

"Yes, I know," said the Colonel; "I know they can't wait for the orders to go to New York and be cashed, but what's the reason they can't get them discounted in Hawkeye?"

"Of course they can. That solves the difficulty. Everybody knows the appropriation's been made and the Company's perfectly good."

So the orders were given and the men appeased, though they grumbled a little at first. The orders went well enough for groceries and such things at a fair discount, and the work danced along gaily for a time. Two or three purchasers put up frame houses at the Landing and moved in, and of course a far-sighted but easy-going journeyman printer wandered along and started the "Napoleon Weekly Telegraph and Literary Repository"—a paper with a Latin motto from the Unabridged dictionary, and plenty of "fat" conversational tales and double-leaded poetry— all for two dollars a year, strictly in advance. Of course the merchants forwarded the orders at once to New York—and never heard of them again.

At the end of some weeks Harry's orders were a drug in the

market[79]—nobody would take them at any discount whatever. The second month closed with a riot.—Sellers was absent at the time, and Harry began an active absence himself with the mob at his heels. But being on horseback, he had the advantage. He did not tarry in Hawkeye, but went on, thus missing several appointments with creditors. He was far on his flight eastward, and well out of danger when the next morning dawned. He telegraphed the Colonel to go down and quiet the laborers—*he* was bound east for money—everything would be right in a week—tell the men so—tell them to rely on him and not be afraid.

Sellers found the mob quiet enough when he reached the Landing. They had gutted the Navigation office, then piled the beautiful engraved stock-books and things in the middle of the floor and enjoyed the bonfire while it lasted. They had a liking for the Colonel, but still they had some idea of hanging him, as a sort of make-shift that might answer, after a fashion, in place of more satisfactory game.

But they made the mistake of waiting to hear what he had to say first. Within fifteen minutes his tongue had done its work and they were all rich men.—He gave every one of them a lot in the suburbs of the city of Stone's Landing, within a mile and a half of the future post office and railway station, and they promised to resume work as soon as Harry got east and started the money along. Now things were blooming and pleasant again, but the men had no money, and nothing to live on. The Colonel divided with them the money he still had in bank—an act which had nothing surprising about it because he was generally ready to divide whatever he had with anybody that wanted it, and it was owing to this very trait that his family spent their days in poverty and at times were pinched with famine.

When the men's minds had cooled and Sellers was gone, they hated themselves for letting him beguile them with fine speeches, but it was too late, now—they agreed to hang him another time—such time as Providence should appoint.

CHAPTER XXVI

பணம் எமத்த அரிதாய் இருக்கிறது

Rumors of ruth's frivolity and worldliness at Fallkill traveled to Philadelphia in due time, and occasioned no little under-talk[80] among the Bolton relatives.

Hannah Shoecraft told another cousin that, for her part, she never believed that Ruth had so much more "mind" than other people; and Cousin Hulda added that she always thought Ruth was fond of admiration, and that was the reason she was unwilling to wear plain clothes and attend Meeting. The story that Ruth was "engaged" to a young gentleman of fortune in Fallkill came with the other news, and helped to give point to the little satirical remarks that went round about Ruth's desire to be a doctor!

Margaret Bolton was too wise to be either surprised or alarmed by these rumors. They might be true; she knew a woman's nature too well to think them improbable, but she also knew how steadfast Ruth was in her purposes, and that, as a brook breaks into ripples and eddies and dances and sports by the way, and yet keeps on to the sea, it was in Ruth's nature to give back cheerful answer to the solicitations of friendliness and pleasure, to appear idly delaying even, and sporting in the sunshine, while the current of her resolution flowed steadily on.

That Ruth had this delight in the mere surface play of life—that she could, for instance, be interested in that somewhat serious by-play called "flirtation," or take any delight in the exercise of those little arts of pleasing and winning which are none the less genuine and charming because they are not intellectual, Ruth, herself, had never suspected until she went to Fallkill. She had believed it her duty to subdue her gaiety of temperament, and let nothing divert her from what are called serious pursuits. In her limited experience she brought everything to the judgment of her own conscience, and settled the affairs of all the world in her own serene judgment hall. Perhaps her mother saw this, and saw also that there was nothing in the Friends' society to prevent her from growing more and more opinionated.

When Ruth returned to Philadelphia, it must be confessed—though it would not have been by her—that a medical career did seem a little less necessary for her than formerly; and coming back in a glow of triumph, as it were, and in the consciousness of the freedom and life in a lively society and in new and sympathetic friendship, she anticipated pleasure in an attempt to break up the stiffness and levelness of the society at home, and infusing into it something of the motion and sparkle which were so agreeable at Fallkill. She expected visits from her new friends, she would have company, the new books and the periodicals about which all the world was talking, and, in short, she would have life.

For a little while she lived in this atmosphere which she had brought with her. Her mother was delighted with this change in her, with the improvement in her health and the interest she exhibited in home affairs. Her father enjoyed the society of his favorite daughter as he did few things besides; he liked her mirthful and teasing ways, and not less a keen battle over something she had read. He had been a great reader all his life, and a remarkable memory had stored his mind with encyclopaedic information. It was one of Ruth's delights to cram herself with some out of the way subject and endeavor to catch her father; but she almost always failed. Mr. Bolton liked company, a house full of it, and the mirth of young people, and he would have willingly entered into any revolutionary plans Ruth might have suggested in relation to Friends' society.

But custom and the fixed order are stronger than the most enthusiastic and rebellious young lady, as Ruth very soon found. In spite of all her brave efforts, her frequent correspondence, and her determined animation, her books and her music, she found herself settling into the clutches of the old monotony, and as she realized the hopelessness of her endeavors, the medical scheme took new hold of her, and seemed to her the only method of escape.

"Mother, thee does not know how different it is in Fallkill, how much more interesting the people are one meets, how much more life there is."

"But thee will find the world, child, pretty much all the same, when thee knows it better. I thought once as thee does now, and had as little thought of being a Friend as thee has. Perhaps when thee has seen more, thee will better appreciate a quiet life."

"Thee married young. I shall not marry young, and perhaps not at all," said Ruth, with a look of vast experience.

"Perhaps thee doesn't know thee own mind; I have known persons of thy age who did not. Did thee see anybody whom thee would like to live with always in Fallkill?"

"Not always," replied Ruth with a little laugh. "Mother, I think I wouldn't say 'always' to any one until I have a profession and am as independent as he is. Then my love would be a free act, and not in any way a necessity."

Margaret Bolton smiled at this new-fangled philosophy. "Thee will find that love, Ruth, is a thing thee won't reason about, when it comes, nor make any bargains about. Thee wrote that Philip Sterling was at Fallkill."

"Yes, and Henry Brierly, a friend of his; a very amusing young fellow and not so serious-minded as Philip, but a bit of a fop maybe."

"And thee preferred the fop to the serious-minded?"

"I didn't prefer anybody, but Henry Brierly was good company, which Philip wasn't always."

"Did thee know thee father had been in correspondence with Philip?"

Ruth looked up surprised and with a plain question in her eyes.

"Oh, it's not about thee."

"What then?" and if there was any shade of disappointment in her tone, probably Ruth herself did not know it.

"It's about some land up in the country. That man Bigler has got father into another speculation."

"That odious man! Why will father have anything to do with him? Is it that railroad?"

"Yes. Father advanced money and took land as security, and whatever has gone with the money and the bonds, he has on his hands a large tract of wild land."

"And what has Philip to do with that?"

"It has good timber, if it could ever be got out, and father says that there must be coal in it; it's in a coal region. He wants Philip to survey it, and examine it for indications of coal."

"It's another of father's fortunes, I suppose," said Ruth. "He has put away so many fortunes for us that I'm afraid we never shall find them."

Ruth was interested in it nevertheless, and perhaps mainly because Philip was to be connected with the enterprise. Mr. Bigler came to dinner with her father next day, and talked a great deal about Mr. Bolton's magnificent tract of land, extolled the sagacity that led him to secure such a property, and led the talk along to another railroad which would open a northern communication to this very land.

"Pennybacker says it's full of coal, he's no doubt of it, and a railroad to strike the Erie would make it a fortune."

"Suppose you take the land and work the thing up, Mr. Bigler; you may have the tract for three dollars an acre."

"You'd throw it away, then," replied Mr. Bigler, "and I'm not the man to take advantage of a friend. But if you'll put a mortgage on it for the northern road, I wouldn't mind taking an interest, if Pennybacker is willing; but Pennybacker, you know, don't go much on land, he sticks to the legislature." And Mr. Bigler laughed.

When Mr. Bigler had gone, Ruth asked her father about Philip's connection with the land scheme.

"There's nothing definite," said Mr. Bolton. "Philip is showing aptitude for his profession. I hear the best reports of him in New York, though those sharpers don't intend to do anything but use him. I've written and offered him employment in surveying and examining the land. We want to know what it is. And if there is anything in it that his enterprise can dig out, he shall have an interest. I should be glad to give the young fellow a lift."

All his life Eli Bolton had been giving young fellows a lift, and shouldering the losses when things turned out unfortunately. His ledger, take it altogether, would not show a balance on the right side; but perhaps the losses on his books will turn out to be credits in a world where accounts are kept on a different basis. The left hand of the ledger will appear the right, looked at from the other side.

Philip wrote to Ruth rather a comical account of the bursting up of the city of Napoleon and the navigation improvement scheme, of Harry's flight and the Colonel's discomfiture. Harry left in such a hurry that he hadn't even time to bid Miss Laura Hawkins good-bye, but he had no doubt that Harry would console himself with the next pretty face he saw—a remark which was thrown in for Ruth's benefit. Col. Sellers had in all probability, by this time, some other equally brilliant speculation in his brain.

As to the railroad, Philip had made up his mind that it was merely kept on foot for speculative purposes in Wall street, and he was about to quit it. Would Ruth be glad to hear, he wondered, that he was coming East? For he was coming, in spite of a letter from Harry in New York, advising him to hold on until he had made some arrangements in regard to contracts, he to be a little careful about Sellers, who was somewhat visionary, Harry said.

The summer went on without much excitement for Ruth. She kept up a correspondence with Alice, who promised a visit in the fall, she read, she earnestly tried to interest herself in home affairs and such people as came to the house; but she found herself falling more and more into reveries, and growing weary of things as they were. She felt that everybody might become in time like two relatives from a Shaker establishment in Ohio, who visited the Boltons about this time, a father and son, clad exactly alike, and alike in manners. The son, however, who was not of age, was more unworldly and sanctimonious than his father; he always addressed his parent as "Brother Plum," and bore himself altogether in such a superior manner that Ruth longed to put bent pins in his chair. Both father and son wore the long, single-breasted collar-less coats of their society; without buttons, before or behind, but with a row of hooks and eyes on either side in front. It was Ruth's suggestion that the coats would be improved by a single hook and eye sewed on in the small of the back where the buttons usually are.

Amusing as this Shaker caricature of the Friends was, it oppressed Ruth beyond measure, and increased her feeling of being stifled.

It was a most unreasonable feeling. No home could be pleasanter than Ruth's. The house, a little out of the city, was one of those elegant country residences, which so much charm visitors to the suburbs of Philadelphia. A modern dwelling and luxurious in everything that wealth could suggest for comfort, it stood in the midst of exquisitely kept lawns, with groups of trees, parterres of flowers massed in colors, with greenhouse, grapery and garden; and on one side, the garden sloped away in undulations to a shallow brook that ran over a pebbly bottom and sang under forest trees. The country about was the perfection of cultivated landscape, dotted with cottages, and stately mansions of Revolutionary date, and sweet as an English country-side, whether seen in the soft bloom of May or in the mellow ripeness of late October.

It needed only the peace of the mind within, to make it a paradise. One riding by on the Old Germantown road, and seeing a young girl swinging in the hammock on the piazza and intent upon some volume of old poetry or the latest novel, would no doubt have envied a life so idyllic. He could not have imagined that the young girl was reading a volume of reports of clinics and longing to be elsewhere.

Ruth could not have been more discontented if all the wealth about her had been as unsubstantial as a dream. Perhaps she so thought it.

"I feel," she once said to her father, "as if I were living in a house of cards."

"And thee would like to turn it into a hospital?"

"No. But tell me father," continued Ruth, not to be put off, "is thee still going on with that Bigler and those other men who come here and entice thee?"

Mr. Bolton smiled, as men do when they talk with women about "business." "Such men have their uses, Ruth. They keep the world active, and I owe a great many of my best operations to such men. Who knows, Ruth, but this new land purchase, which I confess I yielded a little too much to Bigler in, may not turn out a fortune for thee and the rest of the children?"

"Ah, father, thee sees every thing in a rose-colored light. I do believe thee wouldn't have so readily allowed me to begin the study of medicine, if it hadn't had the novelty of an experiment to thee."

"And is thee satisfied with it?"

"If thee means, if I have had enough of it, no. I just begin to see what I can do in it, and what a noble profession it is for a woman.

Would thee have me sit here like a bird on a bough and wait for somebody to come and put me in a cage?"

Mr. Bolton was not sorry to divert the talk from his own affairs, and he did not think it worthwhile to tell his family of a performance that very day which was entirely characteristic of him.

Ruth might well say that she felt as if she were living in a house of cards, although the Bolton household had no idea of the number of perils that hovered over them, any more than thousands of families in America have of the business risks and contingences upon which their prosperity and luxury hang.

A sudden call upon Mr. Bolton for a large sum of money, which must be forthcoming at once, had found him in the midst of a dozen ventures, from no one of which a dollar could be realized. It was in vain that he applied to his business acquaintances and friends; it was a period of sudden panic and no money. "A hundred thousand! Mr. Bolton," said Plumly. "Good God, if you should ask me for ten, I shouldn't know where to get it."

And yet that day Mr. Small (Pennybacker, Bigler and Small) came to Mr. Bolton with a piteous story of ruin in a coal operation, if he could not raise ten thousand dollars. Only ten, and he was sure of a fortune. Without it he was a beggar. Mr. Bolton had already Small's notes for a large amount in his safe, labeled "doubtful"; he had helped him again and again, and always with the same result. But Mr. Small spoke with a faltering voice of his family, his daughter in school, his wife ignorant of his calamity, and drew such a picture of their agony, that Mr. Bolton put by his own more pressing necessity, and devoted the day to scraping together, here and there, ten thousand dollars for this brazen beggar, who had never kept a promise to him nor paid a debt.

Beautiful credit! The foundation of modern society. Who shall say that this is not the golden age of mutual trust, of unlimited reliance upon human promises? That is a peculiar condition of society which enables a whole nation to instantly recognize point and meaning in the familiar newspaper anecdote, which puts into the mouth of a distinguished speculator in lands and mines this remark:—"I wasn't worth a cent two years ago, and now I owe two millions of dollars."

CHAPTER XXVII

ὡς Θἴν τὰ πραχθέντ᾽ ἔβλεπεν, τνφλὸς γεγώς,
οὐ μὴν ὑπέπτηξ᾽ οὐδέν, ἀλλ᾽ ευκαρδίως
βᾶτον τιν᾽ ἄλλην ἤλατ᾽ εἰς ἀκανθίνην,
κάκ᾽ τονδ᾽ ἐγένετ᾽ ἐξαῦθις ἐκ τνφλοῦ βλέπων.

IT WAS A HARD BLOW to poor Sellers to see the work on his darling enterprise stop, and the noise and bustle and confusion that had been such refreshment to his soul, sicken and die out. It was hard to come down to humdrum ordinary life again after being a General Superintendent and the most conspicuous man in the community. It was sad to see his name disappear from the newspapers; sadder still to see it resurrected at intervals, shorn of its aforetime gaudy gear of compliments and clothed on with rhetorical tar and feathers.

But his friends suffered more on his account than he did. He was a cork that could not be kept under the water many moments at a time.

He had to bolster up his wife's spirits every now and then. On one of these occasions he said:

"It's all right, my dear, all right; it will all come right in a little while. There's $200,000 coming, and that will set things booming again. Harry seems to be having some difficulty, but that's to be expected—you can't move these big operations to the tune of Fisher's Hornpipe,[81] you know. But Harry will get it started along presently, and then you'll see! I expect the news every day now."

"But Beriah, you've *been* expecting it every day, all along, haven't you?"

"Well, yes; yes—I don't know but I have. But anyway, the longer it's delayed, the nearer it grows to the time when it will start—same as every day you live brings you nearer to—nearer—"

"The grave?"

"Well, no—not that exactly; but you can't understand these things, Polly dear—women haven't much head for business, you know. You make yourself perfectly comfortable, old lady, and you'll see how we'll trot this right along. Why bless you, *let* the appropriation lag, if it wants to—that's no great matter—there's a bigger thing than that."

"Bigger than $200,000, Beriah?"

"Bigger, child?—why, what's $200,000? Pocket money! Mere pocket money! Look at the railroad! Did you forget the railroad? It ain't many months till spring; it will be coming right along, and the railroad swimming right along behind it. Where'll it be by the middle of summer? Just stop and fancy a moment—just think a little—don't anything suggest itself? Bless your heart, you dear women live right in the present all the time—but a man, why a man lives————"

"In the future, Beriah? But don't we live in the future most too much, Beriah? We do somehow seem to manage to live on next year's crop of corn and potatoes as a general thing while this year is still dragging along, but sometimes it's not a robust diet,— Beriah. But don't look that way, dear—don't mind what I say. I don't mean to fret, I don't mean to worry; and I *don't*, once a month, *do* I, dear? But when I get a little low and feel bad, I get a bit troubled and worrisome, but it don't mean anything in the world. It passes right away. I know you're doing all you can, and I don't want to seem repining and ungrateful—for I'm *not*, Beriah—you know I'm not, don't you?"

"Lord bless you, child, I know you are the very best little woman that ever lived—that ever lived on the whole face of the Earth! And I know that I would be a dog not to work for you and think for you and scheme for you with all my might. And I'll bring things all right yet, honey—cheer up and don't you fear. The railroad————"

"Oh, I *had* forgotten the railroad, dear, but when a body gets blue, a body forgets everything. Yes, the railroad—tell me about the railroad."

"Aha, my girl, don't you see? Things ain't so dark, are they? Now *I* didn't forget the railroad. Now just think for a moment—

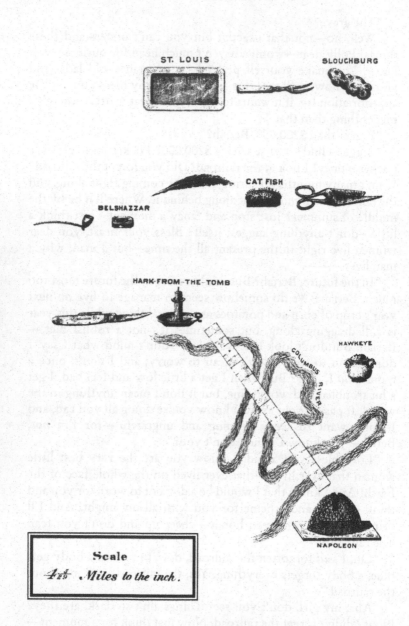

ST. LOUIS

SLOUCHBURG

CAT FISH

BELSHAZZAR

HARK-FROM-THE-TOMB

HAWKEYE

COLUMBUS RIVER

NAPOLEON

Scale
4½ Miles to the inch.

DOODLEVILLE

BRIMSTONE

BABYLON

BLOODY RUN

HAIL COLUMBIA

CORRUPTIONVILLE.

HALLELUJAH

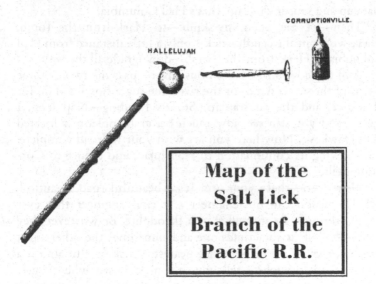

**Map of the
Salt Lick
Branch of the
Pacific R.R.**

just figure up a little on the future dead moral certainties. For instance, call this waiter St. Louis.

"And we'll lay this fork (representing the railroad) from St. Louis to this potato, which is Slouchburg:

"Then with this carving knife we'll continue the railroad from Slouchburg to Doodleville, shown by the black pepper:

"Then we run along the—yes—the comb—to the tumbler—that's Brimstone:

"Thence by the pipe to Belshazzar, which is the salt-cellar:

"Thence to, to—that quill—Catfish—hand me the pin-cushion, Marie Antoinette:

"Thence right along these shears to this horse, Babylon:

"Then by the spoon to Bloody Run—thank you, the ink:

"Thence to Hail Columbia—snuffers, Polly, please—move that cup and saucer close up, that's Hail Columbia:

"Then—let me open my knife—to Hark-from-the-Tomb, where we'll put the candle-stick—only a little distance from Hail Columbia to Hark-from-the-Tomb—downgrade all the way.

"And there we strike Columbus River—pass me two or three skeins of thread to stand for the river; the sugar bowl will do for Hawkeye, and the rat trap for Stone's Landing—Napoleon, I mean—and you can see how much better Napoleon is located than Hawkeye. Now here you are with your railroad complete, and showing its continuation to Hallelujah, and thence to Corruptionville.

"Now then—there your are! It's a beautiful road, beautiful. Jeff Thompson can out-engineer any civil engineer that ever sighted through an aneroid,[82] or a theodolite, or whatever they call it—*he* calls it sometimes one and sometimes the other—just whichever levels off his sentence neatest, I reckon. But ain't it a ripping road, though? I tell you, it'll make a stir when it gets along. Just see what a country it goes through. There's your onions at Slouchburg—noblest onion country that graces God's footstool; and there's your turnip country all around Doodleville—bless my life, what fortunes are going to be made there when they get that contrivance perfected for extracting olive oil out of turnips—if there's any in them; and I reckon there is, because Congress has made an appropriation of money to test the thing, and they wouldn't have done that just on conjecture, of course. And now we come to the Brimstone region—cattle raised there till you can't rest—and corn, and all that sort of thing. Then you've got a little stretch along through Belshazzar that don't produce anything now—at least nothing but rocks—but irrigation will fetch it. Then from Catfish to Babylon it's a little swampy, but there's dead loads of peat down under there somewhere. Next is the Bloody Run and Hail Columbia country—tobacco enough can be raised there to support two such railroads. Next is the sassparilla region. I reckon there's enough of that truck along in there on the line of the pocket-knife, from Hail Columbia to Hark-from-the-Tomb to fat up all the consumptives in all the hospitals from Halifax to the Holy Land. It just grows like weeds! I've got a little belt of sassparilla land in there just tucked away unobtrusively waiting for my little Universal Expectorant[83] to get into shape in my head. And I'll fix that, you know. One of these days I'll have all the nations of the earth expecto—"

"But Beriah, dear—"

"Don't interrupt me, Polly—I don't want you to lose the run of the map—well, *take* your toy-horse, James Fitz-James, if you must have it—and run along with you. Here, now—the soap will do for Babylon. Let me see—where was I? Oh yes—now we run down to Stone's Lan—Napoleon—now we run down to Napoleon. Beautiful road. Look at that, now. Perfectly straight line—straight as the way to the grave. And see where it leaves Hawkeye—clear out in the cold, my dear, clear out in the cold. That town's as bound to die as—well if I owned it I'd get its obituary ready, now, and notify the mourners. Polly, mark my words—in three years from this, Hawkeye'll be a howling wilderness. You'll see. And just look at the river—noblest stream that meanders over the thirsty earth!—calmest, gentlest artery that refreshes her weary bosom! Railroad goes all over it and all through it—wades right along on stilts. Seventeen bridges in three miles and a half—forty-nine bridges from Hark-from-the-Tomb to Stone's Landing altogether—forty-nine bridges, and culvers enough to culvert creation itself! Hadn't skeins of thread enough to represent them all—but you get an idea—perfect trestle-work of bridges for seventy-two miles. Jeff Thompson and I fixed all that, you know; he's to get the contracts and I'm to put them through on the divide. Just oceans of money in those bridges. It's the only part of the railroad I'm interested in,—down along the line—and it's all I want, too. It's enough, I should judge. Now here we are at Napoleon. Good enough country—plenty good enough—all it wants is population. That's all right—that will come. And it's no bad country *now* for calmness and solitude, I can tell you—though there's no money in that, of course. No money, but a man wants rest, a man wants peace—a man don't want to rip and tear around *all* the time. And here we go, now, just as straight as a string for Hallelujah—it's a beautiful angle—handsome upgrade all the way—and then away you go to Corruptionville, the gaudiest country for early carrots and cauliflowers that ever—good missionary field, too. There ain't such another missionary field outside the jungles of Central Africa. And patriotic?—why they named it after Congress itself. Oh, I warn you, my dear, there's a good time coming, and it'll be right along before you know what you're about, too. That railroad's fetching it. You see what it is as far as I've got, and if I had enough bottles and soap and boot-jacks and such things to carry it along to where it joins onto the Union Pacific, fourteen hundred miles from here, I should exhibit to you in that little internal improvement a spectacle of inconceivable sublimity. So, don't you see? We've got the railroad to fall back on; and in the meantime, what are we worrying about that $200,000 appropriation for? That's all right. I'd be willing to bet anything that the very next letter that comes from Harry will—"

The eldest boy entered just in the nick of time and brought a letter, warm from the post-office.

"Things *do* look bright, after all, Beriah. I'm sorry I was blue, but it did seem as if everything had been going against us for whole ages. Open the letter—open it quick, and let's know all about it before we stir out of our places. I am all in a fidget to know what it says."

The letter was opened, without any unnecessary delay.

CHAPTER XXVIII

Hvo der vil kjöbe Pölse af Hunden maa give ham Flesk igjen.

—Mit seinem eignen Verstande wurde Thrasyllus schwerlich durchge-
kommen seyn. Aber in solchen Fällen finden seinesgleichen für ihr Geld
immer einen Spitzbuben, der ihnen seinen Kopf leiht; und dann ist es so
viel als ob sie selbst einen hätten.

Wieland. Die Abderitten.

WHATEVER MAY HAVE BEEN the language of Harry's letter to the
Colonel, the information it conveyed was condensed or ex-
panded, one or the other, from the following episode of his visit
to New York:

He called, with official importance in his mien, at No.——,
Wall street, where a great gilt sign betokened the presence of the
headquarters of the "Columbus River Slack-Water Navigation
Company." He entered and gave a dressy porter his card, and was
requested to wait a moment in a sort of ante-room. The porter returned in a minute, and asked whom he would like to see?

"The president of the company, of course."

"He is busy with some gentlemen, sir; says he will be done
with them directly."

That a copper-plate card with "Engineer-in-Chief" on it
should be received with such tranquility as this, annoyed Mr.
Brierly not a little. But he had to submit. Indeed his annoyance
had time to augment a good deal; for he was allowed to cool his
heels a full half hour in the ante-room before those gentlemen
emerged and he was ushered into the presence. He found a stately
dignitary occupying a very official chair behind a long green
morocco-covered table, in a room sumptuously carpeted and furnished, and well garnished with pictures.

"Good morning, sir; take a seat—take a seat."

"Thank you sir," said Harry, throwing as much chill into his
manner as his ruffled dignity prompted.

"We perceive by your reports and the reports of the Chief

Superintendent, that you have been making gratifying progress with the work.—We are all very much pleased."

"Indeed? We did not discover it from your letters—which we have not received; nor by the treatment our drafts have met with—which were not honored; nor by the reception of any part of the appropriation, no part of it having come to hand."

"Why, my dear Mr. Brierly, there must be some mistake. I am sure we wrote you and also Mr. Sellers, recently—when my clerk comes he will show copies—letters informing you of the ten per cent. assessment."

"Oh, certainly, we got *those* letters. But what we wanted was money to carry on the work—money to pay the men."

"Certainly, certainly—true enough—but we credited you both for a large part of your assessments—I am sure that was in our letters."

"Of course that was in—I remember that."

"Ah, very well then. Now we begin to understand each other."

"Well, I don't see that we do. There's two months' wages due the men, and——"

"How? Haven't you paid the men?"

"Paid them! How are we going to pay them when you don't honor our drafts?"

"Why, my *dear* sir, I cannot see how you can find any fault with us. I am sure we have acted in a perfectly straight forward business way. Now let us look at the thing a moment. You subscribed for 100 shares of the capital stock, at $1,000 a share, I believe?"

"Yes, sir, I did."

"And Mr. Sellers took a like amount?"

"Yes, sir."

"Very well. No concern can get along without money. We levied a ten per cent. assessment. It was the original understanding that you and Mr. Sellers were to have the positions you now hold, with salaries of $600 a month each, while in active service. You were duly elected to these places, and you accepted them. Am I right?"

"Certainly."

"Very well. You were given your instructions and put to work.

By your reports it appears that you have expended the sum of $9,640 upon the said work. Two months salary to you two offi-cers amounts altogether to $2,400—about one-eighth of your ten per cent. assessment, you see; which leaves you in debt to the company for the other seven-eighths of the assessment—viz., something over $8,000 apiece. Now instead of requiring you to forward this aggregate of $16,000 or $17,000 to New York, the company voted unanimously to let you pay it over to the con-tractors, laborers from time to time, and give you credit on the books for it. And they did it without a murmur, too, for they were pleased with the progress you had made, and were glad to pay you that little compliment—and a very neat one it was, too, I am sure. The work you did fell short of $10,000, a trifle. Let me see—$9,640 from $20,000—salary $2,400 added—ah yes, the bal-ance due the company from yourself and Mr. Sellers is $7,960, which I will take the responsibility of allowing to stand for the present, unless you prefer to draw a check now, and thus————"

"Confound it, do you mean to say that instead of the company owing us $2,400, we owe the company $7,960?"

"Well, yes."

"And that we owe the men and the contractors nearly ten thousand dollars besides?"

"Owe them! Oh bless my soul, you can't mean that you have not paid these people?"

"But I *do* mean it!"

The president rose and walked the floor like a man in bodily pain. His brows contracted, he put his hand up and clasped his forehead, and kept saying, "Oh, it is too bad, too bad, too bad! Oh, it is bound to be found out—nothing can prevent it—nothing!"

Then he threw himself into his chair and said:

"My dear Mr. Brierson, this is dreadful—perfectly dreadful. It will be found out. It is bound to tarnish the good name of the company; our credit will be seriously, most seriously impaired. How could you be so thoughtless—the men ought to have been paid though it beggared us all!"

"They ought, ought they? Then why the devil—my name is not Bryerson, by the way—why the mischief didn't the compa—

why what in the nation ever became of the appropriation? Where *is* that appropriation?—if a stockholder may make so bold as to ask."

"The appropriation?—that paltry $200,000, do you mean?"

"Of course—but I didn't know that $200,000 was so very paltry. Though I grant, of course, that it is not a large sum, strictly speaking. But where is it?"

"My dear sir, you surprise me. You surely cannot have had a large acquaintance with this sort of thing. Otherwise you would not have expected much of a result from a mere *initial* appropriation like that. It was never intended for anything but a mere nest egg for the future and *real* appropriations to cluster around."

"Indeed? Well, was it a myth, or was it a reality? Whatever become of it?"

"Why the matter is simple enough. A Congressional appropriation costs money. Just reflect, for instance. A majority of the House Committee, say $10,000 apiece—$40,000; a majority of the Senate Committee, the same each—say $40,000; a little extra to one or two chairmen of one or two such committees, say $10,000 each—$20,000; and there's $100,000 of the money gone, to begin with. Then, seven male lobbyists, at $3,000 each—$21,000; one female lobbyist, $10,000; a high moral Congressman or Senator here and there—the high moral ones cost more, because they give tone to a measure—say ten of these at $3,000 each, is $30,000; then a lot of small-fry country members who won't vote for anything whatever without pay—say twenty at $500 apiece, is $10,000; a lot of dinners to members—say $10,000 altogether; lot of jimcracks for Congressmen's wives and children—those go a long way—you can't spend too much money in that line—well, those things cost in a lump, say $10,000—along there somewhere;—and then comes your printed documents—your maps, your tinted engravings, your pamphlets, your illuminated show cards, your advertisements in a hundred and fifty papers at ever so much a line—because you've *got* to keep the papers all right or you are gone up, you know. Oh, my dear sir, printing bills are destruction itself. Ours, so far amount to—let me see—10; 52; 22; 13;—and then there's 11; 14; 33—well, never mind the details, the total in clean numbers foots up $118,254.42 thus far!"

"What!"

"Oh, yes indeed. Printing's no bagatelle, I can tell you. And then there's your contributions, as a company, to Chicago fires and Boston fires, and orphan asylums and all that sort of thing—head the list, you see, with the company's full name and a thousand dollars set opposite—great card, sir—one of the finest advertisements in the world—the preachers mention it in the pulpit when it's a religious charity—one of the happiest advertisements in the world is your benevolent donation. Ours have amounted to sixteen thousand dollars and some cents up to this time."

"Good heavens!"

"Oh, yes. Perhaps the biggest thing we've done in the advertising line was to get an officer of the U.S. government, of perfectly Himmalayan official altitude, to write up our little internal improvement for a religious paper of enormous circulation—I tell you that makes our bonds go handsomely among the pious poor. Your religious paper is by far the best vehicle for a thing of this kind, because they'll 'lead'[84] your article and put it right in the midst of the reading matter; and if it's got a few Scripture quotations in it, and some temperance platitudes and a bit of gush here and there about Sunday Schools, and a sentimental snuffle now and then about 'God's precious ones, the honest hard-handed poor,' it works the nation like a charm, my dear sir, and never a man suspects that it is an advertisement; but your secular paper sticks you right into the advertising columns and of course you don't take a trick. Give me a religious paper to advertise in, every time; and if you'll just look at their advertising pages, you'll observe that other people think a good deal as I do—especially people who have got little financial schemes to make everybody rich with. Of course I mean your great big metropolitan religious papers that know how to serve God and make money at the same time—that's your sort, sir, that's your sort—a religious paper that isn't run to make money is no use to *us*, sir, as an advertising medium—no use to anybody in our line of business. I guess our next best dodge was sending a pleasure trip of newspaper reporters out to Napoleon. Never paid them a cent; just filled them up with champagne and the fat of the land, put pen, ink and paper before them while they were red-hot, and bless your soul when you come to read their letters you'd have supposed they'd been to heaven. And if a sentimental squeamishness held one or two of them back from taking a less rosy view of Napoleon, our hospitalities tied his tongue, at least, and he said nothing at all and so did us no harm. Let me see—have I stated all the expenses I've been at? No, I was near forgetting one or two items. There's your official salaries—you can't get good men for nothing. Salaries cost pretty lively. And then there's your big high-sounding millionaire names stuck into your advertisements as stockholders—another card,[85] that—and they *are* stockholders, too, but you have to *give* them the stock and non-assessable at that—so they're an expensive lot. Very, very expensive thing, take it all around, is a big internal improvement concern—but you see that yourself, Mr. Bryerman—you see that, yourself, sir."

"But look here. I think you are a little mistaken about it's ever having cost anything for Congressional votes. I happen to know something about that. I've let you say your say—now let me say mine. I don't wish to seem to throw any suspicion on anybody's statements, because we are all liable to be mistaken. But how would it strike you if I were to say that *I* was in Washington all the time this bill was pending?—and what if I added that *I* put the measure through myself? Yes, sir, I did that little thing. And moreover, I never paid a dollar for any man's vote and never promised one. There are some ways of doing a thing that are as good as others which other people don't happen to think about, or don't have the knack of succeeding in, if they do happen to think of them. My dear sir, I am obliged to knock some of your expenses in the head—for never a cent was paid a Congressman or Senator on the part of this Navigation Company."

The president smiled blandly, even sweetly, all through this harangue, and then said:

"Is that so?"

"Every word of it."

"Well it does seem to alter the complexion of things a little. You are acquainted with the members down there, of course, else you could not have worked to such advantage?"

"I know them all, sir. I know their wives, their children, their babies—I even made it a point to be on good terms with their lackeys. I know every Congressman well—even familiarly."

"Very good. Do you know any of their signatures? Do you know their handwriting?"

"Why I know their handwriting as well as I know my own—have had correspondence enough with them, I should think. And their signatures—why I can tell their initials, even."

The president went to a private safe, unlocked it and got out some letters and certain slips of paper. Then he said:

"Now here, for instance; do you believe that that is a genuine letter? Do you know this signature here?—and this one? Do you know who those initials represent—and are they forgeries?"

Harry was stupefied. There were things there that made his brain swim. Presently, at the bottom of one of the letters he saw a signature that restored his equilibrium; it even brought the sunshine of a smile to his face.

The president said:

"That name amuses you. You never suspected him?"

"Of course I ought to have suspected him, but I don't believe it ever really occurred to me. Well, well, well—how did you ever have the nerve to approach him, of all others?"

"Why my friend, we never think of accomplishing anything without his help. He is our mainstay. But how do those letters strike you?"

"They strike me dumb! What a stone-blind idiot I have been!"

"Well, take it all around, I suppose you had a pleasant time in Washington," said the president, gathering up the letters; "of course you must have had. Very few men could go there and get a money bill through without buying a single—"

"Come, now, Mr. President, that's plenty of that! I take back everything I said on *that* head. I'm a wiser man to-day than I was yesterday, I can tell you."

"I think you are. In fact I am satisfied you are. But now I showed you these things in confidence, you understand. Mention facts as much as you want to, but don't mention *names* to *anybody*. I can depend on you for that, can't I?"

"Oh, of course. I understand the necessity of that. I will not betray the names. But to go back a bit, it begins to look as if you never saw any of that appropriation at all?"

"We saw nearly ten thousand dollars of it—and that was all. Several of us took turns at log-rolling in Washington, and if we had charged anything for that service none of that $10,000 would ever have reached New York."

"If you hadn't levied the assessment you would have been in a close place I judge?"

"Close? Have you figured up the total of the disbursements I told you of?"

"No, I didn't think of that."

"Well, let's see:

Spent in Washington, say,	$191,000
Printing, advertising, etc., say,	118,000
Charity, say,	16,000
Total,	$325,000

"The money to do that with, comes from——

Appropriation,	$200,000
Ten per cent. assessment on capital of $1,000,000,	100,000
Total,	$300,000

"Which leaves us in debt some $25,000 at this moment. Salaries of home officers are still going on; also printing and advertising. Next month will show a state of things!"

"And then—burst up, I suppose?"

"By no means. Levy another assessment."

"Oh, I see. That's dismal."

"By no means."

"Why isn't it? What's the road out?"

"Another appropriation, don't you see?"

"Bother the appropriations. They cost more than they come to."

"Not the next one. We'll call for half a million—get it and go for a million the very next month."

"Yes, but the cost of it!"

The president smiled, and patted his secret letters affection-ately. He said:

"All these people are in the next Congress. We shan't have to pay them a cent. And what is more, they will work like beavers for us—perhaps it might be to their advantage."

Harry reflected profoundly a while. Then he said:

"We send many missionaries to lift up the benighted races of other lands. How much cheaper and better it would be if those people could only come here and drink of our civilization at its fountain head."

"I perfectly agree with you, Mr. Beverly. Must you go? Well, good morning. Look in, when you are passing; and whenever I can give you any information about our affairs and prospects, I shall be glad to do it."

Harry's letter was not a long one, but it contained at least the calamitous figures that came out in the above conversation. The Colonel found himself in a rather uncomfortable place—no $1,200 salary forthcoming; and himself held responsible for half of the $9,640 due the workmen, to say nothing of being in debt to the company to the extent of nearly $4,000. Polly's heart was nearly broken; the "blues" returned in fearful force, and she had to go out of the room to hide the tears that nothing could keep back now.

There was mourning in another quarter, too, for Louise had a letter. Washington had refused, at the last moment, to take $40,000 for the Tennessee Land, and had demanded $150,000! So the trade fell through, and now Washington was wailing because he had been so foolish. But he wrote that his man might probably return to the city, soon, and then he meant to sell to him, sure, even if he had to take $10,000. Louise had a good cry—several of them, indeed—and the family charitably forebore to make any comments that would increase her grief.

Spring blossomed, summer came, dragged its hot weeks by, and the Colonel's spirits rose, day by day, for the railroad was making good progress. But by and by something happened. Hawkeye had always declined to subscribe anything toward the railway, imagining that her large business would be a sufficient compulsory influence; but now Hawkeye was frightened; and before Col. Sellers knew what he was about, Hawkeye, in a panic, had rushed to the front and subscribed such a sum that Napoleon's attractions suddenly sank into insignificance and the railroad concluded to follow a comparatively straight course instead of going miles out of its way to build up a metropolis in the muddy desert of Stone's Landing.

The thunderbolt fell. After all the Colonel's deep planning; after all his brain work and tongue work in drawing public attention to his pet project and enlisting interest in it; after all his faithful hard toil with his hands, and running hither and thither on his busy feet; after all his high hopes and splendid prophecies, the fates had turned their backs on him at last, and all in a moment his air-castles crumbled to ruins about him. Hawkeye rose from her fright triumphant and rejoicing, and down went Stone's Landing! One by one its meagre parcel of inhabitants packed up and moved away, as the summer waned and fall approached. Town lots were no longer salable, traffic ceased, a deadly lethargy fell upon the place once more, the "Weekly Telegraph" faded into an early grave, the wary tadpole returned from exile, the bull-frog resumed his ancient song, the tranquil turtle sunned his back upon bank and log and drowsed his grateful life away as in the old sweet days of yore.

CHAPTER XXIX

—Mihma hatak ash osh ilhkolit yakni ya hlopullit *tv*maha holihta
*v*lhpisa ho k*v*shkoa untuklo ho hollissochit holisso afohkit tahli cha.

Chosh. 18. 9.

PHILIP STERLING was on his way to Ilium, in the state of Pennsylvania. Ilium was the railway station nearest to the tract of wild
land which Mr. Bolton had commissioned him to examine.

On the last day of the journey as the railway train Philip was
on was leaving a large city, a lady timidly entered the drawing-
room car, and hesitatingly took a chair that was at the moment
unoccupied. Philip saw from the window that a gentleman had
put her upon the car just as it was starting. In a few moments the
conductor entered, and without waiting an explanation, said
roughly to the lady,

"Now *you* can't sit there. That seat's taken. Go into the other
car."

"I did not intend to take the seat," said the lady rising, "I only
sat down a moment till the conductor should come and give me a
seat."

"There ain't any. Car's full. You'll have to leave."

"But, sir," said the lady, appealingly, "I thought———"

"Can't help what you thought—you must go into the other
car."

"The train is going very fast, let me stand here till we stop."

"The lady can have my seat," cried Philip, springing up. The
conductor turned towards Philip, and coolly and deliberately surveyed him from head to foot, with contempt in every line of his
face, turned his back upon him without a word, and said to the
lady,

"Come, I've got no time to talk. You must go *now*."

The lady, entirely disconcerted by such rudeness, and frightened, moved towards the door, opened it and stepped out. The
train was swinging along at a rapid rate, jarring from side to side;

the step was a long one between the cars and there was no protecting grating. The lady attempted it, but lost her balance, in the
wind and the motion of the car, and fell! She would inevitably
have gone down under the wheels, if Philip, who had swiftly followed her, had not caught her arm and drawn her up. He then assisted her across, found her a seat, received her bewildered thanks,
and returned to his car.

The conductor was still there, taking his tickets, and growling
something about imposition. Philip marched up to him, and burst
out with,

"You are a brute, an infernal brute, to treat a woman that way."

"Perhaps you'd like to make a fuss about it," sneered the conductor.

Philip's reply was a blow, given so suddenly and planted so
squarely in the conductor's face, that it sent him reeling over a fat
passenger, who was looking up in mild wonder that any one
should dare to dispute with a conductor, and against the side of
the car.

He recovered himself, reached the bell rope, "Damn you, I'll
learn you," stepped to the door and called a couple of brakemen,
and then, as the speed slackened, roared out,

"Get off this train."

"I shall not get off. I have as much right here as you."

"We'll see," said the conductor, advancing with the brakemen.
The passengers protested, and some of them said to each other,
"That's too bad," as they always do in such cases, but none of
them offered to take a hand with Philip. The men seized him,
wrenched him from his seat, dragged him along the aisle, tearing
his clothes, thrust him from the car, and then flung his carpet-bag,
overcoat and umbrella after him. And the train went on.

The conductor, red in the face and puffing from his exertion,
swaggered through the car, muttering "Puppy, I'll learn him."
The passengers, when he had gone, were loud in their indignation,
and talked about signing a protest, but they did nothing more
than talk.

The next morning the Hooverville *Patriot and Clarion* had this
"item": —

SLIGHTUALLY OVERBOARD.

"We learn that as the down noon express was leaving H—— yesterday a lady! (God save the mark) attempted to force herself into the already full palatial car. Conductor Slum, who is too old a bird to be caught with chaff, courteously informed her that the car was full, and when she insisted on remaining, he persuaded her to go into the car where she belonged. Thereupon a young sprig, from the East, blustered up, like a Shanghai rooster, and began to sass the conductor with his chin music. That gentleman delivered the young aspirant for a muss one of his elegant little left-handers, which so astonished him that he began to feel for his shooter. Whereupon Mr. Slum gently raised the youth, carried him forth, and set him down just outside the car to cool off. Whether the young blood has yet made his way out of Bascom's swamp, we have not learned. Conductor Slum is one of the most gentlemanly and efficient officers on the road; but he ain't trifled with, not much. We learn that the company have put a new engine on the seven o'clock train, and newly upholstered the drawing-room car throughout. It spares no effort for the comfort of the traveling public."

Philip never had been before in Bascom's swamp, and there was nothing inviting in it to detain him. After the train got out of the way he crawled out of the briars and the mud, and got upon the track. He was somewhat bruised, but he was too angry to mind that. He plodded along over the ties in a very hot condition of mind and body. In the scuffle, his railway check had disappeared, and he grimly wondered, as he noticed the loss, if the company would permit him to walk over their track if they should know he hadn't a ticket.

Philip had to walk some five miles before he reached a little station, where he could wait for a train, and he had ample time for reflection. At first he was full of vengeance on the company. He would sue it. He would make it pay roundly. But then it occurred to him that he did not know the name of a witness he could summon, and that a personal fight against a railway corporation was about the most hopeless in the world. He then thought he would seek out that conductor, lie in wait for him at some station, and thrash him, or get thrashed himself.

But as he got cooler, that did not seem to him a project worthy of a gentleman exactly. Was it possible for a gentleman to get even with such a fellow as that conductor on the latter's own plane? And when he came to this point, he began to ask himself, if he had not acted very much like a fool. He didn't regret striking the fellow—he hoped he had left a mark on him. But, after all, was that the best way? Here was he, Philip Sterling, calling himself a gentleman, in a brawl with a vulgar conductor, about a woman he had never seen before. Why should he have put himself in such a ridiculous position? Wasn't it enough to have offered the lady his seat, to have rescued her from an accident, perhaps from death? Suppose he had simply said to the conductor, "Sir, your conduct is brutal, I shall report you." The passengers, who saw the affair, might have joined in a report against the conductor, and he might really have accomplished something. And, now! Philip looked at his torn clothes, and thought with disgust of his haste in getting into a fight with such an autocrat.

At the little station where Philip waited for the next train, he met a man who turned out to be a justice of the peace in that neighborhood, and told him his adventure. He was a kindly sort of man, and seemed very much interested.

"Dum 'em" said he, when he had heard the story.

"Do you think any thing can be done, sir?"

"Wal, I guess tain't no use. I hain't a mite of doubt of every word you say. But suin's no use. The railroad company owns all these people along here, and the judges on the bench too. Spiled your clothes! Wal, 'least said's soonest mended.' You hain't no chance with the company."

When next morning, he read the humorous account in the *Patriot and Clarion,* he saw still more clearly what chance he would have had before the public in a fight with the railroad company.

Still Philip's conscience told him that it was his plain duty to carry the matter into the courts, even with the certainty of defeat. He confessed that neither he nor any citizen had a right to consult his own feelings or conscience in a case where a law of the land had been violated before his own eyes. He confessed that every citizen's first duty in such a case is to put aside his own business and devote his time and his best efforts to seeing that the infraction is promptly punished; and he knew that no country can be well governed unless its citizens as a body keep religiously before their minds that they are the guardians of the law, and that the law officers are only the machinery for its execution, nothing more. As a finality he was obliged to confess that he was a bad citizen, and also that the general laxity of the time, and the absence of a sense of duty toward any part of the community but the individual himself were ingrained in him, and he was no better than the rest of the people.

The result of this little adventure was that Philip did not reach Ilium till daylight the next morning, when he descended, sleepy and sore, from a way train, and looked about him. Ilium was in a narrow mountain gorge, through which a rapid stream ran. It consisted of the plank platform on which he stood, a wooden house, half painted, with a dirty piazza (unroofed) in front, and a sign board hung on a slanting pole bearing the legend, "Hotel. P. Dusenheimer," a sawmill further down the stream, a blacksmith-shop, and a store, and three or four unpainted dwellings of the slab variety.

As Philip approached the hotel he saw what appeared to be a wild beast crouching on the piazza. It did not stir, however, and he soon found that it was only a stuffed skin. This cheerful invitation to the tavern was the remains of a huge panther which had been killed in the region a few weeks before. Philip examined his ugly visage and strong crooked fore-arm, as he was waiting admittance, having pounded upon the door.

"Vait a bit. I'll shoost put on my trowsers," shouted a voice from the window, and the door was soon opened by the yawning landlord.

"Morgen! Don't hear d' drain oncet. Dem boys geeps me up zo spate. Gom right in."

Philip was shown into a dirty bar-room. It was a small room, with a stove in the middle, set in a long shallow box of sand, for the benefit of the "spitters," a bar across one end—a mere counter with a sliding glass-case behind it containing a few bottles having ambitious labels, and a wash-sink in one corner. On the walls were the bright yellow and black handbills of a traveling circus, with pictures of acrobats in human pyramids, horses flying in long leaps through the air, and sylph-like women in a paradisaic costume, balancing themselves upon the tips of their toes on the bare backs of frantic and plunging steeds, and kissing their hands to the spectators meanwhile.

As Philip did not desire a room at that hour, he was invited to wash himself at the nasty sink, a feat somewhat easier than drying his face, for the towel that hung in a roller over the sink was evidently as much a fixture as the sink itself, and belonged, like the suspended brush and comb, to the traveling public. Philip managed to complete his toilet by the use of his pocket-handkerchief, and declining the hospitality of the landlord, implied in the remark, "You won'd dake notin'?" he went into the open air to wait for breakfast.

The country he saw was wild but not picturesque. The mountain before him might be eight hundred feet high, and was only a portion of a long unbroken range, savagely wooded, which followed the stream. Behind the hotel, and across the brawling brook, was another level-topped, wooded range exactly like it. Ilium itself, seen at a glance, was old enough to be dilapidated, and if it had gained anything by being made a wood and water station of the new railroad, it was only a new sort of grime and rawness. P. Dusenheimer, standing in the door of his uninviting groggery, when the trains stopped for water, never received from the traveling public any patronage except facetious remarks upon his personal appearance. Perhaps a thousand times he had heard the remark, *"Ilium fuit,"*[86] followed in most instances by a hail to himself as "Aeneas,"[87] with the inquiry "Where is old Anchises?"[88] At first he had replied, "Dere ain't no such man"; but irritated by its senseless repetition, he had latterly dropped into the formula of, "You be dam."

Philip was recalled from the contemplation of Ilium by the rolling and growling of the gong within the hotel, the din and clamor increasing till the house was apparently unable to contain it, when it burst out of the front door and informed the world that breakfast was on the table.

The dining room was long, low and narrow, and a narrow table extended its whole length. Upon this was spread a cloth which from appearance might have been as long in use as the towel in the bar-room. Upon the table was the usual service, the heavy, much nicked stone ware, the row of plated and rusty castors, the sugar bowls with the zinc tea-spoons sticking up in them, the piles of yellow biscuits, the discouraged-looking plates of butter. The landlord waited, and Philip was pleased to observe the change in his manner. In the bar-room he was the conciliatory landlord. Standing behind his guests at table, he had an air of peremptory patronage, and the voice in which he shot out the inquiry, as he seized Philip's plate, "Beefsteak or liver?" quite took away Philip's power of choice. He begged for a glass of milk, after trying that green hued compound called coffee, and made his breakfast out of that and some hard crackers which seemed to have been imported into Ilium before the introduction of the iron horse, and to have withstood a ten years siege of regular boarders, Greeks and others.

The land that Philip had come to look at was at least five miles distant from Ilium station. A corner of it touched the railroad, but the rest was pretty much an unbroken wilderness, eight or ten thousand acres of rough country, most of it such a mountain range as he saw at Ilium.

His first step was to hire three woodsmen to accompany him. By their help he built a log hut, and established a camp on the land, and then began his explorations, mapping down his survey as he went along, noting the timber, and the lay of the land, and making superficial observations as to the prospect of coal.

The landlord at Ilium endeavored to persuade Philip to hire the services of a witch-hazel professor[89] of that region, who could walk over the land with his wand and tell him infallibly whether it contained coal, and exactly where the strata ran. But Philip preferred to trust to his own study of the country, and his knowledge of the geological formation. He spent a month in traveling over the land and making calculations; and made up his mind that a fine vein of coal ran through the mountain about a mile from the railroad, and that the place to run in a tunnel was half way towards its summit.

Acting with his usual promptness, Philip, with the consent of Mr. Bolton, broke ground there at once, and, before snow came, had some rude buildings up, and was ready for active operations in the spring. It was true that there were no outcroppings of coal at the place, and the people at Ilium said he "mought as well dig for plug terbaccer there"; but Philip had great faith in the uniformity of nature's operations in ages past, and he had no doubt that he should strike at this spot the rich vein that had made the fortune of the Golden Briar Company.

CHAPTER XXX

—"Gran pensier volgo; e, se tu lui secondi,
Seguiranno gli effetti alle speranze:
Tessi la tela, ch' io ti mostro ordita,
Di cauto vecchio esecutrice ardita."

"Belle domna vostre socors
M'agra mestier, s'a vos plagues."
B. de Ventador.

ONCE MORE LOUISE had good news from her Washington—
Senator Dilworthy was going to sell the Tennessee Land to the
government! Louise told Laura in confidence. She had told her
parents, too, and also several bosom friends; but all of these
people had simply looked sad when they heard the news, except
Laura. Laura's face suddenly brightened under it—only for an instant, it is true, but poor Louise was grateful for even that fleeting
ray of encouragement. When next Laura was alone, she fell into a
train of thought something like this:

"If the Senator has really taken hold of this matter, I may look
for that invitation to his house at any moment. I am perishing to
go! I do long to know whether I am only simply a large-sized
pigmy among these pigmies here, who tumble over so easily when
one strikes them, or whether I am really—." Her thoughts drifted
into other channels, for a season. Then she continued: —"He said
I could be useful in the great cause of philanthropy, and help in
the blessed work of uplifting the poor and the ignorant, if he
found it feasible to take hold of our Land. Well, that is neither
here nor there; what I want, is to go to Washington and find out
what I am. I want money, too; and if one may judge by what she
hears, there are chances there for a—." For a fascinating woman,
she was going to say, perhaps, but she did not.

Along in the fall the invitation came, sure enough. It came officially through brother Washington, the private Secretary, who
appended a postscript that was brimming with delight over the

prospect of seeing the Duchess again. He said it would be happiness enough to look upon her face once more—it would be almost too much happiness when to it was added the fact that she would bring messages with her that were fresh from Louise's lips.

In Washington's letter were several important enclosures. For instance, there was the Senator's check for $2,000—"to buy suitable clothing in New York with!" It was a loan to be refunded when the Land was sold. Two thousand—this was fine indeed. Louise's father was called rich, but Laura doubted if Louise had ever had $400 worth of new clothing at one time in her life. With the check came two through tickets—good on the railroad from Hawkeye to Washington via New York—and they were "dead-head" tickets, too, which had been given to Senator Dilworthy by the railway companies. Senators and representatives were paid thousands of dollars by the government for traveling expenses, but they always traveled "dead-head" both ways, and then did as any honorable, high-minded men would naturally do—declined to receive the mileage tendered them by the government. The Senator had plenty of railway passes, and could easily spare two to Laura—one for himself and one for a male escort. Washington suggested that she get some old friend of the family to come with her, and said the Senator would "dead-head" him home again as soon as he had grown tired of the sights of the capital. Laura thought the thing over. At first she was pleased with the idea, but presently she began to feel differently about it. Finally she said, "No, our staid, steady-going Hawkeye friends' notions and mine differ about some things—they respect me, now, and I respect them—better leave it so—I will go alone; I am not afraid to travel by myself." And so communing with herself, she left the house for an afternoon walk.

Almost at the door she met Col. Sellers. She told him about her invitation to Washington.

"Bless me!" said the Colonel. "I have about made up my mind to go there myself. You see we've got to get another appropriation through, and the Company want me to come east and put it through Congress. Harry's there, and he'll do what he can, of course; and Harry's a good fellow and always does the very best he knows how, but then he's young—rather young for some parts of such work, you know—and besides he talks too much, talks a good deal too much; and sometimes he appears to be a little bit visionary, too, I think—the worst thing in the world for a business man. A man like that always exposes his cards, sooner or later. This sort of thing wants an old, quiet, steady hand—wants an old cool head, you know, that knows men, through and through, and is used to large operations. I'm expecting my salary, and also some dividends from the company, and if they get along in time, I'll go along with you Laura—take you under my wing—you mustn't travel alone. Lord I wish I had the money right now.—But there'll be plenty soon—plenty."

Laura reasoned with herself that if the kindly, simple-hearted Colonel was going anyhow, what could she gain by traveling alone and throwing away his company? So she told him she accepted his offer gladly, gratefully. She said it would be the greatest of favors if he would go with her and protect her—not at his own expense as far as railway fares were concerned, of course; she could not expect him to put himself to so much trouble for her and pay his fare besides. But he wouldn't hear of her paying his fare—it would be only a pleasure to him to serve her. Laura insisted on furnishing the tickets; and finally, when argument failed, she said the tickets cost neither her nor any one else a cent—she had two of them—she needed but one—and if he would not take the other she would not go with him. That settled the matter. He took the ticket. Laura was glad that she had the check for new clothing, for she felt very certain of being able to get the Colonel to borrow a little of the money to pay hotel bills with, here and there.

She wrote Washington to look for her and Col. Sellers toward the end of November; and at about the time set the two travelers arrived safe in the capital of the nation, sure enough.

CHAPTER XXXI

Deh! ben fôra all' incontro ufficio umano,
   E bed n'avresti tu gioja c diletto,
Se la pietosa tua medica mano
Avvicinassi al valoroso petto.
                                    Tasso.

She, gracious lady, yet no paines did spare
To doe him ease, or doe him remedy:
Many restoratives of vertues rare
And costly cordialles she did apply,
To mitigate his stubborne malady.
                  Spenser's Faerie Queene.

MR. HENRY BRIERLY was exceedingly busy in New York, so he wrote Col. Sellers, but he would drop everything and go to Washington.

The Colonel believed that Harry was the prince of lobbyists, a little too sanguine, may be, and given to speculation, but, then, he knew everybody; the Columbus River navigation scheme was got through almost entirely by his aid. He was needed now to help through another scheme, a benevolent scheme in which Col. Sellers, through the Hawkinses, had a deep interest.

"I don't care, you know," he wrote to Harry, "so much about the niggroes. But if the government will buy this land, it will set up the Hawkins family—make Laura an heiress—and I shouldn't wonder if Beriah Sellers would set up his carriage again. Dilworthy looks at it different, of course. He's all for philanthropy, for benefiting the colored race. There's old Balaam, was in the Interior—used to be the Rev. Orson Balaam of Iowa—he's made the riffle[90] on the Injun; great Injun pacificator and land dealer. Balaam's got the Injun to himself, and I suppose that Senator Dilworthy feels that there is nothing left him but the colored man. I do reckon he is the best friend the colored man has got in Washington."

Though Harry was in a hurry to reach Washington, he stopped

in Philadelphia, and prolonged his visit day after day, greatly to the detriment of his business both in New York and Washington. The society at the Boltons' might have been a valid excuse for neglecting business much more important than his. Philip was there; he was a partner with Mr. Bolton now in the new coal venture, concerning which there was much to be arranged in preparation for the Spring work, and Philip lingered week after week in the hospitable house. Alice was making a winter visit. Ruth only went to town twice a week to attend lectures, and the household was quite to Mr. Bolton's taste, for he liked the cheer of company and something going on evenings. Harry was cordially asked to bring his traveling-bag there, and he did not need urging to do so. Not even the thought of seeing Laura at the capital made him restless in the society of the two young ladies; two birds in hand are worth one in the bush certainly.

Philip was at home—he sometimes wished he were not so much so. He felt that too much or not enough was taken for granted. Ruth had met him, when he first came, with a cordial frankness, and her manner continued entirely unrestrained. She neither sought his company nor avoided it, and this perfectly level treatment irritated him more than any other could have done. It was impossible to advance much in love-making with one who offered no obstacles, had no concealments and no embarrassments, and whom any approach to sentimentality would be quite likely to set into a fit of laughter.

"Why, Phil," she would say, "what puts you in the dumps today? You are as solemn as the upper bench in Meeting. I shall have to call Alice to raise your spirits; my presence seems to depress you."

"It's not your presence, but your absence when you *are* present," began Philip, dolefully, with the idea that he was saying a rather deep thing. "But you won't understand me."

"No, I confess I cannot. If you really are so low as to think I am absent when I am present, it's a frightful case of aberration; I shall ask father to bring out Dr. Jackson. Does Alice appear to be present when she is absent?"

"Alice has some human feeling, anyway. She cares for something besides musty books and dry bones. I think, Ruth, when I die," said Philip, intending to be very grim and sarcastic, "I'll leave you my skeleton. You might like that."

"It might be more cheerful than you are at times," Ruth replied with a laugh. "But you mustn't do it without consulting Alice. She might not like it."

"I don't know why you should bring Alice up on every occasion. Do you think I am in love with her?"

"Bless you, no. It never entered my head. Are you? The thought of Philip Sterling in love is too comical. I thought you were only in love with the Ilium coal mine, which you and father talk about half the time."

This is a specimen of Philip's wooing. Confound the girl, he would say to himself, why does she never tease Harry and that young Shepley who comes here?

How differently Alice treated him. She at least never mocked him, and it was a relief to talk with one who had some sympathy with him. And he did talk to her, by the hour, about Ruth. The blundering fellow poured all his doubts and anxieties into her ear, as if she had been the impassive occupant of one of those little wooden confessionals in the Cathedral on Logan Square. Has a confessor, if she is young and pretty, any feeling? Does it mend the matter by calling her your sister?

Philip called Alice his good sister, and talked to her about love and marriage, meaning Ruth, as if sisters could by no possibility have any personal concern in such things. Did Ruth ever speak of him? Did she think Ruth cared for him? Did Ruth care for anybody at Fallkill? Did she care for anything except her profession? And so on.

Alice was loyal to Ruth, and if she knew anything she did not betray her friend. She did not, at any rate, give Philip too much encouragement. What woman, under the circumstances, would?

"I can tell you one thing, Philip," she said, "if ever Ruth Bolton loves, it will be with her whole soul, in a depth of passion that will sweep everything before it and surprise even herself."

A remark that did not much console Philip, who imagined that only some grand heroism could unlock the sweetness of such a heart; and Philip feared that he wasn't a hero. He did not know out of what materials a woman can construct a hero, when she is in the creative mood.

Harry skipped into this society with his usual lightness and gaiety. His good nature was inexhaustible, and though he liked to relate his own exploits, he had a little tact in adapting himself to the tastes of his hearers. He was not long in finding out that Alice liked to hear about Philip, and Harry launched out into the career of his friend in the West, with a prodigality of invention that would have astonished the chief actor. He was the most generous fellow in the world, and picturesque conversation was the one thing in which he never was bankrupt. With Mr. Bolton he was the serious man of business, enjoying the confidence of many of the monied men in New York, whom Mr. Bolton knew, and engaged with them in railway schemes and government contracts. Philip, who had so long known Harry, never could make up his mind that Harry did not himself believe that he was a chief actor in all these large operations of which he talked so much.

Harry did not neglect to endeavor to make himself agreeable to Mrs. Bolton, by paying great attention to the children, and by professing the warmest interest in the Friends' faith. It always seemed to him the most peaceful religion; he thought it must be easier to live by an internal light than by a lot of outward rules; he had a dear Quaker aunt in Providence of whom Mrs. Bolton constantly reminded him. He insisted upon going with Mrs. Bolton and the children to the Friends Meeting on First Day, when Ruth and Alice and Philip, "world's people,"[91] went to a church in town, and he sat through the hour of silence with his hat on, in most exemplary patience. In short, this amazing actor succeeded so well with Mrs. Bolton, that she said to Philip one day,

"Thy friend, Henry Brierly, appears to be a very worldly-minded young man. Does he believe in anything?"

"Oh, yes," said Philip laughing, "he believes in more things than any other person I ever saw."

To Ruth Harry seemed to be very congenial. He was never moody for one thing, but lent himself with alacrity to whatever her fancy was. He was gay or grave as the need might be. No one apparently could enter more fully into her plans for an independent career.

"My father," said Harry, "was bred a physician, and practiced a little before he went into Wall street. I always had a leaning to the study. There was a skeleton hanging in the closet of my father's study when I was a boy, that I used to dress up in old clothes. Oh, I got quite familiar with the human frame."

"You must have," said Philip. "Was that where you learned to play the bones?[92] He is a master of those musical instruments, Ruth; he plays well enough to go on the stage."

"Philip hates science of any kind, and steady application," retorted Harry. He didn't fancy Philip's banter, and when the latter had gone out, and Ruth asked,

"Why don't you take up medicine, Mr. Brierly?"

Harry said, "I have it in mind. I believe I would begin attending lectures this winter if it weren't for being wanted in Washington. But medicine is particularly women's province."

"Why so?" asked Ruth, rather amused.

"Well, the treatment of disease is a good deal a matter of sympathy. A woman's intuition is better than a man's. Nobody knows anything, really, you know, and a woman can guess a good deal nearer than a man."

"You are very complimentary to my sex."

"But," said Harry frankly, "I should want to choose my doctor; an ugly woman would ruin me, the disease would be sure to strike in and kill me at sight of her. I think a pretty physician, with engaging manners, would coax a fellow to live through almost anything."

"I am afraid you are a scoffer, Mr. Brierly."

"On the contrary, I am quite sincere. Wasn't it old what's his name? that said only the beautiful is useful?"[93]

Whether Ruth was anything more than diverted with Harry's company, Philip could not determine. He scorned at any rate to advance his own interest by any disparaging communications about Harry, both because he could not help liking the fellow himself, and because he may have known that he could not more surely create a sympathy for him in Ruth's mind. That Ruth was in no danger of any serious impression he felt pretty sure, felt certain of it when he reflected upon her severe occupation with her profession. Hang it, he would say to himself, she is nothing but pure intellect anyway. And he only felt uncertain of it when she was in one of her moods of raillery, with mocking mischief in her eyes. At such times she seemed to prefer Harry's society to his. When Philip was miserable about this, he always took refuge with Alice, who was never moody, and who generally laughed him out of his sentimental nonsense. He felt at his ease with Alice, and was never in want of something to talk about; and he could not account for the fact that he was so often dull with Ruth, with whom, of all persons in the world, he wanted to appear at his best.

Harry was entirely satisfied with his own situation. A bird of passage is always at its ease, having no house to build, and no responsibility. He talked freely with Philip about Ruth, an almighty fine girl, he said, but what the deuce she wanted to study medicine for, he couldn't see.

There was a concert one night at the Musical Fund Hall and the four had arranged to go in and return by the Germantown cars. It was Philip's plan, who had engaged the seats, and promised himself an evening with Ruth, walking with her, sitting by her in the hall, and enjoying the feeling of protecting that a man always has of a woman in a public place. He was fond of music, too, in a sympathetic way; at least, he knew that Ruth's delight in it would be enough for him.

Perhaps he meant to take advantage of the occasion to say some very serious things. His love for Ruth was no secret to Mrs. Bolton, and he felt almost sure that he should have no opposition in the family. Mrs. Bolton had been cautious in what she said, but Philip inferred everything from her reply to his own questions, one day, "Has thee ever spoken thy mind to Ruth?"

Why shouldn't he speak his mind, and end his doubts! Ruth had been more tricksy than usual that day, and in a flow of spirits quite inconsistent, it would seem, in a young lady devoted to grave studies.

Had Ruth a premonition of Philip's intention, in his manner? It may be, for when the girls came down stairs, ready to walk to the cars,[94] and met Philip and Harry in the hall, Ruth said, laughing,

"The two tallest must walk together," and before Philip knew how it happened Ruth had taken Harry's arm, and his evening was spoiled. He had too much politeness and good sense and kindness to show in his manner that he was hit. So he said to Harry,

"That's your disadvantage in being short." And he gave Alice no reason to feel during the evening that she would not have been his first choice for the excursion. But he was none the less chagrined, and not a little angry at the turn the affair took.

The Hall was crowded with the fashion of the town.— The concert was one of those fragmentary drearinesses that people endure because they are fashionable; *tours de force* on the piano, and fragments from operas, which have no meaning without the setting, with weary pauses of waiting between; there is the comic basso who is so amusing and on such familiar terms with the audience, and always sings the Barber;[95] the attitudinizing tenor, with his languishing "Oh, Summer Night";[96] the soprano with her "Batti Batti,"[97] who warbles and trills and runs and fetches her breath, and ends with a noble scream that brings down a tempest of applause in the midst of which she backs off the stage smiling and bowing. It was this sort of concert, and Philip was thinking that it was the most stupid one he ever sat through, when just as the soprano was in the midst of that touching balled, "Comin' thro' the Rye" (the soprano always sings "Comin' thro' the Rye" on an encore—the Black Swan[98] used to make it irresistible, Philip remembered, with her arch, "If a body kiss a body") there was a cry of Fire!

The hall is long and narrow, and there is only one place of egress. Instantly the audience was on its feet, and a rush began for the door. Men shouted, women screamed, and panic seized the swaying mass. A second's thought would have convinced everyone that getting out was impossible, and that the only effect of a rush would be to crush people to death. But a second's thought was not given. A few cried "Sit down, sit down," but the mass was turned towards the door. Women were down and trampled on in the aisles, and stout men, utterly lost to self-control, were mounting the benches, as if to run a race over the mass to the entrance.

Philip who had forced the girls to keep their seats saw, in a flash, the new danger, and sprang to avert it. In a second more those infuriated men would be over the benches and crushing

Ruth and Alice under their boots. He leaped upon the bench in front of them and struck out before him with all his might, felling one man who was rushing on him, and checking for an instant the movement, or rather parting it, and causing it to flow on either side of him. But it was only for an instant; the pressure behind was too great, and the next Philip was dashed backwards over the seat.

And yet that instant of arrest had probably saved the girls, for as Philip fell, the orchestra struck up "Yankee Doodle" in the liveliest manner. The familiar tune caught the ear of the mass, which paused in wonder, and gave the conductor's voice a chance to be heard—"It's a false alarm!"

The tumult was over in a minute, and the next, laughter was heard, and not a few said, "I knew it wasn't anything." "What fools people are at such a time."

The concert was over, however. A good many people were hurt, some of them seriously, and among them Philip Sterling was found bent across the seat, insensible, with his left arm hanging limp and a bleeding wound on his head.

When he was carried into the air he revived, and said it was nothing. A surgeon was called, and it was thought best to drive at once to the Boltons', the surgeon supporting Philip, who did not speak the whole way. His arm was set and his head dressed, and the surgeon said he would come round all right in his mind by morning; he was very weak. Alice who was not much frightened while the panic lasted in the hall, was very much unnerved by seeing Philip so pale and bloody. Ruth assisted the surgeon with the utmost coolness and with skillful hands helped to dress Philip's wounds. And there was a certain intentness and fierce energy in what she did that might have revealed something to Philip if he had been in his senses.

But he was not, or he would not have murmured "Let Alice do it, she is not too tall."

It was Ruth's first case.

CHAPTER XXXII

Lo, swiche sleightes and subtiltees
In women ben; for ay as besy as bees
Ben they us sely men for to deceive,
And from a sothe wol they ever weive.
                                    Chaucer.

WASHINGTON'S DELIGHT in his beautiful sister was measureless.
He said that she had always been the queenliest creature in the
land, but that she was only commonplace before, compared to
what she was now, so extraordinary was the improvement
wrought by rich fashionable attire.

"But your criticisms are too full of brotherly partiality to be
depended on, Washington. Other people will judge differently."

"Indeed they won't. You'll see. There will never be a woman in
Washington that can compare with you. You'll be famous within
a fortnight, Laura. Everybody will want to know you. You wait—
you'll see."

Laura wished in her heart that the prophecy might come true;
and privately she even believed it might—for she had brought all
the women whom she had seen since she left home under sharp
inspection, and the result had not been unsatisfactory to her.

During a week or two Washington drove about the city every
day with her and familiarized her with all of its salient features.
She was beginning to feel very much at home with the town itself,
and she was also fast acquiring ease with the distinguished people
she met at the Dilworthy table, and losing what little of country
timidity she had brought with her from Hawkeye. She noticed
with secret pleasure the little start of admiration that always
manifested itself in the faces of the guests when she entered the
drawing-room arrayed in evening costume:—she took comforting note of the fact that these guests directed a very liberal share
of their conversation toward her; she observed with surprise, that
famous statesmen and soldiers did not talk like gods, as a general
thing, but said rather commonplace things for the most part; and

she was filled with gratification to discover that she, on the contrary, was making a good many shrewd speeches and now and then a really brilliant one, and furthermore, that they were beginning to be repeated in social circles about the town.

Congress began its sittings, and every day or two Washington escorted her to the galleries set apart for lady members of the households of Senators and Representatives. Here was a larger field and a wider competition, but still she saw that many eyes were uplifted toward her face, and that first one person and then another called a neighbor's attention to her; she was not too dull to perceive that the speeches of some of the younger statesmen were delivered about as much and perhaps more at her than to the presiding officer; and she was not sorry to see that the dapper young Senator from Iowa[99] came at once and stood in the open space before the president's desk to exhibit his feet as soon as she entered the gallery, whereas she had early learned from common report that his usual custom was to prop them on his desk and enjoy them himself with a selfish disregard of other people's longings.

Invitations began to flow in upon her and soon she was fairly "in society." "The season" was now in full bloom, and the first select reception was at hand—that is to say, a reception confined to invited guests.

Senator Dilworthy had become well convinced, by this time, that his judgment of the country-bred Missouri girl had not deceived him—it was plain that she was going to be a peerless missionary in the field of labor he designed her for, and therefore it would be perfectly safe and likewise judicious to send her forth well panoplied for her work.—So he had added new and still richer costumes to her wardrobe, and assisted their attractions with costly jewelry—loans on the future land sale.

This first select reception took place at a cabinet minister's—or rather a cabinet secretary's[100]—mansion. When Laura and the Senator arrived, about half past nine or ten in the evening, the place was already pretty well crowded, and the white-gloved negro servant at the door was still receiving streams of guests.—The drawing-rooms were brilliant with gaslight, and as hot as ovens. The host and hostess stood just within the door of entrance;

Laura was presented, and then she passed on into the maelstrom of be-jeweled and richly attired low-necked ladies and white-kid-gloved and steel pen-coated[101] gentlemen—and wherever she moved she was followed by a buzz of admiration that was grateful to all her senses—so grateful, indeed, that her white face was tinged and its beauty heightened by a perceptible suffusion of color. She caught such remarks as, "Who is she?" "Superb woman!" "That is the new beauty from the west," etc., etc.

Whenever she halted, she was presently surrounded by Ministers, Generals, Congressmen, and all manner of aristocratic people. Introductions followed, and then the usual original question, "How do you like Washington, Miss Hawkins?" supplemented by that other usual original question, "Is this your first visit?"

These two exciting topics being exhausted, conversation generally drifted into calmer channels, only to be interrupted at frequent intervals by new introductions and new inquiries as to how Laura liked the capital and whether it was her first visit or not. And thus for an hour or more the Duchess moved through the crush in a rapture of happiness, for her doubts were dead and gone, now—she knew she could conquer here. A familiar face appeared in the midst of the multitude and Harry Brierly fought his difficult way to her side, his eyes shouting their gratification, so to speak:

"Oh, this *is* a happiness! Tell me, my dear Miss Hawkins—"

"Sh! I know what you are going to ask. I *do* like Washington—I like it ever so much!"

"No, but I was going to ask—"

"Yes, I am coming to it, coming to it as fast as I can. It *is* my first visit. I think you should know that yourself."

And straightway a wave of the crowd swept her beyond his reach.

"Now what can the girl mean? Of course she likes Washington—I'm not such a dummy as to have to ask her that. And as to its being her first visit, why hang it, she knows that I *knew* it was. Does she think I have turned idiot? Curious girl, anyway. But how they do swarm about her! She is the reigning belle of Washington after this night. She'll know five hundred of the heaviest

guns in the town before this night's nonsense is over. And this
isn't even the beginning. Just as I used to say—she'll be a card[102]
in the matter of—yes *sir!* She shall turn the men's heads and I'll
turn the women's! What a team that will be in politics here. I
wouldn't take a quarter of a million for what I can do in this present session—no indeed I wouldn't. Now, here—I don't altogether
like this. That insignificant secretary of legation is—why, she's
smiling on him as if he—and now on the Admiral! Now she's il-
luminating that stuffy Congressman from Massachusetts—vulgar
ungrammatical shovel-maker—greasy knave of spades.[103] I don't
like this sort of thing. She doesn't appear to be much distressed
about *me*—she hasn't looked this way once. All right, my bird of
Paradise, if it suits you, go on. But I think I know your sex. *I'll* go
to smiling around a little, too, and see what effect *that* will have
on you."

And he did "smile around a little," and got as near to her as he
could to watch the effect, but the scheme was a failure—he could
not get her attention. She seemed wholly unconscious of him, and
so he could not flirt with any spirit; he could only talk disjointedly; he could not keep his eyes on the charmers he talked to; he
grew irritable, jealous, and very unhappy. He gave up his enterprise, leaned his shoulder against a fluted pilaster and pouted
while he kept watch upon Laura's every movement. His other
shoulder stole the bloom from many a lovely cheek that brushed
him in the surging crush, but he noted it not. He was too busy
cursing himself inwardly for being an egotistical imbecile. An
hour ago he had thought to take this country lass under his protection and show her "life" and enjoy her wonder and delight
and here she was, immersed in the marvel up to her eyes, and just
a trifle more at home in it than he was himself. And now his angry comments ran on again:

"Now she's sweetening old Brother Balaam; and he—well he
is inviting her to the Congressional prayer-meeting, no doubt—
better let old Dilworthy alone to see that she doesn't overlook
that. And now its Splurge, of New York; and now its Batters of
New Hampshire—and now the Vice President! Well I may as well
adjourn. I've got enough."

But he hadn't. He got as far as the door—and then struggled

back to take one more look, hating himself all the while for his weakness.

Toward midnight, when supper was announced, the crowd thronged to the supper room where a long table was decked out with what seemed a rare repast, but which consisted of things better calculated to feast the eye than the appetite. The ladies were soon seated in files along the wall, and in groups here and there, and the colored waiters filled the plates and glasses and the male guests moved hither and thither conveying them to the privileged sex.

Harry took an ice and stood up by the table with other gentlemen, and listened to the buzz of conversation while he ate.

From these remarks he learned a good deal about Laura that was news to him. For instance, that she was of a distinguished western family; that she was highly educated; that she was very rich and a great landed heiress; that she was not a professor of religion, and yet was a Christian in the truest and best sense of the word, for her whole heart was devoted to the accomplishment of a great and noble enterprise—none other than the sacrificing of her landed estates to the uplifting of the down-trodden negro and the turning of his erring feet into the way of light and righteousness. Harry observed that as soon as one listener had absorbed the story, he turned about and delivered it to his next neighbor and the latter individual straightway passed it on. And thus he saw it travel the round of the gentlemen and overflow rearward among the ladies. He could not trace it backward to its fountain head, and so he could not tell who it was that started it.

One thing annoyed Harry a great deal; and that was the reflection that he might have been in Washington days and days ago and thrown his fascinations about Laura with permanent effect while she was new and strange to the capital, instead of dawdling in Philadelphia to no purpose. He feared he had "missed a trick," as he expressed it.

He only found one little opportunity of speaking again with Laura before the evening's festivities ended, and then, for the first time in years, his airy self-complacency failed him, his tongue's easy confidence forsook it in a great measure, and he was conscious of an unheroic timidity. He was glad to get away and find a place where he could despise himself in private and try to grow his clipped plumes again.

When Laura reached home she was tired but exultant, and Senator Dilworthy was pleased and satisfied. He called Laura "my daughter," next morning, and gave her some "pin money," as he termed it, and she sent a hundred and fifty dollars of it to her mother and loaned a trifle to Col. Sellers. Then the Senator had a long private conference with Laura, and unfolded certain plans of his for the good of the country, and religion, and the poor, and temperance, and showed her how she could assist him in developing these worthy and noble enterprises.

CHAPTER XXXIII

—Itancan Ihduhomni eciyapi, Itancan Tohanokihi-eca eciyapi, Itancan
Iapiwaxte eciyapi, he hunkakewicaye cin etanhan otonwe kin caxtonpi;
nakun Akicita Wicaxta-ceji-skuya, Akicita Anogite, Akicita Taku-kaxta—

> pe richeste wifmen alle: pat were in londe,
> and pere hehere monnen dohtere. . . . .
> pere wes moni pal hende: on faire pā uolke.
> par was mochel honde: of manicunnes londe,
> for ech wende to beon: betere pan *oper.*
>
> *Layamon.*

LAURA SOON DISCOVERED that there were three distinct aristocracies in Washington. One of these, (nick-named the Antiques,)
consisted of cultivated, high-bred old families who looked back
with pride upon an ancestry that had been always great in the nation's councils and its wars from the birth of the republic downward. Into this select circle it was difficult to gain admission. No.
2 was the aristocracy of the middle ground—of which, more
anon. No. 3 lay beyond; of it we will say a word here. We will call
it the Aristocracy of the Parvenus[104]—as, indeed, the general public did. Official position, no matter how obtained, entitled a man
to a place in it, and carried his family with him, no matter whence
they sprang. Great wealth gave a man a still higher and nobler
place in it than did official position. If this wealth had been acquired by conspicuous ingenuity, with just a pleasant little spice
of illegality about it, all the better. This aristocracy was "fast," and
not averse to ostentation. The aristocracy of the Antiques ignored
the aristocracy of the Parvenus; the Parvenus laughed at the Antiques, (and secretly envied them).

There were certain important "society" customs which one in
Laura's position needed to understand. For instance, when a lady
of any prominence comes to one of our cities and takes up her residence, all the ladies of her grade favor her in turn with an initial
call, giving their cards to the servant at the door by way of introduction. They come singly, sometimes; sometime in couples;—

and always in elaborate full dress. They talk two minutes and a quarter and then go. If the lady receiving the call desires a further acquaintance, she must return the visit within two weeks; to neglect it beyond that time means "let the matter drop." But if she does return to visit within two weeks, it then becomes the other party's privilege to continue the acquaintance or drop it. She signifies her willingness to continue it by calling again any time within twelve months; after that, if the parties go on calling upon each other once a year, in our large cities, that is sufficient, and the acquaintanceship holds good. The thing goes along smoothly, now. The annual visits are made and returned with peaceful regularity and bland satisfaction, although it is not necessary that the two ladies shall actually *see* each other oftener than once every few years. Their cards preserve the intimacy and keep the acquaintanceship intact.

For instance, Mrs. A. pays her annual visit, sits in her carriage and sends in her card with the lower right hand corner turned down, which signifies that she has "called in person;" Mrs. B. sends down word that she is "engaged" or "wishes to be excused"—or if she is a Parvenu and low-bred, she perhaps sends word that she is "not at home." Very good; Mrs. A. drives on happy and content. If Mrs. A.'s daughter marries, or a child is born to the family, Mrs. B. calls, sends in her card with the upper left hand corner turned down, and then goes along about her affairs—for that inverted corner means "Congratulations." If Mrs. B.'s husband falls down stairs and breaks his neck, Mrs. A. calls, leaves her card with the upper right hand corner turned down, and then takes her departure; this corner means "Condolence." It is very necessary to get the corners right, else one may unintentionally condole with a friend on a wedding or congratulate her upon a funeral. If either lady is about to leave the city, she goes to the other's house and leaves her card with "P.P.C."[105] engraved under the name—which signifies, "Pay Parting Call." But enough of etiquette. Laura was early instructed in the mysteries of society life by a competent mentor, and thus was preserved from troublesome mistakes.

The first fashionable call she received from a member of the ancient nobility, otherwise the Antiques, was of a pattern with all she received from that limb of the aristocracy afterward. This call was paid by Mrs. Major-General Fulke-Fulkerson and daughter. They drove up at one in the afternoon in a rather antiquated vehicle with a faded coat of arms on the panels, an aged white-wooled negro coachman on the box and a younger darkey beside him—the footman. Both of these servants were dressed in dull brown livery that had seen considerable service.

The ladies entered the drawing-room in full character; that is to say, with Elizabethan stateliness on the part of the dowager, and an easy grace and dignity on the part of the young lady that had a nameless something about it that suggested conscious superiority. The dresses of both ladies were exceedingly rich, as to material, but as notably modest as to color and ornament. All parties having seated themselves, the dowager delivered herself of a remark that was not unusual in its form, and yet it came from her lips with the impressiveness of Scripture:

"The weather has been unpropitious of late, Miss Hawkins."

"It has indeed," said Laura. "The climate seems to be variable."

"It is its nature of old, here," said the daughter—stating it apparently as a fact, only, and by her manner waving aside all personal responsibility on account of it. "Is it not so, mamma?"

"Quite so, my child. Do you like winter, Miss Hawkins?" She said "like" as if she had an idea that its dictionary meaning was "approve of."

"Not as well as summer—though I think all seasons have their charms."

"It is a very just remark. The general held similar views. He considered snow in winter proper; sultriness in summer legitimate; frosts in the autumn the same, and rains in spring not objectionable. He was not an exacting man. And I call to mind now that he always admired thunder. You remember, child, your father always admired thunder?"

"He adored it."

"No doubt it reminded him of battle," said Laura.

"Yes, I think perhaps it did. He had a great respect for Nature. He often said there was something striking about the ocean. You remember his saying that, daughter?"

"Yes, often, mother. I remember it very well."

"And hurricanes. He took a great interest in hurricanes. And animals. Dogs, especially—hunting dogs. Also comets. I think we all have our predilections. I think it is this that gives variety to our tastes." Laura coincided with this view. "Do you find it hard and lonely to be so far from your home and friends, Miss Hawkins?"

"I do find it depressing sometimes, but then there is so much about me here that is novel and interesting that my days are made up more of sunshine than shadow."

"Washington is not a dull city in the season," said the young lady. "We have some very good society indeed, and one need not be at a loss for means to pass the time pleasantly. Are you fond of watering-places, Miss Hawkins?"

"I have really had no experience of them, but I have always felt a strong desire to see something of fashionable watering-place life."

"We of Washington are unfortunately situated in that respect," said the dowager. "It is a tedious distance to Newport.[106] But there is no help for it."

Laura said to herself, "Long Branch[107] and Cape May[108] are nearer than Newport; doubtless these places are low; I'll feel my way a little and see." Then she said aloud:

"Why I thought that Long Branch—"

There was no need to "feel" any further—there was that in both faces before her which made that truth apparent. The dowager said:

"Nobody goes *there*, Miss Hawkins—at least only persons of no position in society. And the President." She added that with tranquility.

"Newport is damp, and cold, and windy and excessively disagreeable," said the daughter, "but it is very select. One cannot be fastidious about minor matters when one has no choice."

The visit had spun out nearly three minutes, now. Both ladies rose with grave dignity, conferred upon Laura a formal invitation to call, and then retired from the conference. Laura remained in the drawing-room and left them to pilot themselves out of the house—an inhospitable thing, it seemed to her, but then she was following her instructions. She stood, steeped in reverie, a while, and then she said:

"I think I could always enjoy icebergs—as scenery—but not as company."

Still, she knew these two people by reputation, and was aware that they were not icebergs when they were in their own waters and amid their legitimate surroundings, but on the contrary were people to be respected for their stainless characters and esteemed for their social virtues and their benevolent impulses. She thought it a pity that they had to be such changed and dreary creatures on occasions of state.

The first call Laura received from the other extremity of the Washington aristocracy followed close upon the heels of the one we have just been describing. The callers this time were the Hon. Mrs. Oliver Higgins, the Hon. Mrs. Patrique Oreillé (pronounced O-re*lay*,) Miss Bridget (pronounced Breezhay) Oreillé, Mrs. Peter Gashly, Miss Gashly, and Miss Emmeline Gashly.

The three carriages arrived at the same moment from different directions. They were new and wonderfully shiny, and the brasses on the harness were highly polished and bore complicated monograms. There were showy coats of arms, too, with Latin mottoes. The coachmen and footmen were clad in bright new livery, of striking colors, and they had black rosettes with shaving-brushes[109] projecting above them, on the sides of their stovepipe hats.

When the visitors swept into the drawing-room they filled the place with a suffocating sweetness procured at the perfumer's. Their costumes, as to architecture, were the latest fashion intensified; they were rainbow-hued; they were hung with jewels—chiefly diamonds. It would have been plain to any eye that it had cost something to upholster these women.

The Hon. Mrs. Oliver Higgins was the wife of a delegate from a distant territory—a gentleman who had kept the principal "saloon," and sold the best whiskey in the principal village in his wilderness, and so, of course, was recognized as the first man of his commonwealth and its fittest representative. He was a man of paramount influence at home, for he was public spirited, he was chief of the fire department, he had an admirable command of profane language, and had killed several "parties." His shirt fronts were always immaculate; his boots daintily polished, and no man could lift a foot and fire a dead shot at a stray speck of dirt on it with a white handkerchief with a finer grace than he; his watch chain weighed a pound; the gold in his finger ring was worth forty-five dollars; he wore a diamond cluster-pin and he parted his hair behind. He had always been regarded as the most elegant gentleman in his territory, and it was conceded by all that no man thereabouts was anywhere near his equal in the telling of an obscene story except the venerable white-haired governor himself. The Hon. Higgins had not come to serve his country in Washington for nothing. The appropriation which he had engineered through Congress for the maintenance of the Indians in his Territory would have made all those savages rich if it had ever got to them.

The Hon. Mrs. Higgins was a picturesque woman, and a fluent talker, and she held a tolerably high station among the Parvenus. Her English was fair enough, as a general thing—though, being of New York origin, she had the fashion peculiar to many natives of that city of pronouncing saw and law as if they were spelt sawr and lawr.

Petroleum was the agent that had suddenly transformed the Gashlys from modest hard-working country village folk into "loud" aristocrats and ornaments of the city.

The Hon. Patrique Oreillé was a wealthy Frenchman from Cork. Not that he was wealthy when he first came from Cork, but just the reverse. When he first landed in New York with his wife, he had only halted at Castle Garden[110] for a few minutes to receive and exhibit papers showing that he had resided in this country two years—and then he voted the democratic ticket and went up town to hunt a house. He found one and then went to work as assistant to an architect and builder, carrying a hod all day and studying politics evenings. Industry and economy soon enabled him to start a low rum shop in a foul locality, and this gave him political influence. In our country it is always our first care to see that our people have the opportunity of voting for their choice of men to represent and govern them—we do not permit our great officials to appoint the little officials. We prefer to have so tremendous a power as that in our own hands. We hold it safest to elect our judges and everybody else. In our cities, the ward meetings elect delegates to the nominating conventions and instruct them whom to nominate. The publicans and their retainers rule the ward meetings (for everybody else hates the worry of politics and stays at home); the delegates from the ward meetings organize as a nominating convention and make up a list of candidates—one convention offering a democratic and another a republican list of—incorruptibles; and then the great meek public come forward at the proper time and make unhampered choice and bless Heaven that they live in a free land where no form of despotism can ever intrude.

Patrick O'Riley (as his name then stood) created friends and influence very fast, for he was always on hand at the police courts to give straw bail[111] for his customers or establish an *alibi* for them in case they had been beating anybody to death on his premises. Consequently he presently became a political leader, and was elected to a petty office under the city government. Out of a meager salary he soon saved money enough to open quite a stylish liquor saloon higher up town, with a faro bank attached and plenty of capital to conduct it with. This gave him fame and great respectability. The position of alderman was forced upon him, and it was just the same as presenting him a gold mine. He had fine horses and carriages, now, and closed up his whiskey mill.

By and by he became a large contractor for city work, and was a bosom friend of the great and good Wm. M. Weed[112] himself, who had stolen $20,000,000 from the city and was a man so envied, so honored, so adored, indeed, that when the sheriff went to his office to arrest him as a felon, that sheriff blushed and apologized, and one of the illustrated papers made a picture of the scene and spoke of the matter in such a way as to show that the editor regretted that the offense of an arrest had been offered to so exalted a personage as Mr. Weed.

Mr. O'Riley furnished shingle nails to the new Court House at three thousand dollars a keg, and eighteen gross of 60-cent thermometers at fifteen hundred dollars a dozen; the controller and the board of audit passed the bills, and a mayor, who was simply ignorant but not criminal, signed them. When they were paid, Mr. O'Riley's admirers gave him a solitaire diamond pin of the size of a filbert, in imitation of the liberality of Mr. Weed's friends, and then Mr. O'Riley retired from active service and amused himself with buying real estate at enormous figures and holding it in other people's names. By and by the newspapers came out with exposures and called Weed and O'Riley "thieves,"—whereupon the people rose as one man (voting repeatedly) and elected the two gentlemen to their proper theatre of action, the New York legislature. The newspapers clamored, and the courts proceeded to try the new legislators for their small irregularities. Our admirable jury system enabled the persecuted ex-officials to secure a jury of nice gentlemen from a neighboring asylum and three graduates from Sing-Sing, and presently they walked forth with characters vindicated. The legislature was called upon to spew them forth— a thing which the legislature declined to do. It was like asking children to repudiate their own father. It was a legislature of the modern pattern.

Being now wealthy and distinguished, Mr. O'Riley, still bearing the legislative "Hon." attached to his name (for titles never die in America, although we *do* take a republican pride in poking fun at such trifles), sailed for Europe with his family. They traveled all about, turning their noses up at every thing, and not finding it a difficult thing to do, either, because nature had originally given those features a cast in that direction; and finally they established themselves in Paris, that Paradise of Americans of their sort.— They staid there two years and learned to speak English with a foreign accent—not that it hadn't always had a foreign accent (which was indeed the case) but now the nature of it was changed. Finally they returned home and became ultra fashionables. They landed here as the Hon. Patrique Oreillé and family, and so are known unto this day.

Laura provided seats for her visitors and they immediately launched forth into a breezy, sparkling conversation with that easy confidence which is to be found only among persons accustomed to high life.

"I've been intending to call sooner, Miss Hawkins," said the Hon. Mrs. Oreillé, "but the weather's been *so* horrid.—How do you like Washington?"

Laura liked it very well indeed.

Mrs. Gashly—"Is it your first visit?"

Yes, it was her first.

All—"Indeed?"

Mrs. Oreillé—"I'm afraid you'll despise the weather, Miss Hawkins. It's perfectly awful. It always is. I tell Mr. Oreillé I can't and I won't put up with any such a climate. If we were obliged to do it, I wouldn't mind it; but we are *not* obliged to, and so I don't see the use of it. Sometimes it's real pitiful the way the children pine for Parry—don't look *so* sad, Bridget, *ma chere*—poor child, she can't hear Parry mentioned without getting the blues."

Mrs. Gashly—"Well I should think so, Mrs. Oreillé. A body *lives* in Paris, but a body only *stays* here. I dote on Paris; I'd druther scrimp along on ten thousand dollars a year there, than suffer and worry here on a real decent income."

Miss Gashly—"Well then I wish you'd take us back, mother; I'm sure *I* hate this stoopid country enough, even if it *is* our dear native land."

Miss Emmeline Gashly—"What, and leave poor Johnny Peterson behind?" [An airy general laugh applauded this sally].

Miss Gashly—"Sister, I should think you'd be ashamed of yourself!"

Miss Emmeline—"Oh, you needn't ruffle your feathers so. I was only joking. He don't mean anything by coming to the house every evening—only comes to see mother. Of course that's all!" [General laughter].

Miss G. prettily confused—"Emmeline, how *can* you!"

Mrs. G.,—"Let your sister alone, Emmeline.—I never saw such a tease!"

Mrs. Oreillé—"What lovely corals you have, Miss Hawkins! Just look at them, Bridget, dear. I've a great passion for corals—it's a pity they're getting a little common. I have some elegant ones—not as elegant as yours, though—but of course I don't wear them now."

Laura—"I suppose they are rather common, but still I have a great affection for these, because they were given to me by a dear old friend of our family named Murphy. He was a very charming man, but very eccentric. We always supposed he was an Irishman, but after he got rich he went abroad for a year or two, and when he came back you would have been amused to see how interested he was in a potato. He asked what it was! Now you know that when Providence shapes a mouth especially for the accommodation of a potato you can detect that fact at a glance when that mouth is in repose—foreign travel can never remove *that* sign. But he was a very delightful gentleman, and his little foible did not hurt him at all. We all have our shams—I suppose there is a sham somewhere about every individual, if we could manage to ferret it out. I would so like to go to France. I suppose our society here compares very favorably with French society does it not, Mrs. Oreillé?"

Mrs. O.—"Not by any means, Miss Hawkins! French society is much more elegant—much more so."

Laura—"I am sorry to hear that. I suppose ours has deteriorated of late."

Mrs. O.—"Very much indeed. There are people in society here that have really no more money to live on than what some of us pay for servant hire. Still I won't say but what some of them are very good people—and respectable, too."

Laura—"The old families seem to be holding themselves aloof, from what I hear. I suppose you seldom meet in society now, the people you used to be familiar with twelve or fifteen years ago?"

Mrs. O.—"Oh, no—hardly ever."

Mr. Riley kept his first rum-mill and protected his customers from the law in those days, and this turn of the conversation was rather uncomfortable to madame than otherwise.

Hon. Mrs. Higgins—"Is François' health good now, Mrs. Oreillé?"

Mrs. O.—(*Thankful for the intervention*)—"Not very. A body couldn't expect it. He was always delicate—especially his lungs—and this odious climate tells on him strong, now, after Parry, which is so mild."

Mrs. H.—"I should think so. Husband says Percy'll die if he don't have a change; and so I'm going to swap round a little and see what can be done. I saw a lady from Florida last week, and she recommended Key West. I told her Percy couldn't abide winds, as he was threatened with a pulmonary affection, and then she said try St. Augustine. It's an awful distance—ten or twelve hundred miles, they say—but then in a case of this kind a body can't stand back for trouble, you know."

Mrs. O.—"No, of course that's so. If François don't get better soon we've got to look out for some other place, or else Europe. We've thought some of the Hot Springs,[113] but I don't know. It's a great responsibility and a body wants to go cautious. Is Hildebrand about again, Mrs. Gashly?"

Mrs. G.—"Yes, but that's about all. It was indigestion, you know, and it looks as if it was chronic. And you know I do dread dyspepsia. We've all been worried a good deal about him. The doctor recommended baked apple and spoiled meat, and I think it done him good. It's about the only thing that will stay on his stomach now-a-days. We have Dr. Shovel now. Who's your doctor, Mrs. Higgins?"

Mrs. H.—"Well, we had Dr. Spooner a good while, but he runs so much to emetics, which I think are weakening, that we changed off and took Dr. Leathers. We like him very much. He has a fine European reputation, too. The first thing he suggested for Percy was to have him taken out in the back yard for an airing, every afternoon, with nothing at all on."

Mrs. O. and Mrs. G.—"What!"

Mrs. H.—"As true as I'm sitting here. And it actually helped him for two or three days; it did indeed. But after that the doctor said it seemed to be too severe and so he has fell back on hot footbaths at night and cold showers in the morning. But I don't think there can be any good sound help for him in such a climate as this. I believe we are going to lose him if we don't make a change."

Mrs. O.—"I suppose you heard of the fright we had two weeks ago last Saturday? No? Why that is strange—but come to remember, you've all been away to Richmond. François tumbled from the sky light in the second-story hall clean down to the first floor—"

Everybody—"Mercy!"

Mrs. O.—"Yes indeed—and broke two of his ribs—"

Everybody—"What!"

Mrs. O.—"Just as true as you live. First we thought he must be injured internally. It was fifteen minutes past 8 in the evening. Of course we were all distracted in a moment—everybody was flying everywhere, and nobody doing anything *worth* anything. By and by I flung out next door and dragged in Dr. Sprague, President of the Medical University—no time to go for our own doctor of course—and the minute he saw François he said, 'Send for your own physician, madam'—said it as cross as a bear, too, and turned right on his heel and cleared out without doing a thing!"

Everybody—"The mean, contemptible brute!"

Mrs. O.—"Well, you may say it. I was nearly out of my wits by this time. But we hurried off the servants after our own doctor and telegraphed mother—she was in New York and rushed down on the first train; and when the doctor got there, lo and behold you he found François had broke one of his legs, too!"

Everybody—"Goodness!"

Mrs. O.—"Yes. So he set his leg and bandaged it up, and fixed his ribs and gave him a dose of something to quiet down his excitement and put him to sleep—poor thing he was trembling and frightened to death and it was pitiful to see him. We had him in my bed—Mr. Oreillé slept in the guest room and I laid down beside François—but not to sleep—bless you no. Bridget and I set up all night, and the doctor staid till two in the morning, bless his old heart.—When mother got there she was so used up with anxiety that she had to go to bed and have the doctor; but when she found that François was not in immediate danger she rallied, and by night she was able to take a watch herself. Well for three days and nights we three never left that bedside only to take an hour's nap at a time. And then the doctor said François was out of danger and if ever there was a thankful set, in this world, it was us."

Laura's respect for these women had augmented during this conversation, naturally enough; affection and devotion are qualities that are able to adorn and render beautiful a character that is otherwise unattractive, and even repulsive.

Mrs. Gashly—"I do believe I should a died if I had been in your place, Mrs. Oreillé. The time Hildebrand was so low with the pneumonia Emmeline and me were all alone with him most of the time and we never took a minute's sleep for as much as two days and nights. It was at Newport and we wouldn't trust hired nurses. One afternoon he had a fit, and jumped up and run out on the portico of the hotel with nothing in the world on and the wind a blowing like ice and we after him scared to death; and when the ladies and gentlemen saw that he had a fit, every lady scattered for her room and not a gentleman lifted his hand to help, the wretches! Well after that his life hung by a thread for as much as ten days, and the minute he was out of danger Emmeline and me just went to bed sick and worn out. *I* never want to pass through such a time again. Poor dear François—which leg did he break, Mrs. Oreillé?"

Mrs. O.—"It was his right hand hind leg. Jump down, François dear, and show the ladies what a cruel limp you've got yet."

François demurred, but being coaxed and delivered gently upon the floor, he performed very satisfactorily, with his "right hand hind leg" in the air. All were affected—even Laura—but hers was an affection of the stomach. The country-bred girl had not suspected that the little whining ten-ounce black and tan reptile, clad in a red embroidered pigmy blanket and reposing in Mrs. Oreillé's lap all through the visit was the individual whose sufferings had been stirring the dormant generosities of her nature. She said:

"Poor little creature! You might have lost him!"

Mrs. O.—"O pray don't mention it, Miss Hawkins—it gives me such a turn!"

Laura—"And Hildebrand and Percy—are they—are they like this one?"

Mrs. G.—"No, Hilly has considerable Skye blood in him, I believe."

Mrs. H.—"Percy's the same, only he is two months and ten days older and has his ears cropped.—His father, Martin Farquhar Tupper,[114] was sickly, and died young, but he was the sweetest disposition.—His mother had heart disease but was very gentle and resigned, and a wonderful ratter."*

---

* As impossible and exasperating as this conversation may sound to a person who is not an idiot, it is scarcely in any respect an exaggeration of one which one of us actually listened to in an American drawing room—otherwise we could not venture to put such a chapter into a book which professes to deal with social possibilities. —THE AUTHORS

So carried away had the visitors become by their interest attaching to this discussion of family matters, that their stay had been prolonged to a very improper and unfashionable length; but they suddenly recollected themselves now and took their departure.

Laura's scorn was boundless. The more she thought of these people and their extraordinary talk, the more offensive they seemed to her; and yet she confessed that if one must choose between the two extreme aristocracies it might be best, on the whole, looking at things from a strictly business point of view, to herd with the Parvenus; she was in Washington solely to compass a certain matter and to do it at any cost, and these people might be useful to her, while it was plain that her purposes and her schemes for pushing them would not find favor in the eyes of the Antiques. If it came to choice—and it might come to that, sooner or later—she believed she could come to a decision without much difficulty or many pangs.

But the best aristocracy of the three Washington castes, and really the most powerful, by far, was that of the Middle Ground. It was made up of the families of public men from nearly every state in the Union—men who held positions in both the executive and legislative branches of the government, and whose characters had for years been blemishless, both at home and at the capital. These gentlemen and their households were unostentatious people; they were educated and refined; they troubled themselves but little about the two other orders of nobility, but moved serenely in their wide orbit, confident in their own strength and well aware of the potency of their influence. They had no troublesome appearances to keep up, no rivalries which they cared to distress themselves about, no jealousies to fret over. They could afford to mind their own affairs and leave other combinations to do the same or do otherwise, just as they chose. They were people who were beyond reproach, and that was sufficient.

Senator Dilworthy never came into collision with any of these factions. He labored for them all and with them all. He said that all men were brethren and all were entitled to the honest unselfish help and countenance of a Christian laborer in the public vineyard.

Laura concluded, after reflection, to let circumstances determine the course it might be best for her to pursue as regarded the several aristocracies.

Now it might occur to the reader that perhaps Laura had been somewhat rudely suggestive in her remarks to Mrs. Oreillé when the subject of corals was under discussion, but it did not occur to Laura herself. She was not a person of exaggerated refinement; indeed the society and the influences that had formed her character had not been of a nature calculated to make her so; she thought that "give and take was fair play," and that to parry an offensive thrust with a sarcasm was a neat and legitimate thing to do. She sometimes talked to people in a way which some ladies would consider actually shocking; but Laura prided herself upon some of her exploits of that character. We are sorry we cannot make her a faultless heroine; but we cannot, for the reason that she was human.

She considered herself a superior conversationist. Long ago, when the possibility had first been brought before her mind that some day she might move in Washington society, she had recognized the fact that practiced conversational powers would be a necessary weapon in that field; she had also recognized the fact that since her dealings there must be mainly with men, and men whom she supposed to be exceptionally cultivated and able, she would need heavier shot in her magazine than mere brilliant "society" nothings; whereupon she had at once entered upon a tireless and elaborate course of reading, and had never since ceased to devote every unoccupied moment to this sort of preparation. Having now acquired a happy smattering of various information, she used it with good effect—she passed for a singularly well informed woman in Washington. The quality of her literary tastes had necessarily undergone constant improvement under this regimen, and as necessarily, also, the quality of her language had improved, though it cannot be denied that now and then her former condition of life betrayed itself in just perceptible inelegancies of expression and lapses of grammar.

CHAPTER XXXIV

Eet Jomfru Haar drager staerkere end ti Par Öxen.

WHEN LAURA HAD BEEN in Washington three months, she was still the same person, in one respect, that she was when she first arrived there—that is to say, she still bore the name of Laura Hawkins. Otherwise she was perceptibly changed.—

She had arrived in a state of grievous uncertainty as to what manner of woman she was, physically and intellectually, as compared with eastern women; she was well satisfied, now, that her beauty was confessed, her mind a grade above the average, and her powers of fascination rather extraordinary. So she was at ease upon those points. When she arrived, she was possessed of habits of economy and not possessed of money; now she dressed elaborately, gave but little thought to the cost of things, and was very well fortified financially.—She kept her mother and Washington freely supplied with money, and did the same by Col. Sellers— who always insisted upon giving his note for loans—with interest; he was rigid upon that; she *must* take interest; and one of the Colonel's greatest satisfactions was to go over his accounts and note what a handsome sum this accruing interest amounted to, and what a comfortable though modest support it would yield Laura in case reverses should overtake her. In truth he could not help feeling that he was an efficient shield for her against poverty: and so, if her expensive ways ever troubled him for a brief moment, he presently dismissed the thought and said to himself, "Let her go on—even if she loses everything she is still safe—this interest will always afford her a good easy income."

Laura was on excellent terms with a great many members of Congress, and there was an undercurrent of suspicion in some quarters that she was one of that detested class known as "lobbyists"; but what belle could escape slander in such a city? Fair-minded people declined to condemn her on mere suspicion, and so the injurious talk made no very damaging headway. She was very gay, now, and very celebrated, and she might well expect to be assailed by many kinds of gossip. She was growing used to celebrity, and could already sit calm and seemingly unconscious, under the fire of fifty lorgnettes in a theatre, or even overhear the low voice "That's she!" as she passed along the street without betraying annoyance.

The whole air was full of a vague vast scheme which was to eventuate in filling Laura's pockets with millions of money; some had one idea of the scheme, and some another, but nobody had any exact knowledge upon the subject. All that any one felt sure about, was that Laura's landed estates were princely in value and extent, and that the government was anxious to get hold of them for public purposes, and that Laura was willing to make the sale but not at all anxious about the matter and not at all in a hurry. It was whispered that Senator Dilworthy was a stumbling block in the way of an immediate sale, because he was resolved that the government should not have the lands except with the understanding that they should be devoted to the uplifting of the negro race; Laura did not care what they were devoted to, it was said, (a world of very different gossip to the contrary notwithstanding), but there were several other heirs and they would be guided entirely by the Senator's wishes; and finally, many people averred that while it would be easy to sell the lands to the government for the benefit of the negro, by resorting to the usual methods of influencing votes, Senator Dilworthy was unwilling to have so noble a charity sullied by any taint of corruption—he was resolved that not a vote should be bought. Nobody could get anything definite from Laura about these matters, and so gossip had to feed itself chiefly upon guesses. But the effect of it all was, that Laura was considered to be very wealthy and likely to be vastly more so in a little while. Consequently she was much courted and as much envied. Her wealth attracted many suitors. Perhaps they came to worship her riches, but they remained to worship her. Some of the noblest men of the time succumbed to her fascinations. She frowned upon no lover when he made his first advances, but by and by when he was hopelessly enthralled, he learned from her own lips that she had formed a resolution never to marry. Then he would go away hating and cursing the whole sex, and she would calmly add his scalp to her string, while she mused upon the bitter day that Col. Selby trampled her love and her pride in the dust. In time it came to be said that her way was paved with broken hearts.

Poor Washington gradually woke up to the fact that he too was an intellectual marvel as well as his gifted sister. He could not conceive how it had come about (it did not occur to him that the gossip about his family's great wealth had anything to do with it). He could not account for it by any process of reasoning, and was simply obliged to accept the fact and give up trying to solve the riddle. He found himself dragged into society and courted, wondered at and envied very much as if he were one of those foreign barbers who flit over here now and then with a self-conferred title of nobility and marry some rich fool's absurd daughter. Sometimes at a dinner party or a reception he would find himself the centre of interest, and feel unutterably uncomfortable in the discovery. Being obliged to say something, he would mine his brain and put in a blast and when the smoke and flying debris had cleared away the result would be what seemed to him but a poor little intellectual clod of dirt or two, and then he would be astonished to see everybody as lost in admiration as if he had brought up a ton or two of virgin gold. Every remark he made delighted his hearers and compelled their applause; he overhead people say he was exceedingly bright—they were chiefly mammas and marriageable young ladies. He found that some of his good things were being repeated about the town. Whenever he heard of an instance of this kind, he would keep that particular remark in mind and analyze it at home in private. At first he could not see that the remark was anything better than a parrot might originate; but by and by he began to feel that perhaps he underrated his powers; and after that he used to analyze his good things with a deal of comfort, and find in them a brilliancy which would have been unapparent to him in earlier days—and then he would make a note of that good thing and say it again the first time he found himself in a new company. Presently he had saved up quite a repertoire of brilliancies; and after that he confined himself to repeating these and ceased to originate any more, lest he might injure his reputation by an unlucky effort.

He was constantly having young ladies thrust upon his notice at receptions, or left upon his hands at parties, and in time he began to feel that he was being deliberately persecuted in this way; and after that he could not enjoy society because of his constant dread of these female ambushes and surprises. He was distressed to find that nearly every time he showed a young lady a polite attention he was straightway reported to be engaged to her; and as some of these reports got into the newspapers occasionally, he had to keep writing to Louise that they were lies and she must believe in him and not mind them or allow them to grieve her.

Washington was as much in the dark as anybody with regard to the great wealth that was hovering in the air and seemingly on the point of tumbling into the family pocket. Laura would give him no satisfaction. All she would say, was:

"Wait. Be patient. You will see."

"But will it be soon, Laura?"

"It will not be very long, I think."

"But what makes you think so?"

"I have reasons—and good ones. Just wait, and be patient."

"But is it going to be as much as people say it is?"

"What do they say it is?"

"Oh, ever so much. Millions!"

"Yes, it will be a great sum."

"But *how* great, Laura? Will it be millions?"

"Yes, you may call it that. Yes, it *will* be millions. There, now—does that satisfy you?"

"Splendid! I can wait. I can wait patiently—ever so patiently. Once I was near selling the land for twenty thousand dollars; once for thirty thousand dollars; once after that for seven thousand dollars; and once for forty thousand dollars—but something always told me not to do it. What a fool I would have been to sell it for such a beggarly trifle! It *is* the land that's to bring the money, isn't it Laura? You can tell me that much, can't you?"

"Yes, I don't mind saying that much. It *is* the land. But mind—don't ever hint that you got it from me. Don't mention me in the matter at all, Washington."

"All right—I won't. Millions! Isn't it splendid! I mean to look around for a building lot; a lot with fine ornamental shrubbery and all that sort of thing. I will do it to-day. And I might as well see an architect, too, and get him to go to work at a plan for a house. I don't intend to spare any expense; I mean to have the noblest house that money can build." Then after a pause—he did not notice Laura's smiles—"Laura, would you lay the main hall in encaustic tiles, or just in fancy patterns of hard wood?"

Laura laughed a good old-fashioned laugh that had more of her former natural self about it than any sound that had issued from her mouth in many weeks. She said:

"*You* don't change, Washington. You still begin to squander a fortune right and left the instant you hear of it in the distance; you never wait till the foremost dollar of it arrives within a hundred miles of you,"—and she kissed her brother good bye and left him weltering in his dreams, so to speak.

He got up and walked the floor feverishly during two hours; and when he sat down he had married Louise, built a house, reared a family, married them off, spent upwards of eight hundred thousand dollars on mere luxuries, and died worth twelve millions.

CHAPTER XXXV

"Mi-x-in tzakcaamah, x-in tzakcolobch chirech nu zaki caam, nu zaki colo. nu chincu, nu galgab, nu zalmet" . . . . .

Rabinal-Achi.

Chascus hom a sas palmas deves se meteys viradas.

LAURA WENT DOWNSTAIRS, knocked at the study door, and entered, scarcely waiting for the response. Senator Dilworthy was alone—with an open Bible in his hand, upside down. Laura smiled, and said, forgetting her acquired correctness of speech,

"It is only me."

"Ah, come in, sit down," and the Senator closed the book and laid it down. "I wanted to see you. Time to report progress from the committee of the whole," and the Senator beamed with his own congressional wit.

"In the committee of the whole things are working very well. We have made ever so much progress in a week. I believe that you and I together could run this government beautifully, uncle."

The Senator beamed again. He liked to be called "uncle" by this beautiful woman.

"Did you see Hopperson last night after the congressional prayer meeting?"

"Yes. He came. He's a kind of—"

"Eh? he is one of my friends, Laura. He's a fine man, a very fine man. I don't know any man in Congress I'd sooner go to for help in any Christian work. What did he say?"

"Oh, he beat around a little. He said he should like to help the negro, his heart went out to the negro, and all that—plenty of them say that—but he was a little afraid of the Tennessee Land bill; if Senator Dilworthy wasn't in it, he should suspect there was a fraud on the government."

"He said that, did he?"

"Yes. And he said he felt he couldn't vote for it. He was shy."

"Not shy, child, cautious. He's a very cautious man. I have

been with him a great deal on conference committees. He wants reasons, good ones. Didn't you show him he was in error about the bill?"

"I did. I went over the whole thing. I had to tell him some of the side arrangements, some of the—"

"You didn't mention me?"

"Oh, no. I told him you were daft about the negro and the philanthropy part of it, as you are."

"Daft is a little strong, Laura. But you know that I wouldn't touch this bill if it were not for the public good, and for the good of the colored race, much as I am interested in the heirs of this property, and would like to have them succeed."

Laura looked a little incredulous, and the Senator proceeded.

"Don't misunderstand *me*, Laura. I don't deny that it is for the interest of all of us that this bill should go through, and it will. I have no concealments from you. But I have one principle in my public life, which I should like you to keep in mind; it has always been my guide. I never push a private interest if it is not justified and ennobled by some larger public good. I doubt if a Christian would be justified in working for his own salvation if it was not to aid in the salvation of his fellow men."

The Senator spoke with feeling, and then added,

"I hope you showed Hopperson that our motives were pure?"

"Yes, and he seemed to have a new light on the measure. I think he will vote for it."

"I hope so; his name will give tone and strength to it. I knew you would only have to show him that it was just and pure, in order to secure his cordial support."

"I think I convinced him. Yes, I am perfectly sure he will vote right now."

"That's good, that's good," said the Senator, smiling, and rubbing his hands. "Is there anything more?"

"You'll find some changes in that I guess," handing the Senator a printed list of names. "Those checked off are all right."

"Ah—'m —'m," running his eye down the list. "That's encouraging. What is the 'C' before some of the names and the 'B. B.'?"

"Those are my private marks. That 'C' stands for 'convinced,' with argument. The 'B. B.' is a general sign for a relative. You see it stands before three of the Hon. Committee. I expect to see the chairman of the committee to-day, Mr. Buckstone."

"So you must, he ought to be seen without any delay. Buckstone is a worldly sort of a fellow, but he has charitable impulses. If we secure him we shall have a favorable report by the committee, and it will be a great thing to be able to state that fact quietly where it will do good."

"Oh, I saw Senator Balloon."

"He will help us, I suppose? Balloon is a whole-hearted fellow. I can't *help* loving that man, for all his drollery and waggishness. He puts on an air of levity sometimes, but there ain't a man in the senate knows the scriptures as he does. He did not make any objections?"

"Not exactly, he said—shall I tell you what he said?" asked Laura glancing furtively at him.

"Certainly."

"He said he had no doubt it was a good thing; if Senator Dilworthy was in it, it would pay to look into it."

The Senator laughed, but rather feebly, and said, "Balloon is always full of his jokes."

"I explained it to him. He said it was all right, he only wanted a word with you," continued Laura. "He is a handsome old gentleman, and he is gallant for an old man."

"My daughter," said the Senator, with a grave look, "I trust there was nothing free in his manner?"

"Free?" repeated Laura, with indignation in her face. "With *me!*"

"There, there, child. I meant nothing. Balloon talks a little freely sometimes, with men. But he is right at heart. His term expires next year and I fear we shall lose him."

"He seemed to be packing the day I was there. His rooms were full of dry-goods boxes, into which his servant was crowding all manner of old clothes and stuff. I suppose he will paint 'Pub. Docs' on them and frank them home. That's good economy, isn't it?"

"Yes, yes, but child, all Congressmen do that. It may not be strictly honest, indeed it is not unless he had some public documents mixed in with the clothes."

"It's a funny world. Good-bye, uncle. I'm going to see that chairman."

And humming a cheery opera air, she departed to her room to dress for going out. Before she did that, however, she took out her note book and was soon deep in its contents, marking, dashing, erasing, figuring, and talking to herself.

"Free! I wonder what Dilworthy *does* think of me anyway? One ... two ... eight ... seventeen ... twenty-one, ... 'm'm ... it takes a heap for a majority. Wouldn't Dilworthy open his eyes if he knew some of the things Balloon *did* say to me. There. ... Hopperson's influence ought to count twenty .... the sanctimonious old curmudgeon. Son-in-law .... sinecure in the negro institution. ... That about gauges *him*. .... The three committeemen .... sons-in-law. Nothing like a son-in-law here in Washington .... or a brother-in law .... And everybody has 'em. .... Let's see .... sixty-one .... with places; .... twenty-five ... persuaded—it is getting on; .... we'll have two-thirds of Congress in time. .... Dilworthy must surely know I understand him. Uncle Dilworthy .... Uncle Balloon! ... Tells very amusing stories .... when ladies are not present. ... I should think so. ... 'm ... 'm. Eighty-five. ... There. I must find that chairman. Queer .... Buckstone acts. .... Seemed to be in love. .... I was *sure* of it. He promised to come here. ... and he hasn't. ... Strange. *Very* strange. ... I must chance to meet him today."

Laura dressed and went out, thinking she was perhaps too early for Mr. Buckstone to come from the house, but as he lodged near the bookstore she would drop in there and keep a look out for him.

While Laura is on her errand to find Mr. Buckstone, it may not be out of the way to remark that she knew quite as much of Washington life as Senator Dilworthy gave her credit for, and more than she thought proper to tell him. She was acquainted by this time with a good many of the young fellows of Newspaper Row, and exchanged gossip with them to their mutual advantage.

They were always talking in the Row, everlastingly gossiping, bantering and sarcastically praising things, and going on in a style which was a curious commingling of earnest and persiflage. Col. Sellers liked this talk amazingly, though he was sometimes a little at sea in it—and perhaps that didn't lessen the relish of the conversation to the correspondents.

It seems that they had got hold of the dry-goods box packing story about Balloon, one day, and were talking it over when the Colonel came in. The Colonel wanted to know all about it, and Hicks told him. And then Hicks went on, with a serious air,

"Colonel, if you register a letter, it means that it is of value, doesn't it? And if you pay fifteen cents for registering it, the government will have to take extra care of it and even pay you back its full value if it is lost. Isn't that so?"

"Yes. I suppose it's so."

"Well Senator Balloon put fifteen cents worth of stamps on each of those seven huge boxes of old clothes, and shipped that ton of second-hand rubbish, old boots and pantaloons and what not through the mails as registered matter! It was an ingenious thing and it had a genuine touch of humor about it, too. I think there is more real talent among our public men of to-day than there was among those of old times—a far more fertile fancy, a much happier ingenuity. Now, Colonel, can you picture Jefferson, or Washington or John Adams franking their wardrobes through the mails and adding the facetious idea of making the government responsible for the cargo for the sum of one dollar and five cents? Statesmen were dull creatures in those days. I have a much greater admiration for Senator Balloon."

"Yes, Balloon is a man of parts, there is no denying it."

"I think so. He is spoken of for the post of Minister to China, or Austria, and I hope will be appointed. What we want abroad is good examples of the national character. John Jay and Benjamin Franklin were well enough in their day, but the nation has made progress since then. Balloon is a man we know and can depend on to be true to—himself."

"Yes, and Balloon has had a good deal of public experience. He is an old friend of mine. He was governor of one of the territories a while, and was very satisfactory."

"Indeed he was. He was ex-officio Indian agent, too. Many a man would have taken the Indian appropriation and devoted the money to feeding and clothing the helpless savages, whose land had been taken from them by the white man in the interests of civilization; but Balloon knew their needs better. He built a government saw-mill on the reservation with the money, and the lumber sold for enormous prices—a relative of his did all the work free of charge—that is to say he charged nothing more than the lumber would bring."

"But the poor Injuns—not that I care much for Injuns—what did he do for them?"

"Gave them the outside slabs to fence in the reservation with. Governor Balloon was nothing less than a father to the poor Indians. But Balloon is not alone, we have many truly noble statesmen in our country's service like Balloon. The Senate is full of them. Don't you think so Colonel?"

"Well, I dunno. I honor my country's public servants as much as any one can. I meet them, sir, every day, and the more I see of them the more I esteem them and the more grateful I am that our institutions give us the opportunity of securing their services. Few lands are so blest."

"That is true, Colonel. To be sure you can buy now and then a Senator or a Representative; but they do not know it is wrong, and so they are not ashamed of it. They are gentle, and confiding and childlike, and in my opinion these are qualities that ennoble them far more than any amount of sinful sagacity could. I quite agree with you, Col. Sellers."

"Well"—hesitated the Colonel—"I am afraid some of them do buy their seats—yes, I am afraid they do—but as Senator Dilworthy himself said to me, it is sinful,—it is very wrong—it is shameful; Heaven protect *me* from such a charge. That is what Dilworthy said. And yet when you come to look at it you cannot deny that we would have to go without the services of some of our ablest men, sir, if the country were opposed to—to—bribery. It is a harsh term. I do not like to use it."

The Colonel interrupted himself at this point to meet an engagement with the Austrian minister, and took his leave with his usual courtly bow.

CHAPTER XXXVI

"Bataïnadon nin-masinaiganan, kakina gaie onijishinon."—"Missawa onijish-ining kakina o masinaiganan, kawin gwetch o-wabandansinan."
Baraga.

புத்தகங்கள்

IN DUE TIME Laura alighted at the book store, and began to look at the titles of the handsome array of books on the counter. A dapper clerk of perhaps nineteen or twenty years, with hair accurately parted and surprisingly slick, came bustling up and leaned over with a pretty smile and an affable—

"Can I—was there any particular book you wished to see?"

"Have you Taine's England?"[115]

"Beg pardon?"

"Taine's Notes on England."

The young gentleman scratched the side of his nose with a cedar pencil[116] which he took down from its bracket on the side of his head, and reflected a moment:

"Ah—I see," [with a bright smile] —"Train, you mean—not Taine. George Francis Train.[117] No, ma'm we—"

"I mean *Taine*—if I may take the liberty."

The clerk reflected again—then:

"Taine. . . . Taine. . . . Is it hymns?"

"No, it isn't hymns. It is a volume that is making a deal of talk just now, and is very widely known—except among parties who sell it."

The clerk glanced at her face to see if a sarcasm might not lurk somewhere in that obscure speech, but the gentle simplicity of the beautiful eyes that met his, banished that suspicion. He went away and conferred with the proprietor. Both appeared to be nonplussed. They thought and talked, and talked and thought by turns. Then both came forward and the proprietor said:

"Is it an American book, ma'm?"

"No, it is an American reprint of an English translation."

"Oh! Yes—yes—I remember, now. We are expecting it every day. It isn't out yet."

"I think you must be mistaken, because you advertised it a week ago."

"Why no—can that be so?"

"Yes, I am sure of it. And besides, here is the book itself, on the counter."

She bought it and the proprietor retired from the field. Then she asked the clerk for the Autocrat of the Breakfast Table—and was pained to see the admiration her beauty had inspired in him fade out of his face. He said with cold dignity, that cook books were somewhat out of their line, but he would order it if she desired it. She said, no, never mind. Then she fell to conning the titles again, finding a delight in the inspection of the Hawthornes, the Longfellows, the Tennysons, and other favorites of her idle hours. Meantime the clerk's eyes were busy, and no doubt his admiration was returning again—or may be he was only gauging her probable literary tastes by some sagacious system of admeasurement only known to his guild. Now he began to "assist" her in making a selection; but his efforts met with no success—indeed they only annoyed her and unpleasantly interrupted her meditations. Presently, while she was holding a copy of "Venetian Life"[118] in her hand and running over a familiar passage here and there, the clerk said, briskly, snatching up a paper-covered volume and striking the counter a smart blow with it to dislodge the dust:

"Now here is a work that we've sold a lot of. Everybody that's read it likes it"—and he intruded it under her nose; "it's a book that I can recommend—'The Pirate's Doom, or the Last of the Buccaneers.' I think it's one of the best things that's come out this season."

Laura pushed it gently aside with her hand and went on filching from "Venetian Life."

"I believe I do not want it," she said.

The clerk hunted around awhile, glancing at one title and then another, but apparently not finding what he wanted. However, he succeeded at last. Said he:

"Have you ever read this, ma'm? I am sure you'll like it. It's by the author of 'The Hooligans of Hackensack.' It is full of love troubles and mysteries and all sorts of such things. The heroine strangles her own mother. Just glance at the title please,— 'Gonderil the Vampire, or The Dance of Death.' And here is 'The Jokist's Own Treasury, or, The Phunny Phellow's Bosom Phriend.' The funniest thing!—I've read it four times, ma'm, and I can laugh at the very sight of it yet. And 'Gonderil,'—I assure you it is the most splendid book I ever read. I know you will like these books, ma'm, because I've read them myself and I know what they are."

"Oh, I was perplexed—but I see how it is, now. You must have thought I asked you to tell me what sort of books I wanted—for I am apt to say things which I don't really mean, when I am absent minded. I suppose I did ask you, didn't I?"

"No ma'm,—but I—"

"Yes, I must have done it, else you would not have offered your services, for fear it might be rude. But don't be troubled—it was all my fault. I ought not to have been so heedless—I ought not to have asked you."

"But you didn't ask me, ma'm. We always help customers all we can. You see our experience—living right among books all the time—that sort of thing makes us able to help a customer make a selection, you know."

"Now does it, indeed? It is part of your business, then?"

"Yes'm, we always help."

"How good it is of you. Some people would think it rather obtrusive, perhaps, but I don't—think it is real kindness—even charity. Some people jump to conclusions without any thought—you have noticed that?"

"O yes," said the clerk, a little perplexed as to whether to feel comfortable or the reverse; "oh yes, indeed, I've often noticed that, ma'm."

"Yes, they jump to conclusions with an absurd heedlessness. Now some people would think it odd that because you, with the budding tastes and the innocent enthusiasms natural to your time of life, enjoyed the Vampires and the volume of nursery jokes, you should imagine that an older person would delight in them too—but I do not think it odd at all. I think it natural—perfectly natural—in you. And kind, too. You look like a person who not

only finds a deep pleasure in any little thing in the way of literature that strikes you forcibly, but is willing and glad to share that
pleasure with others—and that, I think, is noble and admirable—
very noble and admirable. I think we ought all to share our pleasures with others, and do what we can to make each other happy,
do not you?"

"Oh, yes. Oh, yes, indeed. Yes, you are quite right, ma'm."

But he was getting unmistakably uncomfortable, now, notwithstanding Laura's confiding sociability and almost affectionate tone.

"Yes, indeed. Many people would think that what a book-
seller—or perhaps his clerk—knows about literature *as* literature,
in contradistinction to its character as merchandise, would hardly
be of much assistance to a person—that is, to an adult, of course—
in the selection of food for the mind—except of course wrapping
paper, or twine, or wafers, or something like that—but I never feel
that way. I feel that whatever service you offer me, you offer with
a good heart, and I am as grateful for it as if it were the greatest
boon to me. And it *is* useful to me—it is bound to be so.—It cannot be otherwise. If you show me a book which you have read—
not skimmed over or merely glanced at, but *read*—and you tell
me that *you* enjoyed it and that *you* could read it three or four
times, then I know what book I want—"

"Thank you! —th—"

—"to avoid. Yes indeed. I think that no information ever
comes amiss in this world. Once or twice I have traveled in the
cars—and there you know, the peanut boy always measures you
with his eye, and hands you out a book of murders if you are fond
of theology; or Tupper[119] or a dictionary or T. S. Arthur[120] if you
are fond of poetry; or he hands you a volume of distressing jokes
or a copy of the American Miscellany[121] if you particularly dislike
that sort of literary fatty degeneration of the heart—just for the
world like a pleasant-spoken well-meaning gentleman in any
bookstore—. But here I am running on as if business men had
nothing to do but listen to women talk. You must pardon me, for
I was not thinking.—And you must let me thank you again for
helping me. I read a good deal, and shall be in nearly every day;
and I would be sorry to have you think me a customer who talks

too much and buys too little. Might I ask you to give me the time? Ah—two—twenty-two. Thank you very much. I will set mine while I have the opportunity."

But she could not get her watch open, apparently. She tried, and tried again. Then the clerk, trembling at his own audacity, begged to be allowed to assist. She allowed him. He succeeded, and was radiant under the sweet influences of her pleased face and her seductively worded acknowledgments with gratification. Then he gave her the exact time again, and anxiously watched her turn the hands slowly till they reached the precise spot without accident or loss of life, and then he looked as happy as a man who had helped a fellow being through a momentous undertaking, and was grateful to know that he had not lived in vain. Laura thanked him once more. The words were music to his ear; but what were they compared to the ravishing smile with which she flooded his whole system? When she bowed her adieu and turned away, he was no longer suffering torture in the pillory where she had had him trussed up during so many distressing moments, but he belonged to the list of her conquests and was a flattered and happy thrall, with the dawn-light of love breaking over the eastern elevations of his heart.

It was about the hour, now, for the chairman of the House Committee on Benevolent Appropriations to make his appearance, and Laura stepped to the door to reconnoitre. She glanced up the street, and sure enough—

CHAPTER XXXVII

𒀭 𒂠 𒐼 𒐊 𒐉 𒐈 𒐌 𒑊

Usa ogn' artela donna, onde sia cólto
Nella sua rete alcun novello amante;
Nè con tutti, nè sempre un stesso volto
Serba, ma cangia a tempo atti e sembiante.
Tasso.

THAT CHAIRMAN was nowhere in sight. Such disappointments seldom occur in novels, but are always happening in real life.

She was obliged to make a new plan. She sent him a note, and asked him to call in the evening—which he did.

She received the Hon. Mr. Buckstone with a sunny smile, and said:

"I don't know how I ever dared to send you a note, Mr. Buckstone, for you have the reputation of not being very partial to our sex."

"Why I am sure my reputation does me wrong, then, Miss Hawkins. I have been married once—is that nothing in my favor?"

"Oh, yes—that is, it may be and it may not be. If you have known what perfection is in woman, it is fair to argue that inferiority cannot interest you now."

"Even if that were the case it could not affect *you*, Miss Hawkins," said the chairman gallantly. "Fame does not place you in the list of ladies who rank below perfection."

This happy speech delighted Mr. Buckstone as much as it seemed to delight Laura. But it did not confuse him as much as it apparently did her.

"I wish in all sincerity that I could be worthy of such a felicitous compliment as that. But I am a woman, and so I am gratified for it just as it is, and would not have it altered."

"But it is not merely a compliment—that is, an empty compliment—it is the truth. All men will endorse that."

Laura looked pleased, and said:

"It is very kind of you to say it. It is a distinction indeed, for a country-bred girl like me to be so spoken of by people of brains and culture. You are so kind that I know you will pardon my putting you to the trouble to come this evening."

"Indeed it was no trouble. It was a pleasure. I am alone in the world since I lost my wife, and I often long for the society of your sex, Miss Hawkins, notwithstanding what people may say to the contrary."

"It is pleasant to hear you say that. I am sure it must be so. If I feel lonely at times, because of my exile from old friends, although surrounded by new ones who are already very dear to me, how much more lonely must you feel, bereft as you are, and with no wholesome relief from the cares of state that weigh you down. For your own sake, as well as for the sake of others, you ought to go into society oftener. I seldom see you at a reception, and when I do you do not usually give me very much of your attention."

"I never imagined that you wished it or I would have been very glad to make myself happy in that way.—But one seldom gets an opportunity to say more than a sentence to you in a place like that. You are always the centre of a group—a fact which you may have noticed yourself. But if one might come here—"

"Indeed you would always find a hearty welcome, Mr. Buckstone. I have often wished you would come and tell me more about Cairo and the Pyramids, as you once promised me you would."

"Why, do you remember that yet, Miss Hawkins? I thought ladies' memories were more fickle than that."

"Oh, they are not so fickle as gentlemen's promises. And besides, if I had been inclined to forget, I—did you not give me something by way of a remembrancer?"

"Did I?"

"Think."

"It does seem to me that I did; but I have forgotten what it was now."

"Never, never call a lady's memory fickle again! Do you recognize this?"

"A little spray of box![122] I am beaten—I surrender. But have you kept that all this time?"

Laura's confusion was very pretty. She tried to hide it, but the more she tried the more manifest it became and withal the more captivating to look upon. Presently she threw the spray of box from her with an annoyed air, and said:

"I forgot myself. I have been very foolish. I beg that you will forget this absurd thing."

Mr. Buckstone picked up the spray, and sitting down by Laura's side on the sofa, said:

"Please let me keep it, Miss Hawkins. I set a very high value upon it now."

"Give it to me, Mr. Buckstone, and do not speak so. I have been sufficiently punished for my thoughtlessness. You cannot take pleasure in adding to my distress. Please give it to me."

"Indeed I do not wish to distress you. But do not consider the matter so gravely; you have done yourself no wrong. You probably forgot that you had it; but if you had given it to me I would have kept it—and not forgotten it."

"Do not talk so, Mr. Buckstone. Give it to me, please, and forget the matter."

"It would not be kind to refuse, since it troubles you so, and so I restore it. But if you would give me part of it and keep the rest—"

"So that you might have something to remind you of me when you wished to laugh at my foolishness?"

"Oh, by no means, no! Simply that I might remember that I had once assisted to discomfort you, and be reminded to do so no more."

Laura looked up, and scanned his face a moment. She was about to break the twig, but she hesitated and said:

"If I were sure that you—" She threw the spray away, and continued: "This is silly! We will change the subject. No, do not insist—I must have my way in this."

Then Mr. Buckstone drew off his forces and proceeded to make a wily advance upon the fortress under cover of carefully-contrived artifices and stratagems of war. But he contended with an alert and suspicious enemy; and so at the end of two hours it was manifest to him that he had made but little progress. Still, he had made some; he was sure of that.

Laura sat alone and communed with herself;

"He is fairly hooked, poor thing. I can play him at my leisure and land him when I choose. He was all ready to be caught, days and days ago—I saw that, very well. He will vote for our bill—no fear about that; and moreover he will work for it, too, before I am done with him. If he had a woman's eyes he would have noticed that the spray of box had grown three inches since he first gave it to me, but a man never sees anything and never suspects. If I had shown him a whole bush he would have thought it was the same. Well, it is a good night's work: the committee is safe. But this is a desperate game I am playing in these days—a wearing, sordid, heartless game. If I lose, I lose everything—even myself. And if I win the game, will it be worth its cost after all? I do not know. Sometimes I doubt. Sometimes I half wish I had not begun. But no matter; I *have* begun, and I will never turn back; never while I live."

Mr. Buckstone indulged in a reverie as he walked homeward:

"She is shrewd and deep, and plays her cards with considerable discretion—but she will lose, for all that. There is no hurry; I shall come out winner, all in good time. She *is* the most beautiful woman in the world; and she surpassed herself to-night. I suppose I must vote for that bill, in the end maybe; but that is not a matter of much consequence—the government can stand it. She is bent on capturing me, that is plain; but she will find by and by that what she took for a sleeping garrison was an ambuscade."

CHAPTER XXXVIII

Now this surprising news scaus'd her fall in a trance,
Life as she were dead, no limbs she could advance,
Then her dear brother came, her from the ground he took
And she spake up and said, O my poor heart is broke.
The Barnardcastle Tragedy.

"DON'T YOU THINK he is distinguished looking?"

"What! That gawky looking person, with Miss Hawkins?"

"There. He's just speaking to Mrs. Schoonmaker. Such high-bred negligence and unconsciousness. Nothing studied. See his fine eyes."

"Very. They are moving this way now. Maybe he is coming here. But he looks as helpless as a rag baby. Who is he, Blanche?"

"Who is he? And you've been here a week, Grace, and don't know? He's the catch of the season. That's Washington Hawkins—her brother."

"No, is it?"

"Very old family, old Kentucky family I believe. He's got enormous landed property in Tennessee, I think. The family lost everything, slaves and that sort of thing, you know, in the war. But they have a great deal of land, minerals, mines and all that. Mr. Hawkins and his sister too are very much interested in the amelioration of the condition of the colored race; they have some plan, with Senator Dilworthy, to convert a large part of their property to something another[123] for the freedmen."

"You don't say so? I thought he was some guy from Pennsylvania. But he *is* different from others. Probably he has lived all his life on his plantation."

It was a day reception of Mrs. Representative Schoonmaker, a sweet woman, of simple and sincere manners. Her house was one of the most popular in Washington. There was less ostentation there than in some others, and people liked to go where the atmosphere reminded them of the peace and purity of home. Mrs. Schoonmaker was as natural and unaffected in Washington society as she was in her own New York house, and kept up the spirit of home-life there, with her husband and children. And that was the reason, probably, why people of refinement liked to go there.

Washington is a microcosm, and one can suit himself with any sort of society within a radius of a mile. To a large portion of the people who frequent Washington or dwell there, the ultra fashion, the shoddy, the jobbery are as utterly distasteful as they would be in a refined New England City. Schoonmaker was not exactly a leader in the House, but he was greatly respected for his fine talents and his honesty. No one would have thought of offering to carry National Improvement Directors Relief stock for him.

These day receptions were attended by more women than men, and those interested in the problem might have studied the costumes of the ladies present, in view of this fact, to discover whether women dress more for the eyes of women or for effect upon men. It is a very important problem, and has been a good deal discussed, and its solution would form one fixed, philosophical basis, upon which to estimate woman's character. We are inclined to take a medium ground, and aver that woman dresses to please herself, and in obedience to a law of her own nature.

"They are coming this way," said Blanche. People who made way for them to pass, turned to look at them. Washington began to feel that the eyes of the public were on him also, and his eyes rolled about, now towards the ceiling, now towards the floor, in an effort to look unconscious.

"Good morning, Miss Hawkins. Delighted. Mr. Hawkins. My friend, Miss Medlar."

Mr. Hawkins, who was endeavoring to square himself for a bow, put his foot through the train of Mrs. Senator Poplin, who looked round with a scowl, which turned into a smile as she saw who it was. In extricating himself, Mr. Hawkins, who had the care of his hat as well as the introduction on his mind, shambled against Miss Blanche, who said *pardon*, with the prettiest accent, as if the awkwardness were her own. And Mr. Hawkins righted himself.

"Don't you find it very warm to-day, Mr. Hawkins?" said Blanche, by way of a remark.

"It's awful hot," said Washington.

"It's warm for the season," continued Blanche pleasantly. "But I suppose you are accustomed to it," she added, with a general idea that the thermometer always stands at 90° in all parts of the late slave states. "Washington weather generally cannot be very congenial to you?"

"It's congenial," said Washington brightening up, "when it's not congealed."

"That's very good. Did you hear, Grace, Mr. Hawkins says it's congenial when it's not congealed."

"What is, dear?" said Grace, who was talking with Laura.

The conversation was now finely under way. Washington launched out an observation of his own.

"Did you see those Japs,[124] Miss Leavitt?"

"Oh, yes, aren't they queer. But so high-bred, so picturesque. Do you think that color makes any difference, Mr. Hawkins? I used to be so prejudiced against color."

"Did you? I never was. I used to think my old mammy was handsome."

"How interesting your life must have been! I should like to hear about it."

Washington was about settling himself into his narrative style, when Mrs. Gen. McFingal caught his eye.

"Have you been at the Capitol to-day, Mr. Hawkins?"

Washington had not. "Is anything uncommon going on?"

"They say it was very exciting. The Alabama business[125] you know. Gen. Sutler,[126] of Massachusetts, defied England, and they say he wants war."

"He wants to make himself conspicuous more like," said Laura. "He always, you have noticed, talks with one eye on the gallery, while the other is on the speaker."

"Well, my husband says, its nonsense to talk of war, and wicked. *He* knows what war is. If we *do* have war, I hope it will be for the patriots of Cuba. Don't you think we want Cuba, Mr. Hawkins?"

"I think we want it bad," said Washington. "And Santo Domingo. Senator Dilworthy says, we are bound to extend our religion over the isles of the sea. We've got to round out our territory, and"

Washington's further observations were broken off by Laura, who whisked him off to another part of the room, and reminded him that they must make their adieux.

"How stupid and tiresome these people are," she said. "Let's go."

They were turning to say good-by to the hostess, when Laura's attention was arrested by the sight of a gentleman who was just speaking to Mrs. Schoonmaker. For a second her heart stopped beating. He was a handsome man of forty and perhaps more, with grayish hair and whiskers, and he walked with a cane, as if he were slightly lame. He might be less than forty, for his face was worn into hard lines, and he was pale.

No. It could not be, she said to herself. It is only a resemblance. But as the gentleman turned and she saw his full face, Laura put out her hand and clutched Washington's arm to prevent herself from falling.

Washington, who was not minding anything, as usual looked 'round in wonder. Laura's eyes were blazing fire and hatred; he had never seen her look so before; and her face was livid.

"Why, what is it, sis? Your face is as white as paper."

"It's he, it's he. Come, come," and she dragged him away.

"It's who?" asked Washington, when they had gained the carriage.

"It's nobody, it's nothing. Did I say he? I was faint with the heat. Don't mention it. Don't you speak of it," she added earnestly, grasping his arm.

When she had gained her room she went to the glass and saw a pallid and haggard face.

"My God," she cried, "this will never do. I should have killed him, if I could. The scoundrel still lives, and dares to come here. I ought to kill him. He has no right to live. How I hate him. And yet I loved him. Oh heavens, how I did love that man. And why didn't he kill me? He might better. He did kill all that was good in me. Oh, but he shall not escape. He shall not escape this time. He may have forgotten. He will find that a woman's hate doesn't forget. The law? What would the law do but protect him and make me an outcast? How all Washington would gather up its virtuous skirts and avoid me, if it knew. I wonder if he hates me as I do him?"

So Laura raved, in tears and in rage by turns, tossed in a tumult of passion, which she gave way to with little effort to control.

A servant came to summon her to dinner. She had a headache. The hour came for the President's reception. She had a raving headache, and the Senator must go without her.

That night of agony was like another night she recalled. How vividly it all came back to her. And at that time she remembered she thought she might be mistaken. He might come back to her. Perhaps he loved her, a little, after all. *Now,* she knew he did not. Now, she knew he was a cold-blooded scoundrel, without pity. Never a word in all these years. She had hoped he was dead. Did his wife live, she wondered. She caught at that, and it gave a new current to her thoughts. Perhaps, after all—she must see him. She could not live without seeing him. Would he smile as in the old days when she loved him so; or would he sneer as when she last saw him? If he looked so, she hated him. If he should call her "Laura, darling," and look *so!* She must find him. She must end her doubts.

Laura kept her room for two days, on one excuse and another—a nervous headache, a cold—to the great anxiety of the Senator's household. Callers, who went away, said she had been too gay—they did not say "fast," though some of them may have thought it. One so conspicuous and successful in society as Laura could not be out of the way two days, without remarks being made, and not all of them complimentary.

When she came down she appeared as usual, a little pale may be, but unchanged in manner. If there were any deepened lines about the eyes they had been concealed. Her course of action was quite determined.

At breakfast she asked if any one had heard any unusual noise during the night? Nobody had. Washington never heard any noise of any kind after his eyes were shut. Some people thought he never did when they were open either.

Senator Dilworthy said he had come in late. He was detained in a little consultation after the Congressional prayer meeting. Perhaps it was his entrance.

No, Laura said. She heard that. It was later. She might have been nervous, but she fancied somebody was trying to get into the house.

Mr. Brierly humorously suggested that it might be, as none of the members were occupied in night session.

The Senator frowned, and said he did not like to hear that kind of newspaper slang. There might be burglars about.

Laura said that very likely it was only her nervousness. But she thought she would feel safer if Washington would let her take one of his pistols. Washington brought her one of his revolvers, and instructed her in the art of loading and firing it.

During the morning Laura drove down to Mrs. Schoonmaker's to pay a friendly call.

"Your receptions are always delightful," she said to that lady, "the pleasant people all seem to come here."

"It's pleasant to hear you say so, Miss Hawkins. I believe my friends like to come here. Though society in Washington is mixed; we have a little of everything."

"I suppose, though, you don't see much of the old rebel element?" said Laura with a smile.

If this seemed to Mrs. Schoonmaker a singular remark for a lady to make, who was meeting "rebels" in society every day, she did not express it in any way, but only said,

"You know we don't say 'rebel' anymore. Before we came to Washington I thought rebels would look unlike other people. I find we are very much alike, and that kindness and good nature wear away prejudice. And then you know there are all sorts of common interests. My husband sometimes says that he doesn't see but confederates are just as eager to get at the treasury as Unionists. You know that Mr. Schoonmaker is on the appropriations."

"Does he know many Southerners?"

"Oh, yes. There were several at my reception the other day. Among others a confederate Colonel—a stranger—handsome man with gray hair, probably you didn't notice him, uses a cane in walking. A very agreeable man. I wondered why he called. When my husband came home and looked over the cards, he said he had a cotton claim.[127] A real southerner. Perhaps you might know him if I could think of his name. Yes, here's his card—Louisiana."

Laura took the card, looked at it intently till she was sure of the address, and then laid it down, with,

"No, he is no friend of ours."

That afternoon, Laura wrote and dispatched the following note. It was in a round hand, unlike her flowing style, and it was directed to a number and street in Georgetown:—

"A Lady at Senator Dilworthy's would like to see Col. George Selby, on business connected with the Cotton Claims. Can he call Wednesday at three o'clock P. M.?"

On Wednesday at 3 P. M. no one of the family was likely to be in the house except Laura.

CHAPTER XXXIX

—Belhs amics, tornatz,
Per merce, vas me de cors.
Alphonse II.

Ala khambiatü da zure deseiña?
Hitz eman zenereitan,
Ez behin, bal berritan,
Enia zinela.
—Ohikua nüzü;
Enüzü khambiatü,
Bihotzian beinin hartü,
Eta zü maithatü.
Maitia, nun zira?

COL. SELBY HAD JUST COME to Washington, and taken lodgings in Georgetown.[128] His business was to get pay for some cotton that was destroyed during the war. There were many others in Washington on the same errand, some of them with claims as difficult to establish as his. A concert of action was necessary, and he was not, therefore, at all surprised to receive the note from a lady asking him to call at Senator Dilworthy's.

At a little after three on Wednesday he rang the bell of the Senator's residence. It was a handsome mansion on the Square opposite the President's house. The owner must be a man of great wealth, the Colonel thought; perhaps, who knows, said he with a smile, he may have got some of my cotton in exchange for salt and quinine after the capture of New Orleans. As this thought passed through his mind he was looking at the remarkable figure of the Hero of New Orleans,[129] holding itself by main strength from sliding off the back of the rearing bronze horse, and lifting its hat in the manner of one who acknowledges the playing of that martial air: "See, the Conquering Hero Comes!" "Gad," said the Colonel to himself, "Old Hickory ought to get down and give his seat to Gen. Sutler—but they'd have to tie him on."[130]

Laura was in the drawing room. She heard the bell, she heard the steps in the hall, and the emphatic thud of the supporting cane. She had risen from her chair and was leaning against the piano, pressing her left hand against the violent beating of her heart. The door opened and the Colonel entered, standing in the full light of the opposite window. Laura was more in the shadow and stood for an instant, long enough for the Colonel to make the inward observation that she was a magnificent woman. She then advanced a step.

"Col. Selby, is it not?"

The Colonel staggered back, caught himself by a chair, and turned towards her a look of terror.

"Laura? My God!"

"Yes, your wife!"

"Oh, no, it can't be. How came you here? I thought you were—"

"You thought I was dead? You thought you were rid of me? Not so long as you live, Col. Selby, not so long as you live," Laura in her passion was hurried on to say.

No man had ever accused Col. Selby of cowardice. But he was a coward before this woman. May be he was not the man he once was. Where was his coolness? Where was his sneering, imperturbable manner, with which he could have met, and would have met, any woman he had wronged, if he had only been forewarned. He felt now that he must temporize, that he must gain time. There was danger in Laura's tone. There was something frightful in her calmness. Her steady eyes seemed to devour him.

"You have ruined my life," she said; "and I was so young, so ignorant, and loved you so. You betrayed me, and left me, mocking me and trampling me into the dust, a soiled cast-off. You might better have killed me then. Then I should not have hated you."

"Laura," said the Colonel, nerving himself, but still pale, and speaking appealingly, "don't say that. Reproach me. I deserve it. I was a scoundrel. I was everything monstrous. But your beauty made me crazy. You are right. I was a brute in leaving you as I did. But what could I do? I was married, and—"

"And your wife still lives?" asked Laura, bending a little forward in her eagerness.

The Colonel noticed the action, and he almost said "no," but he thought of the folly of attempting concealment.

"Yes. She is here."

What little color had wandered back into Laura's face forsook it again. Her heart stood still, her strength seemed going from her limbs. Her last hope was gone. The room swam before her for a moment, and the Colonel stepped towards her, but she waved him back, as hot anger again coursed through her veins, and said,

"And you dare come with her, *here*, and tell me of it, here and mock me with it! And you think I will have it, George? You think I will let you live with that woman? You think I am as powerless as that day I fell dead at your feet?"

She raged now. She was in a tempest of excitement. And she advanced towards him with a threatening mien. She would kill me if she could, thought the Colonel; but he thought at the same moment, how beautiful she is. He had recovered his head now. She was lovely when he knew her, then a simple country girl. Now she was dazzling, in the fullness of ripe womanhood, a superb creature, with all the fascination that a woman of the world has for such a man as Col. Selby. Nothing of this was lost on him. He stepped quickly to her, grasped both her hands in his, and said,

"Laura, stop! think! Suppose I loved you yet! Suppose I hated my fate! What can I do? I am broken by the war. I have lost everything almost. I had as lief be dead and done with it."

The Colonel spoke with a low remembered voice that thrilled through Laura. He was looking into her eyes as he had looked in those old days, when no birds of all those that sang in the groves where they walked sang a note of warning. He was wounded. He had been punished. Her strength forsook her with her rage, and she sank upon a chair, sobbing,

"Oh! my God, I thought I hated him!"

The Colonel knelt beside her. He took her hand and she let him keep it. She looked down into his face, with a pitiable tenderness, and said in a weak voice,

"And you do love me a little?"

The Colonel vowed and protested. He kissed her hand and her lips. He swore his false soul into perdition.

She wanted love, this woman. Was not her love for George

Selby deeper than any other woman's could be? Had she not a right to him? Did he not belong to her by virtue of her overmastering passion? His wife—she was not his wife, except by the law. She could not be. Even with the law she could have no right to stand between two souls that were one. It was an infamous condition in society that George should be tied to *her*.

Laura thought this, believed it, because she desired to believe it. She came to it as an original proposition, founded on the requirements of her own nature. She may have heard, doubtless she had, similar theories that were prevalent at that day, theories of the tyranny of marriage and of the freedom of marriage. She had even heard women lecturers say that marriage should only continue so long as it pleased either party to it—for a year, or a month, or a day. She had not given much heed to this. But she saw its justice now in a flash of revealing desire. It must be right. God would not have permitted her to love George Selby as she did, and him to love her, if it was right for society to raise up a barrier between them. He belonged to her. Had he not confessed it himself?

Not even the religious atmosphere of Senator Dilworthy's house had been sufficient to instill into Laura that deep Christian principle which had been somehow omitted in her training. Indeed in that very house had she not heard women, prominent before the country and besieging Congress, utter sentiments that fully justified the course she was marking out for herself?[131]

They were seated now, side by side, talking with more calmness. Laura was happy, or thought she was. But it was that feverish sort of happiness which is snatched out of the black shadow of falsehood, and is at the moment recognized as fleeting and perilous, and indulged tremblingly. She loved. She was loved. That is happiness certainly. And the black past and the troubled present and the uncertain future could not snatch that from her.

What did they say as they sat there? What nothings do people usually say in such circumstances, even if they are three-score and ten? It was enough for Laura to hear his voice and be near him. It was enough for him to be near her, and avoid committing himself as much as he could. Enough for him was the present also. Had there not always been some way out of such scrapes?

And yet Laura could not be quite content without prying into to-morrow. *How* could the Colonel manage to free himself from his wife? Would it be long? Could he not go into some State where it would not take much time? He could not say exactly. That they must think of. That they must talk over. And so on. Did this seem like a damnable plot to Laura against the life, maybe, of a sister, a woman like herself? Probably not. It was right that this man should be hers, and there were some obstacles in the way. That was all. There are as good reasons for bad actions as for good ones, to those who commit them. When one has broken the tenth commandment, the others are not of much account.

Was it unnatural, therefore, that when George Selby departed, Laura should watch him from the window, with an almost joyful heart as he went down the sunny square? "I shall see him tomorrow," she said, "and the next day, and the next. He is mine now."

"Damn the woman," said the Colonel as he picked his way down the steps. "Or," he added, as his thoughts took a new turn, "I wish my wife was in New Orleans."

CHAPTER XL

Open your ears; for which of you will stop
The vent of hearing, when loud Rumor speaks?
I, from the orient to the drooping west,
Making the wind my post-horse, still unfold
The acts commenced on this ball of earth:
Upon my tongues continual slanders ride;
The which in every language I pronounce,
Stuffing the ears of men with false reports.
King Henry IV.

AS MAY BE READILY BELIEVED, Col. Beriah Sellers was by this time one of the best known men in Washington. For the first time in his life his talents had a fair field.

He was now at the centre of the manufacture of gigantic schemes, of speculations of all sorts, of political and social gossip. The atmosphere was full of little and big rumors and of vast, undefined expectations. Everybody was in haste, too, to push on his private plan, and feverish in his haste, as if in constant apprehension that to-morrow would be Judgment Day. Work while Congress is in session, said the uneasy spirit, for in the recess there is no work and no device.

The Colonel enjoyed this bustle and confusion amazingly; he thrived in the air of indefinite expectation. All his own schemes took larger shape and more misty and majestic proportions; and in this congenial air, the Colonel seemed even to himself to expand into something large and mysterious. If he respected himself before, he almost worshiped Beriah Sellers now, as a superior being. If he could have chosen an official position out of the highest, he would have been embarrassed in the selection. The presidency of the republic seemed *too* limited and cramped in the constitutional restrictions. If he could have been Grand Llama of the United States, that might have come the nearest to his idea of a position. And next to that he would have luxuriated in the irresponsible omniscience of the Special Correspondent.

Col. Sellers knew the President very well, and had access to his presence when officials were kept cooling their heels in the waiting-room. The President liked to hear the Colonel talk, his voluble ease was a refreshment after the decorous dullness of men who only talked business and government, and overlastingly expounded their notions of justice and the distribution of patronage. The Colonel was as much a lover of farming and of horses as Thomas Jefferson was. He talked to the President by the hour about his magnificent stud, and his plantation at Hawkeye, a kind of principality he represented it. He urged the President to pay him a visit during the recess, and see his stock farm.

"This President's table is well enough," he used to say, to the loafers who gathered about him at Willard's,[132] "well enough for a man on a salary, but God bless my soul, I should like him to see a little old-fashioned hospitality—open house, you know. A person seeing me at home might think I paid no attention to what was in the house, just let things flow in and out. He'd be mistaken. What I look to is quality, sir. The President has variety enough, but the quality! Vegetables of course you can't expect here. I'm very particular about mine. Take celery, now—there's only one spot in this country where celery will grow. But I *am* surprised about the wines. I should think they were manufactured in the New York Custom House.[133] I must send the President some from my cellar. I was really mortified the other day at dinner to see Blacque Bey[134] leave his standing in the glasses."

When the Colonel first came to Washington he had thoughts of taking the mission to Constantinople, in order to be on the spot to look after the dissemination of his Eye Water, but as that invention was not yet quite ready, the project shrank a little in the presence of vaster schemes. Besides he felt that he could do the country more good by remaining at home. He was one of the Southerners who were constantly quoted as heartily "accepting the situation."

"I'm whipped," he used to say with a jolly laugh, "the government was too many for me; I'm cleaned out, done for, except my plantation and private mansion. We played for a big thing, and lost it, and I don't whine, for one. I go for putting the old flag on all the vacant lots. I said to the President, says I, 'Grant, why don't you take Santo Domingo,[135] annex the whole thing, and settle the bill afterwards.' That's my way. I'd take the job to manage Congress. The South would come into it. You've got to conciliate the South, consolidate the two debts,[136] pay 'em off in greenbacks[137] and go ahead. That's my notion. Boutwell's[138] got the right notion about the value of paper, but he lacks courage. I *should* like to run the treasury department about six months. I'd make things plenty, and business look up."

The Colonel had access to the departments. He knew all the senators and representatives, and especially the lobby. He was consequently a great favorite in Newspaper Row, and was often lounging in the offices there, dropping bits of private, official information, which were immediately caught up and telegraphed all over the country. But it used to surprise even the Colonel when he read it, it was embellished to that degree that he hardly recognized it, and the hint was not lost on him. He began to exaggerate his heretofore simple conversation to suit the newspaper demand.

People used to wonder in the winters of 187— and 187—, where the "Specials" got that remarkable information with which they every morning surprised the country, revealing the most secret intentions of the President and his cabinet, the private thoughts of political leaders, the hidden meaning of every movement. This information was furnished by Col. Sellers.

When he was asked, afterwards, about the stolen copy of the Alabama Treaty which got into the "New York Tribune," he only looked mysterious, and said that neither he nor Senator Dilworthy knew anything about it. But those whom he was in the habit of meeting occasionally felt almost certain that he did know.

It must not be supposed that the Colonel in his general patriotic labors neglected his own affairs. The Columbus River Navigation Scheme absorbed only a part of his time, so he was enabled to throw quite a strong reserve force of energy into the Tennessee Land plan, a vast enterprise commensurate with his abilities, and in the prosecution of which he was greatly aided by Mr. Henry Brierly, who was buzzing about the capitol and the hotels day and night, and making capital for it in some mysterious way.

"We must create a public opinion," said Senator Dilworthy. "My only interest in it is a public one, and if the country wants the institution, Congress will have to yield."

It may have been after a conversation between the Colonel and Senator Dilworthy that the following special despatch was sent to a New York newspaper: —

"We understand that a philanthropic plan is on foot in relation to the colored race that will, if successful, revolutionize the whole character of southern industry. An experimental institution is in contemplation in Tennessee which will do for that state what the Industrial School at Zurich did for Switzerland. We learn that approaches have been made to the heirs of the late Hon. Silas Hawkins of Missouri, in reference to a lease of a portion of their valuable property in East Tennessee. Senator Dilworthy, it is understood, is inflexibly opposed to any arrangement that will not give the government absolute control. Private interests must give way to the public good. It is to be hoped that Col. Sellers, who represents the heirs, will be led to see the matter in this light."

When Washington Hawkins read his despatch, he went to the Colonel in some anxiety. He was for a lease, he didn't want to surrender anything. What did he think the government would offer? Two millions?

"May be three, may be four," said the Colonel, "it's worth more than the bank of England."

"If they will not lease," said Washington, "let 'em make it two millions for an undivided half. I'm not going to throw it away, not the whole of it."

Harry told the Colonel that they must drive the thing through, he couldn't be dallying round Washington when Spring opened. Phil wanted him, Phil had a great thing on hand up in Pennsylvania.

"What is that?" inquired the Colonel, always ready to interest himself in anything large.

"A mountain of coal; that's all. He's going to run a tunnel into it in the Spring."

"Does he want any capital?" asked the Colonel, in the tone of a man who is given to calculating carefully before he makes an investment.

"No. Old man Bolton's behind him. He has capital, but I judged that he wanted my experience in starting."

"If he wants me, tell him I'll come, after Congress adjourns. I should like to give him a little lift. He lacks enterprise—now, about that Columbus River. He doesn't see his chances. But he's a good fellow, and you can tell him that Sellers won't go back on him."

"By the way," asked Harry, "who is that rather handsome party that's hanging 'round Laura? I see him with her everywhere, at the Capitol, in the horse cars, and he comes to Dilworthy's. If he weren't lame, I should think he was going to run off with her."

"Oh, that's nothing. Laura knows her business. He has a cotton claim. Used to be at Hawkeye during the war—Selby's his name, was a Colonel. Got a wife and family. Very respectable people, the Selbys."

"Well, that's all right," said Harry, "if it's business. But if a woman looked at me as I've seen her at Selby, I should understand it. And it's talked about, I can tell you."

Jealousy had no doubt sharpened this young gentleman's observation. Laura could not have treated him with more lofty condescension if she had been the Queen of Sheba, on a royal visit to the great republic. And he resented it, and was "huffy" when he was with her, and ran her errands, and brought her gossip, and bragged of his intimacy with the lovely creature among the fellows at Newspaper Row.

Laura's life was rushing on now in the full stream of intrigue and fashionable dissipation. She was conspicuous at the balls of the fastest set, and was suspected of being present at those doubtful suppers that began late and ended early. If Senator Dilworthy remonstrated about appearances, she had a way of silencing him. Perhaps she had some hold on him, perhaps she was necessary to his plan for ameliorating the condition of the colored race.

She saw Col. Selby, when the public knew and when it did not know. She would see him, whatever excuses he made, and however he avoided her. She was urged on by a fever of love and hatred and jealousy, which alternately possessed her. Sometimes she petted him, and coaxed him and tried all her fascinations. And again she threatened him and reproached him. What was he doing? Why had he taken no steps to free himself? Why didn't he send his wife home? She should have *money* soon. They could go to Europe,—anywhere. What did she care for talk?

And he promised, and lied, and invented fresh excuses for delay, like a cowardly gambler and roué as he was, fearing to break with her, and half the time unwilling to give her up.

"That woman doesn't know what fear is," he said to himself, "and she watches me like a hawk."

He told his wife that this woman was a lobbyist, whom he had to tolerate and use in getting through his claims, and that he should pay her and have done with her, when he succeeded.

CHAPTER XLI

وَزِادَهُ كَلَفًا فِى الحُبِّ أَنْ مَنَعَتْ
وَحُبُّ شَيْئًا اَلَى الاِنْسَانِ مَا مُنِعَا

Táj el'-Aroos.

Egundano yçan daya ni baydienetacoric?
Ny amoriac enu mayte, nic hura ecin gayecxi.
Bern. d'Echeparre.

HENRY BRIERLY was at the Dilworthy's constantly and on such terms of intimacy that he came and went without question. The Senator was not an inhospitable man, he liked to have guests in his house, and Harry's gay humor and rattling way entertained him; for even the most devout men and busy statesmen must have hours of relaxation.

Harry himself believed that he was of great service in the University business, and that the success of the scheme depended upon him to a great degree. He spent many hours in talking it over with the Senator after dinner. He went so far as to consider whether it would be worth his while to take the professorship of civil engineering in the new institution.

But it was not the Senator's society nor his dinners—at which this scapegrace remarked that there was too much grace and too little wine—which attracted him to the house. The fact was the poor fellow hung around there day after day for the chance of seeing Laura for five minutes at a time. For her presence at dinner he would endure the long bore of the Senator's talk afterwards, while Laura was off at some assembly, or excused herself on the plea of fatigue. Now and then he accompanied her to some reception, and rarely, on off nights, he was blessed with her company in the parlor, when he sang, and was chatty and vivacious and performed a hundred little tricks of imitation and ventriloquism, and made himself as entertaining as a man could be.

It puzzled him not a little that all his fascinations seemed to go for so little with Laura; it was beyond his experience with women. Sometimes Laura was exceedingly kind and petted him a little, and took the trouble to exert her powers of pleasing, and to entangle him deeper and deeper. But this, it angered him afterwards to think, was in private; in public she was beyond his reach, and never gave occasion to the suspicion that she had any affair with him. He was never permitted to achieve the dignity of a serious flirtation with her in public.

"Why do you treat me so?" he once said, reproachfully.

"Treat you how?" asked Laura in a sweet voice, lifting her eyebrows.

"You know well enough. You let other fellows monopolize you in society, and you are as indifferent to me as if we were strangers."

"Can I help it if they are attentive, can I be rude? But we are such old friends, Mr. Brierly, that I didn't suppose you would be jealous."

"I think I must be a very old friend, then, by your conduct towards me. By the same rule I should judge that Col. Selby must be very new."

Laura looked up quickly, as if about to return an indignant answer to such impertinence, but she only said, "Well, what of Col. Selby, sauce-box?"

"Nothing, probably, you'll care for. Your being with him so much is the town talk, that's all?"

"What do people say?" asked Laura calmly.

"Oh, they say a good many things. You are offended, though, to have me speak of it?"

"Not in the least. You are my true friend. I feel that I can trust you. You wouldn't deceive me, Harry?" throwing into her eyes a look of trust and tenderness that melted away all his petulance and distrust. "What do they say?"

"Some say that you've lost your head about him; others that you don't care any more for him than you do for a dozen others, but that he is completely fascinated with you and about to desert his wife; and others say it is nonsense to suppose you would entangle yourself with a married man, and that your intimacy only arises from the matter of the cotton claims, for which he wants your influence with Dilworthy. But you know everybody is talked about more or less in Washington. I shouldn't care; but I wish you wouldn't have so much to do with Selby, Laura," continued Harry, fancying that he was now upon such terms that his advice would be heeded.

"And you believed these slanders?"

"I don't believe anything against you, Laura, but Col. Selby does not mean you any good. I know you wouldn't be seen with him if you knew his reputation."

"Do you know him?" Laura asked, as indifferently as she could.

"Only a little. I was at his lodgings in Georgetown a day or two ago, with Col. Sellers. Sellers wanted to talk with him about some patent remedy he has, Eye Water, or something of that sort, which he wants to introduce into Europe. Selby is going abroad very soon."

Laura started, in spite of her self-control.

"And his wife? Does he take his family? Did you see his wife?"

"Yes. A dark little woman, rather worn—must have been pretty once though. Has three or four children, one of them a baby. They'll all go, of course. She said she should be glad enough to get away from Washington. You know Selby has got his claim allowed, and they say he has had a run of luck lately at Morrissey's."[139]

Laura heard all this in a kind of stupor, looking straight at Harry, without seeing him. Is it possible, she was thinking, that this base wretch, after all his promises, will take his wife and children and leave me? Is it possible the town is saying all these things about me? And—a look of bitterness coming into her face—does the fool think he can escape so?

"You are angry with me, Laura," said Harry, not comprehending in the least what was going on in her mind.

"Angry?" she said, forcing herself to come back to his presence. "With you? Oh, no. I'm angry with the cruel world, which pursues an independent woman as it never does a man. I'm grateful to you, Harry; I'm grateful to you for telling me of that odious man."

And she rose from her chair and gave him her pretty hand, which the silly fellow took, and kissed and clung to. And he said many silly things, before she disengaged herself gently, and left him, saying it was time to dress, for dinner.

And Harry went away, excited, and a little hopeful, but only a little. The happiness was only a gleam, which departed and left him thoroughly miserable. She never would love him, and she was going to the devil, besides. He couldn't shut his eyes to what he saw, nor his ears to what he heard of her.

What had come over this trifling young lady-killer? It was a pity to see such a gay butterfly broken on a wheel. Was there something good in him, after all, that had been touched? He was in fact madly in love with this woman. It is not for us to analyze the passion and say whether it was a worthy one. It absorbed his whole nature and made him wretched enough. If he deserved punishment, what more would you have? Perhaps this love was kindling a new heroism in him.

He saw the road on which Laura was going clear enough, though he did not believe the worst he heard of her. He loved her too passionately to credit that for a moment. And it seemed to him that if he could compel her to recognize her position, and his own devotion, she might love him, and that he could save her. His love was so far ennobled, and become a very different thing from its beginning in Hawkeye. Whether he ever thought that if he could save her from ruin, he could give her up himself, is doubtful. Such a pitch of virtue does not occur often in real life, especially in such natures as Harry's, whose generosity and unselfishness were matters of temperament rather than habits or principles.

He wrote a long letter to Laura, an incoherent, passionate letter, pouring out his love as he could not do in her presence, and warning her as plainly as he dared of the dangers that surrounded her, and the risks she ran of compromising herself in many ways.

Laura read the letter, with a little sigh may be, as she thought of other days, but with contempt also, and she put it into the fire with the thought, "They are all alike."

Harry was in the habit of writing to Philip freely, and boasting also about his doings, as he could not help doing and remain himself. Mixed up with his own exploits, and his daily triumphs as a lobbyist, especially in the matter of the new University, in which

Harry was to have something handsome, were amusing sketches of Washington society, hints about Dilworthy, stories about Col. Sellers, who had become a well-known character, and wise remarks upon the machinery of private legislation for the public good, which greatly entertained Philip in his convalescence.

Laura's name occurred very often in these letters, at first in casual mention as the belle of the season, carrying everything before her with her wit and beauty, and then more seriously, as if Harry did not exactly like so much general admiration of her, and was a little nettled by her treatment of him. This was so different from Harry's usual tone about women, that Philip wondered a good deal over it. Could it be possible that he was seriously affected? Then came stories about Laura, town talk, gossip which Harry denied the truth of indignantly; but he was evidently uneasy, and at length wrote in such miserable spirits that Philip asked him squarely what the trouble was; was he in love?

Upon this, Harry made a clean breast of it, and told Philip all he knew about the Selby affair, and Laura's treatment of him, sometimes encouraging him and then throwing him off, and finally his belief that she would go to the bad if something was not done to arouse her from her infatuation. He wished Philip was in Washington. He knew Laura, and she had a great respect for his character, his opinions, his judgment. Perhaps he, as an uninterested person in whom she would have some confidence, and as one of the public, could say something to her that would show her where she stood.

Philip saw the situation clearly enough. Of Laura he knew not much, except that she was a woman of uncommon fascination, and he thought from what he had seen of her in Hawkeye, her conduct towards him and towards Harry, of not too much principle. Of course he knew nothing of her history; he knew nothing seriously against her, and if Harry was desperately enamored of her, why should he not win her if he could. If, however, she had already become what Harry uneasily felt she might become, was it not his duty to go to the rescue of his friend and try to save him from any rash act on account of a woman that might prove to be entirely unworthy of him; for trifler and visionary as he was, Harry deserved a better fate than this.

Philip determined to go to Washington and see for himself. He had other reasons also. He began to know enough of Mr. Bolton's affairs to be uneasy. Pennybacker had been there several times during the winter, and he suspected that he was involving Mr. Bolton in some doubtful scheme. Pennybacker was in Washington, and Philip thought he might perhaps find out something about him, and his plans, that would be of service to Mr. Bolton.

Philip had enjoyed his winter very well, for a man with his arm broken and his head smashed. With two such nurses as Ruth and Alice, illness seemed to him rather a nice holiday, and every moment of his convalescence had been precious and all too fleeting. With a young fellow of the habits of Philip, such injuries cannot be counted on to tarry long, even for the purpose of love-making, and Philip found himself getting strong with even disagreeable rapidity.

During his first weeks of pain and weakness, Ruth was unceasing in her ministrations; she quietly took charge of him, and with a gentle firmness resisted all attempts of Alice or any one else to share to any great extent the burden with her. She was clear, decisive and peremptory in whatever she did; but often when Philip opened his eyes in those first days of suffering and found her standing by his bedside, he saw a look of tenderness in her anxious face that quickened his already feverish pulse, a look that remained in his heart long after he closed his eyes. Sometimes he felt her hand on his forehead, and did not open his eyes for fear she would take it away. He watched for her coming to his chamber; he could distinguish her light footstep from all others. If this is what is meant by women practicing medicine, thought Philip to himself, I like it.

"Ruth," said he one day when he was getting to be quite himself, "I believe in it?"

"Believe in what?"

"Why, in women physicians."

"Then, I'd better call in Mrs. Dr. Longstreet."

"Oh, no. One will do, one at a time. I think I should be well tomorrow, if I thought I should never have any other."

"Thy physician thinks thee mustn't talk, Philip," said Ruth putting her finger on his lips.

"But, Ruth, I want to tell you that I should wish I never had got well if—"

"There, there, thee must *not* talk. Thee is wandering again," and Ruth closed his lips, with a smile on her own that broadened into a merry laugh as she ran away.

Philip was not weary, however, of making these attempts, he rather enjoyed it. But whenever he inclined to be sentimental, Ruth would cut him off, with some such gravely conceived speech as, "Does thee think that thy physician will take advantage of the condition of a man who is as weak as thee is? I will call Alice, if thee has any dying confessions to make."

As Philip convalesced, Alice more and more took Ruth's place as his entertainer, and read to him by the hour, when he did not want to talk—to talk about Ruth, as he did a good deal of the time. Nor was this altogether unsatisfactory to Philip. He was always happy and contented with Alice. She was the most restful person he knew. Better informed than Ruth and with a much more varied culture, and bright and sympathetic, he was never weary of her company, if he was not greatly excited by it. She had upon his mind that peaceful influence that Mrs. Bolton had when, occasionally, she sat by his bedside with her work. Some people have this influence, which is like an emanation. They bring peace to a house, they diffuse serene content in a room full of mixed company, though they may say very little, and are apparently unconscious of their own power.

Not that Philip did not long for Ruth's presence all the same. Since he was well enough to be about the house, she was busy again with her studies. Now and then her teasing humor came again. She always had a playful shield against his sentiment. Philip used sometimes to declare that she had no sentiment; and then he doubted if he should be pleased with her after all if she were at all sentimental; and he rejoiced that she had, in such matters, what he called the airy grace of sanity. She was the most gay serious person he ever saw.

Perhaps he was not so much at rest or so contented with her as with Alice. But then he loved her. And what have rest and contentment to do with love?

CHAPTER XLII

Subtle. Would I were hang'd then! I'll conform myself.
Dol. Will you, sir? do so then, and quickly: swear.
Sub. What should I swear?
Dol. To leave your faction, sir,
   And labour kindly in the common work.
                                             The Alchemist.

Eku edue mfine, mfine ata eku: miduehe mfine, mfine itaha.
                                             Epik Proverb.

MR. BUCKSTONE'S CAMPAIGN was brief—much briefer than he
supposed it would be. He began it purposing to win Laura without being won himself; but his experience was that of all who had
fought on that field before him; he diligently continued his effort
to win her, but he presently found that while as yet he could not
feel entirely certain of having won her, it was very manifest that
she had won him. He had made an able fight, brief as it was, and
that at least was to his credit. He was in good company, now; he
walked in a leash of conspicuous captives. These unfortunates followed Laura helplessly, for whenever she took a prisoner he remained her slave henceforth. Sometimes they chafed in their
bondage; sometimes they tore themselves free and said their serf-
dom was ended; but sooner or later they always came back peni-
tent and worshiping. Laura pursued her usual course: she
encouraged Mr. Buckstone by turns, and by turns she harassed
him; she exalted him to the clouds at one time, and at another she
dragged him down again. She constituted him chief champion of
the Knobs University bill, and he accepted the position, at first reluctantly, but later as a valued means of serving her—he even
came to look upon it as a piece of great good fortune, since it
brought him into such frequent contact with her.

Through him she learned that the Hon. Mr. Trollop was a bitter enemy of her bill. He urged he not to attempt to influence Mr.
Trollop in any way, and explained that whatever she might at-

tempt in that direction would surely be used against her and with damaging effect.

She at first said she knew Mr. Trollop, "and was aware that he had a Blank-Blank";* but Mr. Buckstone said that while he was not able to conceive what so curious a phrase as Blank-Blank might mean, and had no wish to pry into the matter, since it was probably private, he "would nevertheless venture the blind assertion that *nothing* would answer in this particular case and during this particular session but to be exceedingly wary and keep clear away from Mr. Trollop; any other course would be fatal."

It seemed that nothing could be done. Laura was seriously troubled. Everything was looking well, and yet it was plain that one vigorous and determined enemy might eventually succeed in overthrowing all her plans. A suggestion came into her mind presently and she said:

"Can't you fight against his great Pension bill and bring him to terms?"

"Oh, never; he and I are sworn brothers on that measure; we work in harness and are very loving—I do everything I possibly can for him there. But I work with might and main against his Immigration bill,—as pertinaciously and as vindictively, indeed, as he works against our University. We hate each other through half a conversation and are all affection through the other half. We understand each other. He is an admirable worker outside the capitol; he will do more for the Pension bill than any other man could do; I wish he would make the great speech on it which he wants to make—and then I would make another and we would be safe."

"Well if he wants to make a great speech why doesn't he do it?"

Visitors interrupted the conversation and Mr. Buckstone took his leave. It was not of the least moment to Laura that her question had not been answered, inasmuch as it concerned a thing which did not interest her; and yet, human being like, she thought she would have liked to know. An opportunity occurring presently, she put the same question to another person and got an answer that satisfied her. She pondered a good while, that night,

---

* Her private figure of speech for Brother—or Son-in-law.

after she had gone to bed, and when she finally turned over to go to sleep, she had thought out a new scheme. The next evening at Mrs. Gloverson's party, she said to Mr. Buckstone:

"I want Mr. Trollop to make his great speech on the Pension bill."

"*Do* you! But you remember I was interrupted, and did not explain to you—"

"Never mind, I know. You must make him make that speech. I very particularly desire it."

"Oh, it is easy to say make him do it, but *how* am I to make him?"

"It is perfectly easy; I have thought it all out."

She then went into the details. At length Mr. Buckstone said:

"I see now. I can manage it, I am sure. Indeed I wonder he never thought of it himself—there are no end of precedents. But how is this going to benefit you, after I *have* managed it? There is where the mystery lies."

"But I will take care of that. It will benefit me a great deal."

"I only wish I could see how; it is the oddest freak. You seem to go the furthest around to get at a thing—but you are in earnest, aren't you?"

"Yes, I am, indeed."

"Very well, I will do it—but why not tell me how you imagine it is going to help you?"

"I will, by and by.—Now there is nobody talking to him. Go straight and do it, there's a good fellow."

A moment or two later the two sworn friends of the Pension bill were talking together, earnestly, and seemingly unconscious of the moving throng about them. They talked an hour, and then Mr. Buckstone came back and said:

"He hardly fancied it at first, but he fell in love with it after a bit. And we have made a compact, too. I am to keep his secret and he is to spare me, in future, when he gets ready to denounce the supporters of the University bill—and I can easily believe he will keep his word on this occasion."

A fortnight elapsed, and the University bill had gathered to itself many friends, meantime. Senator Dilworthy began to think the harvest was ripe. He conferred with Laura privately. She was able to tell him exactly how the House would vote. There was a majority—the bill would pass, unless weak members got frightened at the last, and deserted—a thing pretty likely to occur. The Senator said:

"I wish we had one more good strong man. Now Trollop ought to be on our side, for he is a friend of the negro. But he is against us, and is our bitterest opponent. If he would simply vote No, but keep quiet and not molest us, I would feel perfectly cheerful and content. But perhaps there is no use in thinking of that."

"Why I laid a little plan for his benefit two weeks ago. I think he will be tractable, maybe. He is to come here to-night."

"Look out for him, my child! He means mischief, sure. It is said that he claims to know of improper practices having been used in the interest of this bill, and he thinks he sees a chance to make a great sensation when the bill comes up. Be wary. Be very, very careful, my dear. Do your very ablest talking, now. You can convince a man of anything, when you try. You must convince him that if anything improper has been done, you at least are ignorant of it and sorry for it. And if you *could* only persuade him out of his hostility to the bill, too—but don't overdo the thing; don't seem too anxious, dear."

"I won't; I'll be ever so careful. I'll talk as sweetly to him as if he were my own child! You may trust me—indeed you may."

The door-bell rang.

"That is the gentleman now," said Laura. Senator Dilworthy retired to his study.

Laura welcomed Mr. Trollop, a grave, carefully dressed and very respectable looking man, with a bald head, standing collar and old fashioned watch seals.

"Promptness is a virtue, Mr. Trollop, and I perceive that you have it. You are always prompt with me."

"I always meet my engagements, of every kind, Miss Hawkins."

"It is a quality which is rarer in the world than it has been, I believe. I wished to see you on business, Mr. Trollop."

"I judged so. What can I do for you?"

"You know my bill—the Knobs University bill?"

"Ah, I believe it *is* your bill. I had forgotten. Yes, I know the bill."

"Well, would you mind telling me your opinion of it?"

"Indeed, since you seem to ask it without reserve, I am obliged to say that I do not regard it favorably. I have not seen the bill itself, but from what I can hear, it—it—well, it has a bad look about it. It—"

"Speak it out—never fear."

"Well, it—they say it contemplates a fraud upon the government."

"Well?" said Laura tranquilly.

"Well! *I* say, 'Well?' too."

"Well, suppose it *were* a fraud—which I feel able to deny—would it be the first one?"

"You take a body's breath away! Would you—did you wish me to vote for it? Was that what you wanted to see me about?"

"Your instinct is correct. I *did* want you—I *do* want you to vote for it."

"Vote for a fr—for a measure which is generally believed to be at least questionable? I am afraid we cannot come to an understanding, Miss Hawkins."

"No, I am afraid not—if you have resumed your principles, Mr. Trollop."

"Did you send for me merely to insult me? It is time for me to take my leave, Miss Hawkins."

"No—wait a moment. Don't be offended at a trifle. Do not be offish and unsociable. The Steamship Subsidy bill[140] was a fraud on the government. You voted for it, Mr. Trollop, though you always opposed the measure until after you had an interview one evening with a certain Mrs. McCarter at her house. She was my agent. She was acting for me. Ah, that is right—sit down again. You can be sociable, easily enough if you have a mind to. Well? I am waiting. Have you nothing to say?"

"Miss Hawkins, I voted for that bill because when I came to examine into it—"

"Ah yes. When you came to examine into it. Well, I only want you to examine into *my* bill. Mr. Trollop, you would not sell your vote on that subsidy bill—which was perfectly right—but you accepted of some of the stock, with the understanding that it was to stand in your brother-in-law's name."

"There is no pr—I mean, this is utterly groundless, Miss Hawkins." But the gentleman seemed somewhat uneasy, nevertheless.

"Well, not entirely so, perhaps. I and a person whom we will call Miss Blank (never mind the real name,) were in a closet at your elbow all the while."

Mr. Trollop winced—then he said with dignity:

"Miss Hawkins is it possible that you were capable of such a thing as that?"

"It was bad; I confess that. It *was* bad. Almost as bad as selling one's vote for—but I forget; you did not sell your vote—you only accepted a little trifle, a small token of esteem, for your brother-in-law. Oh, let us come out and be frank with each other. I know you, Mr. Trollop. I have met you on business three or four times; true, I never offered to corrupt your principles—never hinted such a thing; but always when I had finished sounding you, I manipulated you through an agent. Let us be frank. Wear this comely disguise of virtue before the public—it will count there; but here it is out of place. My dear sir, by and by there is going to be an investigation into that National Internal Improvement Directors' Relief Measure of a few years ago, and you know very well that you will be a crippled man, as likely as not, when it is completed."

"It cannot be shown that a man is a knave merely for owning that stock. I am not distressed about the National Improvement Relief Measure."

"Oh indeed I am not trying to distress you. I only wished to make good my assertion that I knew you. Several of you gentlemen bought of that stock (without paying a penny down), received dividends from it, (think of the happy idea of receiving dividends, and very large ones, too, from stock one hasn't paid for!) and all the while your names never appeared in the transaction; if ever you took the stock at all, you took it in other people's names. Now you see, you had to know one of two things; namely, you either knew that the idea of all this preposterous generosity was to bribe you into future legislative friendship, or you *didn't* know it. That is to say, you had to be either a knave or a—well, a fool—there was no middle ground. *You* are not a fool, Mr. Trollop."

"Miss Hawkins you flatter me. But seriously, you do not forget that some of the best and purest men in Congress took that stock in that way?"

"Did Senator Blank?"

"Well, no—I believe not."

"Of course you believe not. Do you suppose he was ever approached, on the subject?"

"Perhaps not."

"If *you* had approached him, for instance, fortified with the fact that some of the best men in Congress, and the purest, etc., etc., what would have been the result?"

"Well, what *would* have been the result?"

"He would have shown you to the door! For Mr. Blank is neither a knave *nor* a fool. There are other men in the Senate and the House whom no one would have been hardy enough to approach with that Relief Stock in that peculiarly generous way, but they are not of the class that *you* regard as the best and purest. No, I say I know you Mr. Trollop. That is to say, one may suggest a thing to Mr. Trollop which it would not do to suggest to Mr. Blank. Mr. Trollop, you are pledged to support the Indigent Congressmen's Retroactive Appropriation which is to come up, either in this or the next session. You do not deny that, even in public. The man that will vote for that bill will break the eighth commandment in any *other* way, sir!"

"But he will not vote for *your* corrupt measure, nevertheless, madam!" exclaimed Mr. Trollop, rising from his seat in a passion.

"Ah, but he will. Sit down again, and let me explain why. Oh, come, don't behave so. It is very unpleasant. Now be good, and you shall have the missing page of your great speech. Here it is!"—and she displayed a sheet of manuscript.

Mr. Trollop turned immediately back from the threshold. It might have been gladness that flashed into his face; it might have been something else; but at any rate there was much astonishment mixed with it.

"Good! Where did you get it? Give it me!"

"Now there is no hurry. Sit down; sit down and let us talk and be friendly."

The gentleman wavered. Then he said:

"No, this is only a subterfuge. I will go. It is not the missing page."

Laura tore off a couple of lines from the bottom of the sheet.

"Now," she said, "you will know whether this is the handwriting or not. You know it *is* the handwriting. Now if you will listen, you will know that this must be the list of statistics which was to be the 'nub' of your great effort, and the accompanying blast the beginning of the burst of eloquence which was continued on the next page—and you will recognize that there was where you broke down."

She read the page. Mr. Trollop said:

"This is perfectly astounding. Still, what is all this to me? It is nothing. It does not concern me. The speech is made, and there an end. I *did* break down for a moment, and in a rather uncomfortable place, since I had led up to those statistics with some grandeur; the hiatus was pleasanter to the House and the galleries than it was to me. But it is no matter now. A week has passed; the jests about it ceased three or four days ago. The whole thing is a matter of indifference to me, Miss Hawkins."

"But you apologized, and promised the statistics for next day. Why didn't you keep your promise?"

"The matter was not of sufficient consequence. The time was gone by to produce an effect with them."

"But I hear that other friends of the Soldiers' Pension Bill desire them very much. I think you ought to let them have them."

"Miss Hawkins, this silly blunder of my copyist evidently has more interest for you than it has for me. I will send my private secretary to you and let him discuss the subject with you at length."

"Did he copy your speech for you?"

"Of course he did. Why all these questions? Tell me—how did you get hold of that page of manuscript? *That* is the only thing that stirs a passing interest in my mind."

"I'm coming to that." Then she said, much as if she were talking to herself: "It does seem like taking a deal of unnecessary pains, for a body to hire another body to construct a great speech for him and then go and get still another body to copy it before it can be read in the House."

"Miss Hawkins, what do you mean by such talk as that?"

"Why I am sure I mean no harm—no harm to anybody in the world. I am certain that I overheard the Hon. Mr. Buckstone either promise to write your great speech for you or else get some other competent person to do it."

"This is perfectly absurd, madam, perfectly absurd!" and Mr. Trollop affected a laugh of derision.

"Why, the thing has occurred before now. I mean that I have heard that Congressmen have sometimes hired literary grubs to build speeches for them. Now didn't I overhear a conversation like that I spoke of?"

"Pshaw! Why of course you may have overheard some such jesting nonsense. But would one be in earnest about so farcical a thing?"

"Well if it was only a joke, why did you make a serious matter of it? Why did you get the speech written for you, and then read it in the House without ever having it copied?"

Mr. Trollop did not laugh, this time; he seemed seriously perplexed. He said:

"Come, play out your jest, Miss Hawkins. I can't understand what you are contriving—but it seems to entertain you—so please go on."

"I will, I assure you; but I hope to make the matter entertaining to you, too. Your private secretary never copied your speech."

"Indeed? Really you seem to know my affairs better than I do myself."

"I believe I do. You can't name your own amanuensis, Mr. Trollop."

"That is sad, indeed. Perhaps Miss Hawkins can?"

"Yes, I *can*. *I* wrote your speech myself, and you read it from my manuscript. There, now!"

Mr. Trollop did not spring to his feet and smite his brow with his hand while a cold sweat broke out all over him and the color forsook his face—no, he only said, "Good God!" and looked greatly astonished.

Laura handed him her commonplace-book and called his attention to the fact that the handwriting there and the handwriting of this speech were the same. He was shortly convinced. He laid the book aside and said, composedly:

"Well, the wonderful tragedy is done, and it transpires that I am indebted to you for my late eloquence. What of it? What was all this for, and what does it amount to, after all? What do you propose to do about it?"

"Oh, nothing. It is only a bit of pleasantry. When I overheard that conversation I took an early opportunity to ask Mr. Buckstone if he knew of anybody who might want a speech written— I had a friend, and so forth and so on. *I* was the friend, myself; I thought I might do you a good turn then and depend on you to do me one by and by. I never let Mr. Buckstone have the speech till the last moment, and when you hurried off to the House with it, you did not know there was a missing page, of course, but I did."

"And now perhaps you think that if I refuse to support your bill, you will make a grand exposure?"

"Well I had not thought of that. I only kept back the page for the mere fun of the thing; but since you mention it, I don't know but I might do something if I were angry."

"My dear Miss Hawkins, if you were to give out that you composed my speech, you know very well that people would say it was only your raillery, your fondness for putting a victim in the pillory and amusing the public at his expense. It is too flimsy, Miss Hawkins, for a person of your fine inventive talent— contrive an abler device than that. Come!"

"It is easily done, Mr. Trollop. I will hire a man, and pin this page on his breast, and label it, 'The Missing Fragment of the Hon. Mr. Trollop's Great Speech—which speech was written and composed by Miss Laura Hawkins under a secret understanding for one hundred dollars—and the money has not been paid.' And I will pin round about it notes in my handwriting, which I will procure from prominent friends of mine for the occasion; also your printed speech in the *Globe*, showing the connection between its bracketed hiatus and my Fragment; and I give you my word of honor that I will stand that human bulletin board in the rotunda of the capitol and make him stay there a week! You see you are premature, Mr. Trollop, the wonderful tragedy is not done yet, by any means. Come, now, doesn't it improve?"

Mr. Trollop opened his eyes rather widely at this novel aspect of the case. He got up and walked the floor and gave himself a moment for reflection. Then he stopped and studied Laura's face a while, and ended by saying:

"Well, I am obliged to believe you *would* be reckless enough to do that."

"Then don't put me to the test, Mr. Trollop. But let's drop the matter. I have had my joke and you've borne the infliction becomingly enough. It spoils a jest to harp on it after one has had one's laugh. I would much rather talk about my bill."

"So would I, now, my clandestine amanuensis. Compared with some other subjects, even your bill is a pleasant topic to discuss."

"Very good indeed! I thought I could persuade you. Now I am sure you will be generous to the poor negro and vote for that bill."

"Yes, I feel more tenderly toward the oppressed colored man than I did. Shall we bury the hatchet and be good friends and respect each other's little secrets, on condition that I vote Aye on the measure?"

"With all my heart, Mr. Trollop. I give you my word of that."

"It is a bargain. But isn't there something else you could give me, too?"

Laura looked at him inquiringly a moment, and then she comprehended.

"Oh, yes! You may have it now. I haven't any more use for it." She picked up the page of manuscript, but she reconsidered her intention of handing it to him, and said, "But never mind; I will keep it close; no one shall see it; you shall have it as soon as your vote is recorded."

Mr. Trollop looked disappointed. But presently made his adieux, and had got as far as the hall, when something occurred to Laura. She said to herself, "I don't simply want his vote, under compulsion—he might vote aye, but work against the bill in secret, for revenge; that man is unscrupulous enough to do anything. I must have his hearty co-operation as well as his vote. There is only one way to get that."

She called him back, and said;

"I value your vote, Mr. Trollop, but I value your influence more. You are able to help a measure along in many ways, if you choose.—I want to ask you to work for the bill as well as vote for it."

"It takes so much of one's time, Miss Hawkins—and time is money, you know."

"Yes, I know it is—especially in Congress. Now there is no use in you and I dealing in pretenses and going at matters in roundabout ways. We know each other—disguises are nonsense. Let us be plain. I will make it an object to you to work for the bill."

"Don't make it unnecessarily plain, please. There are little proprieties that are best preserved. What do you propose?"

"Well, this." She mentioned the names of several prominent Congressmen. "Now," said she, "these gentlemen are to vote and work for the bill, simply out of love for the negro—and out of pure generosity I have put in a relative of each as a member of the University incorporation. They will handle a million or so of money, officially, but will receive no salaries.—A larger number of statesmen are to vote and work for the bill—also out of love for the negro—gentlemen of but moderate influence, these—and out of pure generosity I am to see that relatives of theirs have positions in the University, *with* salaries, and good ones, too. You will vote and work for the bill, from mere affection for the negro, and I desire to testify my gratitude becomingly. Make free choice. Have you any friend whom you would like to present with a salaried or unsalaried position in our institution?"

"Well, I have a brother-in-law—"

"That same old brother-in-law, you good unselfish provider! I have heard of him often, through my agents. How regularly he does 'turn up,' to be sure. He could deal with those millions virtuously, and withal with ability, too—but of course you would rather he had a salaried position?"

"Oh, no," said the gentleman, facetiously, "we are very humble, very humble in our desires; we want no money; we labor solely for our country and require no reward but the luxury of an applauding conscience. Make him one of those poor hard working unsalaried corporators and let him do every body good with those millions—and go hungry himself! I will try to exert a little influence in favor of the bill."

Arrived at home, Mr. Trollop sat down and thought it all over—something after this fashion: it is about the shape it might have taken if he had spoken it aloud.

"My reputation is getting a little damaged, and I meant to clear it up brilliantly with an exposure of this bill at the supreme moment, and ride back into Congress on the éclat of it; and if I had that bit of manuscript, I would do it yet. It would be more money in my pocket, in the end, than my brother-in-law will get out of that incorporatorship, fat as it is. But that sheet of paper is out of my reach—she will never let that get out of her hands. And what a mountain it is! It blocks up *my* road, completely. She was going to hand it to me, once. Why *didn't* she! Must be a deep woman. Deep devil! That is what she is; a beautiful devil—and perfectly fearless, too. The idea of her pinning that paper on a man and standing him up in the rotunda looks absurd at a first glance. But she would do it! She is capable of doing anything. I went there hoping she would try to bribe me—good solid capital that would be in the exposure. Well, my prayer was answered; she did try to bribe me; and I made the best of a bad bargain and let her. I am check-mated. I must contrive something fresh to get back to Congress on. Very well; a bird in the hand is worth two in the bush; I will work for the bill—the incorporatorship will be a very good thing."

As soon as Mr. Trollop had taken his leave, Laura ran to Senator Dilworthy and began to speak, but he interrupted her and said distressfully, without even turning from his writing to look at her:

"Only half an hour! You gave it up early, child. However, it was best, it was best—I'm sure it was best—and safest."

"Give it up! *I!*"

The Senator sprang up, all aglow:

"My child, you can't mean that you—"

"I've made him promise on honor to think about a compromise to-night and come and tell me his decision in the morning."

"Good! There's hope yet that—"

"Nonsense, uncle. I've made him engage to let the Tennessee Land bill utterly alone!"

"*Impossible!* You—"

"I've made him promise to vote with us!"

"INCREDIBLE! Abso—"

"I've made him swear that he'll *work* for us!"

"PRE---POSTEROUS!—Utterly pre—break a window, child, before I suffocate!"

"No matter, it's true anyway. Now we can march into Congress with drums beating and colors flying!"

"Well—well—well. I'm sadly bewildered, sadly bewildered. I can't understand it at all—the most extraordinary woman that ever—it's a great day, it's a great day. There—there—let me put my hand in benediction on this precious head. Ah, my child, the poor negro will bless—"

"Oh bother the poor negro, uncle! Put it in your speech. Good-night, good-bye—we'll marshal our forces and march with the dawn!"

Laura reflected a while, when she was alone, and then fell to laughing, peacefully.

"Everybody works for me,"—so ran her thought. "It was a good idea to make Buckstone lead Mr. Trollop on to get a great speech written for him; and it was a happy part of the same idea for me to copy the speech after Mr. Buckstone had written it, and then keep back a page. Mr. B. was very complimentary to me when Trollop's break-down in the House showed him the *object* of my mysterious scheme; I think he will say still finer things when I tell him the triumph the sequel to it has gained for us.

"But what a coward the man was, to believe I would have exposed that page in the rotunda, and so exposed myself. However, I don't know—I don't know. I will think a moment. Suppose he voted no; suppose the bill failed; that is to suppose this stupendous game lost forever, that I have played so desperately for; suppose people came around pitying me—odious! And he could have saved me by his single voice. Yes, I *would* have exposed him! What would I care for the talk that that would have made about me when I was gone to Europe with Selby and all the world was busy with my history and my dishonor? It would be almost happiness to spite somebody at such a time."

CHAPTER XLIII

"Ikkaké gidiamuttu Wamallitakoanti likissitu anissia ukunnaria ni rubu kurru naussa abbanu aboahüddunnua namonnua."

THE VERY NEXT DAY, sure enough, the campaign opened. In due course, the Speaker of the House reached that Order of Business which is termed "Notices of Bills," and then the Hon. Mr. Buckstone rose in his place and gave notice of a bill "To Found and Incorporate the Knobs Industrial University," and then sat down without saying anything further. The busy gentlemen in the reporters' gallery jotted a line in their note-books, ran to the telegraphic desk in a room which communicated with their own writing-parlor, and then hurried back to their places in the gallery; and by the time they had resumed their seats, the line which they had delivered to the operator had been read in telegraphic offices in towns and cities hundreds of miles away. It was distinguished by frankness of language as well as by brevity:

> "The child is born. Buckstone gives notice of the thieving Knobs University job. It is said the noses have been counted and enough votes have been bought to pass it."

For some time the correspondents had been posting their several journals upon the alleged disreputable nature of the bill, and furnishing daily reports of the Washington gossip concerning it. So the next morning, nearly every newspaper of character in the land assailed the measure and hurled broadsides of invective at Mr. Buckstone. The Washington papers were more respectful, as usual—and conciliatory, also, as usual. They generally supported measures, when it was possible; but when they could not they "deprecated" violent expressions of opinion in other journalistic quarters. They always deprecated, when there was trouble ahead.

However, *The Washington Daily Love-Feast* hailed the bill with warm approbation. This was Senator Balaam's paper—or rather, "Brother" Balaam, as he was popularly called, for he had been a clergyman, in his day; and he himself and all that he did still emitted an odor of sanctity now that he had diverged into journalism and politics. He was a power in the Congressional prayer meeting, and in all movements that looked to the spread of religion and temperance. His paper supported the new bill with gushing affection; it was a noble measure, it was a just measure, it was a generous measure; it was a pure measure; and that surely should recommend it in these corrupt times; and finally, if the nature of the bill were not known at all, the *Love-Feast* would support it anyway, and unhesitatingly, for the fact that Senator Dilworthy was the originator of the measure was a guaranty that it contemplated a worthy and righteous work.

Senator Dilworthy was so anxious to know what the New York papers would say about the bill, that he had arranged to have synopses of their editorials telegraphed to him; he could not wait for the papers themselves to crawl along down to Washington by a mail train which has never run over a cow since the road was built, for the reason that it has never been able to overtake one. It carries the usual "cow-catcher" in front of the locomotive, but this is mere ostentation. It ought to be attached to the rear car, where it could do some good; but instead, no provision is made there for the protection of the traveling public, and hence it is not a matter of surprise that cows so frequently climb aboard that train and among the passengers.

The Senator read his dispatches aloud at the breakfast table. Laura was troubled beyond measure at their tone, and said that that sort of comment would defeat the bill; but the Senator said:

"Oh, not at all, not at all, my child. It is just what we want. Persecution is the one thing needful, now—all the other forces are secured. Give us newspaper persecution enough, and we are safe. Vigorous persecution will alone carry a bill sometimes, dear; and when you start with a strong vote in the first place, persecution comes in with double effect. It scares off some of the weak supporters, true, but it soon turns strong ones into stubborn ones. And then, presently, it changes the tide of public opinion. The great public is weak-minded; the great public is sentimental; the great public always turns around and weeps for an odious murderer, and prays for him, and carries flowers to his prison and besieges the governor with appeals to his clemency, as soon as the papers begin to howl for that man's blood.—In a word, the great putty-hearted public loves to 'gush,' and there is no such darling opportunity to gush as a case of persecution affords."

"Well, uncle, dear, if your theory is right, let us go into raptures, for nobody can ask a heartier persecution than these editorials are furnishing."

"I am not so sure of that, my daughter. I don't entirely like the tone of some of these remarks. They lack vim, they lack venom. Here is one calls it a 'questionable measure.' Bah, there is no strength in that. This one is better; it calls it 'highway robbery.' That sounds something like. But now this one seems satisfied to call it an 'iniquitous scheme!'—'Iniquitous' does not exasperate anybody; it is weak—puerile. The ignorant will imagine it to be intended for a compliment. But this other one—the one I read last—has the true ring: 'This vile, dirty effort to rob the public treasury, by the kites and vultures that now infest the filthy den called Congress'—that is admirable, admirable! We must have more of that sort. But it will come—no fear of that; they're not warmed up, yet. A week from now you'll see."

"Uncle, you and Brother Balaam are bosom friends—why don't you get his paper to persecute us, too?"

"It isn't worth while, my daughter. His support doesn't hurt a bill. Nobody reads his editorials but himself. But I wish the New York papers would talk a little plainer. It is annoying to have to wait a week for them to warm up. I expected better things at their hands—and time is precious, now."

At the proper hour, according to his previous notice, Mr. Buckstone duly introduced his bill entitled "An Act to Found and Incorporate the Knobs Industrial University," moved its proper reference, and sat down.

The Speaker of the House rattled off this observation:

"Fnobjectionbilltakuzhlcourssoreferred!"

Habitués of the House comprehended that this long, lightning-heeled word signified that if there was no objection, the bill would take the customary course of a measure of its nature, and be referred to the Committee on Benevolent Appropriations, and that it was accordingly so referred. Strangers merely supposed that the Speaker was taking a gargle for some affection of the throat.

The reporters immediately telegraphed the introduction of the bill.—And they added:

> "The assertion that the bill will pass was premature. It is said that many favorers of it will desert when the storm breaks upon them from the public press."

The storm came, and during ten days it waxed more and more violent day by day. The great "Negro University Swindle" became the one absorbing topic of conversation throughout the Union. Individuals denounced it, journals denounced it, public meetings denounced it, the pictorial papers caricatured its friends, the whole nation seemed to be growing frantic over it. Meantime the Washington correspondents were sending such telegrams as these abroad in the land: Under date of—

> SATURDAY. "Congressmen Jex and Fluke are wavering; it is believed they will desert the execrable bill."
> MONDAY. "Jex and Fluke *have* deserted!"
> THURSDAY. "Tubbs and Huffy left the sinking ship last night."

Later on:

> "Three desertions. The University thieves are getting scared, though they will not own it."

Later:

> "The leaders are growing stubborn—they swear they can carry it, but it is now almost certain that they no longer have a majority!"

After a day or two of reluctant and ambiguous telegrams:

> "Public sentiment seems changing, a trifle, in favor of the bill—but only a trifle."

And still later:

"It is whispered that the Hon. Mr. Trollop has gone over to the pirates. It is probably a canard. Mr. Trollop has all along been the bravest and most efficient champion of virtue and the people against the bill, and the report is without doubt a shameless invention."

Next day:

"With characteristic treachery, the truckling and pusillanimous reptile, Crippled-Speech Trollop, has gone over to the enemy. It is contended, now, that *he has been a friend to the bill, in secret, since the day it was introduced,* and has had bankable reasons for being so; but he himself declares that he has gone over because the malignant persecution of the bill by the newspapers caused him to study its provisions with more care than he had previously done, and this close examination revealed the fact that the measure is one in every way worthy of support. (Pretty thin!) It cannot be denied that this desertion has had a damaging effect. Jex and Fluke have returned to their iniquitous allegiance, with six or eight others of lesser calibre, and it is reported and believed that Tubbs and Huffy are ready to go back. It is feared that the University swindle is stronger to-day than it has ever been before."

Later—midnight:

"It is said that the committee will report the bill back to-morrow. Both sides are marshaling their forces, and the fight on this bill is evidently going to be the hottest of the session.—All Washington is boiling."

CHAPTER XLIV

Capienda rebus in malis praeceps via est.
—*Seneca.*

Et enim ipse se impellunt, ubi semel à ratione discessum est: ipsaque sibi imbecillitas indulget, in altumque provebitur imprudenter: nec reperet locum consistendi.

—*Cicero.*

"It's easy enough for another fellow to talk," said Harry, despondingly, after he had put Philip in possession of his view of the case. "It's easy enough to say 'give her up,' if you don't care for her. What am I going to do to give her up?"

It seemed to Harry that it was a situation requiring some active measures. He couldn't realize that he had fallen hopelessly in love without some rights accruing to him for the possession of the object of his passion. Quiet resignation under relinquishment of any thing he wanted was not in his line. And when it appeared to him that his surrender of Laura would be the withdrawal of the one barrier that kept her from ruin, it was unreasonable to expect that he could see how to give her up.

Harry had the most buoyant confidence in his own projects always; he saw everything connected with himself in a large way and in rosy hues. This predominance of the imagination over the judgment gave that appearance of exaggeration to his conversation and to his communications with regard to himself, which sometimes conveyed the impression that he was not speaking the truth. His acquaintances had been known to say that they invariably allowed a half for shrinkage in his statements, and held the other half under advisement for confirmation.

Philip in this case could not tell from Harry's story exactly how much encouragement Laura had given him, nor what hopes he might justly have of winning her. He had never seen him desponding before. The "brag" appeared to be all taken out of him,

311

and his airy manner only asserted itself now and then in a comical imitation of its old self.

Philip wanted time to look about him before he decided what to do. He was not familiar with Washington, and it was difficult to adjust his feelings and perceptions to its peculiarities. Coming out of the sweet sanity of the Bolton household, this was by contrast the maddest Vanity Fair one could conceive. It seemed to him a feverish, unhealthy atmosphere in which lunacy would be easily developed. He fancied that everybody attached to himself an exaggerated importance, from the fact of being at the national capital, the center of political influence, the fountain of patronage, preferment, jobs and opportunities.

People were introduced to each other as from this or that state, not from cities or towns, and this gave a largeness to their representative feeling. All the women talked politics as naturally and glibly as they talk fashion or literature elsewhere. There was always some exciting topic at the Capitol, or some huge slander was rising up like a miasmatic exhalation from the Potomac, threatening to settle no one knew exactly where. Every other person was an aspirant for a place, or, if he had one, for a better place, or more pay; almost every other one had some claim or interest or remedy to urge; even the women were all advocates for the advancement of some person, and they violently espoused or denounced this or that measure as it would affect some relative, acquaintance or friend.

Love, travel, even death itself, waited on the chances of the dies daily thrown in the two Houses, and the committee rooms there. If the measure went through, love could afford to ripen into marriage, and longing for foreign travel would have fruition; and it must have been only eternal hope springing in the breast that kept alive numerous old claimants who for years had besieged the doors of Congress, and who looked as if they needed not so much an appropriation of money as six feet of ground. And those who stood so long waiting for success to bring them death were usually those who had a just claim.

Representing states and talking of national and even international affairs, as familiarly as neighbors at home talk of poor crops and the extravagance of their ministers, was likely at first to impose upon Philip as to the importance of the people gathered here.

There was a little newspaper editor from Phil's native town, the assistant on a Peddletonian[141] weekly, who made his little annual joke about the "first egg laid on our table," and who was the menial of every tradesman in the village and under bonds to him for frequent "puffs," except the undertaker, about whose employment he was recklessly facetious. In Washington he was an important man, correspondent, and clerk of two house committees, a "worker" in politics, and a confident critic of every woman and every man in Washington. He would be a consul no doubt by and by, at some foreign port, of the language of which he was ignorant; though if ignorance of language were a qualification he might have been a consul at home. His easy familiarity with great men was beautiful to see, and when Philip learned what a tremendous underground influence this little ignoramus had, he no longer wondered at the queer appointments and the queerer legislation.

Philip was not long in discovering that people in Washington did not differ much from other people; they had the same meannesses, generosities, and tastes. A Washington boarding house had the odor of a boarding house the world over.

Col. Sellers was as unchanged as any one Philip saw whom he had known elsewhere. Washington appeared to be the native element of this man. His pretentions were equal to any he encountered there. He saw nothing in its society that equalled that of Hawkeye, he sat down to no table that could not be unfavorably contrasted with his own at home; the most airy scheme inflated in the hot air of the capital only reached in magnitude some of his lesser fancies, the by-play of his constructive imagination.

"The country is getting along very well," he said to Philip, "but our public men are too timid. What we want is more money. I've told Boutwell so. Talk about basing the currency on gold; you might as well base it on pork. Gold is only one product. Base it on everything! You've got to do something for the West. How am I to move my crops? We must have improvements. Grant's got the idea. We want a canal from the James River to the Mississippi. Government ought to build it."

It was difficult to get the Colonel off from these large themes when he was once started, but Philip brought the conversation round to Laura and her reputation in the City.

"No," he said, "I haven't noticed much. We've been so busy about this University. It will make Laura rich with the rest of us, and she has done nearly as much as if she were a man. She has great talent, and will make a big match. I see the foreign ministers and that sort after her. Yes, there is talk, always will be about a pretty woman so much in public as she is. Tough stories come to me, but I put 'em away. 'Tain't likely one of Si. Hawkins's children would do that—for she is the same as a child of his. I told her, though, to go slow," added the Colonel, as if that mysterious admonition from him would set everything right.

"Do you know anything about a Col. Selby?"

"Know all about him. Fine fellow. But he's got a wife; and I told him, as a friend, he'd better sheer off from Laura. I reckon he thought better of it and did."

But Philip was not long in learning the truth. Courted as Laura was by a certain class and still admitted into society, that, nevertheless, buzzed with disreputable stories about her, she had lost character with the best people. Her intimacy with Selby was open gossip, and there were winks and thrustings of the tongue in any group of men when she passed by. It was clear enough that Harry's delusion must be broken up, and that no such feeble obstacle as his passion could interpose would turn Laura from her fate. Philip determined to see her, and put himself in possession of the truth, as he suspected it, in order to show Harry his folly.

Laura, after her last conversation with Harry, had a new sense of her position. She had noticed before the signs of a change in manner towards her, a little less respect perhaps from men, and an avoidance by women. She had attributed this latter partly to jealousy of her, for no one is willing to acknowledge a fault in himself when a more agreeable motive can be found for the estrangement of his acquaintances. But, now, if society had turned on her, she would defy it. It was not in her nature to shrink. She knew she had been wronged, and she knew that she had no remedy.

What she heard of Col. Selby's proposed departure alarmed her more than anything else, and she calmly determined that if he was deceiving her the second time it should be the last. Let society finish the tragedy if it liked; she was indifferent what came after. At the first opportunity, she charged Selby with his intention to abandon her. He unblushingly denied it. He had not thought of going to Europe. He had only been amusing himself with Sellers's schemes. He swore that as soon as she succeeded with her bill, he would fly with her to any part of the world.

She did not quite believe him, for she saw that he feared her, and she began to suspect that his were the protestations of a coward to gain time. But she showed him no doubts. She only watched his movements day by day, and always held herself ready to act promptly.

When Philip came into the presence of this attractive woman, he could not realize that she was the subject of all the scandal he had heard. She received him with quite the old Hawkeye openness and cordiality, and fell to talking at once of their little acquaintance there; and it seemed impossible that he could ever say to her what he had come determined to say. Such a man as Philip has only one standard by which to judge women.

Laura recognized that fact no doubt. The better part of her woman's nature saw it. Such a man might, years ago, not now, have changed her nature, and made the issue of her life so different, even after her cruel abandonment. She had a dim feeling of this, and she would like now to stand well with him. The spark of truth and honor that was left in her was elicited by his presence. It was this influence that governed her conduct in this interview.

"I have come," said Philip in his direct manner, "from my friend Mr. Brierly. You are not ignorant of his feeling towards you?"

"Perhaps not."

"But perhaps you do not know, you who have so much admiration, how sincere and overmastering his love is for you?" Philip would not have spoken so plainly, if he had in mind anything except to draw from Laura something that would end Harry's passion.

"And is sincere love so rare, Mr. Sterling?" asked Laura, moving her foot a little, and speaking with a shade of sarcasm.

"Perhaps not in Washington," replied Philip, tempted into a

similar tone. "Excuse my bluntness," he continued, "but would the knowledge of his love, would his devotion, make any difference to you in your Washington life?"

"In respect to what?" asked Laura quickly.

"Well, to others. I won't equivocate—to Col. Selby?"

Laura's face flushed with anger, or shame; she looked steadily at Philip and began,

"By what right, sir,—"

"By the right of friendship," interrupted Philip stoutly. "It may matter little to you. It is everything to him. He has a Quixotic notion that you would turn back from what is before you for his sake. You cannot be ignorant of what all the city is talking of." Philip said this determinedly and with some bitterness.

It was a full minute before Laura spoke. Both had risen, Philip as if to go, and Laura in suppressed excitement. When she spoke her voice was very unsteady, and she looked down.

"Yes, I know. I perfectly understand what you mean. Mr. Brierly is nothing—simply nothing. He is a moth singed, that is all—the trifler with women thought he was a wasp. I have no pity for him, not the least. You may tell him not to make a fool of himself, and to keep away. I say this on your account, not his. You are not like him. It is enough for me that you want it so. Mr. Sterling," she continued, looking up, and there were tears in her eyes that contradicted the hardness of her language, "you might not pity him if you knew my history; perhaps you would not wonder at some things you hear. No; it is useless to ask me why it must be so. You can't make a life over—society wouldn't let you if you would—and mine must be lived as it is. There, sir, I'm not offended; but it is useless for you to say anything more."

Philip went away with his heart lightened about Harry, but profoundly saddened by the glimpse of what this woman might have been. He told Harry all that was necessary of the conversation—she was bent on going her own way, he had not the ghost of a chance—he was a fool, she had said, for thinking he had.

And Harry accepted it meekly, and made up his own mind that Philip didn't know much about women.

CHAPTER XLV

—Nakila cu ch'y cu yao chike, chi ka togobah cu y vach, x-e u chax-cut?—Utz, chi ka ya puvak chyve, x-e cha-cu ri amag.

Popul Vuh.

THE GALLERIES OF THE HOUSE were packed, on the momentous day, not because the reporting of an important bill back by a committee was a thing to be excited about, if the bill were going to take the ordinary course afterward; it would be like getting excited over the impaneling of a coroner's jury in a murder case, instead of saving up one's emotions for the grander occasion of the hanging of the accused, two years later, after all the tedious forms of law had been gone through with.

But suppose you understand that this coroner's jury is going to turn out to be a vigilance committee in disguise, who will hear testimony for an hour and then hang the murderer on the spot? That puts a different aspect upon the matter. Now it was whispered that the legitimate forms of procedure usual in the House, and which keep a bill hanging along for days and even weeks, before it is finally passed upon, were going to be overruled, in this case, and short work made of the measure; and so, what was beginning as a mere inquest might turn out to be something very different.

In the course of the day's business the Order of "Reports of Committees" was finally reached and when the weary crowds heard that glad announcement issue from the Speaker's lips they ceased to fret at the dragging delay, and plucked up spirit. The Chairman of the Committee on Benevolent Appropriations rose and made his report, and just then a blue-uniformed brass-mounted little page put a note into his hand. It was from Senator Dilworthy, who had appeared upon the floor of the House for a moment and flitted away again:

"Everybody expects a grand assault in force; no doubt you believe, as I certainly do, that it is the thing to do; we are strong, and everything is hot for the contest. Trollop's espousal of our cause has im-

317

mensely helped us and we grow in power constantly. Ten of the opposition were called away from town about noon (*but*—so it is said—*only for one day*). Six others are sick, but expect to be about again *to-morrow or next day,* a friend tells me. A bold onslaught is worth trying. Go for a suspension of the rules! You will find we can swing a two-thirds vote—I am perfectly satisfied of it. The Lord's truth will prevail.

"Dilworthy."

Mr. Buckstone had reported the bills from his committee, one by one, leaving *the* bill to the last. When the House had voted upon the acceptance or rejection of the report upon all but it, and the question now being upon *its* disposal—

Mr. Buckstone begged that the House would give its attention to a few remarks which he desired to make. His committee had instructed him to report the bill favorably; he wished to explain the nature of the measure, and thus justify the committee's action; the hostility roused by the press would then disappear, and the bill would shine forth in its true and noble character. He said that its provisions were simple. It incorporated the Knobs Industrial University, locating it in East Tennessee, declaring it open to all persons without distinction of sex, color or religion, and committing its management to a board of perpetual trustees, with power to fill vacancies in their own number. It provided for the erection of certain buildings for the University, dormitories, lecture-halls, museums, libraries, laboratories, workshops, furnaces, and mills. It provided also for the purchase of sixty-five thousand acres of land, (fully described) for the purposes of the University, in the Knobs of East Tennessee. And it appropriated [blank] dollars for the purchase of the Land, which should be the property of the national trustees in trust for the uses named.

Every effort had been made to secure the refusal of the whole amount of the property of the Hawkins heirs in the Knobs, some seventy-five thousand acres Mr. Buckstone said. But Mr. Washington Hawkins (one of the heirs) objected. He was, indeed, very reluctant to sell any part of the land at any price; and indeed this reluctance was justifiable when one considers how constantly and how greatly the property is rising in value.

What the South needed, continued Mr. Buckstone, was skilled labor. Without that it would be unable to develop its mines, build its roads, work to advantage and without great waste its fruitful land, establish manufactures or enter upon a prosperous industrial career. Its laborers were almost altogether unskilled. Change them into intelligent, trained workmen, and you increased at once the capital, the resources of the entire South, which would enter upon a prosperity hitherto unknown. In five years the increase in local wealth would not only reimburse the government for the outlay in this appropriation, but pour untold wealth into the treasury.

. This was the material view, and the least important in the honorable gentleman's opinion. [Here he referred to some notes furnished him by Senator Dilworthy, and then continued.] God had given us the care of these colored millions. What account should we render to Him of our stewardship? We had made them free. Should we leave them ignorant? We had cast them upon their own resources. Should we leave them without tools? We could not tell what the intentions of Providence are in regard to these peculiar people, but our duty was plain. The Knobs Industrial University would be a vast school of modern science and practice, worthy of a great nation. It would combine the advantages of Zurich, Freiburg, Creuzot and the Sheffield Scientific.[142] Providence had apparently reserved and set apart the Knobs of East Tennessee for this purpose. What else were they for? Was it not wonderful that for more than thirty years, over a generation, the choicest portion of them had remained in one family, untouched, as if consecrated for some great use!

It might be asked why the government should buy this land, when it had millions of acres, more than the railroad companies desired, which it might devote to this purpose? He answered, that the government had no such tract of land as this. It had nothing comparable to it for the purposes of the University. This was to be a school of mining, of engineering, of the working of metals, of chemistry, zoology, botany, manufactures, agriculture, in short of all the complicated industries that make a state great. There was no place for the location of such a school like the Knobs of East

Tennessee. The hills abounded in metals of all sorts, iron in all its combinations, copper, bismuth, gold and silver in small quantities, platinum he believed, tin, aluminium; it was covered with forests and strange plants; in the woods were found the coon, the opossum, the fox, the deer and many other animals who roamed in the domain of natural history; coal existed in enormous quantity and no doubt oil; it was such a place for the practice of agricultural experiments that any student who had been successful there would have an easy task in any other portion of the country.

No place offered equal facilities for experiments in mining, metallurgy, engineering. He expected to live to see the day when the youth of the South would resort to its mines, its workshops, its laboratories, its furnaces and factories for practical instruction in all the great industrial pursuits.

A noisy and rather ill-natured debate followed, now, and lasted hour after hour. The friends of the bill were instructed by the leaders to *make no effort to check this;* it was deemed better strategy to tire out the opposition; it was decided to vote down every proposition to adjourn, and so continue the sitting into the night; opponents might desert, then, one by one and weaken their party, for they had no personal stake in the bill.

Sunset came, and still the fight went on; the gas was lit, the crowd in the galleries began to thin, but the contest continued; the crowd returned, by and by, with hunger and thirst appeased, and aggravated the hungry and thirsty House by looking contented and comfortable; but still the wrangle lost nothing of its bitterness. Recesses were moved plaintively by the opposition, and invariably voted down by the University army.

At midnight the House presented a spectacle calculated to interest a stranger. The great galleries were still thronged—though only with men, now; the bright colors that had made them look like hanging gardens were gone, with the ladies. The reporters' gallery was merely occupied by one or two watchful sentinels of the quill-driving guild; the main body cared nothing for a debate that had dwindled to a mere vaporing of dull speakers and now and then a brief quarrel over a point of order; but there was an unusually large attendance of journalists in the reporters' waiting-room, chatting, smoking, and keeping on the *qui vive* for the general irruption of the Congressional volcano that must come when the time was ripe for it. Senator Dilworthy and Philip were in the Diplomatic Gallery; Washington sat in the public gallery, and Col. Sellers was not far away. The Colonel had been flying about the corridors and button-holing Congressmen all the evening, and believed that he had accomplished a world of valuable service; but fatigue was telling upon him, now, and he was quiet and speechless—for once. Below, a few Senators lounged upon the sofas set apart for visitors, and talked with idle Congressmen. A dreary member was speaking; the presiding officer was nodding; here and there little knots of members stood in the aisles, whispering together; all about the House others sat in all the various attitudes that express weariness; some, tilted back, had one or more legs disposed upon their desks; some sharpened pencils indolently; some scribbled aimlessly; some yawned and stretched; a great many lay upon their breasts upon the desks, sound asleep and gently snoring. The flooding gaslight from the fancifully wrought roof poured down upon the tranquil scene. Hardly a sound disturbed the stillness, save the monotonous eloquence of the gentleman who occupied the floor. Now and then a warrior of the opposition broke down under the pressure, gave it up and went home.

Mr. Buckstone began to think it might be safe, now, to "proceed to business." He consulted with Trollop and one or two others. Senator Dilworthy descended to the floor of the House and they went to meet him. After a brief comparison of notes, the Congressmen sought their seats and sent pages about the House with messages to friends. These latter instantly roused up, yawned, and began to look alert. The moment the floor was unoccupied, Mr. Buckstone rose, with an injured look, and said it was evident that the opponents of the bill were merely talking against time, hoping in this unbecoming way to tire out the friends of the measure and so defeat it. Such conduct might be respectable enough in a village debating society, but it was trivial among statesmen, it was out of place in so august an assemblage as the House of Representatives of the United States. The friends of the bill had been not only willing that its opponents should express their opinions, but had strongly desired it. They courted the fullest and freest discussion; but it seemed to him that this fairness was but illy appreciated, since gentlemen were capable of taking advantage of it for selfish and unworthy ends. This trifling had gone far enough. He called for the question.

The instant Mr. Buckstone sat down, the storm burst forth. A dozen gentlemen sprang to their feet.

"Mr. Speaker!"

"Mr. Speaker!"

"Mr. Speaker!"

"Order! Order! Order! Question! Question!"

The sharp blows of the Speaker's gavel rose above the din.

The "previous question," that hated gag, was moved and carried. All debate came to a sudden end, of course. Triumph No. 1.

Then the vote was taken on the adoption of the report and it carried by a surprising majority.

Mr. Buckstone got the floor again and moved that the rules be suspended and the bill read a first time.

Mr. Trollop—"Second the motion!"

The Speaker—"It is moved and—"

Clamor of Voices. "Move we adjourn! Second the motion! Adjourn! Adjourn! Order! Order!"

The Speaker, (after using his gavel vigorously)—"It is moved and seconded that the House do now adjourn. All those in favor—"

Voices—"Division! Division! Ayes and nays! Ayes and nays!"

It was decided to vote upon the adjournment by ayes and nays. This was war in earnest. The excitement was furious. The galleries were in commotion in an instant, the reporters swarmed to their places, idling members of the House flocked to their seats, nervous gentlemen sprang to their feet, pages flew hither and thither, life and animation were visible everywhere, all the long ranks of faces in the building were kindled.

"This thing decides it!" thought Mr. Buckstone; "but let the fight proceed."

The voting began, and every sound ceased but the calling of the names and the "Aye!" "No!" "No!" "Aye!" of the responses. There was not a movement in the House; the people seemed to hold their breath.

The voting ceased, and then there was an interval of dead silence while the clerk made up his count. There was a two-thirds vote on the University side—and two over!

The Speaker—"The rules are suspended, the motion is carried—first reading of the *bill!*"

By one impulse the galleries broke forth into stormy applause, and even some of the members of the House were not wholly able to restrain their feelings. The Speaker's gavel came to the rescue and his clear voice followed:

"Order, gentlemen! The House will come to order! If spectators offend again, the Sergeant-at-arms will clear the galleries!"

Then he cast his eyes aloft and gazed at some object attentively for a moment. All eyes followed the direction of the Speaker's, and then there was a general titter. The Speaker said:

"Let the Sergeant-at-arms inform the gentleman that his conduct is an infringement of the dignity of the House—and one which is not warranted by the state of the weather."

Poor Sellers was the culprit. He sat in the front seat of the gallery, with his arms and his tired body overflowing the balustrade—sound asleep, dead to all excitements, all disturbances. The fluctuations of the Washington weather had influenced his dreams, perhaps, for during the recent tempest of applause he had hoisted his gingham umbrella and calmly gone on with his slumbers. Washington Hawkins had seen the act, but was not near enough at hand to save his friend, and no one who was near enough desired to spoil the effect. But a neighbor stirred up the Colonel, now that the House had its eye upon him, and the great speculator furled his tent like the Arab. He said:

"Bless my soul, I'm so absent-minded when I get to thinking! I never wear an umbrella in the house—did anybody notice it? What—asleep? Indeed? And did you wake me sir? Thank you— thank you very much indeed. It might have fallen out of my hands and been injured. Admirable article, sir—present from a friend in Hong Kong; one doesn't come across silk like that in this country—it's the real Young Hyson,[143] I'm told."

By this time the incident was forgotten, for the House was at war again. Victory was almost in sight, now, and the friends of the bill threw themselves into their work with enthusiasm. They soon moved and carried its second reading, and after a strong, sharp fight, carried a motion to go into Committee of the whole. The Speaker left his place, of course, and a chairman was appointed.

Now the contest raged hotter than ever—for the authority that compels order when the House sits *as* a House, is greatly diminished when it sits as a Committee. The main fight came upon the filling of the blanks with the sum to be appropriated for the purchase of the land, of course.

Mr. Buckstone—"Mr. Chairman, I move you, sir, that the words *three millions of* be inserted."

Mr. Hadley—"Mr. Chairman, I move that the words *two and a half dollars* be inserted."

Mr. Clawson—"Mr. Chairman, I move the insertion of the words *five and twenty cents,* as representing the true value of this barren and isolated tract of desolation."

The question, according to rule, was taken upon the smallest sum first. It was lost.

Then upon the next smallest sum. Lost, also.

And then upon the three millions. After a vigorous battle that lasted a considerable time, this motion was carried.

Then, clause by clause the bill was read, discussed, and amended in trifling particulars, and now the Committee rose and reported.

The moment the House had resumed its functions and received the report, Mr. Buckstone moved and carried the third reading of the bill.

The same bitter war over the sum to be paid was fought over again, and now that the ayes and nays could be called and placed on record, every man was compelled to vote by name on the three millions, and indeed on every paragraph of the bill from the enacting clause straight through. But as before, the friends of the measure stood firm and voted in a solid body every time, and so did its enemies.

The supreme moment was come, now, but so sure was the result that not even a voice was raised to interpose an adjournment. The enemy were totally demoralized. The bill was put upon its final passage almost without dissent, and the calling of the ayes and nays began. When it was ended the triumph was complete—the two-thirds vote held good, and a veto was impossible, as far as the House was concerned!

Mr. Buckstone resolved that now that the nail was driven home, he would clinch it on the other side and make it stay forever. He moved a reconsideration of the vote by which the bill had passed. The motion was lost, of course, and the great Industrial University act was an accomplished fact as far as it was in the power of the House of Representatives to make it so.

There was no need to move an adjournment. The instant the last motion was decided, the enemies of the University rose and flocked out of the Hall, talking angrily, and its friends flocked after them jubilant and congratulatory. The galleries disgorged their burden, and presently the House was silent and deserted.

When Col. Sellers and Washington stepped out of the building they were surprised to find that the daylight was old and the sun well up. Said the Colonel:

"Give me your hand, my boy! You're all right at last! You're a millionaire! At least you're going to be. The thing is dead sure. Don't you bother about the Senate. Leave me and Dilworthy to take care of that. Run along home, now, and tell Laura. Lord, it's magnificent news—perfectly magnificent! Run, now. I'll telegraph my wife. She must come here and help me build a house. Everything's all right now!"

Washington was so dazed by his good fortune and so bewildered by the gaudy pageant of dreams that was already trailing its long ranks through his brain, that he wandered he knew not where, and so loitered by the way that when at last he reached home he woke to a sudden annoyance in the fact that his news must be old to Laura, now, for of course Senator Dilworthy must have already been home and told her an hour before. He knocked at her door, but there was no answer.

"That is like the Duchess," said he. "Always cool. A body can't excite her—can't keep her excited, anyway. Now she has gone off to sleep again, as comfortably as if she were used to picking up a million dollars every day or two."

Then he went to bed. But he could not sleep; so he got up and wrote a long, rapturous letter to Louise, and another to his mother. And he closed both to much the same effect:

"Laura will be queen of America, now, and she will be applauded, and honored and petted by the whole nation. Her name will be in every one's mouth more than ever, and how they will court her and quote her bright speeches. And mine, too, I suppose; though they do that more already, than they really seem to deserve. Oh, the world is so bright, now, and so cheery; the clouds are all gone, our long struggle is ended, our troubles are all over. Nothing can ever make us unhappy any more. You dear faithful ones will have the reward of your patient waiting now. How father's wisdom is proven at last! And how I repent me, that there have been times when I lost faith and said the blessing he stored up for us a tedious generation ago was but a long-drawn curse, a blight upon us all. But everything is well, now—we are done with poverty, and toil, weariness and heart-breakings; all the world is filled with sunshine."

CHAPTER XLVI

Forte è l'aceto di vin dolce.

Ne bið swylc cwénlíc þeaw
idese to efnanne,
þeáh ðe hió aenlícu sy,
þaette freoðu-webbe
feores onsaece,
aefter lig-torne,
leófne mannan.

Beowulf.

PHILIP LEFT THE CAPITOL and walked up Pennsylvania Avenue in company with Senator Dilworthy. It was a bright spring morning, the air was soft and inspiring; in the deepening wayside green, the pink flush of the blossoming peach trees, the soft suffusion on the heights of Arlington, and the breath of the warm south wind was apparent the annual miracle of the resurrection of the earth.

The Senator took off his hat and seemed to open his soul to the sweet influences of the morning. After the heat and noise of the chamber, under its dull gas-illuminated glass canopy, and the all night struggle of passion and feverish excitement there, the open, tranquil world seemed like Heaven. The Senator was not in an exultant mood, but rather in a condition of holy joy, befitting a Christian statesman whose benevolent plans Providence has made its own and stamped with approval. The great battle had been fought, but the measure had still to encounter the scrutiny of the Senate, and Providence sometimes acts differently in the two Houses. Still the Senator was tranquil, for he knew that there is an *esprit de corps* in the Senate which does not exist in the House, the effect of which is to make the members complaisant towards the projects of each other, and to extend a mutual aid which in a more vulgar body would be called "log-rolling."

"It is, under Providence, a good night's work, Mr. Sterling. The government has founded an institution which will remove half the difficulty from the Southern problem. And it is a good thing for the Hawkins heirs, a very good thing. Laura will be almost a millionaire."

"Do you think, Mr. Dilworthy, that the Hawkinses will get much of the money?" asked Philip innocently, remembering the fate of the Columbus River appropriation.

The Senator looked at his companion scrutinizingly for a moment to see if he meant any thing personal, and then replied,

"Undoubtedly, undoubtedly. I have had their interests greatly at heart. There will of course be a few expenses, but the widow and orphans will realize all that Mr. Hawkins dreamed of for them."

The birds were singing as they crossed the Presidential Square,[144] now bright with its green turf and tender foliage. After the two had gained the steps of the Senator's house they stood a moment, looking upon the lovely prospect.

"It is like the peace of God," said the Senator devoutly.

Entering the house, the Senator called a servant and said, "Tell Miss Laura that we are waiting to see her. I ought to have sent a messenger on horseback half an hour ago," he added to Philip, "she will be transported with our victory. You must stop to breakfast, and see the excitement." The servant soon came back, with a wondering look and reported,

"Miss Laura ain't dah, sah. I reckon she hain't been dah all night."

The Senator and Philip both started up. In Laura's room there were the marks of a confused and hasty departure, drawers half open, little articles strewn on the floor. The bed had not been disturbed. Upon inquiry it appeared that Laura had not been at dinner, excusing herself to Mrs. Dilworthy on the plea of a violent headache; that she made a request to the servants that she might not be disturbed.

The Senator was astounded. Philip thought at once of Col. Selby. Could Laura have run away with him? The Senator thought not. In fact it could not be. Gen. Leffenwell, the member from New Orleans, had casually told him at the house last night that Selby and his family went to New York yesterday morning and were to sail for Europe to-day.

Philip had another idea which he did not mention. He seized

his hat, and saying that he would go and see what he could learn, ran to the lodgings of Harry, whom he had not seen since yesterday afternoon, when he left him to go to the House.

Harry was not in. He had gone out with a hand-bag before six o'clock yesterday, saying that he had to go to New York, but should return next day. In Harry's room on the table Philip found this note:—

"Dear Mr. Brierly:—Can you meet me at the six o'clock train, and be my escort to New York? I have to go about this University bill, the vote of an absent member we must have here. Senator Dilworthy cannot go.

Yours &c.,   L. H."

"Confound it," said Philip, "the noodle has fallen into her trap. And she promised me she would let him alone."

He only stopped to send a note to Senator Dilworthy, telling him what he had found, and that he should go at once to New York, and then hastened to the railway station. He had to wait an hour for a train, and when it did start it seemed to go at a snail's pace.

Philip was devoured with anxiety. Where could they have gone? What was Laura's object in taking Harry? Had the flight anything to do with Selby? Would Harry be such a fool as to be dragged into some public scandal?

It seemed as if the train would never reach Baltimore. Then there was a long delay at Havre de Grace. A hot box[115] had to be cooled at Wilmington. Would it never get on? Only in passing around the city of Philadelphia did the train not seem to go slow. Philip stood upon the platform and watched for the Boltons' house, fancied he could distinguish its roof among the trees, and wondered how Ruth would feel if she knew he was so near her.

Then came Jersey, everlasting Jersey, stupid irritating Jersey, where the passengers are always asking which line they are on, and where they are to come out, and whether they have yet reached Elizabeth. Launched into Jersey, one has a vague notion that he is on many lines and no one in particular, and that he is liable at any moment to come to Elizabeth. He has no notion what

Elizabeth is, and always resolves that the next time he goes that way he will look out of the window and see what it is like; but he never does. Or if he does, he probably finds that it is Princeton or something of that sort. He gets annoyed, and never can see the use of having different names for stations in Jersey. By and by there is Newark, three or four Newarks apparently; then marshes, then long rock cuttings devoted to the advertisements of patent medicines and ready-made clothing, and New York tonics for Jersey agues, and—Jersey City is reached.

On the ferry-boat Philip bought an evening paper from a boy crying "'Ere's the *Evening Gram*,[146] all about the murder," and with breathless haste ran his eyes over the following:—

SHOCKING MURDER!!!

TRAGEDY IN HIGH LIFE!! A BEAUTIFUL WOMAN SHOOTS A DISTIN-
GUISHED CONFEDERATE SOLDIER AT THE SOUTHERN HOTEL!!! JEAL-
OUSY THE CAUSE!!!!

This morning occurred another of those shocking murders which have become the almost daily food of the newspapers, the direct result of the socialistic doctrines and woman's rights agitations,[147] which have made every woman the avenger of her own wrongs, and all society the hunting ground for her victims.

About nine o'clock a lady deliberately shot a man dead in the public parlor of the Southern Hotel, coolly remarking, as she threw down her revolver and permitted herself to be taken into custody, "He brought it on himself." Our reporters were immediately dispatched to the scene of the tragedy, and gathered the following particulars.

Yesterday afternoon arrived at the hotel from Washington, Col. George Selby and family, who had taken passage and were to sail at noon to-day in the steamer Scotia for England. The Colonel was a handsome man about forty, a gentleman of wealth and high social position, a resident of New Orleans. He served with distinction in the confederate army, and received a wound in the leg from which he has never entirely recovered, being obliged to use a cane in locomotion.

This morning at about nine o'clock, a lady, accompanied by a gentleman, called at the office of the hotel and asked for Col. Selby. The Colonel was at breakfast. Would the clerk tell him that a lady and a gentleman wished to see him for a moment in the parlor? The clerk says that the gentleman asked her, "What do you want to see *him* for?" and that she replied, "He is going to Europe, and I ought to just say good by."

Col. Selby was informed, and the lady and gentleman were shown to the parlor, in which were at the time three or four other persons. Five minutes after two shots were fired in quick succession, and there was a rush to the parlor from which the reports came.

Col. Selby was found lying on the floor, bleeding, but not dead. Two gentlemen, who had just come in, had seized the lady, who made no resistance, and she was at once given in charge of a police officer who arrived. The persons who were in the parlor agree substantially as to what occurred. They had happened to be looking towards the door when the man—Col. Selby—entered with his cane, and they looked at him, because he stopped as if surprised and frightened, and made a backward movement. At the same moment the lady in the bonnet advanced towards him and said something like, "George, will you go with me?" He replied, throwing up his hand and retreating, "My God! I can't, don't fire," and the next instant two shots were heard and he fell. The lady appeared to be beside herself with rage or excitement, and trembled very much when the gentlemen took hold of her; it was them she said, "He brought it on himself."

Col. Selby was carried at once to his room and Dr. Puffer, the eminent surgeon, was sent for. It was found that he was shot through the breast and through the abdomen. Other aid was summoned, but the wounds were mortal, and Col. Selby expired in an hour, in pain, but his mind was clear to the last, and he made a full deposition. The substance of it was that his murderess is a Miss Laura Hawkins, whom he had known at Washington as a lobbyist, and had had some business with her. She had followed him with her attentions and solicitations, and had endeavored to make him desert his wife and go to Europe with her. When he resisted and avoided her, she had threatened him. Only the day before he left Washington she had declared that he should never go out of the city alive without her.

It seems to have been a deliberate and premeditated murder, the woman following him from Washington on purpose to commit it.

We learn that the murderess, who is a woman of dazzling and transcendent beauty and about twenty-six or seven, is a niece of Senator Dilworthy, at whose house she has been spending the winter. She belongs to a high Southern family, and has the reputation of being an heiress. Like some other great beauties and belles in Washington however there have been whispers that she had something to do with the lobby. If we mistake not we have heard her name mentioned in connection with the sale of the Tennessee Lands to the Knobs University, the bill for which passed the House last night.

Her companion is Mr. Harry Brierly, a New York dandy, who has been in Washington. His connection with her and with this tragedy is not known, but he was also taken into custody, and will be detained at least as a witness.

P.S. One of the persons present in the parlor says that after Laura Hawkins had fired twice, she turned the pistol towards herself, but that Brierly sprang and caught it from her hand, and that it was he who threw it on the floor.

Further particulars with full biographies of all the parties in our next edition.

Philip hastened at once to the Southern Hotel, where he found still a great state of excitement, and a thousand different and exaggerated stories passing from mouth to mouth. The witnesses of the event had told it over so many times that they worked it up into a most dramatic scene, and embellished it with whatever could heighten its awfulness. Outsiders had taken up invention also. The Colonel's wife had gone insane, they said. The children had rushed into the parlor and rolled themselves in their father's blood. The hotel clerk said that he noticed there was murder in the woman's eye when he saw her. A person who had met the woman on the stairs felt a creeping sensation. Some thought Brierly was an accomplice, and that he had set the woman on to kill his rival. Some said the woman showed the calmness and indifference of insanity.

Philip learned that Harry and Laura had both been taken to the city prison, and he went there; but he was not admitted. Not being a newspaper reporter, he could not see either of them that night; but the officer questioned him suspiciously and asked him who he was. He might perhaps see Brierly in the morning.

The latest editions of the evening papers had the result of the inquest. It was a plain enough case for the jury, but they sat over it a long time, listening to the wrangling of the physicians. Dr. Puffer insisted that the man died from the effects of the wound in the chest. Dr. Dobb as strongly insisted that the wound in the abdomen caused death. Dr. Golightly suggested that in his opinion death ensued from a complication of the two wounds and perhaps other causes. He examined the table waiter, as to whether Col. Selby ate any breakfast, and what he ate, and if he had any appetite.

The jury finally threw themselves back upon the indisputable fact that Selby was dead, that either wound would have killed him (admitted by the doctors), and rendered a verdict that he died from pistol-shot wounds inflicted by a pistol in the hands of Laura Hawkins.

The morning papers blazed with big type, and overflowed with details of the murder. The accounts in the evening papers were only the premonitory drops to this mighty shower. The scene was dramatically worked up in column after column. There were sketches, biographical and historical. There were long "specials" from Washington, giving a full history of Laura's career there, with the names of men with whom she was said to be intimate, a description of Senator Dilworthy's residence and of his family, and of Laura's room in his house, and a sketch of the Senator's appearance and what he said. There was a great deal about her beauty, her accomplishments and her brilliant position in society, and her doubtful position in society. There was also an interview with Col. Sellers and another with Washington Hawkins, the brother of the murderess. One journal had a long dispatch from Hawkeye, reporting the excitement in that quiet village and the reception of the awful intelligence.

All the parties had been "interviewed."[148] There were reports of conversations with the clerk at the hotel; with the call-boy; with the waiter at table, with all the witnesses, with the policeman, with the landlord (who wanted it understood that nothing of that sort had ever happened in his house before, although it had always been frequented by the best Southern society), and with Mrs. Col. Selby. There were diagrams illustrating the scene of the shooting, and views of the hotel and street, and portraits of the parties.

There were three minute and different statements from the doctors about the wounds, so technically worded that nobody could understand them. Harry and Laura had also been "interviewed" and there was a statement from Philip himself, which a reporter had knocked him up out of bed at midnight to give, though how he found him, Philip never could conjecture.

What some of the journals lacked in suitable length for the occasion, they made up in encyclopaedic information about other similar murders and shootings.

The statement from Laura was not full, in fact it was fragmentary, and consisted of nine parts of the reporter's valuable observations to one of Laura's, and it was, as the reporter significantly remarked, "incoherent." But it appeared that Laura claimed to be Selby's wife, or to have been his wife, that he had deserted her and betrayed her, and that she was going to follow him to Europe. When the reporter asked:

"What made you shoot him, Miss Hawkins?" Laura's only reply was, very simply,

"Did I shoot him? Do they say I shot him?" And she would say no more.

The news of the murder was made the excitement of the day. Talk of it filled the town. The facts reported were scrutinized, the standing of the parties was discussed, the dozen different theories of the motive, broached in the newspapers, were disputed over.

During the night subtle electricity had carried the tale over all the wires of the continent and under the sea; and in all villages and towns of the Union, from the Atlantic to the territories, and away up and down the Pacific slope, and as far as London and Paris and Berlin, that morning the name of Laura Hawkins was spoken by millions and millions of people, while the owner of it—the sweet child of years ago, the beautiful queen of Washington drawing rooms—sat shivering on her cot-bed in the darkness of a damp cell in the Tombs.

CHAPTER XLVII

—Mana qo c'u x-opon-vi ri v'oyeualal, ri v'achihilal! ahcarroc cah, ahcarroc uleu! la quitzih varal in camel, in zachel varal chuxmut cah, chuxmut uleu!

Rabinal-Achi.

PHILIP'S FIRST EFFORT was to get Harry out of the Tombs. He gained permission to see him, in the presence of an officer, during the day, and he found that hero very much cast down.

"I never intended to come to such a place as this, old fellow," he said to Philip; "it's no place for a gentleman, they've no idea how to treat a gentleman. Look at that provender," pointing to his uneaten prison ration. "They tell me I am detained as a witness, and I passed the night among a lot of cut-throats and dirty rascals—a pretty witness I'd be in a month spent in such company."

"But what under heavens," asked Philip, "induced you to come to New York with Laura! What was it for?"

"What for? Why, she wanted me to come. I didn't know anything about that cursed Selby. She said it was lobby business for the University. I'd no idea what she was dragging me into that confounded hotel for. I suppose she knew that the Southerners all go there, and thought she'd find her man. Oh! Lord, I wish I'd taken your advice. You might as well murder somebody and have the credit of it, as get into the newspapers the way I have. She's pure devil, that girl. You ought to have seen how sweet she was on me; what an ass I am."

"Well, I'm not going to dispute a poor prisoner. But the first thing is to get you out of this. I've brought the note Laura wrote you, for one thing, and I've seen your uncle, and explained the truth of the case to him. He will be here soon."

Harry's uncle came, with other friends, and in the course of the day made such a showing to the authorities that Harry was released, on giving bonds to appear as a witness when wanted. His spirits rose with their usual elasticity as soon as he was out of

Centre Street,[149] and he insisted on giving Philip and his friends a royal supper at Delmonico's, an excess which was perhaps excusable in the rebound of his feelings, and which was committed with his usual reckless generosity. Harry ordered the supper, and it is perhaps needless to say that Philip paid the bill.

Neither of the young men felt like attempting to see Laura that day, and she saw no company except the newspaper reporters, until the arrival of Col. Sellers and Washington Hawkins, who had hastened to New York with all speed.

They found Laura in a cell in the upper tier of the women's department. The cell was somewhat larger than those in the men's department, and might be eight feet by ten square, perhaps a little longer. It was of stone, floor and all, and the roof was oven shaped. A narrow slit in the roof admitted sufficient light, and was the only means of ventilation; when the window was opened there was nothing to prevent the rain coming in. The only means of heating being from the corridor, when the door was ajar, the cell was chilly and at this time damp. It was whitewashed and clean, but it had a slight jail odor; its only furniture was a narrow iron bedstead, with a tick of straw and some blankets, not too clean.

When Col. Sellers was conducted to this cell by the matron and looked in, his emotions quite overcame him, the tears rolled down his cheeks and his voice trembled so that he could hardly speak. Washington was unable to say anything; he looked from Laura to the miserable creatures who were walking in the corridor with unutterable disgust. Laura was alone calm and self-contained, though she was not unmoved by the sight of the grief of her friends.

"Are you comfortable, Laura?" was the first word the Colonel could get out.

"You see," she replied. "I can't say it's exactly comfortable."

"Are you cold?"

"It is pretty chilly. The stone floor is like ice. It chills me through to step on it. I have to sit on the bed."

"Poor thing, poor thing. And can you eat any thing?"

"No, I am not hungry. I don't know that I could eat any thing, I can't eat *that*."

"Oh dear," continued the Colonel, "it's dreadful. But cheer up, dear, cheer up"; and the Colonel broke down entirely.

"But," he went on, "we'll stand by you. We'll do everything for you. I know you couldn't have meant to do it, it must have been insanity, you know, or something of that sort. You never did anything of the sort before."

Laura smiled very faintly and said,

"Yes, it was something of that sort. It's all a whirl. He was a villain; you don't know."

"I'd rather have killed him myself, in a duel you know, all fair. I wish I had. But don't you be down. We'll get you off—the best counsel, the lawyers in New York can do anything; I've read of cases. But you must be comfortable now. We've brought some of your clothes, at the hotel. What else can we get for you?"

Laura suggested that she would like some sheets for her bed, a piece of carpet to step on, and her meals sent in; and some books and writing materials if it was allowed. The Colonel and Washington promised to procure all these things, and then took their sorrowful leave, a great deal more affected than the criminal was, apparently, by her situation.

The Colonel told the matron as he went away that if she would look to Laura's comfort a little it shouldn't be the worse for her; and to the turnkey who let them out he patronizingly said,

"You've got a big establishment here, a credit to the city. I've got a friend in there—I shall see you again, sir."

By the next day something more of Laura's own story began to appear in the newspapers, colored and heightened by reporters' rhetoric. Some of them cast a lurid light upon the Colonel's career, and represented his victim as a beautiful avenger of her murdered innocence; and others pictured her as his willing paramour and pitiless slayer. Her communications to the reporters were stopped by her lawyers as soon as they were retained and visited her, but this fact did not prevent—it may have facilitated—the appearance of casual paragraphs here and there which were likely to beget popular sympathy for the poor girl.

The occasion did not pass without "improvement" by the leading journals; and Philip preserved the editorial comments of three or four of them which pleased him most. These he used to read aloud to his friends afterwards and ask them to guess from which journal each of them had been cut. One began in this simple manner:—

> History never repeats itself, but the Kaleidoscopic combinations of the pictured present often seem to be constructed out of the broken fragments of antique legends. Washington is not Corinth, and Lais, the beautiful daughter of Timandra, might not have been the prototype of the ravishing Laura, daughter of the plebeian house of Hawkins; but the orators and statesmen who were the purchasers of the favors of the one, may have been as incorruptible as the Republican statesmen who learned how to love and how to vote from the sweet lips of the Washington lobbyist; and perhaps the modern Lais would never have departed from the national Capital if there had been there even one republican Xenocrates who resisted her blandishments. But here the parallel fails. Lais, wandering away with the youth Hippostratus, is slain by the women who are jealous of her charms. Laura, straying into her Thessaly with the youth Brierly, slays her other lover and becomes the champion of the wrongs of her sex.[150]

Another journal began its editorial with less lyrical beauty, but with equal force. It closed as follows:—

> With Laura Hawkins, fair, fascinating and fatal, and with the dissolute Colonel of a lost cause, who has reaped the harvest he sowed, we have nothing to do. But as the curtain rises on this awful tragedy, we catch a glimpse of the society at the capital under this Adminstration, which we cannot contemplate without alarm for the fate of the Republic.

A third newspaper took up the subject in a different tone. It said:—

> Our repeated predictions are verified. The pernicious doctrines which we have announced as prevailing in American society have been again illustrated. The name of the city is becoming a reproach. We may have done something in averting its ruin in our resolute exposure of the Great Frauds;[151] we shall not be deterred from insisting that the outraged laws for the protection of human

life shall be vindicated now, so that a person can walk the streets or
enter the public houses, at least in the daytime, without the risk of
a bullet through his brain.

A fourth journal began its remarks as follows:—

The fullness with which we present our readers this morning the
details of the Selby-Hawkins homicide is a miracle of modern
journalism. Subsequent investigation can do little to fill out the
picture. It is the old story. A beautiful woman shoots her abscond-
ing lover in cold-blood; and we shall doubtless learn in due time
that if she was not as mad as a hare in this month of March, she was
at least laboring under what is termed "momentary insanity."

It would not be too much to say that upon the first publication
of the facts of the tragedy, there was an almost universal feeling of
rage against the murderess in the Tombs, and that reports of her
beauty only heightened the indignation. It was as if she presumed
upon that and upon her sex, to defy the law, and there was a fer-
vent hope that the law would take its plain course.

Yet Laura was not without friends, and some of them very influential too. She had in her keeping a great many secrets and a
great many reputations, perhaps. Who shall set himself up to
judge human motives? Why, indeed, might we not feel pity for a
woman whose brilliant career had been so suddenly extinguished
in misfortune and crime? Those who had known her so well in
Washington might find it impossible to believe that the fascinating woman could have had murder in her heart, and would readily give ear to the current sentimentality about the temporary
aberration of mind under the stress of personal calamity.

Senator Dilworthy was greatly shocked, of course, but he was
full of charity for the erring.

"We shall all need mercy," he said. "Laura as an inmate of my
family was a most exemplary female, amiable, affectionate and
truthful, perhaps too fond of gaiety, and neglectful of the exter-
nals of religion, but a woman of principle. She may have had experiences of which I am ignorant, but she could not have gone to
this extremity if she had been in her own right mind."

To the Senator's credit be it said, he was willing to help Laura and her family in this dreadful trial. She, herself, was not without money, for the Washington lobbyist is not seldom more fortunate than the Washington claimant, and she was able to procure a good many luxuries to mitigate the severity of her prison life. It enabled her also to have her own family near her, and to see some of them daily. The tender solicitude of her mother, her childlike grief, and her firm belief in the real guiltlessness of her daughter, touched even the custodians of the Tombs who are enured to scenes of pathos.

Mrs. Hawkins had hastened to her daughter as soon as she received money for the journey. She had no reproaches, she had only tenderness and pity. She could not shut out the dreadful facts of the case, but it had been enough for her that Laura had said, in their first interview, "Mother, I did not know what I was doing." She obtained lodgings near the prison and devoted her life to her daughter, as if she had been really her own child. She would have remained in the prison day and night if it had been permitted. She was aged and feeble, but this great necessity seemed to give her new life.

The pathetic story of the old lady's ministrations, and her simplicity and faith, also got into the newspapers in time, and probably added to the pathos of this wrecked woman's fate, which was beginning to be felt by the public. It was certain that she had champions who thought that her wrongs ought to be placed against her crime, and expressions of this feeling came to her in various ways. Visitors came to see her, and gifts of fruit and flowers were sent, which brought some cheer into her hard and gloomy cell.

Laura had declined to see either Philip or Harry, somewhat to the former's relief, who had a notion that she would necessarily feel humiliated by seeing him after breaking faith with him, but to the discomfiture of Harry, who still felt her fascination, and thought her refusal heartless. He told Philip that of course he had got through with such a woman, but he wanted to see her.

Philip, to keep him from some new foolishness, persuaded him to go with him to Philadelphia, and give his valuable services in the mining operations at Ilium.

The law took its course with Laura. She was indicted for murder in the first degree, and held for trial at the summer term. The two most distinguished criminal lawyers in the city had been retained for her defence, and to that the resolute woman devoted her days, with a courage that rose as she consulted with her counsel and understood the methods of criminal procedure in New York.

She was greatly depressed, however, by the news from Washington. Congress adjourned and her bill had failed to pass the Senate. It must wait for the next session.

CHAPTER XLVIII

—In our working, nothing us availle;
For lost is all our labour and travaille,
And all the cost a twenty devil way
Is lost also, which we upon it lay.
                                        Chaucer.

He moonihoawa ka aie.
Hawaiian Proverb.

IT HAD BEEN a bad winter, somehow, for the firm of Penny-backer, Bigler and Small. These celebrated contractors usually made more money during the session of the legislature at Harrisburg than upon all their summer work, and this winter had been unfruitful. It was unaccountable to Bigler.

"You see, Mr. Bolton," he said, and Philip was present at the conversation, "it puts us all out. It looks as if politics was played out. We'd counted on the year of Simon's re-election.[152] And, now, he's re-elected, and I've yet to see the first man who's the better for it."

"You don't mean to say," asked Philip, "that he went in without paying anything?"

"Not a cent, not a dash cent, as I can hear," repeated Mr. Bigler, indignantly. "I call it a swindle on the state. How it was done gets me. I never saw such a tight time for money in Harrisburg."

"Were there no combinations, no railroad jobs, no mining schemes put through in connection with the election?"

"Not that I know," said Bigler, shaking his head in disgust. "In fact it was openly said, that there was no money in the election. It's perfectly unheard of."

"Perhaps," suggested Philip, "it was effected on what the insurance companies call the 'endowment,' or the 'paid up' plan, by which a policy is secured after a certain time without further payment."

"You think then," said Mr. Bolton smiling, "that a liberal and sagacious politician might own a legislature after a time, and not be bothered with keeping up his payments?"

"Whatever it is," interrupted Mr. Bigler, "it's devilish ingenious, and goes ahead of my calculations; it's cleaned me out, when I thought we had a dead sure thing. I tell you what it is, gentlemen, I shall go in for reform. Things have got pretty mixed when a legislature will give away a United States senatorship."

It was melancholy, but Mr. Bigler was not a man to be crushed by one misfortune, or to lose his confidence in human nature, on one exhibition of apparent honesty. He was already on his feet again, or would be if Mr. Bolton could tide him over shoal water for ninety days.

"We've got something with money in it," he explained to Mr. Bolton, "got hold of it by good luck. We've got the entire contract for Dobson's Patent Pavement[153] for the city of Mobile. See here."

Mr. Bigler made some figures; contract so much, cost of work and materials so much, profits so much. At the end of three months the city would owe the company three hundred and seventy-five thousand dollars—two hundred thousand of that would be profits. The whole job was worth at least a million to the company—it might be more. There could be no mistake in these figures; here was the contract, Mr. Bolton knew what materials were worth and what the labor would cost.

Mr. Bolton knew perfectly well from sore experience that there was always a mistake in figures when Bigler or Small made them, and he knew that he ought to send the fellow about his business. Instead of that, he let him talk.

They only wanted to raise fifty thousand dollars to carry on the contract—that expended they would have city bonds. Mr. Bolton said he hadn't the money. But Bigler could raise it on his name. Mr. Bolton said he had no right to put his family to that risk. But the entire contract could be assigned to him—the security was ample—it was a fortune to him if it was forfeited. Besides Mr. Bigler had been unfortunate, he didn't know where to look for the necessaries of life for his family. If he could only have one more chance, he was sure he could right himself. He begged for it.

And Mr. Bolton yielded. He could never refuse such appeals. If he had befriended a man once and been cheated by him, that man appeared to have a claim upon him forever. He shrank, however, from telling his wife what he had done on this occasion, for he knew that if any person was more odious than Small to his family it was Bigler.

"Philip tells me," Mrs. Bolton said that evening, "that the man Bigler has been with thee again to-day. I hope thee will have nothing more to do with him."

"He has been very unfortunate," replied Mr. Bolton, uneasily.

"He is always unfortunate, and he is always getting thee into trouble. But thee didn't listen to him again?"

"Well, mother, his family is in want, and I lent him my name— but I took ample security. The worst that can happen will be a little inconvenience."

Mrs. Bolton looked grave and anxious, but she did not complain or remonstrate; she knew what a "little inconvenience" meant, but she knew there was no help for it. If Mr. Bolton had been on his way to market to buy a dinner for his family with the only dollar he had in the world in his pocket, he would have given it to a chance beggar who asked him for it. Mrs. Bolton only asked (and the question showed that she was no more provident than her husband where her heart was interested),

"But has thee provided money for Philip to use in opening the coal mine?"

"Yes, I have set apart as much as it ought to cost to open the mine, as much as we can afford to lose if no coal is found. Philip has the control of it, as equal partner in the venture, deducting the capital invested. He has great confidence in his success, and I hope for his sake he won't be disappointed."

Philip could not but feel that he was treated very much like one of the Bolton family—by all except Ruth. His mother, when he went home after his recovery from his accident, had affected to be very jealous of Mrs. Bolton, about whom and Ruth she asked a thousand questions—an affectation of jealousy which no doubt concealed a real heartache, which comes to every mother when her son goes out into the world and forms new ties. And to Mrs. Sterling, a widow, living on a small income in a remote Massachusetts village, Philadelphia was a city of many splendors. All its inhabitants seemed highly favored, dwelling in ease and surrounded by superior advantages. Some of her neighbors had relations living in Philadelphia, and it seemed to them somehow a guarantee of respectability to have relations in Philadelphia. Mrs. Sterling was not sorry to have Philip make his way among such well-to-do people, and she was sure that no good fortune could be too good for his deserts.

"So, sir," said Ruth, when Philip came from New York, "you have been assisting in a pretty tragedy. I saw your name in the papers. Is this woman a specimen of your western friends?"

"My only assistance," replied Philip, a little annoyed, "was in trying to keep Harry out of a bad scrape and I failed after all. He walked into her trap, and he has been punished for it. I'm going to take him up to Ilium to see if he won't work steadily at one thing, and quit his nonsense."

"Is she as beautiful as the newspapers say she is?"

"I don't know, she has a kind of beauty—she is not like—"

"Not like Alice?"

"Well, she is brilliant; she was called the handsomest woman in Washington—dashing, you know, and sarcastic and witty. Ruth, do you believe a woman ever becomes a devil?"

"Men do, and I don't know why women shouldn't. But I never saw one."

"Well, Laura Hawkins comes very near it. But it is dreadful to think of her fate."

"Why, do you suppose they will hang a woman? Do you suppose they will be so barbarous as that?"

"I wasn't thinking of that—it's doubtful if a New York jury would find a woman guilty of any such crime. But to think of her life if she is acquitted."

"It is dreadful," said Ruth, thoughtfully, "but the worst of it is that you men do not want women educated to do anything, to be able to earn an honest living by their own exertions. They are educated as if they were always to be petted and supported, and there was never to be any such thing as misfortune. I suppose, now, that you would all choose to have me stay idly at home, and give up my profession."

"Oh, no," said Philip, earnestly, "I respect your resolution. But, Ruth, do you think you would be happier or do more good in following your profession than in having a home of your own?"

"What is to hinder having a home of my own?"

"Nothing, perhaps, only you never would be in it—you would be away day and night, if you had any practice; and what sort of a home would that make for your husband?"

"What sort of a home is it for the wife whose husband is always away riding about in his doctor's gig?"

"Ah, you know that is not fair. The woman makes the home."

Philip and Ruth often had this sort of discussion, to which Philip was always trying to give a personal turn. He was now about to go to Ilium for the season, and he did not like to go without some assurance from Ruth that she might perhaps love him some day, when he was worthy of it, and when he could offer her something better than a partnership in his poverty.

"I should work with a great deal better heart, Ruth," he said the morning he was taking leave, "if I knew you cared for me a little."

Ruth was looking down; the color came faintly to her cheeks, and she hesitated. She needn't be looking down, he thought, for she was ever so much shorter than tall Philip.

"It's not much of a place, Ilium," Philip went on, as if a little geographical remark would fit in here as well as anything else, "and I shall have plenty of time to think over the responsibility I have taken, and—" his observation did not seem to be coming out any where.

But Ruth looked up, and there was a light in her eyes that quickened Phil's pulse. She took his hand, and said with serious sweetness:

"Thee mustn't lose heart, Philip." And then she added, in another mood, "Thee knows I graduate in the summer and shall have my diploma. And if any thing happens—mines explode sometimes—thee can send for me. Farewell."

The opening of the Ilium coal mine was begun with energy, but without many omens of success. Philip was running a tunnel into the breast of the mountain, in faith that the coal stratum ran there as it ought to. How far he must go in he believed he knew, but no one could tell exactly. Some of the miners said that they should probably go through the mountain, and that the hole could be used for a railway tunnel. The mining camp was a busy place at any rate. Quite a settlement of board and log shanties had gone up, with a blacksmith shop, a small machine shop, and a temporary store for supplying the wants of the workmen. Philip and Harry pitched a commodious tent, and lived in the full enjoyment of the free life.

There is no difficulty in digging a hole in the ground, if you have money enough to pay for the digging, but those who try this sort of work are always surprised at the large amount of money necessary to make a small hole. The earth is never willing to yield one product, hidden in her bosom, without an equivalent for it. And when a person asks of her coal, she is quite apt to require gold in exchange.

It was exciting work for all concerned in it. As the tunnel advanced into the rock every day promised to be the golden day. This very blast might disclose the treasure.

The work went on week after week, and at length during the night as well as the daytime. Gangs relieved each other, and the tunnel was every hour, inch by inch and foot by foot, crawling into the mountain. Philip was on the stretch of hope and excitement. Every pay day he saw his funds melting away, and still there was only the faintest show of what the miners call "signs."

The life suited Harry, whose buoyant hopefulness was never disturbed. He made endless calculations, which nobody could understand, of the probable position of the vein. He stood about among the workmen with the busiest air. When he was down at Ilium he called himself the engineer of the works, and he used to spend hours smoking his pipe with the Dutch landlord on the hotel porch, and astonishing the idlers there with the stories of his railroad operations in Missouri. He talked with the landlord, too, about enlarging his hotel, and about buying some village lots, in the prospect of a rise, when the mine was opened. He taught the Dutchman how to mix a great many cooling drinks for the summer time, and had a bill at the hotel, the growing length of which Mr. Dusenheimer contemplated with pleasant anticipations. Mr. Brierly was a very useful and cheering person wherever he went.

Midsummer arrived. Philip could report to Mr. Bolton only progress, and this was not a cheerful message for him to send to Philadelphia in reply to inquiries that he thought became more and more anxious. Philip himself was a prey to the constant fear that the money would give out before the coal was struck.

At this time Harry was summoned to New York, to attend the trial of Laura Hawkins. It was possible that Philip would have to go also, her lawyer wrote, but they hoped for a postponement. There was important evidence that they could not yet obtain, and he hoped the judge would not force them to a trial unprepared. There were many reasons for a delay, reasons which of course are never mentioned, but which it would seem that a New York judge sometimes must understand, when he grants a postponement upon a motion that seems to the public altogether inadequate.

Harry went, but he soon came back. The trial was put off. Every week we can gain, said the learned counsel, Braham, improves our chances. The popular rage never lasts long.

CHAPTER XLIX

Солнце заблистало, но не надолго: блеснуло и скрылось.

"Mofère ipa eiye nã." "Aki ije *ofere* li obbè."

"WE'VE STRUCK IT!"

This was the electric announcement at the tent door that woke Philip out of a sound sleep at dead of night, and shook all the sleepiness out of him in a trice.

"What! Where is it? When? Coal? Let me see it. What quality is it?" were some of the rapid questions that Philip poured out as he hurriedly dressed. "Harry, wake up, my boy. The coal train is coming. Struck it, eh? Let's see?"

The foreman put down his lantern, and handed Philip a black lump. There was no mistake about it, it was the hard, shining anthracite, and its freshly fractured surface, glistened in the light like polished steel. Diamond never shone with such lustre in the eyes of Philip.

Harry was exuberant, but Philip's natural caution found expression in his next remark.

"Now, Roberts, you are sure about this?"

"What—sure that it's coal?"

"O, no, sure that it's the main vein."

"Well, yes. We took it to be that."

"Did you from the first?"

"I can't say we did at first. No, we didn't. Most of the indications were there, but not all of them, not all of them. So we thought we'd prospect a bit."

"Well?"

"It was tolerable thick, and looked as if it might be the vein—looked as if it *ought* to be the vein. Then we went down on it a little. Looked better all the time."

"When did you strike it?"

"About ten o'clock."

"Then you've been prospecting about four hours."

349

"Yes, been sinking on it something over four hours."

"I'm afraid you couldn't go down very far in four hours—could you?"

"O yes—it's a good deal broke up, nothing but picking and gadding stuff."

"Well, it *does* look encouraging, sure enough—but then the lacking indications—"

"I'd rather we had them, Mr. Sterling, but I've seen more than one good permanent mine struck without 'em in my time."

"Well, *that* is encouraging too."

"Yes, there was the Union, the Alabama and the Black Mohawk—all good, sound mines, you know—all just exactly like this one when we first struck them."

"Well, I begin to feel a good deal more easy. I guess we've really got it. I remember hearing them tell about the Black Mohawk."

"I'm free to say that *I* believe it, and the men all think so too. They are all old hands at this business."

"Come Harry, let's go up and look at it, just for the comfort of it," said Philip. They came back in the course of an hour, satisfied and happy.

There was no more sleep for them that night. They lit their pipes, put a specimen of the coal on the table, and made it a kind of loadstone of thought and conversation.

"Of course," said Harry, "there will have to be a branch track built, and a 'switch-back' up the hill."

"Yes, there will be no trouble about getting the money for that now. We could sell out to-morrow for a handsome sum. That sort of coal doesn't go begging within a mile of a railroad. I wonder if Mr. Bolton would rather sell out or work it?"

"Oh, work it," says Harry, "probably the whole mountain is coal now you've got to it."

"Possibly it might not be much of a vein after all," suggested Philip.

"Possibly it *is;* I'll bet it's forty feet thick. I told you. I knew the sort of thing as soon as I put my eyes on it."

Philip's next thought was to write to his friends and announce their good fortune. To Mr. Bolton he wrote a short, business letter, as calm as he could make it. They had found coal of excellent quality, but they could not yet tell with absolute certainty what the vein was. The prospecting was still going on. Philip also wrote to Ruth; but though this letter may have glowed, it was not with the heat of burning anthracite. He needed no artificial heat to warm his pen and kindle his ardor when he sat down to write to Ruth. But it must be confessed that the words never flowed so easily before, and he ran on for an hour disporting in all the extravagance of his imagination. When Ruth read it, she doubted if the fellow had not gone out of his senses. And it was not until she reached the postscript that she discovered the cause of the exhilaration. "P. S.—We have found coal."

The news couldn't have come to Mr. Bolton in better time. He had never been so sorely pressed. A dozen schemes which he had in hand, any one of which might turn up a fortune, all languished, and each needed just a little more money to save that which had been invested. He hadn't a piece of real estate that was not covered with mortgages, even to the wild tract which Philip was experimenting on, and which had no marketable value above the incumbrance on it.

He had come home that day early, unusually dejected.

"I am afraid," he said to his wife, "that we shall have to give up our home. I don't care for myself, but for thee and the children."

"That will be the least of misfortunes," said Mrs. Bolton, cheerfully, "if thee can clear thyself from debt and anxiety, which is wearing thee out, we can live any where. Thee knows we were never happier than when we were in a much humbler home."

"The truth is, Margaret, that affair of Bigler and Small's has come on me just when I couldn't stand another ounce. They have made another failure of it. I might have known they would; and the sharpers, or fools, I don't know which, have contrived to involve me for three times as much as the first obligation. The security is in my hands, but it is good for nothing to me. I have not the money to do anything with the contract."

Ruth heard this dismal news without great surprise. She had long felt that they were living on a volcano, that might go in to active operation at any hour. Inheriting from her father an active brain and the courage to undertake new things, she had little of his sanguine temperament which blinds one to difficulties and possible failures. She had little confidence in the many schemes which had been about to lift her father out of all his embarrassments and into great wealth, ever since she was a child; as she grew older, she rather wondered that they were as prosperous as they seemed to be, and that they did not all go to smash amid so many brilliant projects. She was nothing but a woman, and did not know how much of the business prosperity of the world is only a bubble of credit and speculation, one scheme helping to float another which is no better than it, and the whole liable to come to naught and confusion as soon as the busy brain that conceived them ceases its power to devise, or when some accident produces a sudden panic.

"Perhaps, I shall be the stay of the family, yet," said Ruth, with an approach to gaiety. "When we move into a little house in town, will thee let me put a little sign on the door—DR. RUTH BOLTON? Mrs. Dr. Longstreet,[154] thee knows, has a great income."

"Who will pay for the sign, Ruth?" asked Mr. Bolton.

A servant entered with the afternoon mail from the office. Mr. Bolton took his letters listlessly, dreading to open them. He knew well what they contained, new difficulties, more urgent demands for money.

"Oh, here is one from Philip. Poor fellow. I shall feel his disappointment as much as my own bad luck. It is hard to bear when one is young."

He opened the letter and read. As he read his face lightened, and he fetched such a sigh of relief, that Mrs. Bolton and Ruth both exclaimed.

"Read that," he cried, "Philip has found coal!"

The world was changed in a moment. One little sentence had done it. There was no more trouble. Philip had found coal. That meant relief. That meant fortune. A great weight was taken off, and the spirits of the whole household rose magically. Good Money! beautiful demon of Money, what an enchanter thou art! Ruth felt that she was of less consequence in the household, now that Philip had found coal, and perhaps she was not sorry to feel so.

Mr. Bolton was ten years younger the next morning. He went into the city, and showed his letter on change. It was the sort of news his friends were quite willing to listen to. They took a new interest in him. If it was confirmed, Bolton would come right up again. There would be no difficulty about his getting all the money he wanted. The money market did not seem to be half so tight as it was the day before. Mr. Bolton spent a very pleasant day in his office, and went home revolving some new plans, and the execution of some projects he had long been prevented from entering upon by the lack of money.

The day had been spent by Philip in no less excitement. By daylight, with Philip's letters to the mail, word had gone down to Ilium that coal had been found, and very early a crowd of eager spectators had come up to see for themselves.

The "prospecting" continued day and night for upwards of a week, and during the first four or five days the indications grew more and more promising, and the telegrams and letters kept Mr. Bolton duly posted. But at last a change came, and the promises began to fail with alarming rapidity. In the end it was demonstrated without the possibility of a doubt that the great "find" was nothing but a worthless seam.

Philip was cast down, all the more so because he had been so foolish as to send the news to Philadelphia before he knew what he was writing about. And now he must contradict it. "It turns out to be only a mere seam," he wrote, "but we look upon it as an indication of better further in."

Alas! Mr. Bolton's affairs could not wait for "indications." The future might have a great deal in store, but the present was black and hopeless. It was doubtful if any sacrifice could save him from ruin. Yet sacrifice he must make, and that instantly, in the hope of saving something from the wreck of his fortune.

His lovely country home must go. That would bring the most ready money. The house that he had built with loving thought for each one of his family, as he planned its luxurious apartments and adorned it; the grounds that he had laid out, with so much delight in following the tastes of his wife, with whom the country, the cultivation of rare trees and flowers, the care of garden and lawn and conservatories were a passion almost; this home, which he had hoped his children would enjoy long after he had done with it, must go.

The family bore the sacrifice better than he did. They declared in fact—women are such hypocrites—that they quite enjoyed the city (it was in August) after living so long in the country, that it was a thousand times more convenient in every respect; Mrs. Bolton said it was a relief from the worry of a large establishment, and Ruth reminded her father that she should have had to come to town anyway before long.

Mr. Bolton was relieved, exactly as a water-logged ship is lightened by throwing overboard the most valuable portion of the cargo—but the leak was not stopped. Indeed his credit was injured instead of helped by the prudent step he had taken. It was regarded as a sure evidence of his embarrassment, and it was much more difficult for him to obtain help than if he had, instead of retrenching, launched into some new speculation.

Philip was greatly troubled, and exaggerated his own share in the bringing about of the calamity.

"You must not look at it so!" Mr. Bolton wrote him. "You have neither helped nor hindered—but you know you may help by and by. It would have all happened just so, if we had never begun to dig that hole. That is only a drop. Work away. I still have hope that something will occur to relieve me. At any rate we must not give up the mine, so long as we have any show."

Alas! the relief did not come. New misfortunes came instead. When the extent of the Bigler swindle was disclosed there was no more hope that Mr. Bolton could extricate himself, and he had, as an honest man, no resource except to surrender all his property for the benefit of his creditors.

The Autumn came and found Philip working with diminished force but still with hope. He had again and again been encouraged by good "indications," but he had again and again been disappointed. He could not go on much longer, and almost everybody except himself had thought it was useless to go on as long as he had been doing.

When the news came of Mr. Bolton's failure, of course the work stopped. The men were discharged, the tools were housed, the hopeful noise of pickman and driver ceased, and the mining camp had that desolate and mournful aspect which always hovers over a frustrated enterprise.

Philip sat down amid the ruins, and almost wished he were buried in them. How distant Ruth was now from him, now, when she might need him most. How changed was all the Philadelphia world, which had hitherto stood for the exemplification of happiness and prosperity.

He still had faith that there was coal in that mountain. He made a picture of himself living there a hermit in a shanty by the tunnel, digging away with solitary pick and wheelbarrow, day after day and year after year, until he grew gray and aged, and was known in all that region as the old man of the mountain. Perhaps some day—he felt it must be so some day—he should strike coal. But what if he did? Who would be alive to care for it then? What would he care for it then? No, a man wants riches in his youth, when the world is fresh to him. He wondered why Providence could not have reversed the usual process, and let the majority of men begin with wealth and gradually spend it, and die poor when they no longer needed it.

Harry went back to the city. It was evident that his services were no longer needed. Indeed, he had letters from his uncle, which he did not read to Philip, desiring him to go to San Francisco to look after some government contracts in the harbor there.

Philip had to look about him for something to do; he was like Adam; the world was all before him where to choose. He made, before he went elsewhere, a somewhat painful visit to Philadelphia, painful but yet not without its sweetnesses. The family had never shown him so much affection before; they all seemed to think his disappointment of more importance than their own misfortune. And there was that in Ruth's manner—in what she gave him and what she withheld—that would have made a hero of a very much less promising character than Philip Sterling.

Among the assets of the Bolton property, the Ilium tract was sold, and Philip bought it in at the vendue, for a song, for no one cared to even undertake the mortgage on it except himself. He went away the owner of it, and had ample time before he reached home in November, to calculate how much poorer he was by possessing it.

CHAPTER L

þá eymdir stríða á sorgfullt sinn,
og svipur mótgángs um vánga ríða,
og bakivendir þér veröldin,
og vellyst brosir að þínum qvíða;
þeink allt er knöttótt, og hverfast laetr,
sá hló í dag er á morgun graetr;
Alt jafnar sig!

Sigurd Peterson.

IT IS IMPOSSIBLE for the historian, with even the best intentions, to control events or compel the persons of his narrative to act wisely or to be successful. It is easy to see how things might have been better managed; a very little change here and there would have made a very different history of this one now in hand.

If Philip had adopted some regular profession, even some trade, he might now be a prosperous editor or a conscientious plumber, or an honest lawyer, and have borrowed money at the saving's bank and built a cottage, and be now furnishing it for the occupancy of Ruth and himself. Instead of this, with only a smattering of civil engineering, he is at his mother's house, fretting and fuming over his ill-luck, and the hardness and dishonesty of men, and thinking of nothing but how to get the coal out of the Ilium hills.

If Senator Dilworthy had not made that visit to Hawkeye, the Hawkins family and Col. Sellers would not now be dancing attendance upon Congress, and endeavoring to tempt that immaculate body into one of those appropriations, for the benefit of its members, which the members find it so difficult to explain to their constituents; and Laura would not be lying in the Tombs, awaiting her trial for murder, and doing her best, by the help of able counsel, to corrupt the pure fountain of criminal procedure in New York.

If Henry Brierly had been blown up on the first Mississippi steamboat he set foot on, as the chances were that he would be, he and Col. Sellers never would have gone into the Columbus Navigation scheme, and probably never into the East Tennessee Land scheme, and he would not now be detained in New York from very important business operations on the Pacific coast, for the sole purpose of giving evidence to convict of murder the only woman he ever loved half as much as he loves himself.

If Mr. Bolton had said the little word "no" to Mr. Bigler, Alice Montague might now be spending the winter in Philadelphia, and Philip also (waiting to resume his mining operations in the spring); and Ruth would not be an assistant in a Philadelphia hospital, taxing her strength with arduous routine duties, day by day, in order to lighten a little the burdens that weigh upon her unfortunate family.

It is altogether a bad business. An honest historian who had progressed thus far, and traced everything to such a condition of disaster and suspension, might well be justified in ending his narrative and writing—"after this the deluge." His only consolation would be in the reflection that he was not responsible for either characters or events.

And the most annoying thought is that a little money, judiciously applied, would relieve the burdens and anxieties of most of these people; but affairs seem to be so arranged that money is most difficult to get when people need it most.

A little of what Mr. Bolton has weakly given to unworthy people would now establish his family in a sort of comfort, and relieve Ruth of the excessive toil for which she inherited no adequate physical vigor. A little money would make a prince of Col. Sellers; and a little more would calm the anxiety of Washington Hawkins about Laura, for however the trial ended, he could feel sure of extricating her in the end. And if Philip had a little money he could unlock the stone door in the mountain whence would issue a stream of shining riches. It needs a golden wand to strike that rock. If the Knobs University bill could only go through, what a change would be wrought in the condition of most of the persons in this history. Even Philip himself would feel the good effects of it; for Harry would have something and Col. Sellers would have something; and have not both these cautious people expressed a determination to take an interest in the Ilium mine when they catch their larks?

Philip could not resist the inclination to pay a visit to Fallkill. He had not been at the Montagues' since the time he saw Ruth there, and he wanted to consult the Squire about an occupation. He was determined now to waste no more time in waiting on Providence, but to go to work at something, if it were nothing better than teaching in the Fallkill Seminary, or digging clams on Hingham beach.[155] Perhaps he could read law in Squire Montague's office while earning his bread as a teacher in the Seminary.

It was not altogether Philip's fault, let us own, that he was in this position. There are many young men like him in American society, of his age, opportunities, education and abilities, who have really been educated for nothing and have let themselves drift, in the hope that they will find somehow, and by some sudden turn of good luck, the golden road to fortune. He was not idle or lazy, he had energy and a disposition to carve his own way. But he was born into a time when all young men of his age caught the fever of speculation, and expected to get on in the world by the omission of some of the regular processes which have been appointed from of old. And examples were not wanting to encourage him. He saw people, all around him, poor yesterday, rich to-day, who had come into sudden opulence by some means which they could not have classified among any of the regular occupations of life. A war would give such a fellow a career and very likely fame. He might have been a "railroad man," or a politician, or a land speculator, or one of those mysterious people who travel free on all railroads and steamboats, and are continually crossing and re-crossing the Atlantic, driven day and night about nobody knows what, and make a great deal of money by so doing. Probably, at last, he sometimes thought with a whimsical smile, he should end by being an insurance agent, and asking people to insure their lives for his benefit.

Possibly Philip did not think how much the attractions of Fallkill were increased by the presence of Alice there. He had known her so long, she had somehow grown into his life by habit, that he would expect the pleasure of her society without thinking much about it. Latterly he never thought of her without thinking of Ruth, and if he gave the subject any attention, it was probably in an undefined consciousness that he had her sympathy in his love, and that she was always willing to hear him talk about it. If he ever wondered that Alice herself was not in love and never spoke of the possibility of her own marriage, it was a transient thought—for love did not seem necessary, exactly, to one so calm and evenly balanced and with so many resources in herself.

Whatever her thoughts may have been they were unknown to Philip, as they are to these historians; if she was seeming to be what she was not, and carrying a burden heavier than any one else carried, because she had to bear it alone, she was only doing what thousands of women do, with a self-renunciation and heroism of which men, impatient and complaining, have no conception. Have not these big babies with beards filled all literature with their outcries, their griefs and their lamentations? It is always the gentle sex which is hard and cruel and fickle and implacable.

"Do you think you would be contented to live in Fallkill, and attend the county Court?" asked Alice, when Philip had opened the budget of his new programme.

"Perhaps not always," said Philip, "I might go and practice in Boston maybe, or go to Chicago."

"Or you might get elected to Congress."

Philip looked at Alice to see if she was in earnest and not chaffing him. Her face was quite sober. Alice was one of those patriotic women in the rural districts, who think men are still selected for Congress on account of qualifications for the office.

"No," said Philip, "the chances are that a man cannot get into Congress now without resorting to arts and means that should render him unfit to go there; of course there are exceptions; but do you know that I could not go into politics if I were a lawyer, without losing standing somewhat in my profession, and without raising at least a suspicion of my intentions and unselfishness? Why, it is telegraphed all over the country and commented on as something wonderful if a congressman votes honestly and unselfishly and refuses to take advantage of his position to steal from the government."

"But," insisted Alice, "I should think it a noble ambition to go to Congress, if it is so bad, and help reform it. I don't believe it is as corrupt as the English parliament used to be, if there is any truth in the novels, and I suppose that is reformed."

"I'm sure I don't know where the reform is to begin. I've seen a perfectly capable, honest man, time and again, run against an illiterate trickster, and get beaten. I suppose if the people wanted decent members of Congress they would elect them. Perhaps," continued Philip with a smile, "the women will have to vote."

"Well, I should be willing to, if it were a necessity, just as I would go to war and do what I could, if the country couldn't be saved otherwise," said Alice, with a spirit that surprised Philip, well as he thought he knew her. "If I were a young gentleman in these times—"

Philip laughed outright. "It's just what Ruth used to say, 'if she were a man.' I wonder if all the young ladies are contemplating a change of sex."

"No, only a changed sex," retorted Alice; "we contemplate for the most part young men who don't care for anything they ought to care for."

"Well," said Philip, looking humble. "I care for some things, you and Ruth for instance; perhaps I ought not to. Perhaps I ought to care for Congress and that sort of thing."

"Don't be a goose, Philip. I heard from Ruth yesterday."

"Can I see her letter?"

"No, indeed. But I am afraid her hard work is telling on her, together with her anxiety about her father."

"Do you think, Alice," asked Philip with one of those selfish thoughts that are not seldom mixed with real love, "that Ruth prefers her profession to—to marriage?"

"Philip," exclaimed Alice, rising to quit the room, and speaking hurriedly as if the words were forced from her, "you are as blind as a bat; Ruth would cut off her right hand for you this minute."

Philip never noticed that Alice's face was flushed and that her voice was unsteady; he only thought of the delicious words he had heard. And the poor girl, loyal to Ruth, loyal to Philip, went straight to her room, locked the door, threw herself on the bed and sobbed as if her heart would break. And then she prayed that her Father in Heaven would give her strength. And after a time she was calm again, and went to her bureau drawer and took from a hiding place a little piece of paper, yellow with age. Upon it was pinned a four-leaved clover, dry and yellow also. She looked long at this foolish memento. Under the clover leaf was written in a school-girl's hand—*Philip, June, 186—.*"

Squire Montague thought very well of Philip's proposal. It would have been better if he had begun the study of the law as soon as he left college, but it was not too late now, and besides he had gathered some knowledge of the world.

"But," asked the Squire, "do you mean to abandon your land in Pennsylvania?" This tract of land seemed an immense possible fortune to this New England lawyer-farmer. "Hasn't it good timber, and doesn't the railroad almost touch it?"

"I can't do anything with it now. Perhaps I can sometime."

"What is your reason for supposing that there is coal there?"

"The opinion of the best geologist I could consult, my own observation of the country, and the little veins of it we found. I feel certain it is there. I shall find it some day. I know it. If I can only keep the land till I make money enough to try again."

Philip took from his pocket a map of the anthracite coal region, and pointed out the position of the Ilium mountain which he had begun to tunnel.

"Doesn't it look like it?"

"It certainly does," said the Squire, very much interested. It is not unusual for a quiet country gentleman to be more taken with such a venture than a speculator who has had more experience in its uncertainty. It was astonishing how many New England clergymen, in the time of the petroleum excitement, took chances in oil. The Wall street brokers are said to do a good deal of small business for country clergymen, who are moved no doubt with the laudable desire of purifying the New York stock board.

"I don't see that there is much risk," said the Squire, at length. "The timber is worth more than the mortgage; and if that coal seam does run there, it's a magnificent fortune. Would you like to try it again in the spring, Phil?"

Like to try it! If he could have a little help, he would work himself, with pick and barrow, and live on a crust. Only give him one more chance.

And this is how it came about that the cautious old Squire Montague was drawn into this young fellow's speculation, and began to have his serene old age disturbed by anxieties and by the hope of a great stroke of luck.

"To be sure, I only care about it for the boy," he said. The Squire was like everybody else; sooner or later he must "take a chance."

It is probably on account of the lack of enterprise in women that they are not so fond of stock speculations and mine ventures as men. It is only when woman becomes demoralized that she takes to any sort of gambling. Neither Alice nor Ruth were much elated with the prospect of Philip's renewal of his mining enterprise.

But Philip was exultant. He wrote to Ruth as if his fortune were already made, and as if the clouds that lowered over the house of Bolton were already in the deep bosom of a coal mine buried. Towards spring he went to Philadelphia with his plans all matured for a new campaign. His enthusiasm was irresistible.

"Philip has come, Philip has come," cried the children, as if some great good had again come into the household; and the refrain even sang itself over in Ruth's heart as she went the weary hospital rounds. Mr. Bolton felt more courage than he had had in months, at the sight of his manly face and the sound of his cheery voice.

Ruth's course was vindicated now, and it certainly did not become Philip, who had nothing to offer but a future chance against the visible result of her determination and industry, to open an argument with her. Ruth was never more certain that she was right and that she was sufficient unto herself. She, may be, did not much heed the still small voice that sang in her maiden heart as she went about her work, and which lightened it and made it easy, "Philip has come."

"I am glad for father's sake," she said to Philip, "that thee has come. I can see that he depends greatly upon what thee can do. He thinks women won't hold out long," added Ruth with the smile that Philip never exactly understood.

"And aren't you tired sometimes of the struggle?"

"Tired? Yes, everybody is tired I suppose. But it is a glorious profession. And would you want me to be dependent, Philip?"

"Well, yes, a little," said Philip, feeling his way towards what he wanted to say.

"On what, for instance, just now?" asked Ruth, a little maliciously Philip thought.

"Why, on—" he couldn't quite say it, for it occurred to him that he was a poor stick for any body to lean on in the present state of his fortune, and that the woman before him was at least as independent as he was.

"I don't mean depend," he began again. "But I love you, that's all. Am I nothing to you?" And Philip looked a little defiant, and as if he had said something that ought to brush away all the sophistries of obligation on either side, between man and woman.

Perhaps Ruth saw this. Perhaps she saw that her own theories of a certain equality of power, which ought to precede a union of two hearts, might be pushed too far. Perhaps she had felt sometimes her own weakness and the need after all of so dear a sympathy and so tender an interest confessed, as that which Philip could give. Whatever moved her—the riddle is as old as creation—she simply looked up to Philip and said in a low voice,

"Everything."

And Philip clasping both her hands in his, and looking down into her eyes, which drank in all his tenderness with the thirst of a true woman's nature—

"Oh! Philip, come out here," shouted young Eli, throwing the door wide open.

And Ruth escaped away to her room, her heart singing again, and now as if it would burst for joy, "Philip has come."

That night Philip received a dispatch from Harry—"The trial begins to-morrow."

CHAPTER LI

Mpethie ou sagar lou nga thia gawantou kone yoboul goube.
Wolof Proverb.

"Mitsoda eb volna a' te szolgád, hogy illyen nagy dolgot tselekednek?"
Királyok II. K. 8. 13.

DECEMBER, 18—, found Washington Hawkins and Col. Sellers once more at the capitol of the nation, standing guard over the University bill. The former gentleman was despondent, the latter hopeful. Washington's distress of mind was chiefly on Laura's account. The court would soon sit to try her case, he said, and consequently a great deal of ready money would be needed in the engineering of it. The University bill was sure to pass, this time, and that would make money plenty, but might not the help come too late? Congress had only just assembled, and delays were to be feared.

"Well," said the Colonel, "I don't know but you are more or less right, there. Now let's figure up a little on the preliminaries. I think Congress always tries to do as near right as it can, according to its lights. A man can't ask any fairer than that. The first preliminary it always starts out on, is to clean itself, so to speak. It will arraign two or three dozen of its members, or maybe four or five dozen, for taking bribes to vote for this and that and the other bill last winter."

"It goes up into the dozens, does it?"

"Well, yes; in a free country like ours, where any man can run for Congress and anybody can vote for him, you can't expect immortal purity all the time—it ain't in nature.—Sixty or eighty or a hundred and fifty people are bound to get in who are not angels in disguise, as young Hicks the correspondent says; but still it is a very good average; very good indeed. As long as it averages as well as that, I think we can feel very well satisfied. Even in these days, when people growl so much and the newspapers are so out of patience, there is still a very respectable minority of honest men in Congress."

"Why a respectable *minority* of honest men can't do any good, Colonel."

"Oh, yes it can, too."

"Why, how?"

"Oh, in many ways, many ways."

"But what *are* the ways?"

"Well—I don't know—it is a question that requires time; a body can't answer every question right off-hand. But it *does* do good. I am satisfied of that."

"All right, then; grant that it does good; go on with the preliminaries."

"That is what I am coming to. First, as I said, they will try a lot of members for taking money for votes. That will take four weeks."

"Yes, that's like last year; and it is a sheer waste of the time for which the nation pays those men to *work*—that is what that is. And it pinches when a body's got a bill waiting."

"A waste of time, to purify the fountain of public law! Well, I never heard anybody express an idea like that before. But if it were, it would still be the fault of the minority, for the majority don't institute these proceedings. *There* is where that minority becomes an obstruction—but still one can't say it is on the wrong side.—Well, after they have finished the bribery cases, they will take up cases of members who have bought their seats with money. That will take another four weeks."

"Very good; go on. You have accounted for two-thirds of the session."

"Next they will try each other for various smaller irregularities like the sale of appointments to West Point cadetships,[156] and that sort of thing—mere trifling pocket-money enterprises that might better be passed over in silence, perhaps, but then one of our Congresses can never rest easy till it has thoroughly purified itself of all blemishes—and that is a thing to be applauded."

"How long does it take to disinfect itself of these minor impurities?"

"Well, about two weeks, generally."

"So Congress always lies helpless in quarantine ten weeks of a session. That's encouraging. Colonel, poor Laura will never get any benefit from our bill. Her trial will be over before Congress has half purified itself.—And doesn't it occur to you that by the time it has expelled all its impure members there may not be enough members left to do business legally?"

"Why I did not say Congress would expel anybody."

"Well *won't* it expel anybody?"

"Not necessarily. Did it last year? It never does. That would not be regular."

"Then why waste all the session in that tomfoolery of trying members?"

"It is usual; it is customary; the country requires it."

"Then the country is a fool, *I* think."

"Oh, no. The country *thinks* somebody is going to be expelled."

"Well, when nobody *is* expelled, what does the country think then?"

"By that time, the thing has strung out so long that the country is sick and tired of it and glad to have a change on any terms. But all that inquiry is not lost. It has a good moral effect."

"Who does it have a good moral effect on?"

"Well—I don't know. On foreign countries, I think. We have always been under the gaze of foreign countries. There is no country in the world, sir, that pursues corruption as inveterately as we do. There is no country in the world whose representatives try each other as much as ours do, or stick to it as long on a stretch. I think there is something great in being a model for the whole civilized world, Washington."

"You don't mean a model; you mean an example."

"Well, it's all the same; it's just the same thing. It shows that a man can't be corrupt in this country without sweating for it, I can tell you that."

"Hang it, Colonel, you just said we never punish anybody for villainous practices."

"But good God we *try* them, don't we! Is it nothing to show a disposition to sift things and bring people to a strict account? I tell you it has its effect."

"Oh, bother the effect!—What is it they *do* do? How do they proceed? You know perfectly well—and it is all bosh, too. Come, now, how do they proceed?"

"Why they proceed right and regular—and it ain't bosh, Washington, it ain't bosh. They appoint a committee to investigate, and that committee hears evidence three weeks, and all the witnesses on one side swear that the accused took money or stock or something for his vote. Then the accused stands up and testifies that he *may* have done it, but he was receiving and handling a good deal of money at the time and he doesn't remember this particular circumstance—at least with sufficient distinctness to enable him to grasp it tangibly. So of course the thing is not proven—and that is what they say in the verdict. They don't acquit, they don't condemn. They just say, 'Charge not proven.' It leaves the accused in a kind of a shaky condition before the country, it purifies Congress, it satisfies everybody, and it doesn't seriously hurt anybody. It has taken a long time to perfect our system, but it is the most admirable in the world, now."

"So one of those long stupid investigations always turns out in that lame silly way. Yes, you are correct. I thought maybe you viewed the matter differently from other people. Do you think a Congress of ours could convict the devil of anything if he were a member?"

"My dear boy, don't let these damaging delays prejudice you against Congress. Don't use such strong language; you talk like a newspaper. Congress has inflicted frightful punishments on its members—now you know that. When they tried Mr. Fairoaks,[157] and a cloud of witnesses proved him to be—well, you know what they proved him to be—and his own testimony and his own confessions gave him the same character, what did Congress do then?—come!"

"Well, what *did* Congress do?"

"You know that Congress did, Washington. Congress intimated plainly enough, that they considered him almost a stain upon their body; and without waiting ten days, hardly, to think the thing over, they rose up and hurled at him a resolution declaring that they disapproved of his conduct! Now *you* know that, Washington."

"It *was* a terrific thing—there is no denying that. If he had been proven guilty of theft, arson, licentiousness, infanticide, and defiling graves, I believe they would have suspended him for two days."

"You can depend on it, Washington. Congress is vindictive, Congress is savage, sir, when it gets waked up once. It will go to any length to vindicate its honor at such a time."

"Ah well, we have talked the morning through, just as usual in these tiresome days of waiting, and we have reached the same old result; that is to say, we are no better off than when we began. The land bill is just as far away as ever, and the trial is closer at hand. Let's give up everything and die."

"Die and leave the Duchess to fight it out all alone? Oh, no, that won't do. Come, now, don't talk so. It is all going to come out right. Now you'll see."

"It never will, Colonel, never in the world. Something tells me that. I get more tired and more despondent every day. I don't see any hope; life is only just a trouble. I am so miserable these days!"

The Colonel made Washington get up and walk the floor with him, arm in arm. The good old speculator wanted to comfort him, but he hardly knew how to go about it. He made many attempts, but they were lame; they lacked spirit; the words were encouraging, but they were only words—he could not get any heart into them. He could not always warm up, now, with the old Hawkeye fervor. By and by his lips trembled and his voice got unsteady. He said:

"Don't give up the ship, my boy—don't do it. The wind's bound to fetch around and set in our favor. I *know* it."

And the prospect was so cheerful that he wept. Then he blew a trumpet-blast that started the meshes of his handkerchief, and said in almost his breezy old-time way:

"Lord bless us, this is all nonsense! Night doesn't last always; day has got to break some time or other. Every silver lining has a cloud behind it, as the poet says; and that remark has always cheered me, though I never could see any meaning to it. Everybody uses it, though, and everybody gets comfort out of it. I wish they would start something fresh. Come, now, let's cheer up; there's been as good fish in the sea as there are now. It shall never be said that Beriah Sellers—. Come in!"

It was the telegraph boy. The Colonel reached for the message and devoured its contents.

"I said it! Never give up the ship! The trial's postponed till February, and we'll save the child yet. Bless my life, what lawyers they have in New York! Give them money to fight with, and the ghost of an excuse, and they would manage to postpone anything in this world, unless it might be the millennium or something like that. Now for work again, my boy. The trial will last to the middle of March, sure; Congress ends the fourth of March. Within three days of the end of the session they will be done putting through the preliminaries, and then they will be ready for national business. Our bill will go through in forty-eight hours, then, and we'll telegraph a million dollars to the jury—to the lawyers, I mean—and the verdict of the jury will be 'Accidental murder resulting from justifiable insanity'—or something to that effect, something to that effect. Everything is dead sure, now. Come, what is the matter? What are you wilting down like that for? You mustn't be a girl, you know."

"Oh, Colonel, I am become so used to troubles, so used to failures, disappointments, hard luck of all kinds, that a little good news breaks me right down. Everything has been so hopeless that now I can't stand good news at all. It is too good to be true, anyway. Don't you see how our bad luck has worked on me? My hair is getting gray, and many nights I don't sleep at all. I wish it was all over and we could rest. I wish we could lie down and just forget everything, and let it all be just a dream that is done and can't come back to trouble us any more. I am so tired."

"Ah, poor child, don't talk like that—cheer up—there's daylight ahead. Don't give up. You'll have Laura again, and Louise, and your mother, and oceans and oceans of money—and then you can go away, ever so far away somewhere, if you want to, and forget all about this infernal place. And by George I'll go with you! I'll go with you—now there's my word on it. Cheer up. I'll run out and tell the friends the news."

And he wrung Washington's hand and was about to hurry away when his companion, in a burst of grateful admiration said:

"I think you are the best soul and the noblest I ever knew, Colonel Sellers! and if the people only knew you as I do, you would not be tagging around here a nameless man—you would be in Congress."

The gladness died out of the Colonel's face, and he laid his hand upon Washington's shoulder and said gravely:

"I have always been a friend of your family, Washington, and I think I have always tried to do right as between man and man, according to my lights. Now I don't think there has ever been anything in my conduct that should make you feel justified in saying a thing like that."

He turned, then, and walked slowly out, leaving Washington abashed and somewhat bewildered. When Washington had presently got his thoughts into line again, he said to himself, "Why, honestly, I only meant to compliment him—indeed I would not have hurt him for the world."

CHAPTER LII

Aucune chose au monde et plus noble et plus belle
Que la sainte ferveur d'un véritable zèle.
Le Tartuffe, a. 1, sc. 6.

With faire discourse the evening so they pas;
For that olde man of pleasing wordes had store,
And well could file his tongue, as smooth as glas—
Faerie Queene.

—Il prit un air bénin et tendre,
D'un *Laudate Deum* leur prêta le bon jour,
Puis convia le monde au fraternel amour!
Roman du Renard (Prologue).

THE WEEKS DRIFTED by monotonously enough, now. The "preliminaries" continued to drag along in Congress, and life was a dull suspense to Sellers and Washington, a weary waiting which might have broken their hearts, maybe, but for the relieving change which they got out of an occasional visit to New York to see Laura. Standing guard in Washington or anywhere else is not an exciting business in time of peace, but standing guard was all that the two friends had to do; all that was needed of them was that they should be on hand and ready for any emergency that might come up. There was no work to do; that was all finished; this was but the second session of the last winter's Congress, and its action on the bill could have but one result—its passage. The House must do its work over again, of course, but the same membership was there to see that it did it.— The Senate was secure— Senator Dilworthy was able to put all doubts to rest on that head. Indeed it was no secret in Washington that a two-thirds vote in the Senate was ready and waiting to be cast for the University bill as soon as it should come before that body.

Washington did not take part in the gaieties of "the season," as he had done the previous winter. He had lost his interest in such things; he was oppressed with cares, now. Senator Dilworthy said to Washington that an humble deportment, under punishment, was best, and that there was but one way in which the troubled heart might find perfect repose and peace. The suggestion found a response in Washington's breast, and the Senator saw the sign of it in his face.

From that moment one could find the youth with the Senator even oftener than with Col. Sellers. When the statesman presided at great temperance meetings, he placed Washington in the front rank of impressive dignitaries that gave tone to the occasion and pomp to the platform. His bald headed surroundings made the youth the more conspicuous. When the statesman made remarks in these meetings, he not infrequently alluded with effect to the encouraging spectacle of one of the wealthiest and most brilliant young favorites of society forsaking the light vanities of that butterfly existence to nobly and self-sacrificingly devote his talents and his riches to the cause of saving his hapless fellow creatures from shame and misery here and eternal regret hereafter. At the prayer meetings the Senator always brought Washington up the aisle on his arm and seated him prominently; in his prayers he referred to him in the cant terms which the Senator employed, perhaps unconsciously, and mistook, maybe, for religion, and in other ways brought him into notice. He had him out at gatherings for the benefit of the negro, gatherings for the benefit of the Indian, gatherings for the benefit of the heathen in distant lands. He had him out time and again, before Sunday Schools, as an example for emulation. Upon all these occasions the Senator made casual references to many benevolent enterprises which his ardent young friend was planning against the day when the passage of the University bill should make his ample means available for the amelioration of the condition of the unfortunate among his fellow men of all nations and all climes. Thus as the weeks rolled on Washington grew up into an imposing lion once more, but a lion that roamed the peaceful fields of religion and temperance, and revisited the glittering domain of fashion no more. A great moral influence was thus brought to bear in favor of the bill; the weightiest of friends flocked to its standard; its most energetic enemies said it was useless to fight longer; they had tacitly surrendered while as yet the day of battle was not come.

CHAPTER LIII

—He seekes, of all his drifte the aymed end:
Thereto this subtile engins he does bend,
His practick witt and his fayre fyled tongue,
With thousand other sleightes; for well he kend
His credit now in doubtful ballaunce hong:
For hardly could bee hurt, who was already stong.
Faerie Queene.

Selons divers besoins, il est une science
D'étendre les liens de notre conscience,
Et de rectifier le mal de l'action
Avec la pureté de notre intention.
Le Tartuffe, a. 4, sc. 5.

THE SESSION was drawing toward its close. Senator Dilworthy thought he would run out west and shake hands with his constituents and let them look at him. The legislature whose duty it would be to re-elect him to the United States Senate, was already in session. Mr. Dilworthy considered his re-election certain, but he was a careful, painstaking man, and if, by visiting his State he could find the opportunity to persuade a few more legislators to vote for him, he held the journey to be well worth taking. The University bill was safe, now; he could leave it without fear; it needed his presence and his watching no longer. But there was a person in his State legislature who did need watching—a person who, Senator Dilworthy said, was a narrow, grumbling, uncomfortable malcontent—a person who was stolidly opposed to reform, and progress and *him*,—a person who, he feared, had been bought with money to combat him, and through him the commonwealth's welfare and its political purity.

"If this person Noble," said Mr. Dilworthy, in a little speech at a dinner party given him by some of this admirers, "merely desired to sacrifice *me*, I would willingly offer up my political life on the altar of my dear State's weal, I would be glad and grateful to do it; but when he makes of me but a cloak to hide his deeper

designs, when he proposes to strike *through* me at the heart of my
beloved State, all the lion in me is roused—and I say, Here I stand,
solitary and alone, but unflinching, unquailing, thrice armed with
my sacred trust; and whoso passes, to do evil to this fair domain
that looks to me for protection, must do so over my dead body."

He further said that if this Noble were a pure man, and merely
misguided, he could bear it, but that he should succeed in his
wicked designs through a base use of money would leave a blot
upon his State which would work untold evil to the morals of the
people, and *that* he would not suffer; the public morals must not
be contaminated. He would seek this man Noble; he would argue,
he would persuade, he would appeal to his honor.

When he arrived on the ground he found his friends unterri-
fied; they were standing firmly by him and were full of courage.
Noble was working hard, too, but matters were against him, he
was not making much progress. Mr. Dilworthy took an early opportunity to send for Mr. Noble; he had a midnight interview
with him, and urged him to forsake his evil ways; he begged him
to come again and again, which he did. He finally sent the man
away at 3 o'clock one morning; and when he was gone, Mr. Dilworthy said to himself,

"I feel a good deal relieved, now, a great deal relieved."

The Senator now turned his attention to matters touching the
souls of his people. He appeared in church; he took a leading part
in prayer meetings; he met and encouraged the temperance societies; he graced the sewing circles of the ladies with his presence,
and even took a needle now and then and made a stitch or two
upon a calico shirt for some poor Bibleless pagan of the South
Seas, and this act enchanted the ladies, who regarded the garments
thus honored as in a manner sanctified. The Senator wrought in
Bible classes, and nothing could keep him away from the Sunday
Schools—neither sickness nor storms nor weariness. He even
traveled a tedious thirty miles in a poor little rickety stage-coach
to comply with the desire of the miserable hamlet of Cattleville
that he would let its Sunday School look upon him.

All the town was assembled at the stage office when he arrived,
two bonfires were burning, and a battery of anvils was popping
exultant broadsides; for a United States Senator was a sort of god

in the understanding of these people who never had seen any creature mightier than a county judge. To them a United States Senator was a vast, vague colossus, an awe inspiring unreality.

Next day everybody was at the village church a full half hour before time for Sunday School to open; ranchmen and farmers had come with their families from five miles around, all eager to get a glimpse of the great man—the man who had been to Washington; the man who had seen the President of the United States, and had even talked with him; the man who had seen the actual Washington Monument—perhaps touched it with his hands.

When the Senator arrived the Church was crowded, the windows were full, the aisles were packed, so was the vestibule, and so indeed was the yard in front of the building. As he worked his way through to the pulpit on the arm of the minister and followed by the envied officials of the village, every neck was stretched and every eye twisted around intervening obstructions to get a glimpse. Elderly people directed each other's attention and said, "There! that's him, with the grand, noble forehead!" Boys nudged each other and said, "Hi, Johnny, here he is! There, that's him, with the peeled head!"

The Senator took his seat in the pulpit, with the minister on one side of him and the Superintendent of the Sunday School on the other. The town dignitaries sat in an impressive row within the altar railings below. The Sunday School children occupied ten of the front benches, dressed in their best and most uncomfortable clothes, and with hair combed and faces too clean to feel natural. So awed were they by the presence of a living United States Senator, that during three minutes not a "spit-ball" was thrown. After that they began to come to themselves by degrees, and presently the spell was wholly gone and they were reciting verses and pulling hair.

The usual Sunday School exercises were hurried through, and then the minister got up and bored the house with a speech built on the customary Sunday School plan; then the Superintendent put in his oar; then the town dignitaries had their say. They all made complimentary reference to "their friend the Senator," and told what a great and illustrious man he was and what he had done for his country and for religion and temperance, and exhorted the little boys to be good and diligent and try to become like him some day. The speakers won the deathless hatred of the house by these delays, but at last there was an end and hope revived; inspiration was about to find utterance.

Senator Dilworthy rose and beamed upon the assemblage for a full minute in silence. Then he smiled with an access of sweetness upon the children and began:

"My little friends—for I hope that all these bright-faced little people are my friends and will let me be their friend—my little friends, I have traveled much, I have been in many cities and many States, everywhere in our great and noble country, and by the blessing of Providence I have been permitted to see many gatherings like this—but I am proud, I am truly proud to say that I never have looked upon so much intelligence, so much grace, such sweetness of disposition as I see in the charming young countenances I see before me at this moment. I have been asking myself as I sat here, Where am I? Am I in some far-off monarchy, looking upon little princes and princesses? No. Am I in some populous centre of my own country, where the choicest children of the land have been selected and brought together as at a fair for a prize? No. Am I in some strange foreign clime where the children are marvels that we know not of? No. Then where am I? Yes—where am I? I am in a simple, remote, unpretending settlement of my own dear State, and these are the children of the noble and virtuous men who have made me what I am! My soul is lost in wonder at the thought! And I humbly thank Him to whom we are but as worms of the dust, that He has been pleased to call me to serve such men! Earth has no higher, no grander position for me. Let kings and emperors keep their tinsel crowns, I want them not; my heart is here!

"Again, I thought, Is this a theatre? No. Is it a concert or a gilded opera? No. Is it some other vain, brilliant, beautiful temple of soul-staining amusement and hilarity? No. Then what is it? What did my consciousness reply? I ask you, my little friends, What did my consciousness reply? It replied, It is the temple of the Lord! Ah, think of that, now. I could hardly keep the tears back, I was so grateful. Oh, how beautiful it is to see these ranks of sunny little faces assembled here to learn the way of life; to learn to be good; to learn to be useful; to learn to be pious; to learn to be great and glorious men and women; to learn to be props and pillars of the State and shining lights in the councils and the households of the nation; to be bearers of the banner and soldiers of the cross in the rude campaigns of life, and ransomed souls in the happy fields of Paradise hereafter.

"Children, honor your parents and be grateful to them for providing for you the precious privileges of a Sunday School.

"Now my dear little friends, sit up straight and pretty—there, that's it—and give me your attention and let me tell you about a poor little Sunday School scholar I once knew.—He lived in the far west, and his parents were poor. They could not give him a costly education, but they were good and wise and they sent him to the Sunday School. He loved the Sunday School. I hope you love your Sunday School—ah, I see by your faces that you do! That is right.

"Well, this poor little boy was always in his place when the bell rang, and he always knew his lesson; for his teachers wanted him to learn and he loved his teachers dearly. Always love your teachers, my children, for they love you more than you can know, now. He would not let bad boys persuade him to go to play on Sunday. There was one little bad boy who was always trying to persuade him, but he never could.

"So this poor little boy grew up to be a man, and had to go out in the world, far from home and friends to earn his living. Temptations lay all about him, and sometimes he was about to yield, but he would think of some precious lesson he learned in his Sunday School a long time ago, and that would save him. By and by he was elected to the legislature. Then he did everything he could for Sunday Schools. He got laws passed for them; he got Sunday Schools established wherever he could.

"And by and by the people made him governor—and he said it was all owing to the Sunday School.

"After a while the people elected him a Representative to the Congress of the United States, and he grew very famous.—Now temptations assailed him on every hand. People tried to get him to drink wine, to dance, to go to theatres; they even tried to buy his vote; but no, the memory of his Sunday School saved him from all harm; he remembered the fate of the bad little boy who used to try to get him to play on Sunday, and who grew up and became a drunkard and was hanged. He remembered that, and was glad he never yielded and played on Sunday.

"Well, at last, what do you think happened? Why the people gave him a towering, illustrious position, a grand, imposing position. And what do you think it was? What should you say it was, children? It was Senator of the United States! That poor little boy that loved his Sunday School became that man. *That man stands before you!* All that he is, he owes to the Sunday School.

"My precious children, love your parents, love your teachers, love your Sunday School, be pious, be obedient, be honest, be diligent, and then you will succeed in life and be honored of all men. Above all things, my children, be honest. Above all things be pure-minded as the snow. Let us join in prayer."

When Senator Dilworthy departed from Cattleville, he left three dozen boys behind him arranging a campaign of life whose objective point was the United States Senate.

When he arrived at the State capital at midnight Mr. Noble came and held a three-hours' conference with him, and then as he was about leaving said:

"I've worked hard, and I've got them at last. Six of them haven't got quite back-bone enough to slew around and come right out for you on the first ballot to-morrow, but they're going to vote against you on the first for the sake of appearances, and then come out for you all in a body on the second—I've fixed all that! By supper time to-morrow you'll be re-elected. You can go to bed and sleep easy on that."

After Mr. Noble was gone, the Senator said:

"Well, to bring about a complexion of things like this was worth coming West for."

CHAPTER LIV

भेट्त्तमसो ऽष्टाविधो मोह्स्य च ट्ग्राविधो मह्रामोह्ः
तामिस्रो ऽष्टाट्ग्राधा तया भवत्यन्धतामिन'
Sánkhya Káriká, xlvii.

Ny byd ynat nep yr dysc; yr adysco dyn byth ny byd ynat ony byd doethineb
yny callon; yr doethet uyth uo dyn ny byd ynat ony byd dysc gyt ar doethinab.
Cyvreithiau Cymru.

THE CASE OF THE STATE OF NEW YORK against Laura Hawkins
was finally set down for trial on the 15th day of February, less
than a year after the shooting of George Selby.

If the public had almost forgotten the existence of Laura and
her crime, they were reminded of all the details of the murder by
the newspapers, which for some days had been announcing the
approaching trial. But they had not forgotten. The sex, the age,
the beauty of the prisoner; her high social position in Washington,
the unparalleled calmness with which the crime was committed
had all conspired to fix the event in the public mind, although
nearly three hundred and sixty-five subsequent murders had occurred to vary the monotony of metropolitan life.

No, the public read from time to time of the lovely prisoner,
languishing in the city prison, the tortured victim of the law's delay; and as the months went by it was natural that the horror of
her crime should become a little indistinct in memory, while the
heroine of it should be invested with a sort of sentimental interest.
Perhaps her counsel had calculated on this. Perhaps it was by
their advice that Laura had interested herself in the unfortunate
criminals who shared her prison confinement, and had done not a
little to relieve, from her own purse, the necessities of some of the
poor creatures. That she had done this, the public read in the journals of the day, and the simple announcement cast a softening
light upon her character.

The court room was crowded at an early hour, before the arrival of judges, lawyers and prisoner. There is no enjoyment so

keen to certain minds as that of looking upon the slow torture of a human being on trial for life, except it be an execution; there is no display of human ingenuity, wit and power so fascinating as that made by trained lawyers in the trial of an important case, nowhere else is exhibited such subtlety, acumen, address, eloquence.

All the conditions of intense excitement meet in a murder trial. The awful issue at stake gives significance to the lightest word or look. How the quick eyes of the spectators rove from the stolid jury to the keen lawyers, the impassive judge, the anxious prisoner. Nothing is lost of the sharp wrangle of the counsel on points of law, the measured decisions of the bench, the duels between the attorneys and the witnesses. The crowd sways with the rise and fall of the shifting testimony, in sympathetic interest, and hangs upon the dicta of the judge in breathless silence. It speedily takes sides for or against the accused, and recognizes as quickly its favorites among the lawyers. Nothing delights it more than the sharp retort of a witness and the discomfiture of an obnoxious attorney. A joke, even if it be a lame one, is nowhere so keenly relished or quickly applauded as in a murder trial.

Within the bar the young lawyers and the privileged hangers-on filled all the chairs except those reserved at the table for those engaged in the case. Without, the throng occupied all the seats, the window ledges and the standing room. The atmosphere was already something horrible. It was the peculiar odor of a criminal court, as if it were tainted by the presence, in different persons, of all the crimes that men and women can commit.

There was a little stir when the Prosecuting Attorney, with two assistants, made his way in, seated himself at the table, and spread his papers before him. There was more stir when the counsel of the defense appeared. They were Mr. Braham, the senior, and Mr. Quiggle and Mr. O'Keefe, the juniors.

Everybody in the court room knew Mr. Braham, the great criminal lawyer, and he was not unaware that he was the object of all eyes as he moved to his place, bowing to his friends in the bar. A large but rather spare man, with broad shoulders and a massive head, covered with chestnut curls which fell down upon his coat collar and which he had a habit of shaking as a lion is supposed to shake his mane. His face was clean shaven, and he had a wide mouth and rather small dark eyes, set quite too near together. Mr. Braham wore a brown frock coat buttoned across his breast, with a rose-bud in the the upper button-hole, and light pantaloons. A diamond stud was seen to flash from his bosom, and as he seated himself and drew off his gloves a heavy seal ring was displayed upon his white left hand. Mr. Braham having seated himself, deliberately surveyed the entire house, made remark to one of his assistants, and then taking an ivory-handled knife from his pocket began to pare his finger nails, rocking his chair backwards and forwards slowly.

A moment later Judge O'Shaunnessy entered at the rear door and took his seat in one of the chairs behind the bench; a gentleman in black broadcloth, with sandy hair, inclined to curl, a round, reddish and rather jovial face, sharp rather than intellectual, and with a self-sufficient air. His career had nothing remarkable in it. He was descended from a long line of Irish Kings, and he was the first one of them who had ever come into his kingdom—the kingdom of such being the city of New York. He had, in fact, descended so far and so low that he found himself, when a boy, a sort of street Arab in that city; but he had ambition and native shrewdness, and he speedily took to boot-polishing and newspaper hawking, became the office and errand boy of a law firm, picked up knowledge enough to get some employment in police courts, was admitted to the bar, became a rising young politician, went to the legislature, and was finally elected to the bench which he now honored. In this democratic country he was obliged to conceal his royalty under a plebeian aspect. Judge O'Shaunnessy never had a lucrative practice nor a large salary, but he had prudently laid away money—believing that a dependant judge can never be impartial—and he had lands and houses to the value of three or four hundred thousand dollars. Had he not helped to build and furnish this very Court House? Did he not know that the very "spittoon" which his judgeship used cost the city the sum of one thousand dollars?

As soon as the judge was seated, the court was opened, with the "oi yis, oi yis" of the officer in his native language, the case called, and the sheriff was directed to bring in the prisoner. In the midst of a profound hush Laura entered, leaning on the arm of the officer, and was conducted to a seat by her counsel. She was followed by her mother and by Washington Hawkins, who were given seats near her.

Laura was very pale, but this pallor heightened the lustre of her large eyes and gave a touching sadness to her expressive face. She was dressed in simple black, with exquisite taste, and without an ornament. The thin lace veil which partially covered her face did not so much conceal as heighten her beauty. She would not have entered a drawing room with more self-poise, nor a church with more haughty humility. There was in her manner or face neither shame nor boldness, and when she took her seat in full view of half the spectators, her eyes were downcast. A murmur of admiration ran through the room. The newspaper reporters made their pencils fly. Mr. Braham again swept his eyes over the house as if in approval. When Laura at length raised her eyes a little, she saw Philip and Harry within the bar, but she gave no token of recognition.

The clerk then read the indictment, which was in the usual form. It charged Laura Hawkins, in effect, with the premeditated murder of George Selby, by shooting him with a pistol, with a revolver, shot-gun, rifle, repeater, breech-loader, cannon, six-shooter, with a gun, or some other weapon; with killing him with a slung-shot, a bludgeon, carving knife, bowie knife, pen knife, rolling pin, car hook, dagger, hair pin, with a hammer, with a screw-driver, with a nail, and with all other weapons and utensils whatsoever, at the Southern hotel and in all other hotels and places wheresoever, on the thirteenth day of March and all other days of the christian era whensoever.

Laura stood while the long indictment was read, and at the end, in response to the inquiry of the judge, she said in a clear, low voice, "Not guilty." She sat down and the court proceeded to impanel a jury.

The first man called was Michael Lanigan, saloon keeper.

"Have you formed or expressed any opinion on this case, and do you know any of the parties?"

"Not any," said Mr. Lanigan.

"Have you any conscientious objections to capital punishment?"

"No, sir, not to my knowledge."

"Have you read anything about this case?"

"To be sure, I read the papers, y'r Honor."

Objected to by Mr. Braham, for cause, and discharged.

Patrick Coughlin.

"What is your business?"

"Well—I haven't got any particular business."

"Haven't any particular business, eh? Well, what's your general business! What do you do for a living?"

"I own some terriers, sir."

"Own some terriers, eh? Keep a rat pit?"

"Gentlemen comes there to have a little sport. *I* never fit 'em, sir."

"Oh, I see—you are probably the amusement committee of the city council. Have you ever heard of this case?"

"Not till this morning, sir."

"Can you read?"

"Not fine print, y'r Honor."

The man was about to be sworn, when Mr. Braham asked,

"Could your father read?"

"The old gentleman was mighty handy at that, sir."

Mr. Braham submitted that the man was disqualified. Judge thought not. Point argued. Challenged peremptorily, and set aside.

Ethan Dobb, cart-driver.

"Can you read?"

"Yes, but haven't a habit of it."

"Have you heard of this case?"

"I think so—but it might be another. I have no opinion about it."

Dist. A. "Tha—tha—there! Hold on a bit? Did anybody tell you to say you had no opinion about it?"

"N-n-o, sir."

"Take care now, take care. Then what suggested it to you to volunteer that remark?"

"They've always asked that, when I was on juries."

"All right, then. Have you any conscientious scruples about capital punishment?"

"Any which?"

"Would you object to finding a person guilty of murder on evidence?"

"I might, sir, if I thought he wasn't guilty."

The district attorney thought he saw a point.

"Would this feeling rather incline you against a capital conviction?"

The juror said he hadn't any feeling, and didn't know any of the parties. Accepted and sworn.

Dennis Laflin, laborer. Have neither formed nor expressed an opinion. Never had heard of the case. Believed in hangin' for them that deserved it. Could read if it was necessary.

Mr. Braham objected. The man was evidently bloody minded. Challenged peremptorily.

Larry O'Toole, contractor. A showily dressed man of the style known as "vulgar genteel," had a sharp eye and a ready tongue. Had read the newspaper reports of the case, but they made no impression on him. Should be governed by the evidence. Knew no reason why he could not be an impartial juror.

Question by District Attorney.

"How is it that the reports made no impression on you?"

"Never believe anything I see in the newspapers." (Laughter from the crowd, approving smiles from his Honor and Mr. Braham.) Juror sworn in. Mr. Braham whispered to O'Keefe, "That's the man."

Avery Hicks, pea-nut peddler. Did he ever hear of this case? The man shook his head.

"Can you read?"

"No."

"Any scruples about capital punishment?"

"No."

He was about to be sworn, when the district attorney turning to him carelessly, remarked,

"Understand the nature of an oath?"

"Outside," said the man, pointing to the door.

"I say, do you know what an oath is?"

"Five cents," explained the man.

"Do you mean to insult me?" roared the prosecuting officer. "Are you an idiot?"

"Fresh baked. I'm deefe. I don't hear a word you say."

The man was discharged. "He wouldn't have made a bad juror, though," whispered Braham. "I saw him looking at the prisoner sympathizingly. That's a point you want to watch for."

The result of the whole day's work was the selection of only two jurors. These however were satisfactory to Mr. Braham. He had kept off all those he did not know. No one knew better than this great criminal lawyer that the battle was fought on the selection of the jury. The subsequent examination of witnesses, the eloquence expended on the jury are all for effect outside. At least that is the theory of Mr. Braham. But human nature is a queer thing, he admits; sometimes jurors are unaccountably swayed, be as careful as you can in choosing them.

It was four weary days before this jury was made up, but when it was finally complete, it did great credit to the counsel for the defence. So far as Mr. Braham knew, only two could read, one of whom was the foreman, Mr. Braham's friend, the showy contractor. Low foreheads and heavy faces they all had; some had a look of animal cunning, while the most were only stupid. The entire panel formed that boasted heritage commonly described as the "bulwark of our liberties."[158]

The District Attorney, Mr. McFlinn, opened the case for the state. He spoke with only the slightest accent, one that had been inherited but not cultivated. He contented himself with a brief statement of the case. The state would prove that Laura Hawkins, the prisoner at the bar, a fiend in the form of a beautiful woman, shot dead George Selby, a Southern gentleman, at the time and place described. That the murder was in cold blood, deliberate and without provocation; that it had been long premeditated and threatened; that she had followed the deceased from Washington to commit it. All this would be proved by unimpeachable witnesses. The attorney added that the duty of the jury, however painful it might be, would be plain and simple. They were citizens, husbands, perhaps fathers. They knew how insecure life had

become in the metropolis. To-morrow their own wives might be
widows, their own children orphans, like the bereaved family in
yonder hotel, deprived of husband and father by the jealous hand
of some murderous female. The attorney sat down, and the clerk
called,

"Henry Brierly."

CHAPTER LV

*"Dyden i Midten," sagde Fanden, han sad imellem to Procutorer.
Eur breûtaer brâz eo! Ha klevet hoc'h eûz-hu hé vreût?*

HENRY BRIERLY took the stand. Requested by the District Attorney to tell the jury all he knew about the killing, he narrated
the circumstances substantially as the reader already knows them.

He accompanied Miss Hawkins to New York at her request,
supposing she was coming in relation to a bill then pending in
Congress, to secure the attendance of absent members. Her note
to him was here shown. She appeared to be very much excited at
the Washington station. After she had asked the conductor several
questions, he heard her say, "He can't escape." Witness asked her
"Who?" and she replied "Nobody." Did not see her during the
night. They traveled in a sleeping car. In the morning she appeared not to have slept, said she had a headache. In crossing the
ferry she asked him about the shipping in sight; he pointed out
where the Cunarders lay when in port. They took a cup of coffee
that morning at a restaurant. She said she was anxious to reach the
Southern Hotel where Mr. Simons, one of the absent members,
was staying, before he went out. She was entirely self-possessed,
and beyond unusual excitement did not act unnaturally. After she
had fired twice at Col. Selby, she turned the pistol towards her
own breast, and witness snatched it from her. She had been a great
deal with Selby in Washington, appeared to be infatuated with
him.

(Cross-examined by Mr. Braham.) "Mist-er . . . . er Brierly!"
(Mr. Braham had in perfection this lawyer's trick of annoying a
witness, by drawling out the "Mister," as if unable to recall the
name, until the witness is sufficiently aggravated, and then suddenly, with a rising inflection, flinging his name at him with startling unexpectedness.) "Mist-er . . . . er Brierly! What is your
occupation?"

"Civil Engineer, sir."

"Ah, *civil* engineer, (with a glance at the jury). Following that occupation with Miss Hawkins?" (Smiles by the jury.)

"No, sir," said Harry, reddening.

"How long have you known the prisoner?"

"Two years, sir. I made her acquaintance in Hawkeye, Missouri."

"M . . . m . . m. Mist-er . . . . . er Brierly! Were you not a lover of Miss Hawkins?"

Objected to. "I submit, your Honor, that I have the right to establish the relation of this unwilling witness to the prisoner." Admitted.

"Well, sir," said Harry hesitatingly, "we were friends."

"You act like a friend!" (sarcastically.) The jury were beginning to hate this neatly dressed young sprig. "Mister . . . . . er Brierly! Didn't Miss Hawkins refuse you?"

Harry blushed and stammered and looked at the judge. "You must answer, sir," said His Honor.

"She—she—didn't accept me."

"No. I should think not. Brierly! do you dare tell the jury that you had not an interest in the removal of your rival, Col. Selby?" roared Mr. Braham in a voice of thunder.

"Nothing like this, sir, nothing like this," protested the witness.

"That's all, sir," said Mr. Braham severely.

"One word," said the District Attorney. "Had you the least suspicion of the prisoner's intention, up to the moment of the shooting?"

"Not the least," answered Harry earnestly.

"Of course not, of course not," nodded Mr. Braham to the jury.

The prosecution then put upon the stand the other witnesses of the shooting at the hotel, and the clerk and the attending physicians. The fact of the homicide was clearly established. Nothing new was elicited, except from the clerk, in reply to a question by Mr. Braham, the fact that when the prisoner enquired for Col. Selby she appeared excited and there was a wild look in her eyes.

The dying deposition of Col. Selby was then produced. It set forth Laura's threats, but there was a significant addition to it, which the newspaper report did not have. It seemed that after the deposition was taken as reported, the Colonel was told for the first time by his physicians that his wounds were mortal. He appeared to be in great mental agony and fear, and said he had not finished his deposition. He added, with great difficulty and long pauses these words. "I—have—not—told—all. I must tell—put—it—down—I—wronged—her. Years—ago—I—can't—see—O—God—I—deserved—" That was all. He fainted and did not revive again.

The Washington railway conductor testified that the prisoner had asked him if a gentleman and his family went out on the evening train, describing the persons he had since learned were Col. Selby and family.

Susan Cullum, colored servant at Senator Dilworthy's, was sworn. Knew Col. Selby. Had seen him come to the house often, and be alone in the parlor with Miss Hawkins. He came the day but one before he was shot. She let him in. He appeared flustered like. She heard talking in the parlor, 'peared like it was quarrelin.' Was afeared sumfin' was wrong. Just put her ear to the keyhole of the back parlor door. Heard a man's voice, "I can't, I can't, Good God," quite beggin' like. Heard young Miss' voice, "Take your choice, then. If you 'bandon me, you knows what to 'spect." Then he rushes outen the house. I goes in and I says, "Missis did you ring?" She was a standin', like a tiger, her eyes flashin'. I come right out.

This was the substance of Susan's testimony, which was not shaken in the least by a severe cross-examination. In reply to Mr. Braham's question, if the prisoner did not look insane, Susan said, "Lord, no, sir, just mad as a hawnet."

Washington Hawkins was sworn. The pistol, identified by the officer as the one used in the homicide, was produced. Washington admitted that it was his. She had asked him for it one morning, saying she thought she had heard burglars the night before. Admitted that he never had heard burglars in the house. Had anything unusual happened just before that? Nothing that he remembered. Did he accompany her to a reception at Mrs. Schoonmaker's a day or two before? Yes. What occurred? Little by little it was dragged out of the witness that Laura had behaved strangely there, appeared to be sick, and he had taken her home. Upon being pushed he admitted that she had afterwards confessed that she saw Selby there. And Washington volunteered the statement that Selby was a black-hearted villain.

The District Attorney said, with some annoyance, "There—there! That will do."

The defense declined to examine Mr. Hawkins at present. The case for the prosecution was closed. Of the murder there could not be the least doubt, or that the prisoner followed the deceased to New York with a murderous intent. On the evidence the jury must convict, and might do so without leaving their seats. This was the condition of the case two days after the jury had been selected. A week had passed since the trial opened, and a Sunday had intervened. The public who read the reports of the evidence saw no chance for the prisoner's escape. The crowd of spectators who had watched the trial were moved with the most profound sympathy for Laura.

Mr. Braham opened the case for the defense. His manner was subdued, and he spoke in so low a voice that it was only by reason of perfect silence in the court room that he could be heard. He spoke very distinctly, however, and if his nationality could be discovered in his speech it was only in a certain richness and breadth of tone.

He began by saying that he trembled at the responsibility he had undertaken; and he should altogether despair, if he did not see before him a jury of twelve men of rare intelligence, whose acute minds would unravel all the sophistries of the prosecution, men with a sense of honor, which would revolt at the remorseless persecution of this hunted woman by the state, men with hearts to feel for the wrongs of which she was the victim. Far be it from him to cast any suspicion upon the motives of the able, eloquent and ingenious lawyers of the state; they act officially; their business is to convict. It is our business, gentlemen, to see that justice is done.

"It is my duty, gentlemen, to unfold to you one of the most affecting dramas in all the history of misfortune. I shall have to show you a life, the sport of fate and circumstances, hurried along through shifting storm and sun, bright with trusting innocence and anon black with heartless villainy, a career which moves on in love and desertion and anguish, always hovered over by the dark spectre of INSANITY,—an insanity hereditary and induced by mental torture,—until it ends, if end it must in your verdict, by one of those fearful accidents which are inscrutable to men and of which God alone knows the secret.

"Gentlemen, I shall ask you to go with me away from this court room and its minions of the law, away from the scene of this tragedy, to a distant, I wish I could say a happier day. The story I have to tell is of a lovely little girl, with sunny hair and laughing eyes, traveling with her parents, evidently people of wealth and refinement, upon a Mississippi steamboat. There is an explosion, one of those terrible catastrophes, which leave the imprint of an unsettled mind upon the survivors. Hundreds of mangled remains are sent into eternity. When the wreck is cleared away this sweet little girl is found among the panic stricken survivors, in the midst of a scene of horror enough to turn the steadiest brain. Her parents have disappeared. Search even for their bodies is in vain. The bewildered, stricken child—who can say what changes the fearful event wrought in her tender brain?—clings to the first person who shows her sympathy. It is Mrs. Hawkins, this good lady who is still her loving friend. Laura is adopted into the Hawkins family. Perhaps she forgets in time that she is not their child. She is an orphan. No, gentlemen, I will not deceive you, she is *not* an orphan. Worse than that. There comes another day of agony. She knows that her father lives. But who is he, where is he? Alas, I cannot tell you. Through the scenes of this painful history he flits here and there, a lunatic! If he seeks his daughter, it is the purposeless search of a lunatic, as one who wanders bereft of reason, crying, where is my child? Laura seeks her father. In vain! Just as she is about to find him, again and again he disappears, he is gone, he vanishes.

"But this is only the prologue to the tragedy. Bear with me while I relate it. (Mr. Braham takes out his handkerchief, unfolds it slowly, crushes it in his nervous hand, and throws it on the table.) Laura grew up in her humble southern home, a beautiful creature, the joy of the house, the pride of the neighborhood, the loveliest flower in all the sunny South. She might yet have been happy; she was happy. But the destroyer came into this paradise. He plucked the sweetest bud that grew there, and having enjoyed its odor, trampled it in the mire beneath his feet. George Selby, the deceased, a handsome, accomplished Confederate Colonel, was this human fiend. He deceived her with a mock marriage; after some months he brutally abandoned her, and spurned her as if she were a contemptible thing; all the time he had a wife in New Orleans. Laura was crushed. For weeks, as I shall show you by the testimony of her adopted mother and brother, she hovered over death in delirium. Gentlemen, did she ever emerge from this delirium? I shall show you that when she recovered her health, her mind was changed, she was not what she had been. You can judge yourselves whether the tottering reason ever recovered its throne.

"Years pass. She is in Washington, apparently the happy favorite of a brilliant society. Her family have become enormously rich by one of those sudden turns in fortune that the inhabitants of America are familiar with—the discovery of immense mineral wealth in some wild lands owned by them. She is engaged in a vast philanthropic scheme for the benefit of the poor, by the use of this wealth. But, alas, even here and now, the same relentless fate pursued her. The villain Selby appears again upon the scene, as if on purpose to complete the ruin of her life. He appeared to taunt her with her dishonor; he threatened exposure if she did not become again the mistress of his passion. Gentlemen, do you wonder if this woman, thus pursued, lost her reason, was beside herself with fear, and that her wrongs preyed upon her mind until she was no longer responsible for her acts? I turn away my head as one who would not willingly look even upon the just vengeance of Heaven. (Mr. Braham paused as if overcome by his emotions. Mrs. Hawkins and Washington were in tears, as were many of the spectators also. The jury looked scared.)

"Gentlemen, in this condition of affairs it needed but a spark—I do not say a suggestion, I do not say a hint—from this butterfly Brierly, this rejected rival, to cause the explosion. I make no charges, but if this woman was in her right mind when she fled from Washington and reached this city in company with Brierly, then I do not know what insanity is."

When Mr. Braham sat down, he felt that he had the jury with him. A burst of applause followed, which the officer promptly suppressed. Laura, with tears in her eyes, turned a grateful look upon her counsel. All the women among the spectators saw the tears and wept also. They thought as they also looked at Mr. Braham, how handsome he is!

Mrs. Hawkins took the stand. She was somewhat confused to be the target of so many eyes, but her honest and good face at once told in Laura's favor.

"Mrs. Hawkins," said Mr. Braham, "will you be kind enough to state the circumstances of your finding Laura?"

"I object," said Mr. McFlinn, rising to his feet. "This has nothing whatever to do with the case, your honor. I am surprised at it, even after the extraordinary speech of my learned friend."

"How do you propose to connect it, Mr. Braham?" asked the judge.

"If it please the court," said Mr. Braham, rising impressively, "your Honor has permitted the prosecution, and I have submitted without a word, to go into the most extraordinary testimony to establish a motive. Are we to be shut out from showing that the motive attributed to us could not by reason of certain mental conditions exist? I purpose, may it please your Honor, to show the cause and the origin of an aberration of mind, to follow it up with other like evidence, connecting it with the very moment of the homicide, showing a condition of the intellect of the prisoner that precludes responsibility."

"The State must insist upon its objections," said the District Attorney. "The purpose evidently is to open the door to a mass of irrelevant testimony, the object of which is to produce an effect upon the jury your Honor well understands."

"Perhaps," suggested the judge, "the court ought to hear the testimony, and exclude it afterwards, if it is irrelevant."

"Will your honor hear argument on that?"

"Certainly."

And argument his honor did hear, or pretend to, for two whole days, from all the counsel in turn, in the course of which the lawyers read contradictory decisions enough to perfectly establish both sides, from volume after volume, whole libraries in fact, until no mortal man could say what the rules were. The question of insanity in all its legal aspects was of course drawn into the discussion, and its application affirmed and denied. The case was felt to turn upon the admission or rejection of this evidence. It was a sort of test trial of strength between the lawyers. At the end the judge decided to admit the testimony, as the judge usually does in such cases, after a sufficient waste of time in what are called arguments.

Mrs. Hawkins was allowed to go on.

CHAPTER LVI

—Voyre mais (demandoit Trinquamelle) mon amy, comment procedez vous en action criminelle, la partie coupable prinse *flagrante crimine*?— Comme vous aultres Messieurs (respondit Bridoye)—

"Hag eunn drâ-bennâg hoc'h eûz-hu da lavaroud évid hé wennidigez?"

MRS. HAWKINS slowly and conscientiously, as if every detail of her family history was important, told the story of the steamboat explosion, of the finding and adoption of Laura. Silas, that is Mr. Hawkins, and she always loved Laura as if she had been their own child.

She then narrated the circumstances of Laura's supposed marriage, her abandonment and long illness, in a manner that touched all hearts. Laura had been a different woman since then.

Cross-examined. At the time of first finding Laura on the steamboat, did she notice that Laura's mind was at all deranged? She couldn't say that she did. After the recovery of Laura from her long illness, did Mrs. Hawkins think there were any signs of insanity about her? Witness confessed that she did not think of it *then*.

Re-direct examination. "But she was different after that?"

"O, yes, sir."

Washington Hawkins corroborated his mother's testimony as to Laura's connection with Col. Selby. He was at Harding during the time of her living there with him. After Col. Selby's desertion she was almost dead, never appeared to know anything rightly for weeks. He added that he never saw such a scoundrel as Selby. (Checked by District attorney.) Had he noticed any change in Laura after her illness? Oh, yes. Whenever any allusion was made that might recall Selby to mind, she looked awful—as if she could kill him.

"You mean," said Mr. Braham, "that there was an unnatural, insane gleam in her eyes?"

"Yes, certainly," said Washington in confusion.

All this was objected to by the district attorney, but it was got before the jury, and Mr. Braham did not care how much it was ruled out after that.

Beriah Sellers was the next witness called. The Colonel made his way to the stand with majestic, yet bland deliberation. Having taken the oath and kissed the Bible with a smack intended to show his great respect for that book, he bowed to his Honor with dignity, to the jury with familiarity, and then turned to the lawyers and stood in an attitude of superior attention.

"Mr. Sellers, I believe?" began Mr. Braham.

"Beriah Sellers, Missouri," was the courteous acknowledgment that the lawyer was correct.

"Mr. Sellers, you know the parties here, you are a friend of the family?"

"Know them all, from infancy, sir. It was me, sir, that induced Silas Hawkins, Judge Hawkins, to come to Missouri, and make his fortune. It was by my advice and in company with me, sir, that he went into the operation of—"

"Yes, yes. Mr. Sellers, did you know a Major Lackland?"

"Knew him well, sir, knew him and honored him, sir. He was one of the most remarkable men of our country, sir. A member of Congress. He was often at my mansion sir, for weeks. He used to say to me, 'Col. Sellers, if you would go into politics, if I had you for a colleague, we should show Calhoun and Webster that the brain of the country didn't lie east of the Alleganies'. But I said—"

"Yes, yes. I believe Major Lackland is not living, Colonel?"

There was an almost imperceptible sense of pleasure betrayed in the Colonel's face at this prompt acknowledgment of his title.

"Bless you, no. Died years ago, a miserable death, sir, a ruined man, a poor sot. He was suspected of selling his vote in Congress, and probably he did; the disgrace killed him, he was an outcast, sir, loathed by himself and by his constituents. And I think, sir—"

The Judge. "You will confine yourself, Col. Sellers, to the questions of the counsel."

"Of course, your honor. This," continued the Colonel in confidential explanation, "was twenty years ago. I shouldn't have thought of referring to such a trifling circumstance *now*. If I remember rightly, sir"—

A bundle of letters was here handed to the witness.

"Do you recognize that hand-writing?"

"As if it was my own, sir. It's Major Lackland's. I was knowing to these letters when Judge Hawkins received them. [The Colonel's memory was a little at fault here. Mr. Hawkins had never gone into details with him on this subject.] He used to show them to me, and say, 'Col. Sellers you've a mind to untangle this sort of thing.' Lord, how everything comes back to me. Laura was a little thing then. The Judge and I were just laying our plans to buy the Pilot Knob, and—"

"Colonel, one moment. Your Honor, we put these letters in evidence."

The letters were a portion of the correspondence of Major Lackland with Silas Hawkins; parts of them were missing and important letters were referred to that were not here. They related, as the reader knows, to Laura's father. Lackland had come upon the track of a man who was searching for a lost child in a Mississippi steamboat explosion years before. The man was lame in one leg, and appeared to be flitting from place to place. It seemed that Major Lackland got so close track of him that he was able to describe his personal appearance and learn his name. But the letter containing these particulars was lost. Once he heard of him at a hotel in Washington; but the man departed, leaving an empty trunk, the day before the major went there. There was something very mysterious in all his movements.

Col. Sellers, continuing his testimony, said that he saw this lost letter, but could not now recall the name. Search for the supposed father had been continued by Lackland, Hawkins and himself for several years, but Laura was not informed of it till after the death of Hawkins, for fear of raising false hopes in her mind.

Here the District Attorney arose and said,

"Your Honor, I must positively object to letting the witness wander off into all these irrelevant details."

Mr. Braham. "I submit, your Honor, that we cannot be interrupted in this manner. We have suffered the state to have full swing. Now here is a witness, who has known the prisoner from infancy, and is competent to testify upon the one point vital to her safety. Evidently he is a gentleman of character, and his knowledge of the case cannot be shut out without increasing the aspect of persecution which the State's attitude towards the prisoner already has assumed."

The wrangle continued, waxing hotter and hotter. The Colonel seeing the attention of the counsel and Court entirely withdrawn from him, thought he perceived here his opportunity. Turning and beaming upon the jury, he began simply to talk, but as the grandeur of his position grew upon him—his talk broadened unconsciously into an oratorical vein.

"You see how she was situated, gentlemen; poor child, it might have broken her heart to let her mind get to running on such a thing as that. You see, from what we could make out her father was lame in the left leg and had a deep scar on his left forehead. And so ever since the day she found out she *had* another father, she never could run across a lame stranger without being taken all over with a shiver, and almost fainting where she stood. And the next minute she would go right after that man. Once she stumbled on a stranger with a game leg, and she was the most grateful thing in this world—but it was the wrong leg, and it was days and days before she could leave her bed. Once she found a man with a scar on his forehead, and she was just going to throw herself into his arms, but he stepped out just then, and there wasn't anything the matter with his legs. Time and time again, gentlemen of the jury, has this poor suffering orphan flung herself on her knees with all her heart's gratitude in her eyes before some scarred and crippled veteran, but always, always to be disappointed, always to be plunged into new despair—if his legs were right his scar was wrong, if his scar was right his legs were wrong. Never could find a man that would fill the bill. Gentlemen of the jury, you have hearts, you have feelings, you have warm human sympathies, you can feel for this poor suffering child. Gentlemen of the jury, if I had time, if I had the opportunity, if I might be permitted to go on and tell you the thousands and thousands and thousands of mutilated strangers this poor girl has started out of cover, and hunted from city to city, from state to state, from continent to continent, till she has run them down and found they wan't the ones, I know your hearts—"

By this time the Colonel had become so warmed up, that his

voice, had reached a pitch above that of the contending counsel; the lawyers suddenly stopped, and they and the Judge turned towards the Colonel and remained for several seconds too surprised at this novel exhibition to speak. In this interval of silence, an appreciation of the situation gradually stole over the audience, and an explosion of laughter followed, in which even the Court and the bar could hardly keep from joining.

Sheriff. "Order in the Court."

The Judge. "The witness will confine his remarks to answers to questions."

The Colonel turned courteously to the Judge and said,

"Certainly, your Honor, certainly. I am not well acquainted with the forms of procedure in the courts of New York, but in the West, sir, in the West—"

The Judge. "There, there, that will do, that will do!"

"You see, your Honor, there were no questions asked me, and I thought I would take advantage of the lull in the proceedings to explain to the jury a very significant train of—"

The Judge. "That will *do*, sir! Proceed, Mr. Braham."

"Col. Sellers, have you any reason to suppose that this man is still living?"

"Every reason, sir, every reason."

"State why."

"I have never heard of his death, sir. It has never come to my knowledge. In fact, sir, as I once said to Governor—"

"Will you state to the jury what has been the effect of the knowledge of this wandering and evidently unsettled being, supposed to be her father, upon the mind of Miss Hawkins for so many years?"

Question objected to. Question ruled out.

Cross-examined. "Major Sellers, what is your occupation?"

The Colonel looked about him loftily, as if casting in his mind what would be the proper occupation of a person of such multifarious interests, and then said with dignity,

"A gentleman, sir. My father used to always say, sir"—

"Capt. Sellers, did you ever see this man, this supposed father?"

"No, sir. But upon one occasion, old Senator Thompson said to me, it's my opinion, Colonel Sellers"—

"Did you ever see any body who *had* seen him?"

"No, sir. It was reported around at one time, that"—

"That is all."

The defense then spent a day in the examination of medical experts in insanity, who testified, on the evidence heard, that sufficient causes had occurred to produce an insane mind in the prisoner. Numerous cases were cited to sustain this opinion. There was such a thing as momentary insanity, in which the person, otherwise rational to all appearances, was for the time actually bereft of reason, and not responsible for his acts. The causes of this momentary possession could often be found in the person's life. [It afterwards came out that the chief expert for the defense, was paid a thousand dollars for looking into the case.]

The prosecution consumed another day in the examination of experts refuting the notion of insanity. These causes might have produced insanity, but there was no evidence that they have produced it in this case, or that the prisoner was not at the time of the commission of the crime in full possession of her ordinary faculties.

The trial had now lasted two weeks. It required four days now for the lawyers to "sum up." These arguments of the counsel were very important to their friends, and greatly enhanced their reputation at the bar; but they have small interest to us. Mr. Braham in his closing speech surpassed himself; his effort is still remembered as the greatest in the criminal annals of New York.

Mr. Braham re-drew for the jury the picture of Laura's early life; he dwelt long upon that painful episode of the pretended marriage and the desertion. Col. Selby, he said, belonged, gentlemen, to what is called the "upper classes." It is the privilege of the "upper classes" to prey upon the sons and daughters of the people. The Hawkins family, though allied to the best blood of the South, were at the time in humble circumstances. He commented upon her parentage. Perhaps her agonized father, in his intervals of sanity, was still searching for his lost daughter. Would he one day hear that she had died a felon's death? Society had pursued her, fate had pursued her, and in a moment of delirium she had turned and defied fate and society. He dwelt upon the admission of base wrong in Col. Selby's dying statement. He drew a vivid picture of the villain at last overtaken by the vengeance of Heaven. Would the jury say that this retributive justice, inflicted by an outraged, a deluded woman, rendered irrational by the most cruel wrongs, was in the nature of a foul, premeditated murder? "Gentlemen, it is enough for me to look upon the life of this most beautiful and accomplished of her sex, blasted by the heartless villainy of man, without seeing, at the end of it, the horrible spectacle of a gibbet. Gentlemen, we are all human, we have all sinned, we all have need of mercy. But I do not ask mercy of you who are the guardians of society and of the poor waifs, its sometimes wronged victims; I ask only that justice which you and I shall need in that last dreadful hour, when death will be robbed of half its terrors if we can reflect that we have never wronged a human being. Gentlemen, the life of this lovely and once happy girl, this now stricken woman, is in your hands."

The jury were visibly affected. Half the court room was in tears. If a vote of both spectators and jury could have been taken *then*, the verdict would have been, "Let her her go, she has suffered enough."

But the district attorney had the closing argument. Calmly and without malice or excitement he reviewed the testimony. As the cold facts were unrolled, fear settled upon the listeners. There was no escape from the murder or its premeditation. Laura's character as a lobbyist in Washington, which had been made to appear incidentally in the evidence, was also against her. The whole body of the testimony of the defense was shown to be irrelevant, introduced only to excite sympathy, and not giving a color of probability to the absurd supposition of insanity. The attorney then dwelt upon the insecurity of life in the city, and the growing immunity with which women committed murders. Mr. McFlinn made a very able speech, convincing the reason without touching the feelings.

The Judge in his charge reviewed the testimony with great show of impartiality. He ended by saying that the verdict must be acquittal or murder in the first degree. If you find that the prisoner committed a homicide, in possession of her reason and with premeditation, your verdict will be accordingly. If you find she was not in her right mind, that she was the victim of insanity, hereditary or momentary, as it has been explained, your verdict will take that into account.

As the Judge finished his charge, the spectators anxiously watched the faces of the jury. It was not a remunerative study. In the court room the general feeling was in favor of Laura, but whether this feeling extended to the jury, their stolid faces did not reveal. The public outside hoped for a conviction, as it always does; it wanted an example; the newspapers trusted the jury would have the courage to do its duty. When Laura was convicted, then the public would turn around and abuse the governor if he did not pardon her.

The jury went out. Mr. Braham preserved his serene confidence, but Laura's friends were dispirited. Washington and Col. Sellers had been obliged to go to Washington and they had departed under the unspoken fear that the verdict would be unfavorable,—a disagreement was the best they could hope for, and money was needed. The necessity of the passage of the University bill was now imperative.

The Court waited for some time, but the jury gave no signs of coming in. Mr. Braham said it was extraordinary. The Court then took a recess for a couple of hours. Upon again coming in word was brought that the jury had not yet agreed.

But the jury had a question. The point upon which they wanted instruction was this:—They wanted to know if Col. Sellers was related to the Hawkins family. The court then adjourned till morning.

Mr. Braham, who was in something of a pet, remarked to Mr. O'Toole that they must have been deceived—that juryman with the broken nose could read!

CHAPTER LVII

"Wegotogwen ga-ijiwebadogwen; gonima ta-matchi-inakamigad."

THE MOMENTOUS DAY was at hand—a day that promised to make or mar the fortunes of the Hawkins family for all time. Washington Hawkins and Col. Sellers were both up early, for neither of them could sleep. Congress was expiring, and was passing bill after bill as if they were gasps and each likely to be its last. The University was on file for its third reading this day, and to-morrow Washington would be a millionaire and Sellers no longer impecunious; but this day, also, or at farthest the next, the jury in Laura's case would come to a decision of some kind or other—they would find her guilty, Washington secretly feared, and then the care and the trouble would all come back again and there would be wearing months of besieging judges for new trials; on this day, also, the re-election of Mr. Dilworthy to the Senate would take place. So Washington's mind was in a state of turmoil; there were more interests at stake than it could handle with serenity. He exulted when he thought of his millions; he was filled with dread when he thought of Laura. But Sellers was excited and happy. He said:

"Everything is going right, everything's going perfectly right. Pretty soon the telegrams will begin to rattle in, and then you'll see, my boy. Let the jury do what they please; what difference is it going to make? To-morrow we can send a million to New York and set the lawyers at work on the judges; bless your heart they will go before judge after judge and exhort and beseech and pray and shed tears. They always do; and they always win, too. And they will win this time. They will get a writ of habeas corpus, and a stay of proceedings, and a supersedeas,[159] and a new trial and a nolle prosequi, and there you are! That's the routine, and it's no trick at all to a New York lawyer. That's the regular routine—everything's red tape and routine in the law, you see; it's all Greek to you, of course, but to a man who is acquainted with those

403

things it's mere—I'll explain it to you sometime. Everything's going to glide right along easy and comfortable now. You'll see,
Washington, you'll see how it will be. And then, let me think . . . . .
Dilworthy will be elected to-day, and by day after to-morrow
night he will be in New York ready to put in *his* shovel—and you
haven't lived in Washington all this time not to know that the
people who walk right by a Senator whose term is up without
hardly seeing him will be down at the deepo to say 'Welcome
back and God bless you, Senator, I'm glad to see you, sir!' when
he comes along back re-elected, you know. Well, you see, his influence was naturally running low when he left here, but now he
has got a new six-years' start, and his suggestions will simply just
weigh a couple of tons a-piece day after tomorrow. Lord bless
you he could rattle through that habeas corpus and surpersedeas
and all those things for Laura all by himself if he wanted to, when
he gets back."

"I hadn't thought of that," said Washington, brightening, "but
it is so. A newly-elected Senator *is* a power, I know that."

"Yes indeed he is.—Why it is just human nature. Look at me.
When we first came here, I was *Mr.* Sellers, and *Major* Sellers, and
Captain Sellers, but nobody could ever get it right somehow; but
the minute our bill went through the House, I was *Colonel* Sellers
every time. And nobody could do enough for me; and whatever I
said was wonderful, sir, it was always wonderful; I never seemed
to say any flat things at all. It was Colonel won't you come and
dine with us; and Colonel why *don't* we ever see you at our
house; and the Colonel says this; and the Colonel says that; and
we know such-and-such is so-and-so, because husband heard
Col. Sellers *say* so. Don't you see? Well, the Senate adjourned and
left our bill high and dry, and I'll be hanged if I warn't *Old Sellers*
from that day till our bill passed the House again last week. Now
I'm the *Colonel* again; and if I were to eat all the dinners I àm invited to, I reckon I'd wear my teeth down level with my gums in
a couple of weeks."

"Well I do wonder what you will be to-morrow, Colonel, after
the President signs the bill?"

"*General* sir!—General, without a doubt. Yes, sir, to-morrow
it will be General, let me congratulate you, sir; General, you've

done a great work, sir;—you've done a great work for the niggro; Gentlemen, allow me the honor to introduce my friend General Sellers, the humane friend of the niggro. Lord bless me, you'll see the newspapers say, General Sellers and servants arrived in the city last night and is stopping at the Fifth Avenue; and General Sellers has accepted a reception and banquet by the Cosmopolitan Club; you'll see the General's opinions quoted, too—and what the General has to say about the propriety of a new trial and a habeas corpus for the unfortunate Miss Hawkins will not be without weight in influential quarters, I can tell you."

"And I want to be the first to shake your faithful old hand and salute you with your new honors, and I want to do it *now*— General!" said Washington, suiting the action to the word, and accompanying it with all the meaning that a cordial grasp and eloquent eyes could give it.

The Colonel was touched; he was pleased and proud, too; his face answered for that.

Not very long after breakfast the telegrams began to arrive. The first was from Braham, and ran thus:

"We feel certain that the verdict will be rendered to-day. Be it good or bad, let it find us ready to make the next move instantly, whatever it may be."

"That's the right talk," said Sellers. "That Braham's a wonderful man. He was the only man there that really understood me; he told me so himself, afterwards."

The next telegram was from Mr. Dilworthy:

"I have not only brought over the Great Invincible, but through him a dozen more of the opposition. Shall be re-elected to-day by an overwhelming majority."

"Good again!" said the Colonel. "That man's talent for organization is something marvelous. He wanted me to go out there and engineer that thing, but I said, No, Dilworthy, I must be on hand here, both on Laura's account and the bill's—but you've no trifling genius for organization yourself, said I—and I was right. You go ahead, said I—you can fix it—and so he has. But I claim no credit for that—if I stiffened up his back-bone a little, I simply put him in the way to make his fight—didn't make it myself. He has captured Noble—I consider that a splendid piece of diplomacy—Splendid, sir!"

By and by came another dispatch from New York:

> "Jury still out. Laura calm and firm as a statue. The report that the jury have brought her in guilty is false and premature."

"Premature!" gasped Washington, turning white. "Then they all expect that sort of a verdict, when it comes."

And so did he; but he had not had courage enough to put it into words. He had been preparing himself for the worst, but after all his preparation the bare suggestion of the possibility of such a verdict struck him cold as death.

The friends grew impatient, now; the telegrams did not come fast enough; even the lightning could not keep up with their anxieties. They walked the floor talking disjointedly and listening for the door-bell. Telegram after telegram came. Still no result. By and by there was one which contained a single line:

> "Court now coming in after brief recess to hear verdict. Jury ready."

"Oh, I wish they would finish!" said Washington. "This suspense is killing me by inches!"

Then came another telegram:

> "Another hitch somewhere. Jury want a little more time and further instructions."

"Well, well, well, this *is* trying," said the Colonel. And after a pause, "No dispatch from Dilworthy for two hours, now. Even a dispatch from him would be better than nothing, just to vary this thing."

They waited twenty minutes. It seemed twenty hours.

"Come!" said Washington. "I can't wait for the telegraph boy to come all the way up here. Let's go down to Newspaper Row—meet him on the way."

While they were passing along the Avenue, they saw some one putting up a great display-sheet on the bulletin board of a newspaper office, and an eager crowd of men was collecting about the place. Washington and the Colonel ran to the spot and read this:

"Tremendous Sensation! Startling news from Saint's Rest! On first ballot for U.S. Senator, when voting was about to begin, Mr. Noble rose in his place and drew forth a package, walked forward and laid it on the Speaker's desk, saying, 'This contains $7,000 in bank bills and was given me by Senator Dilworthy in his bed-chamber at midnight last night to buy my vote for him—I wish the Speaker to count the money and retain it to pay the expense of prosecuting this infamous traitor for bribery.' The whole legislature was stricken speechless with dismay and astonishment. Noble further said that there were fifty members present with money in their pockets, placed there by Dilworthy to buy their votes. Amidst unparalleled excitement the ballot was now taken, and J. W. Smith elected U.S. Senator; Dilworthy receiving not one vote! *Noble promises damaging exposures concerning Dilworthy and certain measures of his now pending in Congress.*"

"Good heavens and earth!" exclaimed the Colonel.

"To the Capitol!" said Washington. "Fly!"

And they did fly. Long before they got there the newsboys were running ahead of them with Extras, hot from the press, announcing the astounding news.

Arrived in the gallery of the Senate, the friends saw a curious spectacle—every Senator held an Extra in his hand and looked as interested as if it contained news of the destruction of the earth. Not a single member was paying the least attention to the business of the hour.

The Secretary, in a loud voice, was just beginning to read the title of a bill:

"House-Bill-No.-4,231,-An-Act-to-Found-and-Incorporate-the-Knobs-Industrial-University!-Read-first-and-second-time—considered-in-committee-of-the-whole-ordered-engrossed-and-passed-to-third-reading-and-final-passage!"

The President—"Third reading of the *bill!*"

The two friends shook in their shoes. Senators threw down

their extras and snatched a word or two with each other in whispers. Then the gavel rapped to command silence while the names were called on the ayes and nays. Washington grew paler and paler, weaker and weaker while the lagging list progressed; and when it was finished, his head fell helplessly forward on his arms. The fight was fought, the long struggle was over, and he was a pauper. Not a man had voted for the bill!

Col. Sellers was bewildered and well nigh paralyzed, himself. But no man could long consider his own troubles in the presence of such suffering as Washington's. He got him up and supported him—almost carried him indeed—out of the building and into a carriage. All the way home Washington lay with his face against the Colonel's shoulder and merely groaned and wept. The Colonel tried as well as he could under the dreary circumstances to hearten him a little, but it was of no use. Washington was past all hope of cheer, now. He only said:

"Oh, it is all over—it is all over for good, Colonel. We must beg our bread, now. We never can get up again. It was our last chance, and it is gone. They will hang Laura! My God they will hang her! Nothing can save the poor girl now. Oh, I wish with all my soul they would hang me instead!"

Arrived at home, Washington fell into a chair and buried his face in his hands and gave full way to his misery. The Colonel did not know where to turn nor what to do. The servant maid knocked at the door and passed in a telegram, saying it had come while they were gone.

The Colonel tore it open and read with the voice of a man-of-war's broadside:

"VERDICT OF JURY, NOT GUILTY AND LAURA IS FREE!"

CHAPTER LVIII

分 不 白 皂

Papel y tinta y poco justicia.

THE COURT ROOM was packed on the morning on which the verdict of the jury was expected, as it had been every day of the trial, and by the same spectators, who had followed its progress with such intense interest.

There is a delicious moment of excitement which the frequenter of trials well knows, and which he would not miss for the world. It is that instant when the foreman of the jury stands up to give the verdict, and before he has opened his fateful lips.

The court assembled and waited. It was an obstinate jury. It even had another question—this intelligent jury—to ask the judge this morning.

The question was this:—"Were the doctors clear that the deceased had no disease which might soon have carried him off, if he had not been shot?" There was evidently one juryman who didn't want to waste life, and was willing to strike a general average, as the jury always does in a civil case, deciding not according to the evidence but reaching the verdict by some occult mental process.

During the delay the spectators exhibited unexampled patience, finding amusement and relief in the slightest movements of the court, the prisoner and the lawyers. Mr. Braham divided with Laura the attention of the house. Bets were made by the sheriff's deputies on the verdict, with large odds in favor of a disagreement.

It was afternoon when it was announced that the jury was coming in. The reporters took their places and were all attention; the judge and lawyers were in their seats; the crowd swayed and pushed in eager expectancy, as the jury walked in and stood up in silence.

Judge. "Gentlemen, have you agreed upon your verdict?"

Foreman. "We have."

Judge. "What is it?"

Foreman. "NOT GUILTY."

A shout went up from the entire room and a tumult of cheering which the court in vain attempted to quell. For a few moments all order was lost. The spectators crowded within the bar and surrounded Laura who, calmer than anyone else, was supporting her aged mother, who had almost fainted from excess of joy.

And now occurred one of those beautiful incidents which no fiction-writer would dare to imagine, a scene of touching pathos, creditable to our fallen humanity. In the eyes of the women of the audience Mr. Braham was the hero of the occasion; he had saved the life of the prisoner; and besides he was such a handsome man. The women could not restrain their long pent-up emotions. They threw themselves upon Mr. Braham in a transport of gratitude; they kissed him again and again, the young as well as the advanced in years, the married as well as the ardent single women; they improved the opportunity with a touching self-sacrifice; in the words of a newspaper of the day they "lavished him with kisses." It was something sweet to do; and it would be sweet for a woman to remember in after years, that she had kissed Braham! Mr. Braham himself received these fond assaults with the gallantry of his nation, enduring the ugly, and heartily paying back beauty in its own coin.

This beautiful scene is still known in New York as "the kissing of Braham."

When the tumult of congratulation had a little spent itself, and order was restored, Judge O'Shaunnessy said that it now became his duty to provide for the proper custody and treatment of the acquitted. The verdict of the jury having left no doubt that the woman was of an unsound mind, with a kind of insanity dangerous to the safety of the community, she could not be permitted to go at large. "In accordance with the directions of the law in such cases," said the Judge, "and in obedience to the dictates of a wise humanity, I hereby commit Laura Hawkins to the care of the Superintendent of the State Hospital for Insane Criminals, to be held in confinement until the State Commissioners on Insanity shall order her discharge. Mr. Sheriff, you will attend at once to the execution of this decree."

Laura was overwhelmed and terror-stricken. She had expected to walk forth in freedom in a few moments. The revulsion was terrible. Her mother appeared like one shaken with an ague fit. Laura insane! And about to be locked up with madmen! She had never contemplated this. Mr. Braham said he should move at once for a writ of *habeas corpus*.

But the judge could not do less than his duty, the law must have its way. As in the stupor of a sudden calamity, and not fully comprehending it, Mrs. Hawkins saw Laura led away by the officer.

With little space for thought she was rapidly driven to the railway station, and conveyed to the Hospital for Lunatic Criminals. It was only when she was within this vast and grim abode of madness that she realized the horror of her situation. It was only when she was received by the kind physician and read pity in his eyes, and saw his look of hopeless incredulity when she attempted to tell him that she was not insane; it was only when she passed through the ward to which she was consigned and saw the horrible creatures, the victims of a double calamity, whose dreadful faces she was hereafter to see daily, and was locked into the small, bare room that was to be her home, that all her fortitude forsook her. She sank upon the bed, as soon as she was left alone—she had been searched by the matron—and tried to think. But her brain was in a whirl. She recalled Braham's speech, she recalled the testimony regarding her lunacy. She wondered if she *were* not mad; she felt that she soon should be among these loathsome creatures. Better almost to have died, than to slowly go mad in this confinement.

—We beg the reader's pardon. This is not history, which has just been written. It is really what would have occurred if this were a novel. If this were a work of fiction, we should not dare to dispose of Laura otherwise. True art and any attention to dramatic proprieties required it. The novelist who would turn loose upon society an insane murderess could not escape condemnation. Besides, the safety of society, the decencies of criminal procedure, what we call our modern civilization, all would demand that Laura should be disposed of in the manner we have described. Foreigners, who read this sad story, will be unable to understand any other termination of it.

But this is history and not fiction. There is no such law or custom as that to which his Honor is supposed to have referred; Judge O'Shaunnessy would not probably pay any attention to it if there were. There is no Hospital for Insane Criminals; there is no State commission of lunacy. What actually occurred when the tumult in the court room had subsided the sagacious reader will now learn.

Laura left the court room, accompanied by her mother and other friends, amid the congratulations of those assembled, and was cheered as she entered a carriage, and drove away. How sweet was the sunlight, how exhilarating the sense of freedom! Were not these following cheers the expression of popular approval and affection? Was she not the heroine of the hour?

It was with a feeling of triumph that Laura reached her hotel, a scornful feeling of victory over society with its own weapons.

Mrs. Hawkins shared not at all in this feeling; she was broken with the disgrace and the long anxiety.

"Thank God, Laura," she said, "it is over. Now we will go away from this hateful city. Let us go home at once."

"Mother," replied Laura, speaking with some tenderness, "I cannot go with you. There, don't cry, I cannot go back to that life."

Mrs. Hawkins was sobbing. This was more cruel that anything else, for she had a dim notion of what it would be to leave Laura to herself.

"No, mother, you have been everything to me. You know how dearly I love you. But I cannot go back."

A boy brought in a telegraphic dispatch. Laura took it and read:

"The bill is lost. Dilworthy is ruined. (Signed) WASHINGTON."

For a moment the words swam before her eyes. The next her eyes flashed fire as she handed the dispatch to her mother and bitterly said,

"The world is against me. Well, let it be, let it. I am against it."

"This is a cruel disappointment," said Mrs. Hawkins, to whom one grief more or less did not much matter now, "to you and Washington; but we must humbly bear it."

"Bear it," replied Laura scornfully, "I've all my life borne it, and fate has thwarted me at every step."

A servant came to the door to say that there was a gentleman below who wished to speak with Miss Hawkins. "J. Adolphe Griller" was the name Laura read on the card. "I do not know such a person. He probably comes from Washington. Send him up."

Mr. Griller entered. He was a small man, slovenly in dress, his tone confidential, his manner wholly void of animation, all his features below the forehead protruding—particularly the apple of his throat—hair without a kink in it, a hand with no grip, a meek, hang-dog countenance. He was a falsehood done in flesh and blood; for while every visible sign about him proclaimed him a poor, witless, useless weakling; the truth was that he had the brains to plan great enterprises and the pluck to carry them through. That was his reputation, and it was a deserved one.

He softly said:

"I called to see you on business, Miss Hawkins. You have my card?"

Laura bowed.

Mr. Griller continued to purr, as softly as before:

"I will proceed to business. I am a business man. I am a lecture-agent, Miss Hawkins, and as soon as I saw that you were acquitted, it occurred to me that an early interview would be mutually beneficial."

"I don't understand you, sir," said Laura coldly.

"No? You see, Miss Hawkins, this is your opportunity. If you will enter the lecture field under good auspices, you will carry everything before you."

"But, sir, I never lectured, I haven't any lecture, I don't know anything about it."

"Ah, madam, that makes no difference—no real difference. It is not necessary to be able to lecture in order to go into the lecture field. If one's name is celebrated all over the land, especially, and if she is also beautiful, she is certain to draw large audiences."

"But what should I lecture about?" asked Laura, beginning in spite of herself to be a little interested as well as amused.

"Oh, why, woman—something about woman, I should say; the marriage relation, woman's fate, anything of that sort. Call it The Revelations of a Woman's Life; now, there's a good title. I wouldn't want any better title than that. I'm prepared to make you an offer, Miss Hawkins, a liberal offer,—twelve thousand dollars for thirty nights."

Laura thought. She hesitated. Why not? It would give her employment, money. She must do something:

"I will think of it, and let you know soon. But still, there is very little likelihood that I—however, we will not discuss it further now."

"Remember, that the sooner we get to work the better, Miss Hawkins, public curiosity is so fickle. Good day, madam."

The close of the trial released Mr. Harry Brierly and left him free to depart upon his long talked of Pacific-coast mission. He was very mysterious about it, even to Philip.

"It's confidential, old boy," he said, "a little scheme we have hatched up. I don't mind telling you that it's a good deal bigger thing than that in Missouri, and a sure thing. I wouldn't take a half a million just for my share. And it will open something for you, Phil. You will hear from me."

Philip did hear from Harry a few months afterward. Everything promised splendidly, but there was a little delay. Could Phil let him have a hundred, say for ninety days?

Philip himself hastened to Philadelphia, and, as soon as the spring opened, to the mine at Ilium, and began transforming the loan he had received from 'Squire Montague into laborers' wages. He was haunted with many anxieties; in the first place, Ruth was overtaxing her strength in her hospital labors, and Philip felt as if he must move heaven and earth to save her from such toil and suffering. His increased pecuniary obligation oppressed him. It seemed to him also that he had been one cause of the misfortune to the Bolton family, and that he was dragging into loss and ruin everybody who associated with him. He worked on day after day and week after week, with a feverish anxiety.

It would be wicked, thought Philip, and impious, to pray for luck; he felt that perhaps he ought not to ask a blessing upon the sort of labor that was only a venture; but yet in that daily petition, which this very faulty and not very consistent young Christian gentleman put up, he prayed earnestly enough for Ruth and for the Boltons and for those whom he loved and who trusted in him, and that his life might not be a misfortune to them and a failure to himself.

Since this young fellow went out into the world from his New England home, he had done some things that he would rather his mother should not know, things maybe that he would shrink from telling Ruth. At a certain green age young gentlemen are sometimes afraid of being called milksops, and Philip's associates had not always been the most select, such as these historians would have chosen for him, or whom at a later period he would have chosen for himself. It seemed inexplicable, for instance, that his life should have been thrown so much with his college acquaintance, Henry Brierly.

Yet, this was true of Philip, that in whatever company he had been he had never been ashamed to stand up for the principles he learned from his mother, and neither raillery nor looks of wonder turned him from that daily habit he learned at his mother's knees. Even flippant Harry respected this, and perhaps it was one of the reasons why Harry and all who knew Philip trusted him implicitly. And yet it must be confessed that Philip did not convey the impression to the world of a very serious young man, or of a man who might not rather easily fall into temptation. One looking for a real hero would have to go elsewhere.

The parting between Laura and her mother was exceedingly painful to both. It was as if two friends parted on a wide plain, the one to journey towards the setting and the other towards the rising sun, each comprehending that every step henceforth must separate their lives wider and wider.

CHAPTER LIX

Ebok imana ebok ofut idibi.

Epik Proverb.

'Ο καρκίνος ὧδ' εφα
Χαλᾷ τὸν ὄφιν λαβών·
Εὐθὺν χρὴ τον ἑταῖρον ἔμμεν,
Καὶ μὴ σκολιὰ φρονεῖν.

Mishittoonaeog noowaog
ayeuuhkone neen,
Nashpe nuskesukqunnonut
ho, ho, nunnaumunun.

WHEN MR. NOBLE'S BOMBSHELL FELL in Senator Dilworthy's camp, the statesman was disconcerted for a moment.—For a moment; that was all. The next moment he was calmly up and doing. From the centre of our country to its circumference, nothing was talked of but Mr. Noble's terrible revelation, and the people were furious. Mind, they were not furious because bribery was uncommon in our public life, but merely because here was *another* case. Perhaps it did not occur to the nation of good and worthy people that while they continued to sit comfortably at home and leave the true source of our political power (the "primaries,") in the hands of saloon-keepers, dog-fanciers and hod-carriers, they could go on expecting "another" case of this kind, and even dozens and hundreds of them, and never be disappointed. However, they may have thought that to sit at home and grumble would some day right the evil.

Yes, the nation was excited, but Senator Dilworthy was calm—what was left of him after the explosion of the shell. Calm, and up and doing. What did he do first? What would you do first, after you had tomahawked your mother at the breakfast table for putting too much sugar in your coffee? You would "ask for a suspension of public opinion." That is what Senator Dilworthy did. It is the custom. He got the usual amount of suspension. Far and wide he was called a thief, a briber, a promoter of steamship subsidies,

416

railway swindles, robberies of the government in all possible forms and fashions. Newspapers and everybody else called him a pious hypocrite, a sleek, oily fraud, a reptile who manipulated temperance movements, prayer meetings, Sunday schools, public charities, missionary enterprises, all for his private benefit. And as these charges were backed up by what seemed to be good and sufficient evidence, they were believed with national unanimity.

Then Mr. Dilworthy made another move. He moved instantly to Washington and "demanded an investigation." Even this could not pass without comment. Many papers used language to this effect:

> "Senator Dilworthy's remains have demanded an investigation. This sounds fine and bold and innocent; but when we reflect that they demand it at the hands of the Senate of the United States, it simply becomes matter for derision. One might as well set the gentlemen detained in the public prisons to trying each other. This investigation is likely to be like all other Senatorial 'investigations'— amusing but not useful. Query. Why does the Senate still stick to this pompous word, 'Investigation?' One does not blindfold one's self in order to investigate an object."

Mr. Dilworthy appeared in his place in the Senate and offered a resolution appointing a committee to investigate his case. It carried, of course, and the committee was appointed. Straightway the newspapers said:

> "Under the guise of appointing a committee to investigate the late Mr. Dilworthy, the Senate yesterday appointed a committee to *investigate his accuser, Mr. Noble*. This is the exact spirit and meaning of the resolution, and the committee cannot try anybody but Mr. Noble without overstepping its authority. That Mr. Dilworthy had the effrontery to offer such a resolution will surprise no one; and that the Senate could entertain it without blushing and pass it without shame will surprise no one. We are now reminded of a note which we have received from the notorious burglar Murphy, in which he finds fault with a statement of ours to the effect that he had served one term in the penitentiary and also one in the U.S. Senate. He says, 'The latter statement is untrue and does me great injustice.' After an unconscious sarcasm like that, further comment is unnecessary."

And yet the Senate was roused by the Dilworthy trouble. Many speeches were made. One Senator (who was accused in the public prints of selling his chances of re-election to his opponent for $50,000 and had not yet denied the charge) said that, "the presence in the Capital of such a creature as this man Noble, to testify against a brother member of their body, was an insult to the Senate."

Another Senator said, "Let the investigation go on; and let it make an example of this man Noble; let it teach him and men like him that they could not attack the reputation of a United States Senator with impunity."

Another said he was glad the investigation was to be had, "for it was high time that the Senate should crush some cur like this man Noble, and thus show his kind that it was able and resolved to uphold its ancient dignity."

A by-stander laughed, at this finely delivered peroration, and said,

"Why, this is the Senator who franked his baggage home through the mails last week—registered, at that. However, perhaps he was merely engaged in 'upholding the ancient dignity of the Senate,' then."

"No, the modern dignity of it," said another by-stander. "It don't resemble its ancient dignity, but it fits its modern style like a glove."

There being no law against making offensive remarks about U.S. Senators, this conversation, and others like it, continued without let or hindrance. But our business is with the investigating committee.

Mr. Noble appeared before the Committee of the Senate, and testified to the following effect:

He said that he was a member of the State legislature of the Happy-Land-of-Canaan; that on the——day of——he assembled himself together at the city of Saint's Rest, the capital of the State, along with his brother legislators; that he was known to be a political enemy of Mr. Dilworthy and bitterly opposed to his re-election; that Mr. Dilworthy came to Saint's Rest and was reported to be buying pledges of votes with money; that the said Dilworthy sent for him to come to his room in the hotel at night, and he went; was introduced to Mr. Dilworthy; called two or three times afterward at Dilworthy's request—usually after midnight; Mr. Dilworthy urged him to vote for him; Noble declined; Dilworthy argued; said he was bound to be elected, and could then ruin him (Noble) if he voted no; said he had every railway and every public office and stronghold of political power in the State under his thumb, and could set up or pull down any man he chose; gave instances showing where and how he had used this power; if Noble would vote for him he would make him a Representative in Congress; Noble still declined to vote, and said he did not believe Dilworthy was going to be elected; Dilworthy showed a list of men who would vote for him—a majority of the legislature; gave further proofs of his power by telling Noble everything the opposing party had done or said in secret caucus; claimed that his spies reported everything to him, and that—

Here a member of the Committee objected that this evidence was irrelevant and also in opposition to the spirit of the Committee's instructions, because if these things reflected upon any one it was upon Mr. Dilworthy. The chairman said, let the person proceed with his statement—the Committee could exclude evidence that did not bear upon the case.

Mr. Noble continued. He said that his party would cast him out if he voted for Mr. Dilworthy; Dilworthy said that that would inure to his benefit because he would then be a recognized friend of his (Dilworthy's) and he could consistently exalt him politically and make his fortune; Noble said he was poor, and it was hard to tempt him so; Dilworthy said he would fix that; he said, "Tell me what you want, and say you will vote for me"; Noble could not say; Dilworthy said "I will give you $5,000—"

A Committee man said, impatiently, that this stuff was all outside the case, and valuable time was being wasted; this was all a plain reflection upon a brother Senator. The Chairman said it was the quickest way to proceed, and the evidence need have no weight.

Mr. Noble continued. He said he told Dilworthy that $5,000 was not much to pay for a man's honor, character and everything that was worth having; Dilworthy said he was surprised; he considered $5,000 a fortune for some men; asked what Noble's figure was; Noble said he could not think $10,000 too little; Dilworthy said it was a great deal too much; he would not do it for any other man, but he had conceived a liking for Noble, and where he liked a man his heart yearned to help him; he was aware that Noble was poor, and had a family to support, and that he bore an unblemished reputation at home; for such a man and such a man's influence he could do much, and feel that to help such a man would be an act that would have its reward; the struggles of the poor always touched him; he believed that Noble would make a good use of this money and that it would cheer many a sad heart and needy home; he would give the $10,000; all he desired in return was that when the balloting began, Noble should cast his vote for him and should explain to the legislature that upon looking into the charges against Mr. Dilworthy of bribery, corruption, and forwarding stealing measures in Congress he had found them to be base calumnies upon a man whose motives were pure and whose character was stainless; he then took from his pocket $2,000 in bank bills and handed them to Noble, and got another package containing $5,000 out of his trunk and gave to him also. He—

A Committee man jumped up, and said:

"*At last*, Mr. Chairman, this shameless person has arrived at the point. This is sufficient and conclusive. By his own confession he has received a bribe, and did it deliberately. This is a grave offense, and cannot be passed over in silence, sir. By the terms of our instructions we can now proceed to mete out to him such punishment as is meet for one who has maliciously brought disrespect upon a Senator of the United States. We have no need to hear the rest of his evidence."

The Chairman said it would be better and more regular to proceed with the investigation according to the usual forms. A note would be made of Mr. Noble's admission.

Mr. Noble continued. He said that it was now far past midnight; that he took his leave and went straight to certain legislators, told them everything, made them count the money, and also told them of the exposure he would make in joint convention; he made that exposure, as all the world knew. The rest of the $10,000 was to be paid the day after Dilworthy was elected.

Senator Dilworthy was now asked to take the stand and tell

what he knew about the man Noble. The Senator wiped his mouth with his handkerchief, adjusted his white cravat, and said that but for the fact that public morality required an example, for the warning of future Nobles, he would beg that in Christian charity this poor misguided creature might be forgiven and set free. He said that it was but too evident that this person had approached him in the hope of obtaining a bribe; he had intruded himself time and again, and always with moving stories of his poverty. Mr. Dilworthy said that his heart had bled for him—insomuch that he had several times been on the point of trying to get some one to do something for him. Some instinct had told him from the beginning that this was a bad man, an evil-minded man, but his inexperience of such had blinded him to his real motives, and hence he had never dreamed that his object was to undermine the purity of a United States Senator. He regretted that it was plain, now, that such was the man's object and that punishment could not with safety to the Senate's honor be withheld. He grieved to say that one of those mysterious dispensations of an inscrutable Providence which are decreed from time to time by His wisdom and for His righteous purposes, had given this conspirator's tale a color of plausibility,—but this would soon disappear under the clear light of truth which would now be thrown upon the case.

It so happened, (said the Senator,) that about the time in question, a poor young friend of mine, living in a distant town of my State, wished to establish a bank; he asked me to lend him the necessary money; I said I had no money just then, but would try to borrow it. The day before the election a friend said to me that my election expenses must be very large—especially my hotel bills,—and offered to lend me some money. Remembering my young friend, I said I would like a few thousands now, and a few more by and by; whereupon he gave me two packages of bills said to contain $2,000 and $5,000 respectively; I did not open the packages or count the money; I did not give any note or receipt for the same; I made no memorandum of the transaction, and neither did my friend. That night this evil man Noble came troubling me again. I could not rid myself of him, though my time was very precious. He mentioned my young friend and said he was very anxious to have $7,000 now to begin his banking operations with, and could wait a while for the rest. Noble wished to get the money and take it to him. I finally gave him the two packages of bills; I took no note or receipt from him, and made no memorandum of the matter. I no more look for duplicity and deception in another man than I would look for it in myself. I never thought of this man again until I was overwhelmed the next day by learning what a shameful use he had made of the confidence I had reposed in him and the money I had entrusted to his care. This is all, gentlemen. To the absolute truth of every detail of my statement I solemnly swear, and I call Him to witness who is the Truth and the loving Father of all whose lips abhor false speaking; I pledge my honor as a Senator, that I have spoken but the truth. May God forgive this wicked man—as I do.

Mr. Noble—"Senator Dilworthy, your bank account shows that up to that day, and even on that very day, you conducted all your financial business through the medium of checks instead of bills, and so kept careful record of every moneyed transaction. Why did you deal in bank bills on this particular occasion?"

The Chairman—"The gentleman will please to remember that the Committee is conducting this investigation."

Mr. Noble—"Then will the Committee ask the question?"

The Chairman—"The Committee will—when it desires to know."

Mr. Noble—"Which will not be during this century perhaps."

The Chairman—"Another remark like that, sir, will procure you the attentions of the Sergeant-at-arms."

Mr. Noble—"D——n the Sergeant-at-arms, and the Committee too!"

Several Committeemen—"Mr. Chairman, this is contempt!"

Mr. Noble—"Contempt of whom?"

"Of the Committee! Of the Senate of the United States!"

Mr. Noble—"Then I am become the acknowledged representative of a nation. You know as well as I do that the whole nation hold as much as three-fifths of the United States Senate in entire contempt.—Three-fifths of you are Dilworthys."

The Sergeant-at-arms very soon put a quietus upon the observations of the representative of the nation, and convinced him that he was not in the over-free atmosphere of his Happy-Land-of-Canaan.

The statement of Senator Dilworthy naturally carried conviction to the minds of the committee.—It was close, logical, unanswerable; it bore many internal evidences of its truth.—For instance, it is customary in all countries for business men to loan large sums of money in bank bills instead of checks. It is customary for the lender to make no memorandum of the transaction. It is customary for the borrower to receive the money without making a memorandum of it, or giving a note or a receipt for it—because the borrower is not likely to die or forget about it. It is customary to lend nearly anybody money to start a bank with, especially if you have not the money to lend him and have to borrow it for the purpose. It is customary to carry large sums of money in bank bills about your person or in your trunk. It is customary to hand a large sum in bank bills to a man you have just been introduced to (if he asks you to do it,) to be conveyed to a distant town and delivered to another party. It is not customary to make a memorandum of this transaction; it is not customary for the conveyor to give a note or a receipt for the money; it is not customary to require that he shall get a note or a receipt from the man he is to convey it to in the distant town. It would be at least singular in you to say to the proposed conveyor, "You might be robbed; I will deposit the money in bank and send a check for it to my friend through the mail."

Very well. It being plain that Senator Dilworthy's statement was rigidly true, and this fact being strengthened by his adding to it the support of "his honor as a Senator," the Committee rendered a verdict of "Not proven that a bribe had been offered and accepted." This in a manner exonerated Noble and let him escape.

The Committee made its report to the Senate, and that body proceeded to consider its acceptance. One Senator—indeed, several Senators—objected that the Committee had failed of its duty; they had proved this man Noble guilty of nothing, they had meted out no punishment to him; if the report were accepted, he would go forth free and scathless, glorying in his crime, and it would be a tacit admission that any blackguard could insult the Senate of the United States and conspire against the sacred reputation of its members with impunity; the Senate owed it to the upholding of its ancient dignity to make an example of this man Noble—he should be crushed.

An elderly Senator got up and took another view of the case. This was a Senator of the worn-out and obsolete pattern; a man still lingering among the cobwebs of the past, and behind the spirit of the age. He said that there seemed to be a curious misunderstanding of the case. Gentlemen seemed exceedingly anxious to preserve and maintain the honor and dignity of the Senate.

Was this to be done by trying an obscure adventurer for attempting to trap a Senator into bribing him? Or would not the truer way be to find out whether the Senator was capable of *being* entrapped into so shameless an act, and then try *him?* Why, of course. *Now* the whole idea of the Senate seemed to be to shield the Senator and turn inquiry away from him. The true way to uphold the honor of the Senate was to have none but honorable men in its body. If this Senator had yielded to temptation and had offered a bribe, he was a soiled man and ought to be instantly expelled; therefore he wanted the Senator tried, and not in the usual namby-pamby way, but in good earnest. He wanted to know the truth of this matter. For himself, he believed that the guilt of Senator Dilworthy was established beyond the shadow of a doubt; and he considered that in trifling with his case and shirking it the Senate was doing a shameful and cowardly thing—a thing which suggested that in its willingness to sit longer in the company of such a man, it was acknowledging that it was itself of a kind with him and was therefore not dishonored by his presence. He desired that a rigid examination be made into Senator Dilworthy's case, and that it be continued clear into the approaching extra session if need be. There was no dodging this thing with the lame excuse of want of time.

In reply, an honorable Senator said that he thought it would be as well to drop the matter and accept the Committee's report. He said with some jocularity that the more one agitated this thing, the worse it was for the agitator. He was not able to deny that he believed Senator Dilworthy to be guilty—but what then? Was it such an extraordinary case? For his part, even allowing the Senator to be guilty, he did not think his continued presence during the few remaining days of the Session would contaminate the Senate to a dreadful degree. [This humorous sally was received with smiling admiration—notwithstanding it was not wholly new, having originated with the Massachusetts General in the House a day or two before, upon the occasion of the proposed expulsion of a member for selling his vote for money.]

The Senate recognized the fact that it could not be contaminated by sitting a few days longer with Senator Dilworthy, and so it accepted the committee's report and dropped the unimportant matter.

Mr. Dilworthy occupied his seat to the last hour of the session. He said that his people had reposed a trust in him, and it was not for him to desert them. He would remain at his post till he perished, if need be.

His voice was lifted up and his vote cast for the last time, in support of an ingenious measure contrived by the General from Massachusetts[160] whereby the President's salary was proposed to be doubled and every Congressman paid several thousand dollars extra for work previously done, under an accepted contract, and already paid for once and receipted for.

Senator Dilworthy was offered a grand ovation by his friends at home, who said that their affection for him and their confidence in him were in no wise impaired by the persecutions that had pursued him, and that he was still good enough for them.*

---

* The $7,000 left by Mr. Noble with his state legislature was placed in safe keeping to await the claim of the legitimate owner. Senator Dilworthy made one little effort through his protégé the embryo banker to recover it, but there being no notes of hand or other memoranda to support the claim, it failed. The moral of which is, that when one loans money to start a bank with, one ought to take the party's written acknowledgment of the fact.

CHAPTER LX

ᨠᨶᨺᩤᩢᨩᩮᩦᩃᨶᩲᨩ

"Ow holan whath ythew prowte
kynthoma ogas marowe"—

FOR SOME DAYS Laura had been a free woman once more. During this time, she had experienced—first, two or three days of triumph, excitement, congratulations, a sort of sunburst of gladness, after a long night of gloom and anxiety; then two or three days of calming down, by degrees—a receding of tides, a quieting of the storm-wash to a murmurous surf-beat, a diminishing of devastating winds to a refrain that bore the spirit of a truce—days given to solitude, rest, self-communion, and the reasoning of herself into a realization of the fact that she was actually done with bolts and bars, prison horrors and impending death; then came a day whose hours filed slowly by her, each laden with some remnant, some remaining fragment of the dreadful time so lately ended—a day which, closing at last, left the past a fading shore behind her and turned her eyes toward the broad sea of the future. So speedily do we put the dead away and come back to our place in the ranks to march in the pilgrimage of life again!

And now the sun rose once more and ushered in the first day of what Laura comprehended and accepted as a new life.

The past had sunk below the horizon, and existed no more for her; she was one with it for all time. She was gazing out over the trackless expanses of the future, now, with troubled eyes. Life must be begun again—at eight and twenty years of age. And where to begin? The page was blank, and waiting for its first record; so this was indeed a momentous day.

Her thoughts drifted back, stage by stage, over her career. As far as the long highway receded over the plain of her life, it was lined with the gilded and pillared splendors of her ambition all crumbled to ruin and ivy-grown; every milestone marked a disaster; there was no green spot remaining anywhere in memory of a hope that had found its fruition; the unresponsive earth had uttered no voice of flowers in testimony that one who was blest had gone that road.

Her life had been a failure. That was plain, she said. No more of that. She would now look the future in the face; she would mark her course upon the chart of life, and follow it; follow it without swerving, through rocks and shoals, through storm and calm, to a haven of rest and peace—or, shipwreck. Let the end be what it might, she would mark her course now—to-day—and follow it.

On her table lay six or seven notes. They were from lovers; from some of the prominent names in the land; men whose devotion had survived even the grisly revealments of her character which the courts had uncurtained; men who knew her now, just as she was, and yet pleaded as for their lives for the dear privilege of calling the murderess wife.

As she read these passionate, these worshiping, these supplicating missives, the woman in her nature confessed itself; a strong yearning came upon her to lay her head upon a loyal breast and find rest from the conflict of life, solace for her griefs, the healing of love for her bruised heart.

With her forehead resting upon her hand, she sat thinking, thinking, while the unheeded moments winged their flight. It was one of those mornings in early spring when nature seems just stirring to a half consciousness out of a long, exhausting lethargy; when the first faint balmy airs go wandering about, whispering the secret of the coming change; when the abused brown grass, newly relieved of snow, seems considering whether it can be worth the trouble and worry of contriving its green raiment again only to fight the inevitable fight with the implacable winter and be vanquished and buried once more; when the sun shines out and a few birds venture forth and lift up a forgotten song; when a strange stillness and suspense pervades the waiting air. It is a time when one's spirit is subdued and sad, one knows not why; when the past seems a storm-swept desolation, life a vanity and a burden, and the future but a way to death. It is a time when one is filled with vague longings; when one dreams of flight to peaceful islands in the remote solitudes of the sea, or folds his hands and says, What is the use of struggling, and toiling and worrying any more? let us give it all up.

It was into such a mood as this that Laura had drifted from the musings, which the letters of her lovers had called up. Now she lifted her head and noted with surprise how the day had wasted. She thrust the letters aside, rose up and went and stood at the window. But she was soon thinking again, and was only gazing into vacancy.

By and by she turned; her countenance had cleared; the dreamy look was gone out of her face, all indecision had vanished; the poise of her head and the firm set of her lips told that her resolution was formed. She moved toward the table with all the old dignity in her carriage, and all the old pride in her mien. She took up each letter in its turn, touched a match to it and watched it slowly consume to ashes. Then she said:

"I have landed upon a foreign shore, and burned my ships behind me. These letters were the last thing that held me in sympathy with any remnant or belonging of the old life. Henceforth that life and all that appertains to it are as dead to me and as far removed from me as if I were become a denizen of another world."

She said that love was not for her—the time that it could have satisfied her heart was gone by and could not return; the opportunity was lost, nothing could restore it. She said there could be no love without respect, and she would only despise a man who could content himself with a thing like her. Love, she said, was a woman's first necessity: love being forfeited, there was but one thing left that could give a passing zest to a wasted life, and that was fame, admiration, the applause of the multitude.

And so her resolution was taken. She would turn to that final resort of the disappointed of her sex, the lecture platform. She would array herself in fine attire, she would adorn herself with jewels, and stand in her isolated magnificence before massed audiences and enchant them with her eloquence and amaze them with her unapproachable beauty. She would move from city to city like a queen of romance, leaving marveling multitudes behind her and impatient multitudes awaiting her coming. Her life, during one hour of each day, upon the platform, would be a rapturous intoxication—and when the curtain fell, and the lights were out, and the people gone, to nestle in their homes and forget her, she would find in sleep oblivion of her homelessness, if she could, if not she would brave out the night in solitude and wait for the next day's hour of ecstasy.

So, to take up life and begin again was no great evil. She saw her way. She would be brave and strong; she would make the best of what was left for her among the possibilities.

She sent for the lecture agent, and matters were soon arranged.

Straightway all the papers were filled with her name and all the dead walls flamed with it. The papers called down imprecations upon her head; they reviled her without stint; they wondered if all sense of decency was dead in this shameless murderess, this brazen lobbyist, this heartless seducer of the affections of weak and misguided men; they implored the people, for the sake of their pure wives, their sinless daughters, for the sake of decency, for the sake of public morals, to give this wretched creature such a rebuke as should be an all-sufficient evidence to her and to such as her, that there was a limit where the flaunting of their foul acts and opinions before the world must stop; certain of them, with a higher art, and to her a finer cruelty, a sharper torture, uttered no abuse, but always spoke of her in terms of mocking eulogy and ironical admiration. Everybody talked about the new wonder, canvassed the theme of her proposed discourse, and marveled how she would handle it.

Laura's few friends wrote to her or came and talked with her, and pleaded with her to retire while it was yet time, and not attempt to face the gathering storm. But it was fruitless. She was stung to the quick by the comments of the newspapers; her spirit was roused, her ambition was towering, now. She was more determined than ever. She would show these people what a hunted and persecuted woman could do.

The eventful night came. Laura arrived before the great lecture hall in a close carriage within five minutes of the time set for the lecture to begin. When she stepped out of the vehicle her heart beat fast and her eyes flashed with exultation: the whole street was packed with people, and she could hardly force her way to the hall! She reached the ante-room, threw off her wraps and placed herself before the dressing-glass. She turned herself this way and that—everything was satisfactory, her attire was perfect. She smoothed her hair, re-arranged a jewel here and there, and all the while her heart sang within her, and her face was radiant. She had not been so happy for ages and ages, it seemed to her. Oh, no, she had never been so overwhelmingly grateful and happy in her whole life before. The lecture agent appeared at the door. She waved him away and said:

"Do not disturb me. I want no introduction. And do not fear for me; the moment the hands point to eight I will step upon the platform."

He disappeared. She held her watch before her. She was so impatient that the second-hand seemed whole tedious minutes dragging its way around the circle. At last the supreme moment came, and with head erect and the bearing of an empress she swept through the door and stood upon the stage. Her eyes fell upon—

Only a vast, brilliant emptiness—there were not forty people in the house! There were only a handful of coarse men and ten or twelve still coarser women, lolling upon the benches and scattered about singly and in couples.

Her pulses stood still, her limbs quaked, the gladness went out of her face. There was a moment of silence, and then a brutal laugh and an explosion of cat-calls and hisses saluted her from the audience. The clamor grew stronger and louder, and insulting speeches were shouted at her. A half-intoxicated man rose up and threw something, which missed her but bespattered a chair at her side, and this evoked an outburst of laughter and boisterous admiration. She was bewildered, her strength was forsaking her. She reeled away from the platform, reached the ante-room, and dropped helpless upon a sofa. The lecture agent ran in, with a hurried question upon his lips; but she put forth her hands, and with the tears raining from her eyes said:

"Oh, do not speak! Take me away—please take me away, out of this dreadful place! Oh, this is like all my life—failure, disappointment, misery—always misery, always failure. What have I done, to be so pursued! Take me away, I beg of you, I implore you!"

Upon the pavement she was hustled by the mob, the surging

masses roared her name and accompanied it with every species of insulting epithet; they thronged after the carriage, hooting, jeering, cursing, and even assailing the vehicle with missiles. A stone crushed through a blind, wounding Laura's forehead, and so stunning her that she hardly knew what further transpired during her flight.

It was long before her faculties were wholly restored, and then she found herself lying on the floor by a sofa in her own sitting-room, and alone. So she supposed she must have sat down upon the sofa and afterward fallen. She raised herself up, with difficulty, for the air was chilly and her limbs were stiff. She turned up the gas and sought the glass. She hardly knew herself, so worn and old she looked, and so marred with blood were her features. The night was far spent, and a dead stillness reigned. She sat down by her table, leaned her elbows upon it and put her face in her hands.

Her thoughts wandered back over her old life again and her tears flowed unrestrained.—Her pride was humbled, her spirit was broken. Her memory found but one resting place; it lingered about her young girlhood with a caressing regret; it dwelt upon it as the one brief interval in her life that bore no curse. She saw herself again in the budding grace of her twelve years, decked in her dainty pride of ribbons, consorting with the bees and the butterflies, believing in fairies, holding confidential converse with the flowers, busying herself all day long with airy trifles that were as weighty to her as the affairs that tax the brains of diplomats and emperors. She was without sin, then, and unacquainted with grief; the world was full of sunshine and her heart was full of music. From that—to this!

"If I could only die!" she said. "If I could only go back, and be as I was then, for one hour—and hold my father's hand in mine again, and see all the household about me, as in that old innocent time—and then die! My God, I am humbled, my pride is all gone, my stubborn heart repents—have pity!"

When the spring morning dawned, the form still sat there, the elbows resting upon the table and the face upon the hands. All day long the figure sat there, the sunshine enriching its costly raiment and flashing from its jewels; twilight came, and presently the stars, but still the figure remained; the moon found it there still, and framed the picture with the shadow of the window sash, and flooded it with mellow light; by and by the darkness swallowed it up, and later the gray dawn revealed it again; the new day grew toward its prime, and still the forlorn presence was undisturbed.

But now the keepers of the house had become uneasy; their periodical knockings still finding no response, they burst open the door.

The jury of inquest found that death had resulted from heart disease, and was instant and painless. That was all. Merely heart disease.

CHAPTER LXI

Han ager ikke ilde som veed at vende.
Wanna unyanpi kta. Niye de kta he?
Iapi Oaye, vol. i, no. 7.

CLAY HAWKINS, YEARS gone by, had yielded, after many a struggle, to the migratory and speculative instinct of our age and our people, and had wandered further and further westward upon trading ventures. Settling finally in Melbourne, Australia, he ceased to roam, became a steady-going substantial merchant, and prospered greatly. His life lay beyond the theatre of this tale.

His remittances had supported the Hawkins family, entirely, from the time of his father's death until latterly when Laura by her efforts in Washington had been able to assist in this work. Clay was away on a long absence in some of the eastward islands when Laura's troubles began, trying (and almost in vain,) to arrange certain interests which had become disordered through a dishonest agent, and consequently he knew nothing of the murder till he returned and read his letters and papers. His natural impulse was to hurry to the States and save his sister if possible, for he loved her with a deep and abiding affection.—His business was so crippled now, and so deranged, that to leave it would be ruin; therefore he sold out at a sacrifice that left him considerably reduced in worldly possessions, and began his voyage to San Francisco. Arrived there, he perceived by the newspapers that the trial was near its close. At Salt Lake later telegrams told him of the acquittal, and his gratitude was boundless—so boundless, indeed, that sleep was driven from his eyes by the pleasurable excitement almost as effectually as preceeding weeks of anxiety had done it. He shaped his course straight for Hawkeye, now, and his meeting with his mother and the rest of the household was joyful—albeit he had been away so long that he seemed almost a stranger in his own home.

But the greetings and congratulations were hardly finished when all the journals in the land clamored the news of Laura's miserable death. Mrs. Hawkins was prostrated by this last blow, and it was well that Clay was at her side to stay her with comforting words and take upon himself the ordering of the household with its burden of labors and cares.

Washington Hawkins had scarcely more than entered upon that decade which carries one to the full blossom of manhood which we term the beginning of middle age, and yet a brief sojourn at the capital of the nation had made him old. His hair was already turning gray when the late session of Congress began its sittings; it grew grayer still, and rapidly, after the memorable day that saw Laura proclaimed a murderess; it waxed grayer and still grayer during the lagging suspense that succeeded it and after the crash which ruined his last hope—the failure of his bill in the Senate and the destruction of its champion, Dilworthy. A few days later, when he stood uncovered while the last prayer was pronounced over Laura's grave, his hair was whiter and his face hardly less old than the venerable minister's whose words were sounding in his ears.

A week after this, he was sitting in a double-bedded room in a cheap boarding house in Washington, with Col. Sellers. The two had been living together lately, and this mutual cavern of theirs the Colonel sometimes referred to as their "premises" and sometimes as their "apartments"—more particularly when conversing with persons outside. A canvas-covered modern trunk, marked "G. W. H." stood on end by the door, strapped and ready for a journey; on it lay a small morocco satchel, also marked "G. W. H." There was another trunk close by—a worn, and scarred, and ancient hair relic, with "B. S." wrought in brass nails on its top; on it lay a pair of saddle-bags that probably knew more about the last century than they could tell. Washington got up and walked the floor a while in a restless sort of way, and finally was about to sit down on the hair trunk.

"Stop, don't sit down on that!" exclaimed the Colonel. "There, now—that's all right—the chair's better. I couldn't get another trunk like that—not another like it in America, I reckon."

"I am afraid not," said Washington, with a faint attempt at a smile.

"No indeed; the man is dead that made that trunk and that saddle-bags."

"Are his great-grand-children still living?" said Washington, with levity only in the words, not in the tone.

"Well, I don't know—I hadn't thought of that—but anyway they can't make trunks and saddle-bags like that, if they are—no man can," said the Colonel with honest simplicity. "Wife didn't like to see me going off with that trunk—she said it was nearly certain to be stolen."

"Why?"

"Why? Why, aren't trunks always being stolen?"

"Well, yes—some kinds of trunks are."

"Very well, then; this is some kind of a trunk—and an almighty rare kind, too."

"Yes, I believe it is."

"Well, then, why shouldn't a man want to steal it if he got a chance?"

"Indeed I don't know.—Why should he?"

"Washington, I never heard anybody talk like you. Suppose you were a thief, and that trunk was lying around and nobody watching—wouldn't you steal it? Come, now, answer fair— wouldn't you steal it?"

"Well, now, since you corner me, I don't know but I would *take* it,—but I wouldn't consider it stealing."

"You wouldn't! Well, that beats me. Now what would you call stealing?"

"Why, taking property is stealing."

"Property! Now what a way to talk that is. What do you suppose that trunk is worth?"

"Is it in good repair?"

"Perfect. Hair rubbed a little, but the main structure is perfectly sound."

"Does it leak anywhere?"

"Leak? Do you want to carry water in it? What do you mean by does it leak?"

"Why—a—do the clothes fall out of it when it is—when it is stationary?"

"Confound it, Washington, you are trying to make fun of me. I don't know what has got into you to-day; you act mighty curious. What *is* the matter with you?"

"Well, I'll tell you, old friend. I am almost happy. I am, indeed. It wasn't Clay's telegram that hurried me up so and got me ready to start with you. It was a letter from Louise."

"Good! What is it? What does she say?"

"She says come home—her father has consented, at last."

"My boy, I want to congratulate you; I want to shake you by the hand! It's a long turn that has no lane at the end of it, as the proverb says, or somehow that way. You'll be happy yet, and Beriah Sellers will be there to see, thank God!"

"I believe it. General Boswell is pretty nearly a poor man, now. The railroad that was going to build up Hawkeye made short work of him, along with the rest. He isn't so opposed to a son-in-law without a fortune, now."

"Without a fortune, indeed! Why that Tennessee Land—"

"Never mind the Tennessee Land, Colonel. I am done with that, forever and forever—"

"Why no! You can't mean to say—"

"My father, away back yonder, years ago, bought it for a blessing for his children, and—"

"Indeed he did! Si Hawkins said to me—"

"It proved a curse to him as long as he lived, and never a curse like it was inflicted upon any man's heirs—"

"I'm bound to say there's more or less truth—"

"It began to curse me when I was a baby, and it has cursed every hour of my life to this day—"

"Lord, lord, but it's so! Time and again my wife—"

"I depended on it all through my boyhood and never tried to do an honest stroke of work for my living—"

"Right again—but then you—"

"I have chased it years and years as children chase butterflies. We might all have been prosperous, now; we might all have been happy, all these heart-breaking years, if we had accepted our poverty at first and gone contentedly to work and built up our own weal by our own toil and sweat—"

"It's so, it's so; bless my soul, how often I've told Si Hawkins—"

"Instead of that, we have suffered more than the damned themselves suffer! I loved my father, and I honor his memory and recognize his good intentions; but I grieve for his mistaken ideas of conferring happiness upon his children. I am going to begin my life over again, and begin it and end it with good solid work! I'll leave *my* children no Tennessee Land!"

"Spoken like a man, sir, spoken like a man! Your hand, again my boy! And always remember that when a word of advice from Beriah Sellers can help, it is at your service. I'm going to begin again, too!"

"Indeed!"

"Yes, sir. I've seen enough to show me where my mistake was. The law is what I was born for. I shall begin the study of the law. Heavens and earth, but that Braham's a wonderful man—a wonderful man sir! Such a head! And such a way with him! But I could see that he was jealous of me. The little licks I got in in the course of my argument before the jury—"

"Your argument! Why, you were a witness."

"Oh, yes, to the popular eye, to the popular eye—but *I* knew when I was dropping information and when I was letting drive at the court with an insidious argument. But the court knew it, bless you, and weakened every time! And Braham knew it. I just reminded him of it in a quiet way, and its final result, and he said in a whisper, 'You did it, Colonel, you did it, sir—but keep it mum for *my* sake; and I'll tell you what *you* do,' says he, 'you go into the law, Col. Sellers—go into the law, sir; that's *your* native element!' And into the law the subscriber is going. There's worlds of money in it!—whole worlds of money! Practice first in Hawkeye, then in Jefferson, then in St. Louis, then in New York! In the metropolis of the western world! Climb, and climb, and climb—and wind up on the *Su*preme bench. Beriah Sellers, Chief Justice of the *Su*preme Court of the United States, sir! A made man for all time and eternity! That's the way *I* block it out, sir—and it's as clear as day—clear as the rosy morn!"

Washington had heard little of this. The first reference to Laura's trial had brought the old dejection to his face again, and he stood gazing out of the window at nothing, lost in reverie.

There was a knock—the postman handed in a letter. It was

from Obedstown, East Tennessee, and was for Washington. He opened it. There was a note saying that enclosed he would please find a bill for the current year's taxes on the 75,000 acres of Tennessee Land belonging to the estate of Silas Hawkins, deceased, and added that the money must be paid within sixty days or the land would be sold at public auction for the taxes, as provided by law. The bill was for $180—something more than twice the market value of the land, perhaps.

Washington hesitated. Doubts flitted through his mind. The old instinct came upon him to cling to the land just a little longer and give it one more chance. He walked the floor feverishly, his mind tortured by indecision. Presently he stopped, took out his pocket book and counted his money. Two hundred and thirty dollars—it was all he had in the world.

"One hundred and eighty . . . . from two hundred and thirty," he said to himself. "Fifty left . . . . . . It is enough to get me home . . . . Shall I do it, or shall I not? . . . . I wish I had somebody to decide for me."

The pocket book lay open in his hand, with Louise's small letter in view. His eye fell upon that, and it decided him.

"It shall go for taxes," he said, "and never tempt me or mine any more!"

He opened the window and stood there tearing the tax bill to bits and watching the breeze waft them away, till all were gone.

"The spell is broken, the life-long curse is ended!" he said. "Let us go."

The baggage wagon had arrived; five minutes later the two friends were mounted upon their luggage in it, and rattling off toward the station, the Colonel endeavoring to sing "Homeward Bound," a song whose words he knew, but whose tune, as he rendered it, was a trial to auditors.

CHAPTER LXII

Gedi kanadiben tsannawa.

—La xalog, la xamaih mi-x-ul nu qiza u quïal gih, u quïal agab?
Rabinal-Achi.

PHILIP STERLING'S CIRCUMSTANCES were becoming straitened.
The prospect was gloomy. His long siege of unproductive labor
was beginning to tell upon his spirits; but what told still more
upon them was the undeniable fact that the promise of ultimate
success diminished every day, now. That is to say, the tunnel had
reached a point in the hill which was considerably beyond where
the coal vein should pass (according to all his calculations) if there
were a coal vein there; and so, every foot that the tunnel now progressed seemed to carry it further away from the object of the
search.

Sometimes he ventured to hope that he had made a mistake in
estimating the direction, which the vein should naturally take after crossing the valley and entering the hill. Upon such occasions
he would go into the nearest mine of the vein he was hunting for,
and once more get the bearings of the deposit and mark out its
probable course; but the result was the same every time; his tunnel had manifestly pierced beyond the natural point of junction;
and then his spirits fell a little lower. His men had already lost
faith, and he often overheard them saying it was perfectly plain
that there was no coal in the hill.

Foremen and laborers from neighboring mines, and no end of
experienced loafers from the village, visited the tunnel from time
to time, and their verdicts were always the same and always dis-
heartening—"No coal in that hill." Now and then Philip would
sit down and think it all over and wonder what the mystery
meant; then he would go into the tunnel and ask the men if there
were no signs yet? None—always "none." He would bring out a
piece of rock and examine it, and say to himself, "It is limestone—
it has crinoids and corals in it—the rock is right." Then he would

throw it down with a sigh, and say, "But that is nothing; where coal is, limestone with these fossils in it is pretty certain to lie against its foot casing; but it does not necessarily follow that where this peculiar rock is, coal must lie above it or beyond it; this sign is not sufficient."

The thought usually followed:—"There *is* one infallible sign—if I could only strike *that!*"

Three or four times in as many weeks he said to himself, "Am I a visionary? I *must* be a visionary; everybody is in these days; everybody chases butterflies: everybody seeks sudden fortune and will not lay one up by slow toil. This is not right, I will discharge the men and go at some honest work. There is no coal here. What a fool I have been; I will give it up."

But he never could do it. A half hour of profound thinking always followed; and at the end of it he was sure to get up and straighten himself and say: "There *is* coal there; I will *not* give it up; and coal or no coal I will drive the tunnel clear through the hill; I will not surrender while I am alive."

He never thought of asking Mr. Montague for more money. He said there was now but one chance of finding coal against nine hundred and ninety nine that he would not find it, and so it would be wrong in him to make the request and foolish in Mr. Montague to grant it.

He had been working three shifts of men. Finally, the settling of a weekly account exhausted his means. He could not afford to run in debt, and therefore he gave the men their discharge. They came into his cabin presently, where he sat with his elbows on his knees and his chin in his hands, the picture of discouragement and their spokesman said:

"Mr. Sterling, when Tim was down a week with his fall you kept him on half wages and it was a mighty help to his family; whenever any of us was in trouble you've done what you could to help us out; you've acted fair and square with us every time, and I reckon we are men and know a man when we see him. We haven't got any faith in that hill, but we have a respect for a man that's got the pluck that you've showed; you've fought a good fight, with everybody agin you and if we had grub to go on, I'm d—d if we wouldn't stand by you till the cows come home! That is what the boys say. Now we want to put in one parting blast for luck. We want to work three days more; if we don't find anything, we won't bring in no bill against you. That is what we've come to say."

Philip was touched. If he had had money enough to buy three days' "grub" he would have accepted the generous offer, but as it was, he could not consent to be less magnanimous than the men, and so he declined in a manly speech, shook hands all around and resumed his solitary communings. The men went back to the tunnel and "put in a parting blast for luck" anyhow. They did a full day's work and then took their leave. They called at his cabin and gave him good-bye, but were not able to tell him their day's effort had given things a more promising look.

The next day Philip sold all the tools but two or three sets; he also sold one of the now deserted cabins as old lumber, together with its domestic wares, and made up his mind that he would buy provisions with the trifle of money thus gained and continue his work alone. About the middle of the afternoon he put on his roughest clothes and went to the tunnel. He lit a candle and groped his way in. Presently he heard the sound of a pick or a drill, and wondered what it meant. A spark of light now appeared in the far end of the tunnel. And when he arrived there he found the man Tim at work. Tim said:

"I'm to have a job in the Golden Brier mine by and by—in a week or ten days—and I'm going to work here till then. A man might as well be at some thing, and besides I consider that I owe you what you paid me when I was laid up."

Philip said, Oh, no, he didn't owe anything; but Tim persisted, and then Philip said he had a little provision, now, and would share. So for several days Philip held the drill and Tim did the striking. At first Philip was impatient to see the result of every blast, and was always back and peering among the smoke the moment after the explosion. But there was never any encouraging result; and therefore he finally lost almost all interest, and hardly troubled himself to inspect results at all. He simply labored on, stubbornly and with little hope.

Tim staid with him till the last moment, and then took up his job at the Golden Brier, apparently as depressed by the continued barrenness of their mutual labors as Philip was himself. After that, Philip fought his battle alone, day after day, and slow work it was; he could scarcely see that he made any progress.

Late one afternoon he finished drilling a hole which he had been at work at for more than two hours; he swabbed it out, and poured in the powder and inserted the fuse; then filled up the rest of the hole with dirt and small fragments of stone; tamped it down firmly, touched his candle to the fuse, and ran. By and by the dull report came, and he was about to walk back mechanically and see what was accomplished; but he halted; presently turned on his heel and thought, rather than said:

"No, this is useless, this is absurd. If I found anything it would only be one of those little aggravating seams of coal which doesn't mean anything, and—."

By this time he was walking out of the tunnel. His thought ran on:

"I am conquered......I am out of provisions, out of money.....I have got to give it up......All this hard work lost! But I am *not* conquered! I will go and work for money, and come back and have another fight with fate. Ah me, it may be years, it may be years."

Arrived at the mouth of the tunnel, he threw his coat upon the ground, sat down on a stone, and his eye sought the western sun and dwelt upon the charming landscape which stretched its woody ridges, wave upon wave, to the golden horizon.

Something was taking place at his feet, which did not attract his attention.

His reverie continued, and its burden grew more and more gloomy. Presently he rose up and cast a look far away toward the valley, and his thoughts took a new direction:

"There it is! How good it looks! But down there is not up here. Well, I will go home and pack up—there is nothing else to do."

He moved off moodily toward his cabin. He had gone some distance before he thought of his coat; then he was about to turn back, but he smiled at the thought, and continued his journey—such a coat as that could be of little use in a civilized land. A little further on, he remembered that there were some papers of value in one of the pockets of the relic, and then with a petulant ejaculation he turned back, picked up the coat and put it on.

He made a dozen steps, and then stopped very suddenly. He stood still a moment, as one who is trying to believe something and cannot. He put a hand up over his shoulder and felt his back, and a great thrill shot through him. He grasped the skirt of the coat impulsively and another thrill followed. He snatched the coat from his back, glanced at it, threw it from him and flew back to the tunnel. He sought the spot where the coat had lain—he had to look close, for the light was waning—then to make sure, he put his hand to the ground and a little stream of water swept against his fingers:

"Thank God, I've struck it at last!"

He lit a candle and ran into the tunnel; he picked up a piece of rubbish cast out by the last blast, and said:

"This clayey stuff is what I've longed for—I know what is behind it."

He swung his pick with hearty good will till long after the darkness had gathered upon the earth, and when he trudged home at length he knew he had a coal vein and that it was seven feet thick from wall to wall.

He found a yellow envelope lying on his rickety table, and recognized that it was of a family sacred to the transmission of telegrams.

He opened it, read it, crushed it in his hand and threw it down. It simply said:

"Ruth is very ill."

CHAPTER LXIII

Alaila pomaikai kaua, ola na iwi iloka o ko kaua mau la elemakule.
Laieikawai, 9.

ܘܩܠܐ: ܚܕܬܐ ܟܝܠܐ · ܡܡܕܘܡܝ ܟܘܝܢܐܡܝܗ·
ܕܘܩܢܐ : ܐܘܩܕܐ : ܗܠ

IT WAS EVENING when Philip took the cars at the Ilium station. The news of his success had preceded him, and while he waited for the train, he was the center of a group of eager questioners, who asked him a hundred things about the mine, and magnified his good fortune. There was no mistake this time.

Philip, in luck, had become suddenly a person of consideration, whose speech was freighted with meaning, whose looks were all significant. The words of the proprietor of a rich coal mine have a golden sound, and his common sayings are repeated as if they were solid wisdom.

Philip wished to be alone; his good fortune at this moment seemed an empty mockery, one of those sarcasms of fate, such as that which spreads a dainty banquet for the man who has no appetite. He had longed for success principally for Ruth's sake; and perhaps now, at this very moment of his triumph, she was dying.

"Shust what I said, Mister Sderling," the landlord of the Ilium hotel kept repeating. "I dold Jake Schmidt he find him dere shust so sure as noting."

"You ought to have taken a share, Mr. Dusenheimer," said Philip.

"Yaas, I know. But d'old woman, she say 'You sticks to your pisiness.' So I sticks to 'em. Und I makes noting. Dat Mister Prierly, he don't never come back here no more, ain't it?"

"Why?" asked Philip.

"Vell, dere is so many peers, und so many oder dhrinks, I got 'em all set down, ven he coomes back."

It was a long night for Philip, and a restless one. At any other time the swing of the cars would have lulled him to sleep, and the rattle and clank of wheels and rails, the roar of the whirling iron would have only been cheerful reminders of swift and safe travel. Now they were voices of warning and taunting; and instead of going rapidly the train seemed to crawl at a snail's pace. And it not only crawled, but it frequently stopped; and when it stopped it stood dead still, and there was an ominous silence. Was anything the matter, he wondered. Only a station probably. Perhaps, he thought, a telegraphic station. And then he listened eagerly. Would the conductor open the door and ask for Philip Sterling, and hand him a fatal dispatch?

How long they seemed to wait. And then slowly beginning to move, they were off again, shaking, pounding, screaming through the night. He drew his curtain from time to time and looked out. There was the lurid sky line of the wooded range along the base of which they were crawling. There was the Susquehannah, gleaming in the moonlight. There was a stretch of level valley with silent farm houses, the occupants all at rest, without trouble, without anxiety. There was a church, a graveyard, a mill, a village; and now, without pause or fear, the train had mounted a trestle-work high in air and was creeping along the top of it while a swift torrent foamed a hundred feet below.

What would the morning bring? Even while he was flying to her, her gentle spirit might have gone on another flight, whither he could not follow her. He was full of foreboding. He fell at length into a restless doze. There was a noise in his ears as of a rushing torrent when a stream is swollen by a freshet in the spring. It was like the breaking up of life; he was struggling in the consciousness of coming death: when Ruth stood by his side, clothed in white, with a face like that of an angel, radiant, smiling, pointing to the sky, and saying, "Come." He awoke with a cry—the train was roaring through a bridge, and it shot out into daylight.

When morning came the train was industriously toiling along through the fat lands of Lancaster, with its broad farms of corn and wheat, its mean houses of stone, its vast barns of granaries, built as if for storing the riches of Heliogabalus.[161] Then came the smiling fields of Chester, with their English green, and soon the county of Philadelphia itself, and the increasing signs of the approach to a great city. Long trains of coal cars, laden and unladen, stood upon sidings; the tracks of other roads were crossed; the smoke of other locomotives was seen on parallel lines; factories multiplied; streets appeared; the noise of a busy city began to fill the air; and with a slower and slower clank on the connecting rails and interlacing switches the train rolled into the station and stood still.

It was a hot August morning. The broad streets glowed in the sun, and the white-shuttered houses stared at the hot thoroughfares like closed bakers'-ovens set along the highway. Philip was oppressed with the heavy air; the sweltering city lay as in a swoon. Taking a street car, he rode away to the northern part of the city, the newer portion, formerly the district of Spring Garden, for in this the Boltons now lived, in a small brick house, befitting their altered fortunes.

He could scarcely restrain his impatience when he came in sight of the house. The window shutters were not "bowed"; thank God, for that. Ruth was still living, then. He ran up the steps and rang. Mrs. Bolton met him at the door.

"Thee is very welcome, Philip."

"And Ruth?"

"She is very ill, but quieter than she has been, and the fever is a little abating. The most dangerous time will be when the fever leaves her. The doctor fears she will not have strength enough to rally from it. Yes, thee can see her."

Mrs. Bolton led the way to the little chamber where Ruth lay. "Oh," said her mother, "if she were only in her cool and spacious room in our old home. She says that seems like heaven."

Mr. Bolton sat by Ruth's bedside, and he rose and silently pressed Philip's hand. The room had but one window; that was wide open to admit the air, but the air that came in was hot and lifeless. Upon the table stood a vase of flowers. Ruth's eyes were closed; her cheeks were flushed with fever, and she moved her head restlessly as if in pain.

"Ruth," said her mother, bending over her, "Philip is here."

Ruth's eyes unclosed, there was a gleam of recognition in them, there was an attempt at a smile upon her face, and she tried to raise her thin hand, as Philip touched her forehead with his lips; and he heard her murmur,

"Dear Phil."

There was nothing to be done but to watch and wait for the cruel fever to burn itself out. Dr. Longstreet told Philip that the fever had undoubtedly been contracted in the hospital, but it was not malignant, and would be little dangerous if Ruth were not so worn down with work, or if she had a less delicate constitution.

"It is only her indomitable will that has kept her up for weeks. And if that should leave her now, there will be no hope. You can do more for her now, sir, than I can?"

"How?" asked Philip eagerly.

"Your presence, more than anything else, will inspire her with the desire to live."

When the fever turned, Ruth was in a very critical condition. For two days her life was like the fluttering of a lighted candle in the wind. Philip was constantly by her side, and she seemed to be conscious of his presence, and to cling to him, as one borne away by a swift stream clings to a stretched-out hand from the shore. If he was absent a moment her restless eyes sought something they were disappointed not to find.

Philip so yearned to bring her back to life, he willed it so strongly and passionately, that his will appeared to affect hers and she seemed slowly to draw life from his.

After two days of this struggle with the grasping enemy, it was evident to Dr. Longstreet that Ruth's will was beginning to issue its orders to her body with some force, and that strength was slowly coming back. In another day there was a decided improvement. As Philip sat holding her weak hand and watching the least sign of resolution in her face, Ruth was able to whisper,

"I so want to live, for you, Phil!"

"You will, darling, you must," said Philip in a tone of faith and courage that carried a thrill of determination—of command— along all her nerves.

Slowly Philip drew her back to life. Slowly she came back, as one willing but well nigh helpless. It was new for Ruth to feel this dependence on another's nature, to consciously draw strength of will from the will of another. It was a new but a dear joy, to be lifted up and carried back into the happy world, which was now all aglow with the light of love; to be lifted and carried by the one she loved more than her own life.

"Sweetheart," she said to Philip, "I would not have cared to come back but for thy love."

"Not for thy profession?"

"Oh, thee may be glad enough of that some day, when thy coal bed is dug out and thee and father are in the air again."

When Ruth was able to ride she was taken into the country, for the pure air was necessary to her speedy recovery. The family went with her. Philip could not be spared from her side, and Mr. Bolton had gone up to Ilium to look into that wonderful coal mine and to make arrangements for developing it, and bringing its wealth to market. Philip had insisted on re-conveying the Ilium property to Mr. Bolton, retaining only the share originally contemplated for himself, and Mr. Bolton, therefore, once more found himself engaged in business and a person of some consequence in Third street. The mine turned out even better than was at first hoped, and would, if judiciously managed, be a fortune to them all. This also seemed to be the opinion of Mr. Bigler, who heard of it as soon as anybody, and, with the impudence of his class called upon Mr. Bolton for a little aid in a patent car-wheel he had bought an interest in. That rascal, Small, he said, had swindled him out of all he had.

Mr. Bolton told him he was very sorry, and recommended him to sue Small.

Mr. Small also came with a similar story about Mr. Bigler; and Mr. Bolton had the grace to give him like advice. And he added, "If you and Bigler will procure the indictment of each other, you may have the satisfaction of putting each other in the penitentiary for the forgery of my acceptances."

Bigler and Small did not quarrel however. They both attacked Mr. Bolton behind his back as a swindler, and circulated the story that he had made a fortune by failing.

In the pure air of the highlands, amid the golden glories of ripening September, Ruth rapidly came back to health. How beautiful the world is to an invalid, whose senses are all clarified, who has been so near the world of spirits that she is sensitive to the finest influences, and whose frame responds with a thrill to the subtlest ministrations of soothing nature. Mere life is a luxury, and the color of the grass, of the flowers, of the sky, the wind in the trees, the outlines of the horizon, the forms of clouds, all give a pleasure as exquisite as the sweetest music to the ear famishing for it. The world was all new and fresh to Ruth, as if it had just been created for her, and love filled it, till her heart was overflowing with happiness.

It was golden September also at Fallkill. And Alice sat by the open window in her room at home, looking out upon the meadows where the laborers were cutting the second crop of clover. The fragrance of it floated to her nostrils. Perhaps she did not mind it. She was thinking. She had just been writing to Ruth, and on the table before her was a yellow piece of paper with a faded four-leaved clover pinned on it—only a memory now. In her letter to Ruth she had poured out her heartiest blessings upon them both, with her dear love forever and forever.

"Thank God," she said, "they will never know."

They never would know. And the world never knows how many women there are like Alice, whose sweet but lonely lives of self-sacrifice, gentle, faithful, loving souls, bless it continually.

"She is a dear girl," said Philip, when Ruth showed him the letter.

"Yes, Phil, and we can spare a great deal of love for her, our own lives are so full."

טוב אחרית דבר מראשיתו

APPENDIX

Perhaps some apology to the reader is necessary in view of our failure to find Laura's father. We supposed, from the ease with which lost persons are found in novels, that it would not be difficult. But it was; indeed, it was impossible; and therefore the portions of the narrative containing the record of the search have been stricken out. Not because they were not interesting—for they were; but inasmuch as the man was not found, after all, it did not seem wise to harass and excite the reader to no purpose.

The Authors

EDITOR'S APPENDICES

APPENDIX A

While giving performances in London, Twain read the proof sheets for the edition of The Gilded Age *to be published by Routledge and Sons. Letters to his wife show that he composed this preface alone, if only because there was not enough time to consult Warner by transatlantic mail.*

AUTHOR'S PREFACE TO THE LONDON EDITION

IN AMERICA nearly every man has his dream, his pet scheme, whereby he is to advance himself socially or pecuniarily. It is this all-pervading speculativeness which we have tried to illustrate in "The Gilded Age." It is a characteristic which is both bad and good, for both the individual and the nation. Good, because it allows neither to stand still, but drives both for ever on, toward some point or other which is a-head, not behind nor at one side. Bad, because the chosen point is often badly chosen, and then the individual is wrecked; the aggregation of such cases affects the nation, and so is bad for the nation. Still, it is a trait which it is of course better for a people to have and sometimes suffer from than to be without.

We have also touched upon one sad feature, and it is one which we found little pleasure in handling. That is the shameful corruption which lately crept into our politics, and in a handful of years has spread until the pollution has affected some portion of every State and every Territory in the Union.

But I have a great strong faith in a noble future for my country. A vast majority of the people are straightforward and honest; and this late state of things is stirring them to action. If it would only keep on stirring them until it became the habit of their lives to attend to the politics of the country personally, and put only their very best men into positions of trust and authority! That day will come.

Our improvement has already begun. Mr. Tweed (whom Great Britain furnished to us), after laughing at our laws and courts for a good while, has at last been sentenced to thirteen years' imprisonment, with hard labour. It is simply bliss to think of it. It will be at least two years before any governor will dare to pardon him out, too. A great New York judge, who continued a vile, a shameless career, season after season, defying the legislature and sneering at the newspapers, was brought low at last, stripped of his dignities, and by public sentence debarred from ever again holding any office of honour or profit in the State. Another such judge (furnished to us by Great Britain) had the grace to break his heart and die in the palace built with his robberies when he saw the same blow preparing for his own head and sure to fall upon it.

MARK TWAIN

The Langham Hotel,
London, *Dec.* 11*th*, 1873

APPENDIX B

J. Hammond Trumbell—*a bibliographer, philologist, historian, authority on North American Indians, and Hartford friend of the authors*—*supplied the mottoes for* The Gilded Age. *They were intended, allegedly, to parody the current practice of using mottoes. However, Trumbull aimed to make them relevant to the content of the particular chapter, sometimes but not always ironically. Trumbull's translations were not published until* The Gilded Age *was reset for the Authorized Uniform Edition of Twain's writing in 1899.*

Bryant Morey French, for his excellent edition of The Gilded Age *(Indianapolis: Bobbs-Merrill, 1972), studied Trumbull's manuscript, which gives both some alternative translations and some alternative mottoes. French added some useful notes.*

TRANSLATIONS OF CHAPTER-HEAD MOTTOES
BY
J. HAMMOND TRUMBULL, LL.D., L.H.D.

TITLE

Chinese: Hïe lï shán ching yǔ: tung sin ní pien kin. *Literally*, By combined strength, a mountain becomes gems: by united hearts, mud turns to gold.

[A maxim often painted on the doorposts of a Chinese firm—which may be freely translated—Two heads, working together, out of commonplace materials, bring THE GILDED AGE.]

CHAPTER I
   Chippeway: "He owns much land."—*Baraga.*
CHAPTER II
   Ethiopic: "It behoveth Christian people who have not children, to take up the children of the departed, whether youths or virgins, and to make them as their own children," etc.

                        The Didascalia (translated by T. Platt), 121.
CHAPTER III
   Old French: [Pantagruel and Panurge, on their voyage to the Oracle of Bacbuc, are frightened by seeing afar off, "a huge monstrous physeter." "Poor Panurge began to cry and howl worse than ever:] Babillebabou, said he, [shrugging up his shoulders, quivering with fear, there will be the devil upon dun.] This will be a worse business than that the other day. Let us fly, let us fly! Old Nick take me, if it is not Leviathan, described by the noble prophet Moses, in the life of patient Job. It will swallow us all like a dose of pills. . . . . Look, look, it is upon us. Oh! how horrible and abominable thou art! . . . Oh, oh! Devil, Sathanas, Leviathan! I cannot bear to look upon thee, thou art so abominably ugly."—*Motteux's Translation.*
CHAPTER V
   Sindhi: "Having removed the little daughter, and placed her in their own house, they instructed her."—*Life of Abd-ul-Latif,* 46 (cited in Trumpp's Sindhi grammar, p. 356).
   French Proverb: He would dry snow in the oven, to sell it for table salt.—Quitard, 193.
CHAPTER VI
   Chinese: [*Shap neen tseen sze, ke fan sun.*] The affairs of ten years past, how often have they been new.
   Chippeway:

            "So blooms the human face divine,
               When youth its pride of beauty shows:
            Fairer than Spring the colors shine,
               And sweeter than the virgin rose."

                        Ojibwa Hymns. (Am. Tract Society), p. 78.
CHAPTER IX
   Italian: When I saw thee for the first time, it seemed to me that paradise was opened, and that the angels were coming, one by one, all to

rest on thy lovely face, all to rest on thy beautiful head; Thou bindest me in chains, and I cannot loose myself.

J. Caselli, *Chants popul de l'Italie*, 21.

Choctaw: "Now therefore divide this land for an inheritance."

Joshua, xiii. 7.

Eskimo (Greenland), from Fabricius's translation of Genesis:— "And when he had made an end of commanding his sons, he gathered up his feet into the bed, and yielded up the ghost, and was gathered unto his people."—*First Book of Moses*, xlix. 32.

CHAPTER X

Eskimo:—"And said, 'Whose daughter art thou? tell me, I pray thee.'"—*Gen.* xxiv. 23.

Massachusetts Indian (Eliot's version of Psalm xlv. 10): "Hearken, O daughter, and consider, and incline thine ear; forget also thine own people, and thy father's house."

Italian:—"Jeannette answered: 'Madam, you have taken me from my father and brought me up as your own child, and for this I ought to do all in my power to please you.'"

CHAPTER XI

Japan: Though he eats, he knows not the taste of what he eats.

CHAPTER XII

Egyptian (from the Book of the Dead, or Funereal Ritual, edited by Lepsius from the Turin papyrus; translated by Birch). "The Preparation in the West. The Roads of the West."

CHAPTER XIV

From Thomas Makin's *Description of Pennsylvania* (Descriptio Pennsylvaniae) 1729. Translated [?] by Robert Proud:

"Fair Philadelphia next is rising seen,
Between two rivers plac'd, two miles between;
The Delaware and Sculkil, new to fame,
Both ancient streams, yet of a modern name.
The city, form'd upon a beauteous plan,
Has many houses built, tho' late began;
Rectangular the streets, direct and fair;
And rectilinear all the ranges are."

Italian: translated by Wiffen—from Tasso.

"Of generous thoughts and principles sublime,
Amongst them in the city lived a maid,
The flower of virgins, in her ripest prime,
Supremely beautiful! but that she made
Never her care, or beauty only weighed
In worth with virtue."

            —*Jerusalem Delivered*, c. ii., st. 14.

CHAPTER XV

Latin: [Celsus] I think the healing art ought to be based on reason to be sure, and too that it should be founded on unmistakable evidences, all uncertainties being rejected, not from the serious attention of a physician, but from the very profession itself.

CHAPTER XVI

Egyptian (from the Book of the Dead), in Birch's translation: "I have come." "*Make Road* expresses what I am" (i.e., is my name).

CHAPTER XVIII

Tamachekh (*Touareg*): From an improvisation by a native poet, at Algiers; printed by Hanoteau, *Essai de Grammaise de Langeu Tamachek*, p. 207.

—If she should come to our country (the plains), there is not a man who would not run to see her.

Romance:

—"Enough! she cries, henceforth thou art
The friend and master of my heart.
No other covenant I require
Than this: 'I take thee for my wife.'
That done, enjoy thy heart's desire,
Of me and mine the lord for life."

            A. Bruce Whyte's paraphrase.

CHAPTER XIX

German: from the "Book of Songs" (Angelique, 4) of Heine.

"O how rapidly develop
From mere fugitive sensations
Passions that are fierce and boundless,
Tenderest associations!
Tow'rds this lady grows the bias
Of my heart on each occasion,

And that I'm enamoured of her
Has become my firm persuasion."

CHAPTER XX

Old Irish: From the *Annals of the Four Masters* (vol. vi., p. 2298).
O'Donovan translates:

—"A sweet sounding trumpet; endowed with the gift of eloquence
and address, of sense and counsel, and with the look of amiability in
his countenance, which captivated every one who beheld him."

CHAPTER XXI

[Let each one know how to follow his own path.]

CHAPTER XXII

"Is there on earth such a transport as this,
When the look of the loved one avows her bliss?
Can life an equal joy impart
To the bliss that lives in a lover's heart?
O! he, be assured, hath never proved
Life's holiest joys who hath never loved!
Yet the joys of love, so heavenly fair,
Can exist but when honour and virtue are there."

Translated by Richardson.

Hawaiian: Love is that which excels in attractiveness (is much better than) the dish of *poi* and the *fish-bowl* (the favorite dishes of the Islanders).

CHAPTER XXIV

Sioux-Dakota (from Riggs' translation of Bunyan's *Pilgrim's Progress*).

"*Christian.* This town of Fair-Speech—I have heard of it; and as I
remember, they say it's a wealthy place.

By-Ends. Yes, I assure you that it is; and I have very many rich kindred there."

CHAPTER XXV

Assyrian:—"A place very difficult."

Smith's Assurbanipal, p. 269 (l. 90).

CHAPTER XXVI

Tamul: Money is very scarce.

CHAPTER XXVII

Egyptian: "Things prepare I. I prepare a road."

Book of the Dead, xliv. 117. 1, 2.

Greek (post-classical):
> "And when he saw his eyes were out,
> With all his might and main,
> He jumped into *another* bush,
> And scratched them in again."

CHAPTER XXVIII

Danish proverb: "He who would buy sausage of a dog, must give him bacon in exchange."

German: "Thrasyllus, with his unaided intellect, would not have succeeded; but such worthies can always find rogues who for money will lend brains, which is just as well as to have brains of their own."

CHAPTER XXIX

Choctaw translation of Joshua xviii. 9: "And the men went and passed through the land, and described it [by cities, into seven parts] in a book."

CHAPTER XXX

Italian; in Wiffen's translation:
> "I nurse a mighty project: the design
> But needs thy gentle guidance to commend
> My hopes to sure success; the thread I twine;
> Weave thou the web, the lively colors blend;
> What cautious Age begins, let Dauntless Beauty end."

Provençal: "Fair lady, your help is needful to me, if you please."

CHAPTER XXXI

Italian; from the *Jerusalem Delivered,* c. vi. st. 76:
> "It would be some humanity to stand
> His dutiful physician! what delight
> Would it not be to lay thy healing hand
> Upon the young man's breast!"

Wiffen.

CHAPTER XXXIII

Sioux (Dakota) translation of the *Pilgrim's Progress.* By-Ends names his distinguished friends, in the City of Fair-Speech:

—"My Lord Turn-about, my Lord Time-server, my Lord Fair-speech, from whose ancestors the town first took its name; also Mr. Smooth-man, Mr. Facing-both-ways, Mr. Anything," etc.

Semi-Saxon:
> "The richest women all—that were in the land,
> And the higher men's daughters—
> There was many a rich garment—on the fair folk,
> There was mickle envy—from [all parts of the country],
> For each weened to be—better than others."

CHAPTER XXXIV

Danish proverb: One hair of a maiden's head pulls stronger than ten yoke of oxen.

CHAPTER XXXV

Quiché (Guatemalan), from a native drama, published by Brasseur des Bourbourg:

"I have snared and caught him, I have taken and bound him, with my brilliant snares, with my white noose, with my bracelets of chiseled gold, with my rings, and with my enchantments."

Old French proverb: Every one has the palms of his hands turned *toward himself.*

CHAPTER XXXVI

Tamul: "Books."

Chippeway: "My books are many and they are all good." "Although his books are good, he does not much look into them."

CHAPTER XXXVII

Assyrian (from Smith's Assurbanipal): "Ni-ni-id [dag]-ga ra a-ha-mis, 'We will (help) each other.'"

[Note. The fourth group varies in different copies of the cuneiform record. Mr. Smith puts *dag*, marking it as a variant, and translates by "help." Others may prefer to read *gul*, "to cheat." As philological criticism would have been out of place in the "Gilded Age," and as the passage is a familiar one, it seemed best to omit the questionable group—leaving it to the reader to fill the blank as in his better judgment he might determine.]

Italian, from the *Jerusalem Delivered,* c. iv., st. 78:
> "All arts the enchantress practised to beguile
> Some new admirer in her well-spread snare;
> Nor used with all, nor always, the same wile,
> But shaped to every taste her grace and air."

CHAPTER XXXIX

Provençal: Dear friend, return, for pity's sake, to me, at once.

Basque (*Souletin* dialect); from a popular song, published by Vallaberry: "You gave me your word—not once only, twice—that you would be mine. I am the same as in other times; I have not changed, for I took it to my heart, and I loved you."—*Chants populaires du pays Basque*, pp. 6, 7.

CHAPTER XLI

Arabic:

"And her denying increased his devotion in love:

For lovely, as a thing, to man, is that which is denied him."

From an Arabic poet quoted in the *Táj el-'Aroos* (of the Seyyid Murtada) which, as everybody knows, is a commentary on the *Kámoos*—the Arabic "Webster's Unabridged."

Basque. From the *Poésies Basques* of Bernard d'Echeparre (Bordeaux, 1545), edited by G. Brunet, 1847:

"Was there ever any one so unfortunate as I am?

She whom I adore does not love me at all, and yet I cannot renounce her."

CHAPTER XLII

Efik (or *Old Calabar*) proverb: "The rat enters the trap, the trap catches him; if he did not go into the trap, the trap would not do so." From R. F. Burton's *Wit and Wisdom of West Africa*, p. 367.

CHAPTER XLIII

Arrawak version of Acts xix. 23: "And the same time there arose no small stir (Gr. τάραχος οὐκ ὀλίγος) about that way."

CHAPTER XLIV

Latin (Seneca): "In an evil career a reckless downward course is inevitably taken."

Latin (Cicero): "For men are subject to their own impulses as soon as they have once parted company with reason; and their very weakness gives way to itself, incautiously sails into deep water and finds no place of anchorage."

CHAPTER XLV

Quiché (*Guatemalan*), from the *Popol Vuh*, or Sacred Book, edited by Brasseur de Bourbourg, p. 222:

—" 'What will you give us, then, if we will take pity on you?' they said. 'Ah, well, we will give you silver,' responded the associate [petitioners]."

CHAPTER XLVI

Italian proverb: "Strong is the vinegar of sweet wine."

Anglo-Saxon: "Such is no feminine usage
        for a woman to practise,
        although she be beautiful,—
        that a peace-weaver
        machinate to deprive of life,
        after burning anger,
        a man beloved."

                                —*Thorpe's translation*, 3885–91.

CHAPTER XLVII

Quiché (from a native drama): "My bravery and my power have availed me nothing! Alas, let heaven and earth hear me! Is it true that I must die, that I must die here, between earth and sky?"

CHAPTER XLVIII

"A poison-toothed serpent (*moonihoawa*) is debt."

CHAPTER XLIX

Russian: "The sun began to shine, but not for a long time; it shone for a moment and disappeared."

Yoruba proverb: "I *almost* killed the bird." "Nobody can make a stew of *almost*" (or "*Almost* never made a stew").—

Crowther's Yoruba Proverbs, in Grammar, p. 229.

CHAPTER L

Icelandic, from a modern poem:

    "When anguish wars in thy heavy breast,
        and adverse scourges lash thy cheeks,
        and the world turns her back on thee,
        and pleasure mocketh at thy pain:
        Think *all is round* and easily turns;
        he weeps to-morrow who laughs to-day;
            Time makes all good."

CHAPTER LI

Wolof (Senegambian) proverb: "If you go to the sparrows' ball, take with you some ears of corn for them." R. F. Burton, from Dard's Grammaire Wolofe.

Hungarian, from 2 Kings, viii. 13:

—"Is thy servant a dog, that he should do this great thing?"

CHAPTER LII

French of Molière:

"Nothing in the world is more noble and more beautiful Than the holy fervor of true zeal."—Molière.

French: [The Fox] "assumed a benign and tender expression, He bade them good day with a Laudate Deum, And invited the whole world to share his brotherly love."

CHAPTER LIII

French of Molière: Tartuffe, the hypocrite, is speaking:

"According to differing emergencies, there is a science
Of stretching the limitations of our conscience,
And of compensating the evil of our acts
By the purity of our motives."

CHAPTER LIV

Sanskrit: "The distinctions of obscurity are eightfold, as are also those of illusion; extreme illusion is tenfold; gloom is eighteen-fold, and so is utter darkness."

[This description of a New York jury is from Memorial Verses on the Sankya philosophy, translated by Colebrooke.]

Old Welsh: "Nobody is a judge through learning; although a person may always learn he will not be a judge unless there be wisdom in his heart; however wise a person may be, he will not be a judge unless there be learning with the wisdom."—Ancient Laws of Wales, ii. 207.

CHAPTER LV

Danish proverb: "Virtue in the middle," said the Devil, when he sat down between two lawyers.

Breton: "This is a great pleader! Have you heard him plead?"

—Legonidec's Descrip. de Braham.

CHAPTER LVI

Old French: " 'Yea, but,' asked Trinquamelle, 'how do you proceed, my friend, in criminal causes, the culpable and guilty party being taken and seized upon *flagrante crimine?*' 'Even as your other worships use to do,' answered (Judge) Bridlegoose."

—*Rabelais, Pantagruel,* b. ii, ch. 137.

Breton: "Have you anything to say for her justification?"

—*Legonidec.*

CHAPTER LVII

Chippeway: "I don't know what may have happened; perhaps we shall hear bad news!"—*Baraga.*

CHAPTER LVIII

Chinese (Canton dialect, *Tsow pak păt fun*): "Black and white not distinguished," i.e., Right and wrong not perceived.

Spanish proverb (of a court of law): Paper and ink and little justice.

CHAPTER LIX

Efik (Old Calabar) proverb: "One monkey does not like to see another get his belly full."—*Burton's West African Proverbs.*

Grecian. From the *Greek Anthology:* "When the Crab caught with his claw the Snake, he reproved him for his indirect course." [An old version of what the Pot said to the Kettle.]

Massachusetts Indian, from Eliot's translation of Psalm xxxv., 21: "Yea, they opened their mouth wide against me, and said, Aha, aha, our eye hath seen it!"

CHAPTER LX

Javanese: "Alas!"

Cornish: "My heart yet is proud

Though I am nearly dead."—*The Creation.*

CHAPTER LXI

Danish proverb: "He is a good driver who knows how *to turn.*"

Sioux (Dakota): "Let us go now. Will you go?" [The *Iapi Oaye* is a Dakota newspaper published monthly in the Dakota language.]

CHAPTER LXII

Kanuri (Borneo): "At the bottom of patience there is heaven."

—R. F. Burton's *West African Proverbs.*

Quiché: "Is it in vain, is it without profit, that I am come here to lose so many days, so many nights?"

CHAPTER LXIII

Hawaiian: "Then we two shall be happy, our offspring shall live in the days of our old age."

Syriac (from the Old Testament; the blessing on Naomi transferred to Ruth): "And he shall be unto thee a restorer of thy life [*consolator animae,* as Walton translates from the Syriac version,] and a nourisher of thine old age." Ruth iv., 15.

TAIL-PIECE

Hebrew: "The end of a thing is better than the beginning." Eccles. vii. 8.

EXPLANATORY NOTES

I AM INDEBTED to the notes in Bryant Morey French's edition of *The Gilded Age* (Indianapolis: Bobbs-Merrill, 1972). French tried especially to identify real-life models for characters and places; my notes center on specialized words, turns of speech, and allusions that a modern reader may not understand precisely. Still, because some allusions were extremely topical, even the best-informed reader can now miss them in what was shaped as "A Tale of To-Day" in 1873.

1. Nazareth: A reference to John 1:45–46, which relates—with a flash of almost-modern drollness—how Jesus' first disciples were recruited: "Philip found Nathanael and said to him, 'We have found him of whom Moses in the Law and the Prophets wrote—Jesus of Nazareth, the son of Joseph.' Nathanael said to him, 'Can any good thing come out of Nazareth?'"
2. *linsey-woolsey:* A common, homespun cloth of linen and wool or else of cotton and wool.
3. *stage-plank:* Or gangplank.
4. A mud-valve discharged mud that had collected in a steam boiler.
5. *"bight":* Curve or loop.
6. *verge-staff:* Pole at the bow for displaying a flag or emblem.
7. To skin the cat was to hang by the hands and pass the legs through the circle formed by the support and the upper part of the body.
8. The hog-chains on a steamboat ran from bow to stern like a tension rod.
9. *"night-hawk":* The figure of the bird used as an ensign or symbol of the steamboat line.
10. *"jack-staff":* The flagstaff on the bow of the steamboat.
11. *guards:* Extensions of the deck beyond the hull, especially needed on side-wheel steamboats.
12. *"mark twain":* The leadsman's call for two fathoms of water or twelve feet of depth.
13. Flooding would destroy Napoleon—located where the Arkansas River entered the Mississippi—after Samuel Clemens's piloting days.

14. The fantail denoted part of the stern when it was unusually long.
15. "*Colonel Sellers*": His title is perhaps granted prematurely as well as inflated. Chapter XVIII will state that he served as a "captain" in the "home guards" of his village during the Civil War.
16. The distance from St. Louis to Hannibal, Missouri, the village where Samuel Clemens grew up, is 130 river miles.
17. *Godey's Lady's Book:* A monthly magazine, centered on fashion and manners; its literary content favored sentimental and domestic themes.
18. A Leghorn hat was made of fine, plaited straw and had a broad brim.
19. "*cheapen*": To cheapen was to bargain about the price.
20. "*portmonnaie*": Or purse; literally, a money carrier (from French *porte-monnaie*).
21. "*Yedo*": Also Yeddo; a former name for Tokyo.
22. "*Roderick Dhu*": A chieftain in Sir Walter Scott's once-popular narrative poem *The Lady of the Lake* (1810).
23. "*casters*": Here, small containers of condiments.
24. "*Poniatowski*": Presumably, Sellers has picked up the name of a distinguished Polish lineage, which included a king and a marshal in Napoleon's armies.
25. "*Astor Library*": Established by a bequest from John Jacob Astor, it was folded eventually into the New York Public Library.
26. *Chambers' Street box:* Converted from an opera house, Burton's Chambers' Street Theatre functioned from 1848 to 1864.
27. *Burton:* William E. Burton (1804–1860) was a playwright-manager-actor, perhaps "serious" here because in one of his long-running farces (*The Serious Family*), he played the sanctimonious and lugubrious Aminadab Sleek.
28. "*kindness*": For "The man that lays his hand upon a woman / Save in the way of kindness is a wretch / Whom t'were gross flattery to name a coward," see John Tobin, *The Honeymoon* (1805), act 2, scene 1.
29. *fame:* Compare "Some are born great, some achieve greatness, and some have greatness thrust upon them," from Shakespeare's *Twelfth Night*, act 2, scene 5.
30. *Lt. Strain:* Isaac G. Strain (1821–1857), an officer of the U.S. Navy, explored in Central and South America.
31. *Dr. Kane:* Elisha Kent Kane (1820–1857), U.S. naval surgeon, published gripping accounts of his Arctic expeditions.
32. *bul-bul:* A songbird in Persian poetry.

33. *giant swing:* A complete swing of the body around a horizontal bar.
34. *whipping the devil round the stump:* Avoiding or overcoming a difficult point in a roundabout way.
35. *Dorking Convention:* Doubtless, a topical barb. In 1871 "The Battle of Dorking"—published in *Blackwood's Edinburgh Magazine* and reprinted in the United States in *Littell's Living Age* as a warning to "make defensive preparations" militarily—had a temporary fame; "The American Battle of Dorking"—*Harper's Weekly,* June 29, 1872—ridiculed Horace Greeley's fitness for president of the United States. The *New York Herald* of May 12, 1872, jeered at the number of reformist conventions held during the "past week" and ridiculed in detail the Equal Rights Party that nominated Victoria Woodhull for president. The Universal Peace Union had also met.
36. *Mr. Gringo:* Probably an inside joke for those posted on the political-journalistic gossip of New York City. A plausible target is William Cauldwell, Democratic state senator and co-editor of the *New York Sunday Mercury.*
37. *the Atlas:* The *New York Atlas,* a Sunday newspaper-magazine, had the subtitle of "Literary, Historical and Commercial Reporter."
38. *Broad Street,* in lower Manhattan, was extra-wide because it was originally a canal for drainage and shipping.
39. *Bank of Commerce:* Though banks elsewhere used this name also, Philip probably means the National Bank of Commerce in Manhattan, upgraded from a state bank by the Currency Act of June 3, 1864.
40. *"St. Jo":* St. Joseph, Missouri, at the western border of the state, was a terminal for travel westward.
41. *"Trautwine":* John Cresson Trautwine, *The Civil Engineer's Pocket Book* (1871–1872).
42. *India-rubber:* Later shortened to "rubber."
43. *Profile paper,* ruled horizontally and vertically to scale, was used by engineers.
44. *"Mobile custom house":* As a port of entry, Mobile, Alabama, had an office of the federal Customs Bureau for collecting tariffs, the major source of revenue. For several reasons, such offices, staffed by appointments through the Secretary of the Treasury, had become centers of political patronage and corruption.
45. *"Otard":* A prominent name among producers of French cognac.
46. *"hanging it up":* Here, adding to an account for payment later; more generally, letting a matter lie for the present.

47. *Girard College:* The will of Stephen Girard (1750–1831), who stipulated that no ministers of religion could enter the premises of the school for white orphan boys he was founding, set off lasting controversy. By mid-century, the school was attracting as many tourists as Independence Hall.

48. *Fairmount Water Works and Park:* Long a tourist attraction as a triumph of engineering and civic planning.

49. *St. Girard:* Because of the ongoing controversy over how Girard's bequest was being handled, the irony is ambiguous. Whatever Warner's opinion, Twain admired Girard's anticlericalism but scoffed at glorification of him.

50. *Mint:* The first United States Mint, which activated its imposing building in 1833.

51. *"Arch Street Meeting":* The Society of Friends had erected a large meetinghouse on Arch Street in 1804.

52. *"Kick-a-poos":* Tribe of Algonquin Indians, whose name had become a conversational tag.

53. *"Woman's Medical College":* The first medical school for women; incorporated in 1850.

54. *railroad:* Fictitious, but mixing genuine and allusive place-names.

55. *"Simony":* The buying or selling of sacred objects or privileges; in 1873 an obvious pun on Simon Cameron, political boss of Pennsylvania.

56. *"St. James the Less":* One of the original twelve apostles; he is called "the Less" to distinguish him from St. James the Great, who, along with Peter and John, composed Jesus' innermost circle.

57. *prompter's drawl:* Here, the prompter is someone calling out the steps or other movements.

58. *"Pilot Knob":* Town, south of St. Louis, on a minor river and a railroad line.

59. *Atchison:* As president pro tempore of the U.S. Senate, David R. Atchison (from Missouri) technically became vice-president twice between 1852 and 1854.

60. *wide-awake:* A soft felt hat; called a "wide-awake" because it had no "nap." Its surface was smooth, not hairy or downy.

61. *flavor of rose:* Barbers have long used rose-scented soaps and oils.

62. *"breaking down":* Dancing with energy and gesture.

63. *juba:* A Southern African-American dance with a lively rhythm.

64. *setting poles:* Or punting poles, to propel a boat.

65. *"bilin"*: For "boiling"? Here, figuratively, the complete range of the needed materials.

66. *"Roederer"*: An established brand of champagne from Reims, France.

67. In 1854–1857, Sir George Gore, an Irish baronet, spent around a half-million dollars on a series of buffalo hunts.

68. In 1797, as part of an American delegation to negotiate a loan to the Republic of France, Charles Cotesworth Pinckney protested with "no, no, not a sixpence"—which was later transformed into the now-revered motto.

69. Beatrice Cenci was made famous for readers of English by the verse drama (1819) of Percy Bysshe Shelley. Raped by her father, she hired assassins to kill him. She was executed later by the state.

70. *"opera house"*: In 1873, an obvious allusion to Jim Fisk (James Fisk, Jr.), a manipulator of railroad stock. He spent lavishly on his mistress Josie Mansfield, whose new suitor shot Fisk in 1872.

71. *Jefferson City*: Capital of Missouri.

72. *country dance*: Here, a dance involving at least several couples and a pattern of maneuvers.

73. *Rebecca*: The Independent Order of Odd Fellows, a secret fraternal order, is devoted to public service; the Independent Order of Good Templars once organized temperance lodges; the Cadets of Temperance, a junior adjunct of the Sons of Temperance, pledged to give up tobacco (as did member Samuel Clemens in 1850); the International Association of Rebekah Assemblies, the women's auxiliary of the IOOF, evolved from the Daughters of Rebekah.

74. *The Plough, the Loom, and the Anvil*, respected primarily as an agricultural magazine, aimed at a broad audience in practical science.

75. *Practical Magazine*, started in 1873, had the subtitle of *An Illustrated Cyclopedia of Industrial News, Inventions and Improvements*.

76. *artist*: In 1868, Vinnie Ream emerged into the news through accusations that the commission from Congress for a bronze statue of Abraham Lincoln had resulted from highly partisan politics.

77. *cribs*: An allusion to the slang term for a house of prostitution and therefore to charges that women had to pay for a federal clerkship with sexual favors; less provocatively, "crib" meant feeding trough.

78. *"P.S."*: Permanent Secretary, though Private Secretary is also plausible.

79. *a drug in the market:* Same as the current "drug (or drag) on the market."

80. *undertalk:* Talk at a lower volume than normal or else shielded by a hand; more simply, gossip.

81. *"Fisher's Hornpipe":* By 1840, if not earlier, "Fischer's Hornpipe," a brisk tune, was available as sheet music.

82. *"aneroid":* Or aneroid barometer.

83. *"Expectorant":* Medicine for bringing up phlegm from the throat.

84. *"'lead'":* To give a story better prominence; here it could mean, technically, the printer's practice of inserting more space between lines and therefore making a text more noticeable.

85. *"card":* An impressive point or attraction; more simply, a drawing card.

86. *"Ilium fuit":* Troy is past, or Troy is no more, or Troy has been. From Virgil's *Aeneid*, book 2, line 325.

87. *"Aeneas":* Trojan hero whose descendants, according to tradition, founded Rome.

88. *"Anchises":* Father of Aeneas, who carried him to safety during the sacking of Troy by the Greeks.

89. *witch-hazel professor:* Folk belief uses a divining rod (here, a fork of the witch-hazel shrub) to locate (dowse for) water, gold, etc.

90. *"made the riffle":* Here, raked in money; literally, found gold at the bar or slot of a sluice box.

91. *"world's people":* In the Society of Friends, applied to outsiders.

92. *"play the bones":* Use a pair of bones, held between the fingers, to produce rhythms; once associated with the minstrel show.

93. Garbled deliberately from John Ruskin, *The Stones of Venice* (1851–1853), I, chap. 2, sec. 17: "Remember that the most beautiful things in the world are the most useless; peacocks and lilies for instance. . . ."

94. *cars:* Probably horse-drawn cars, the earliest form of city transportation, though Philadelphia already had steam railroads connecting its suburbs.

95. *the Barber:* Figaro, whose aria "Largo al factotum," in act 1 of Gioacchino Rossini's *Barber of Seville* (1816), is still a favorite part of concerts by baritones.

96. *"Oh, Summer Night":* Probably Ernesto's solo ("Com'è gentil la notte a mezzo Aprile . . ."), opening the final scene of act 3 of Gaetano Donizetti's *Don Pasquale* (1843).

97. *"Batti Batti":* Most probably, Zerlina's aria in act 1, scene 12, of Mozart's *Don Giovanni* (1787).

98. *Black Swan:* Though the career of Elizabeth Taylor Greenfield, born a slave in the United States, was dwindling, she had reached national and international fame with her vocal concerts.

99. *Senator from Iowa:* William Boyd Allison had just entered the U.S. Senate in 1873; in 1867, Twain, observing him in the House of Representatives, jotted in a notebook: "Stands around where women can see him."

100. *secretary's:* The authors are noting the difference between British and American titles for a member of the national "cabinet."

101. *steel pen-coated:* Dressed in formal black coats.

102. *"card":* Here, more clearly (cf. note 85) a drawing card or attractive feature.

103. *"knave of spades":* Jack of spades or the lowest face card; a knave is also a dishonest rascal. Oakes Ames, the congressman from Massachusetts tangled in the scandals of Crédit Mobilier, was a manufacturer of shovels.

104. *Parvenus:* Persons of recent wealth or power who are condescended to by those already established; upstarts.

105. *"P.P.C.":* *Pour prendre congé* (French): to take leave. On a visiting card, it indicated a farewell call.

106. *"Newport":* After the Civil War, Newport, Rhode Island, became the summer playground for wealthy Northern families.

107. *"Long Branch":* On the coast of New Jersey.

108. *"Cape May":* A beach-resort area at the southern end of New Jersey, on Delaware Bay.

109. *shaving-brushes:* Literally, a brush for spreading lather on the face; here, some kind of roughly similar decoration.

110. *Castle Garden:* In Battery Park, at the southern tip of Manhattan; earlier a theater, and from 1855 to 1889 a depot for immigrants.

111. *straw bail:* A bail bond backed by worthless assets.

112. *Wm. M. Weed:* Beyond the transparency of the name, the details given confirm the reference to William M. Tweed, whose swindles of public money in New York City had recently emerged through the headlines and the courts.

113. *"Hot Springs":* Hot Springs, Virginia, was a fashionable resort in the decade after the Civil War.

114. Martin Farquhar Tupper (1810–1889) was popular for his moralizing advice.

115. *"Taine's England":* Hippolyte Taine's *Notes Sur l'Angleterre* (1872) was immediately translated, as *Notes on England*.

116. *cedar pencil:* Pencil with the lead encased in wood from the southern red cedar.
117. George Francis Train (1829–1904) was currently much in the news as a flamboyant entrepreneur in shipping and railroads as well as a political agitator.
118. *Venetian Life:* A travel book (1866) by William Dean Howells, the editor of the *Atlantic Monthly* and a good friend of both Twain and Warner.
119. Tupper's sententious clichés in *Proverbial Philosophy* (1838–1876) used flabby free verse.
120. T. S. Arthur (1809–1895), author of moral tales mostly centered on temperance, is best remembered for *Ten Nights in a Barroom and What I Saw There* (1854).
121. *"American Miscellany":* Published in Boston since 1865, it featured "entertaining" literature.
122. *"spray of box":* Small branch of boxwood (*Buxus sempervirens*) or some similar species or, more generally, of boxberry or similarly named bushes.
123. *"something another":* Today, "something or other" has replaced various similar phrases.
124. *"Japs":* In 1871, thirty Japanese noblemen came to observe "mechanical inventions" in the United States. Still more newsworthy, a delegation of high Japanese officials, along with their retinue, came to the Capital in early 1872; President Grant received its leaders at the White House.
125. *"Alabama business":* From 1869 to 1872, the United States pressed for damages to Northern shipping by raiders, such as the *Alabama,* built in England for the Confederacy. Much controversy swirled over how pugnaciously to insist on these claims.
126. *"Gen. Sutler":* In 1873, readers easily recognized Benjamin F. Butler (1818–1893), long newsworthy as a Democratic politician, a Civil War general, and then a Radical Republican.
127. *"cotton claim":* After the Civil War, fraud and litigation gathered around cotton, which had risen sharply in value. Perhaps Selby had acquired the rights of a "loyal" Southerner whose cotton had been destroyed by Union troops. Union rules and practice had changed often during the war.
128. Georgetown, on the north bank of the Potomac River, was incorporated into the District of Columbia in 1871.
129. *Hero of New Orleans:* At the center of Lafayette Park (originally named Jackson Park) is an equestrian statue of Andrew Jackson

as commanding general at the battle in 1812 that decisively defeated the British.

130. *"tie him on":* Led by mainline New England Republicans, the enemies of portly Benjamin Butler ridiculed him as a military politician, inept in the field.

131. At the time, readers would think first of Victoria Woodhull, then of Elizabeth Cady Stanton, Susan B. Anthony, and Lucy Stone.

132. *Willard's:* A hotel favored by insiders as well as visitors, partly because it was close to the White House.

133. The New York Custom House had a reputation for chicanery as well as corruption; its inspectors decided on the classifying, even labeling, of imported casks of wine.

134. *"Blacque Bey":* The urbane Envoy Extraordinary and Minister Plenipotentiary from Turkey.

135. *" 'Santo Domingo' ":* In 1871, the Senate had rejected a treaty, negotiated with the strong support of President Grant, to annex Santo Domingo (the Dominican Republic).

136. *"two debts":* The Fourteenth Amendment (1868) forbade federal payment of debts incurred by the seceded states. Only a Sellers could hope to add these to the Union war debts or, just as unlikely, the debts incurred by the states undergoing Reconstruction.

137. *"greenbacks":* The ongoing controversy about whether to return to a specie or "hard money" standard and therefore retire the paper currency or "greenbacks" issued to help finance the Civil War divided basically between creditors or holders of Union war bonds and borrowers, such as farmers, who paid more when interest rates went up; fiscal conservatives deplored the greenbacks as cheapening the currency and encouraging speculation.

138. *"Boutwell's":* As Secretary of the Treasury, George S. Boutwell had approved reissuing temporarily $5,000,000 in retired greenbacks (to help "move the crops"); however, he vacillated when challenged.

139. *"Morrissey's":* John Morrissey (1831–1878), former prizefighter who rose to power as a Democrat and was elected to the U.S. House of Representatives from 1867 to 1871, ran well-known gambling houses in New York City and Saratoga.

140. *"Steamship Subsidy bill":* Several sources revealed in 1872 that the Pacific Mail Steamship Company had spent lavishly through lobbyists to get an annual federal subsidy.

141. *Peddletonian:* Evidently generic for an insignificant (peddling?)

town; suggestive also of Piddle-town, whose newspaper would deal in trivia.

142. The Sheffield Scientific School, established at Yale College in 1861, aimed at the excellence in science education reached by the well-known European schools named here.

143. *"Young Hyson"*: Sellers, groggy and surprised, may clutch at the name of a Chinese variety of fine green tea.

144. *Presidential Square*: Or President's Square, which includes the White House grounds, Lafayette Square, and the Ellipse.

145. *hot box*: The overheated bearing on an axle.

146. *"Evening Gram"*: The *New York Evening Telegram*, started in 1867 by James Gordon Bennett, owner of the *New York Herald*, which was perhaps the first daily newspaper to feature stories about crimes.

147. *"woman's rights agitations"*: Rising to a temporary peak in 1872, "equal rights" organizers were arguing for enfranchising white females, for equitable laws about the property of married couples, for more flexible laws on divorce, and even for "free love"— meaning sexual activity without marriage.

148. *"interviewed"*: Interviewing was a very recent form of personalized journalism, looked down on by conservative editors and their readership.

149. *Centre Street*: The location for the city jail, called the Tombs because its site was gloomy and because, built in the Egyptian Revival style, it looked like an ancient tomb to some.

150. As the text of the fictitious quotation admits, it combines "broken fragments of antique legends" and Greek history.

151. *"Great Frauds"*: The staggering swindles of the Tweed ring, exposed first by the *New York Times*.

152. *"re-election"*: Simon Cameron was re-elected to the U.S. Senate in 1872.

153. *"Patent Pavement"*: Inventors were motivated because cities were trying out methods and materials for improving their streets.

154. *"Mrs. Dr. Longstreet"*: Dr. Hannah E. Myers Longshore (1819–1901), a Quaker, was prominent in Philadelphia as a physician, surgeon, and educator.

155. *Hingham beach*: On the south shore of Massachusetts Bay or Boston Harbor.

156. *"cadetships"*: In 1870, the *New York World* and *New York Times* featured charges that members of the House of Representatives

were selling appointments to the U.S. Military Academy and the Naval Academy. Investigation by the House Committee on Military Affairs would confirm that.

157. *"Mr. Fairoaks":* The House of Representatives censured Oakes Ames in 1873 for his part in the Crédit Mobilier dealings. See also note 103.

158. *"bulwark of our liberties":* Once a favored phrase in our political rhetoric; see, for example, a speech by Abraham Lincoln in 1858: "What constitutes the bulwark of our liberty and independence?"

159. *"a supersedeas":* Document issued to halt or delay the action of some process of law.

160. *the General from Massachusetts:* Benjamin Butler had helped lead the so-called Salary Grab Act of March 1873 that raised salaries currently (indeed, retroactively, some argued). The president's salary rose from $50,000 to $100,000; that of congressmen from $5,000 to $7,500.

161. *Heliogabalus:* The name (also Elagabalus) of a sun god that an especially inept Roman emperor, Varius Avitus Bassianus (218–222), adopted.

Read more Mark Twain in Penguin 🐧 Classics

The Adventures of Huckleberry Finn
Introduction by John Seelye
Notes by Guy Cardwell
A novel of immeasurable richness, filled with adventures, ironies, and wonderfully drawn characters, all conveyed with Twain's mastery of humor and language, *Huckleberry Finn* is often regarded as the masterpiece of American literature.　　　　　*ISBN 0-14-243717-4*

The Adventures of Tom Sawyer
Introduction by John Seelye
Evoking life in a small Mississippi River town, *Tom Sawyer* is Twain's hymn to the secure and fantastic world of boyhood and adventure.
ISBN 0 -14-039083-9

A Connecticut Yankee in King Arthur's Court
Edited with an Introduction by Justin Kaplan
This imaginary confrontation of a nineteenth-century American life in sixth-century England is both a rich, extravagant comedy and an apocalyptic vision of terrifying violence and destruction.
ISBN 0-14-043064-4

The Innocents Abroad
Introduction by Tom Quirk
Notes by Guy Cardwell
These irreverent writings on travel in Europe are a burlesque of the sentimental travel books popular in the mid-nineteenth century and launched Twain's career. Bringing his fresh and humorous perspective to bear on hallowed European landmarks, Twain ultimately concludes that, for better or worse, "human nature is very much the same all over the world."
ISBN 0-14-243708-5

Life on the Mississippi
Introduction by James M. Cox
Twain's firsthand portrait of the steamboat age and the science of riverboat piloting recalls the history of the Mississippi River, from its discovery by Europeans to the writer's own time.　*ISBN 0-14-039050-2*

Tales, Speeches, Essays, and Sketches
Edited with an Introduction by Tom Quirk
Masterful short fiction and prose pieces display the variety of Twain's imaginative invention, his diverse talents, and his extraordinary emotional range. The volume includes "Jim Smiley and his Jumping Frog," "The Man That Corrupted Hadleyburg," "Fenimore Cooper's Literary Offenses," and the spectacularly scatological "Date, 1601."　*ISBN 0-14-043417-8*